*Countdown to Contagion*

ALSO BY PETER SWAN

*The Rick Conwright Private Investigator Series*
Past Due
Unnatural Causes
Forest Park

*The Parkinson Fealder Homicide Detective Series*
Fealder's Choice

# COUNTDOWN
# TO
# CONTAGION

# PETER SWAN

PORTLAND•OREGON
INKWATERPRESS.COM

Publisher: Inkwater Press | www.inkwaterpress.com

Paperback ISBN-13 978-1-62901-583-5 | ISBN-10 1-62901-583-0
Kindle      ISBN-13 978-1-62901-584-2 | ISBN-10 1-62901-584-9

1 3 5 7 9 10 8 6 4 2

# PROLOGUE

**T**HEY HAD MOVED THE SACKS OF RICE AND TUBS OF spices closer to the walls to make room for the simple wooden table and the folding chairs. The whitewashed cinderblock walls of the storage room behind the small pasar reflected light from the single bulb hanging from the ceiling. Two geckos clung to the walls undisturbed by the eight Malaysian men solemnly gathered below them. It was humid, even for Penang, and the portable fan did little to relieve the oppressive evening heat in the windowless room.

Word had been passed at prayers the day before, summoning them to their first meeting in ten days. Ali, an unremarkable pharmacist by day, was a clever and determined leader whose fervor inspired the others. He was also a patient man and the evening's meeting was the culmination of months of intensive planning and preparation. When he realized that his nascent group lacked specific resources or skills, Ali had probed and questioned, sometimes through contacts at the mosque, sometimes through murky business connections, and even by using the internet. His greatest find had been Moud, the microbiologist who had just lost his job at a large rubber company, and it was with his help that the Egyptian's concept had been refined and engineered.

Moud had graduated from a technical high school in Kuala Lumpur and went on to the University of Malaysia where he received a degree in Chemistry. His graduate work at Colorado State took him deeply into biochemistry. His first two years there proceeded smoothly enough and seemed to bode well for his career. This was despite his feeling of alienation from the other students who found him irritable and overly sensitive. But then, his dissertation committee had failed to approve his thesis proposal. This development led to a bitter dispute. The chair of his committee was an openly religious Christian and Moud felt sure the woman's beliefs had led to a hostility toward Muslims. From that conviction, it was an easy step for Moud to convince himself that she had influenced the other two professors to reject his proposal. Instead of following the committee's suggestion for a different topic, Moud filed a grievance alleging discrimination. When the university's hearing panel did not support his claim, Moud withdrew from the program.

Two years later, still angry and disillusioned, he received his doctor's degree in microbiology from the University of Cairo. He returned to Malaysia and found work in the laboratory of a rubber plantation. Again, his first two years went well and he was given progressively more responsibility. Then, disagreements with his French supervisor over the scope of his authority escalated to the point where the company released him. His bitterness increased in the months following as he unsuccessfully sought a new science job. Meanwhile, some of the most radical rhetoric at the mosque resonated with Moud and Ali recruited him.

Ali stood behind the table and held his arms outward to get the group's attention. "We are ready at last! The men in Portland have their site ready for Moud's arrival. The nest is ready and we can pack the container tomorrow at Ri's warehouse. Allah has smiled on us. There is a Malaysian ship, the Malaca Trader, sailing for Portland in two days that will take Ri's shipment."

A short, bald man whose goatee made him appear vaguely satanical leaned toward the table and asked "but how do we get an officer on board?"

Ali nodded, "Yes. That's more difficult. We have bribed the agent to make us a copy of the crew list. So we know the identity of the third officer." Ali looked toward a younger man at the back, "Sallah will see that the officer will be involved in a regrettable traffic accident and Sallah knows a man named Krati who will gladly take the officer's place, with another bribe to the ship's agent if need be. Krati is a licensed mate and can fill in easily."

Moud spoke up, "I've seen this Krati fellow a few times at the other mosque. I never talked to him, but he seemed high strung."

"That may be," said Ali, "but Sallah says he will do whatever he is told and won't ask a lot of questions."

The short man turned to question the slender microbiologist, "Are you completely satisfied with the nest, Moud?"

"It is very functional," Moud replied. "The life-support systems are all more than adequate and everything is backed up. Stabilizing it inside the container is important, but I am convinced it can be braced so that it cannot move."

"And your own capability to endure this?" another man asked.

"Allah will give me strength for this task. I know I can make it." He paused looking down for a moment, then straightened and added, "This is my role in our glorious jihad. I shall not fail!"

# ONE

THE SHIP WAS OVER TWO HOURS LATE FOR THE RENDEZ-vous. This was nothing unusual in the work of a pilot, especially when a ship arrived from across the Pacific. The pilots' launch throttled back as it approached the loom of the Malaca Trader through the patchy morning fog. The much larger ship was barely making steerageway to enable its convergence with the launch.

Paul Castner, at forty-four, had been a river pilot most of his working life, as had his father before him. The eyeglasses and his prematurely greying hair gave him a scholarly appearance that belied his extreme fitness and vitality. Paul surveyed the ship's Jacob's ladder against the black hull and began to feel the familiar exhilaration of boarding a ship to conn it up the Columbia River to Portland.

Even at dead slow ahead, coming close along-side the towering hull of a container ship could be a precarious maneuver. Paul clipped into the safety line dropped from the ship's deck. Stepping off the launch's bulwark onto the lower rungs of the ladder took all of Paul's concentration and he was grateful that the ship was not rolling. Safely on the ladder, he thanked the helmsman of the launch and climbed the eighteen feet up to the opening in the Malaca Trader's bulwarks.

The deckhand who had lowered the ladder and safety line offered Paul a hand and welcomed him aboard in broken English. Using a walkie-talkie, the deckhand confirmed to the bridge that the pilot was aboard. As soon as the two craft separated, the ship began to regain speed. Paul walked toward the super-structure topped by the bridge leaving the deckhand to recover the ladder. The hulking banks of grey, white and red containers rose four stories above him as he made his way aft on the weather deck. He proceeded cautiously, stepping around a few tensioners and unused chains that did not look to be properly stowed.

He had almost made it to the aft-most, number five, hold when he was startled to hear a voice speaking softly but deliberately somewhere inboard of his position. Paul guessed the language was Malay and peered toward the sound. The speaker had his back to Paul and was standing well into a narrow athwartships passage between the aft-most two stacks of containers. Seeing no one else, Paul assumed the words had been spoken to him.

"Good morning to you" Paul said a little uncertainly.

The man spun around to face him with an alarmed look. Paul could then see that he held a microphone with an attachment resembling a stethoscope that he pressed against the end of the container in front of him. With an angry sweep of his arm the man, who was dressed like an officer, hissed "Away! Away!"

"OK! OK! But what the devil are you doing?"

"Test. Make test for no shift. Why are you here? Not allowed! Go away now!"

Baffled and put off by this outburst, Paul said, "Yeah, well I've got to get along to the bridge". He turned and headed aft. His thoughts moved on from the odd encounter as he entered the superstructure and summoned the elevator that would take him six stories up to the bridge. It was time to focus on meeting the captain and the helmsman and on taking the conn of the Malaca Trader.

Ten hours later, after a relatively uneventful, but fog-slowed transit up the river, Paul turned on his walkie-talkie and contacted the master of the lead docking tug. "Jay, Paul Castner here. Has your bitch had her litter yet?"

Jay Delmer was one of the senior tugboat skippers serving the Portland-Vancouver waterfront. Delmer and his wife were well-respected breeders of Weimaraners. "Yeah! Two days ago. Seven little beauties, too!"

"Glad to hear it! How do you want to make up?"

"I'll put Charlie on your stern with a line and I'll have my mate push on your bow. I'll be aboard in a jiffy. Does she have bow thrusters?"

"Yes, she does. We'll check you out up here in case you want to use 'em."

Delmer quickly boarded and, after a warm handshake with Paul, familiarized himself with the bridge layout. Another thirty minutes passed as the two tugs, under Delmer's direction, nudged and pushed the ship alongside the pier and the longshore workers made her mooring lines fast. Paul started on some of the obligatory paperwork while the lines were secured and the gangway was deployed. Paul bade the captain goodbye as soon as a Customs official and the husbanding agent for the ship boarded.

Leaving the superstructure, Paul walked forward toward the gangway. He recalled the odd incident of the officer seeming to talk to one of the containers as he passed the hatch closest to the bridge. Curiosity overcame fatigue and he turned into the same athwartships alleyway to look more closely at that area. When he came to the container where the officer had stood, he studied its exterior. The only slightly unusual feature he saw was a five-inch diameter metal disc inserted in the container wall and two small orifices perhaps three-quarters of an inch in diameter. Paul shrugged his shoulders in puzzlement and, as he turned to leave, he looked up and saw the same officer glaring at him from the far end of the alleyway. Feeling the force of that belligerent stare, he smiled sheepishly and said, "looks like a very stable stow."

The man nodded without replying and studied him closely. Slightly unnerved, Paul proceeded to the gangway without looking back and walked down to the pier. He saw the taxi that brought the ship's agent beginning to depart from the pier. He hailed it yelling that he was going to the River Pilots' office. Krati stood at the rail and watched his departure.

Krati was rattled when Paul noticed him at the container. He was even more unnerved when he discovered Paul examining the container after the ship arrived in port. As soon as he finished his obligatory third mate's conference with the supervisor of the longshoremen, he used a pre-paid cell phone to call the number Ali had given him in Penang. He gave a description of their river pilot, told of the pilot"s troubling curiosity, and said the man had headed off to the pilots' office.

Paul's cab was slowed by the traffic that, even in the industrial area along the river, had some rush-hour congestion at 4:30. It was nearly five when the taxi reached the Pilot Association's office. Paul entered the utilitarian suite on the second story of the grey frame building and greeted the Association's long-time secretary. He had to finish and file his paperwork and keyboard a terse summary of the inward voyage for archival purposes, but first he had to make two calls. Pouring himself a cup of the notoriously strong coffee from the office pot, he called his wife, Meg. His second call was to his best friend, Tad Madison.

Tad was in his small, well-equipped kitchen when his phone rang.

"Tad, it's Paul."

"Hi! I've already got the bouillabaisse started. What's up?"

"That's why I called. I'm still in Portland."

"Oh! That's not good! What happened?" Tad asked, thinking Paul sounded tired.

"The ship was a couple of hours late arriving and then this fog slowed us down quite a bit. Meg and I were really looking forward to dinner at your place, but I'd be way too late and I'm sort of bushed."

"Don't worry about it, pal. They have one of

those 'crisis' department meetings at the college. The meeting is running over into the evening and Davi can't make it either. Were you on the Malaca something-or-other?"

"Yeah, that was her. The Malaca Trader."

"Problems beyond the fog?"

"No. Not kept up too well, but she handled okay. Damndest thing though. When I first boarded, I saw one of the officers talking to a container!"

"Oh, right! Some guys get really lonely at sea!"

"No, I'm serious. The container was inboard at the weather-deck level two rows forward of the super-structure. This guy had a little mike device pressed up against the end of the container. He looked guilty when I noticed him and gave me a line of crap about testing for stability! I had to scurry up to the bridge so I sort of forgot about it until we docked. On my way off the ship, I was curious enough that I walked over to look at the container. It had a round disk insert in the end and two small holes nearby. The same man saw me looking at it and really gave me the evil eye! It was truly weird. As I was getting into a cab, I looked back at the ship and there he was: leaning on the bulwark and still watching me! Well, enough of that. Anyway, I'm really sorry about the bad timing on dinner. You going to be at the shop tomorrow?"

"Yeah, I'll be in the store. I'll call you tomorrow afternoon."

"I have a better idea. You all come over to our place and play Scrabble. I can throw some burgers on the grill."

"Deal! I'll check with Davi, but it sounds good!"

It was getting dark as Paul got into one of the

Association's cars that the pilots used to shuttle back to the coast if they did not have an assignment on an outbound ship awaiting them. He had traveled no more than three blocks along the nearly deserted street when he saw a man beside an older Nissan sedan on the shoulder waving a gas can. Realizing it was a bad place for someone to have run out of gas, Paul pulled over and lowered his window. The man who approached him appeared to be of Near Eastern extraction.

"Can I help?" Paul asked.

The man leaned toward the window holding the gas can in his left hand with his right hand out of Paul's sight.

"Thank you. Can you take me to a gas station?" he asked.

"Sure, get in."

The man opened the passenger-side door. It was then that Paul glimpsed a gun-like object in the man's right hand. Paul frantically attempted to put the car in gear, but a blinding pain overwhelmed his body and he was unable to move or speak. Paul saw a second man materialize from behind the Nissan. Through a haze of pain and numbness, he heard the two men speak to each other in a language he could not understand. The two men quickly pulled Paul from his car and roughly pushed him into the Nissan's passenger seat. The first man returned to Paul's car and drove it off in the gathering darkness.

Almost unconscious and still unable to move, Paul realized he was being taken a few miles down a frontage road in the industrial area near the river. The pain was beginning to subside but, before he could speak or move, the car left the road and turned into the delivery bay of a warehouse. The driver made a short call on his cell phone and almost immediately a second Near Eastern man emerged from the warehouse. The last thing Paul knew was that the driver had retrieved a soft pillow from the back seat and that he was going to die.

# T W O

THADEUS "TAD" MADISON GREW UP IN BREMERTON, Washington, where his father served the last fifteen years of his naval career as Chief Procurement Officer for the Naval Shipyard. Tad enrolled in the California Maritime Academy directly after graduation from high school. He received his Third Mate's license upon graduation and, in two more years, earned his all-oceans master's ticket. He was twenty-three when he married Christi, then a clerk in the Registrar's Office at the Academy. They rented an apartment in Daly City and Christi found a job at an insurance agency in San Francisco. But Tad was too many weeks at sea and Christy had a handsome, single boss at the agency. Despite almost daily satellite phone calls from Tad and happy days together between voyages, the temptations remained and eventually led to Christi having an affair. Tad and Christy were divorced soon afterward.

Tad then enlisted in the Coast Guard where his first assignment was as a Special Agent to investigate criminal activity within the service and to support the enforcement function against smugglers and saboteurs. Tad quickly had some impressive successes and received a commendation. He remained in that capacity for three years and it whetted his appetite for investigative work and his growing interest in working for the Federal Bureau of Investigation. Tad resigned his Coast Guard commission and applied to join the FBI.

After completing FBI training at Quantico, Virginia, Tad was assigned to the Counter Terrorism Joint Task Force working out of the Southern District of New York field office. The work required patience and determination. The team he was on often traveled on short notice to Yemen, Pakistan, Somalia, and Sudan. The agents dug through layers of false identities and pursued endless leads. They interviewed hundreds of persons some of whom gave up valuable information while others knew nothing useful or simply refused to reveal anything. It was critically important work, but was also stressful, at times frustrating, and usually meant living in Spartan quarters and subsisting on military MREs.

Tad served for nine years and had risen to be the Assistant Special Agent in Charge in the Atlanta field office. But more and more he wanted to be grounded in a state-side community. He submitted his resignation and returned to the Pacific Northwest. He chose Wilcao, the small, picturesque town on the Oregon Coast very near the mouth of the Columbia River, as a place to live.

Three months later, Tad took another step in a new direction: he signed the papers to buy the only bookstore in Wilcao. Tad had become hooked on Classic Comics at age nine and had read the entire Horatio Hornblower series by the time he was thirteen. He had found time to read most of the great Russian, English and American novelists during his years in the merchant marine. During his bachelor years as an FBI agent, his literary interests had broadened to include history and biographies. He lived relatively simply and books became his most valued possessions. His enduring fascination with reading made the bookstore purchase seem like a sensible investment despite the fact the former owner had not made a success of it. Tad renamed the shop, "The Breakers". Aside from an annual buying trip, he spent his days helping his only employee mind the store.

After eight years of Tad's ownership, The Breakers had become a profitable business and a favorite meeting place for the local book lovers. There were even those who rarely bought books, but just dropped by for friendly, small-town conversation. Tad greatly enjoyed his role as the amiable owner of The Breakers.

Tad's background at sea made for easy conversation when he first met Paul Castner.. Over the years, Tad and Paul had become the best of friends. Paul's friendship had encouraged Tad to hang on through the rough time when, after the Great Recession, The Breakers was nearly insolvent. Tad was far too enthused by the fullness of life to be suicidal, but he was emotionally flat-lined combatting the store's financial problems. Paul saw Tad as a good business man but, at the same time, he saw a friend who was dispirited and somewhat disengaged. Paul knew that an interesting and good-hearted person was to be found under Tad's veneer of stoic determination. As the months passed, the town's economy gradually improved and Tad's reserve began to thaw. Tad and he started fishing together and Meg welcomed her husband's new friend in their home. Tad enjoyed attending their son's junior high school basketball games with them and he and the boy quickly developed an affectionate friendship.

Tad's relationship with Paul became even deeper after an ill-fated cross-country ski trip near Santiam Pass. Paul and Tad decided, in a moment of energetic enthusiasm, to leave the groomed trail and strike out on a course closer to Hayrick Butte. They figured that course would eventually intersect another trail heading back to the road-head where they had parked one of the cars. They reasoned that breaking trail on the new route should have been well within their capabilities and started off. What they, and the weather report they had seen the previous evening, did not foresee was a sudden snowstorm.

They carried a compass, but an unlucky fall by Tad crushed it. The simple trail map they had picked up at the road-head was not topographical and they had not fully appreciated the steepness of the ridge lying in their path between the two groomed trails. Their visibility decreased to less than forty feet as the storm increased in intensity. Three hours passed and they had to face the fact that they were lost and near exhaustion. They tried to call on Paul's cell phone, but discovered they were in a "no service" area.

Tad felt light-headed and had started to shiver. They entered a narrow gully where they found a little respite from the wind. Paul produced a folding shovel from his day pack and started digging a snow cave in a drift between a fallen log and the slope of the gully's side. Paul seemed to tolerate the cold better than Tad and he had fallen less so his clothes were dryer. They knew they would have to bivouac through the night without sleeping bags. Paul cut branches with a hunting knife and covered the mouth of their cave but, even with less wind, Tad could not stop shivering. Fearing Tad was on the threshold of hypothermia, Paul stripped off his own down under-vest and insisted that Tad put it on. They lighted the four candles they carried in their packs and gained a few degrees of warmth. Paul embraced Tad in a bear hug and they pulled their two survival blankets close around themselves.

The storm broke around two in the morning. Tad was weak but had stopped shivering and his head was clear. Paul made Tad eat the candy bars and trail mix they had left in their day packs. They thought they heard a snowplow working as the first light of dawn filtered through the snowed-over boughs that covered their tiny cave. By mid-morning, Tad's strength had returned and they were able to ski through the gully in the general direction of the sound. To their sur-prise and relief, they came upon a graveled road less than a half-mile away.

A Bureau of Land Management employee in a pickup truck stopped when he saw their waving arms. He told them Meg had reported they had not returned from their outing and that a search party was being organized as they spoke. His radio call aborted the organizing and he drove them to their car.

Their adventure, though not one they ever wanted to repeat, strengthened the bond between the two men. And Tad would never forget that Paul's efforts had probably saved his life.

# THREE

IT WAS TWO IN THE MORNING WHEN THE PULSING OF Tad's bedside phone dragged him from deep sleep to adrenalized consciousness.

"Yeah. Wazzit?"

"Oh, Tad, it's Meg! I'm so sorry to wake you up, but I'm worried sick! Paul hasn't come home! He called me from Portland... said he was on his way."

"Whoa, Meg," said Tad, suddenly clear-headed. "He called me too. Told me he was delayed and you guys couldn't make dinner. He sounded a little tired. Any chance he got the nods on the way back and just decided to duck into a motel?"

"Not likely. He's always such a wide-awake driver. Besides, he would certainly have called. Tad, I'm scared!"

"Stay calm! I'll come right over and we'll call the State Police. I'm sure he's okay. Did he have his cell?"

"Yes, he always carries it although sometimes he lets the battery get too low. Thanks, Tad!"

Tad's calls to the State Police revealed no traffic accidents on the highway to the coast or the County road to Wilcao. The Portland police declined to start a missing-person investigation on the grounds it was too soon to merit action. Tad awakened the Pilots' Association secretary. She confirmed that Paul had left at dusk in an Association car, perhaps a little tired, but otherwise his usual, good-natured self. Calls to the emergency rooms of all the hospitals en route revealed that no one admitted to those facilities remotely resembled Paul.

⸺

The two men, Taj and Rudi, had worked with cold efficiency. They stripped Paul's body and started the careful process of dyeing Paul's hair. They threw the cards and licenses from the wallet along with his clothes into a small incinerator. They removed Paul's glasses and dentures and added them to a garbage bag destined for a dumpster four blocks away. After Rudi smashed the cell phone with a hammer, he dropped it into a storm drain. Working quickly, the two men redressed the body with clothes from a Good Will store and splashed it with bourbon. Well aware that the riskiest part of their job lay just ahead, they loaded the body into the Nissan and headed for an unlighted road that ended near a railroad track.

⸺

Tad embraced Meg who sobbed quietly in his arms. He tried to convince her that there would be a benign explanation for Paul's disappearance, but he was nearly as unnerved as Meg. He tried to consider all possible scenarios. By morning, Meg still had no word.

He sensed that she was holding herself together, but only barely. Though he had not said this to Meg, he decided, with both reluctance and fear, to start checking medical examiner's offices. Leaving Meg with a good friend and neighbor, Tad drove to Portland.

Tad reached the Multnomah County morgue just after the end of business hours. The night attendant insisted that he could not help him and that, if the pathologists were able to help, it would have to be in the morning.

## 8:10 AM THURSDAY, NOVEMBER 1ST, PORTLAND

Tad was back at the morgue within minutes of its opening the next morning knowing he had to cover four counties before the day ended. The Assistant Medical Examiner, Dr. Agnasi, met Tad at the reception desk.

"How can we help, Mr. Madison?"

"My best friend never made it home to Wilcao from Portland last night. His wife and I have tried all the hospitals, the State Police, County Sheriffs.... nothing. I... I need to find out from you if he could possibly have had a fatal accident."

"Well, we've only had two fatalities in the last thirty-six hours. One we have an identity for and the other appears to have been an unidentified homeless person that railway workers found last night next to the tracks. What is your friend's name?"

"Paul Castner."

"That's not the man we've identified," said Agnasi.

"This homeless person ... a white male?"

"Well, yes. But the intake form says he was dressed in ill-fitting clothes which reeked of alcohol when the body was found. Doesn't sound at all like your friend."

Tad was relieved but, having pursued it this far, he was not about to walk away without more definitive information. "Have you done an autopsy?"

"No, not yet. Later today. On intake, it appeared to be due to either natural causes or self-inflicted alcohol poisoning. Of course we'll be able to know with reasonable certainty after we do the autopsy."

"My friend was dark haired with a little grey, forty-four years old, wore glasses...."

Dr. Agnasi checked the intake form and interrupted, "the age sounds about right, but this fellow's a blond and no glasses."

"I see. Nevertheless, any chance I could see his face?"

"Well, that's a little irregular, but we'd like to ID this man. I suppose – just in the interest of eliminating any outside possibility – it would be alright."

The two men moved down the hall toward the refrigerated storage area. Dr. Agnasi asked Tad to wait in an anteroom where he gestured toward a television monitor and then passed through another door marked "Staff Only". The anteroom had somber gray walls and was furnished with four armchairs with faded plaid seats. An odor of cigarette butts lingered even though smoking was no longer allowed. Tad waited uneasily until the monitor flickered on. An unseen camera panned a few feet across the autopsy lab and then stopped to focus on a bank of oversize drawers set in the wall. A hand opened one of the drawers. Tad saw a draped body in repose on a pad inside the sliding drawer. The technician drew back the sheet and what he saw hit Tad with a spasm of horror and sadness. Under the blond hair, he unmistakably saw Paul Castner's bloodless face.

Tad pushed the button on the intercom, "That is Paul! I don't understand how it could be, but it is!"

Dr. Agnasi came through the door a minute later looking chagrined. "I'm sorry that it is your friend, Mr. Madison. I took a close look at him and could see marks on the bridge of his nose where his glasses must have pressed. I also took a look at the scalp and I'm fairly sure the hair has been recently dyed. Our intake people should have caught that."

Tad lowered himself into a chair and tried to choke back his emotions enough to talk further with the pathologist. "But why would he have dyed his hair and changed into crummy clothes? And Paul has never ever been drunk in all the years I've known him. This is 'way too strange to be 'natural causes', Dr. Agnasi!"

The doctor eyed Tad sympathetically. A big man, solid frame he thought, but on the edge of losing it over his friend. Well, who would not with that kind of a shock? "Did your friend wear dentures?"

"Huh? Oh, yeah, Paul lost most of his teeth in his thirties... some kind of a gum disease."

"The dentures were missing. And no personal belongings."

"So you're thinking like me. Somebody somehow killed him and tried to make it hard to identify him."

"I think that's really a possibility. I'll have to call Mrs. Castner and bring the local police in right away."

Tad felt a burning anger and knew he was not going to walk away from what he felt sure was the murder of his best friend. "Can you possibly let me know what your findings are, Doctor?"

"I'm sorry, but I can't do that. You can talk to the police and, in due time, Mrs. Castner will know and I'm sure she'll want to tell you."

Tad decided to call in a seasonal employee to help at the book store until he had learned whatever he could about what had caused Paul's death and why. He realized that he might be over-reacting in the sense that, despite his horror and sadness over Paul's murder, there was probably little he could do. Had his anger led him to overestimate what he could accomplish? Was he temporarily deranged by a primitive need for revenge? He had to acknowledge that those emotions could be factors affecting his judgment. But he also had confidence in his FBI training and his ability to solve problems. There was something so macabre about Paul's demise. The circumstances of his death dishonored Paul and Tad felt he had to clear that up. He believed that a week or so of his time spent on that effort was the least he could do for his friend.

He thanked the doctor and told him he would call Meg himself in about twenty minutes. Leaving his cell-phone number with the receptionist, he turned and walked toward his rental car, exhausted, angry, and determined to discover who had done this to Paul.

He was back at his motel slumped in an easy chair trying to formulate a plan to fathom what had happened when two Portland Police detectives knocked on the door. After introductions and presentation of their credentials, they sat on the edge of the bed with weary grunts and started asking questions. They had talked to Dr. Agnasi by telephone, but since he had not had time to do the autopsy, they had decided to visit Tad first. "So did Mr. Castner spend quite a lot of evenings away from home?" the older detective asked.

"No, not at all. When he wasn't on a ship, I think he was always home unless he and Meg had a social engagement or were watching their son play sports."

"And no addictions or compulsions that you know about?"

"No absolutely not! He was as normal and wholesome as you could want."

"You ever get any feeling he led a secret life of any kind? Into high risk or deviant stuff?"

"Those theories are all baloney, gentlemen! Paul never missed a piloting job unless he was seriously sick, and he was happily married and a wonderful father to his son. Hell, except for fishing, he was a real homebody."

"Well, can we be sure that when he was supposed to be fishing, he wasn't doing something funky with a hooker or a secret lover?"

"You can be damn sure! Most of the time he fished with a man in Wilcao, Matt Maloney, and I've gone with him a few times myself. Besides, I told you he called his wife and me and told us both he was off the ship and on his way home. I tell you he was waylaid somehow!"

The detective who had been doing most of the questioning said, "We think you're right about foul play and you may even be right that the killer was a total stranger to him. But why all the trouble to conceal his identity?"

Leaving that question hanging, the second detective asked, "Mind telling us where you were two nights ago?"

Tad wondered if they could possibly suspect him. "As I said earlier, I'd prepared a dinner for Paul and Meg. I live alone and my girlfriend had a last-minute evening meeting and wasn't able to join us. When Paul called to say he was so late that they couldn't make it either, I ate alone, cleaned up the kitchen, and watched a DVD of *Three Days of the Condor.* I was in bed by quarter to ten. I was asleep when Paul's wife, Meg, called."

"Thanks. We would have had to ask you sooner or later. Anyone see you in Wilcao in late afternoon?"

"I picked up some groceries I needed at the Superette on Third Street. The cashier might remember me. We had a short conversation about Walla Walla Sweet onions. I think her name is Mandy or maybe it's Mindy."

Both men glanced at their watches and looked at each other. The man who did most of the questioning stood and closed his notebook.

"Thanks again. Here's our cards if you think of anything else."

Tad looked at names on the cards, "Detective Angel Martinez" and "Detective Bob Peterson." They seemed like good professionals, but they also acted as if they were overworked, almost distracted. He wondered if they would bring all their department's resources to bear on this case.

Tad's next move was to try to locate the Pilot Association's car that Paul had been driving. None of the seven towing services reported picking up such a car so he drove to some fairly obvious places such as waterfront parking lots. A light drizzle had begun, leaving the warehouses and factories with a dirty, gray sheen. After several hours, with nothing to show for his time, he questioned whether his efforts could add anything to the detectives' investigation. But, as he passed a sign directing traffic to the airport, he realized that the airport's long-term parking garage was a possibility he should not overlook. He turned the car around and headed for the Portland Airport.

Tad had to drive slowly enough to view each of the many hundreds of parked cars on either side of the aisle. He had a couple of close encounters with drivers backing out of their stalls as he was looking to the opposite side. Impatient drivers searching for open stalls or wanting to drive home after a long trip honked at him more than once. He was on the fourth level and on the verge of losing his concentration when he saw a gray Chevy sedan like the cars in the small fleet the pilots used. Pulling his car into an empty stall at the end of the aisle, Tad ran back to the Chevrolet. It was the right color and vintage, but how could he be sure? He walked around to the front. That end of the car was in semi-darkness, but Tad had no trouble seeing the creosote-colored scrape on the front right fender. He remembered Paul telling him how he was mad at himself the day he rubbed the car against a telephone pole while backing out of the Association's parking area. Paul had taken considerable kidding from his colleagues that he, a pilot, could not manage to steer his own car past the pole. The Association had never bothered to have the scrape repaired. This was certainly a Pilots Association vehicle and could well be the one Paul was driving the day he was killed. He reached for his cell phone to call Angel Martinez.

After the tow truck left, Tad felt a grim satisfaction that his efforts had led to the recovery of the car. Martinez thanked him, but also told him that they had just sent out a dispatch to all law enforcement with a description of the car and implied that the airport police would have found it later that day anyway. Tad was ravenous by then and drove back to the ocean terminal area where he found a waterfront cafe for a late lunch. The coffee was awful but, to his surprise, the tuna-melt was quite decent. As he ate, he tried to remember anything Paul had said or done in the last few days that might be significant. There was nothing …unless … he thought about Paul's description over the phone of the puzzling incident on the Malaca Trader. What had he said? A guilty look from a mate who was talking into some kind of a device held against a container? And a bullshit explanation from the guy, who later glared at him. Certainly peculiar, but hardly enough to get a man killed. And yet, the effort taken by someone to prevent a quick identification of the body suggested much more than just a random violent encounter.

He paid his bill and headed for the Portland Coast Guard office and his friend, Lieutenant Commander

Bowen Gardiner. They had met six years ago in the course of a marine investigation concerning a cargo ship that had stranded just offshore from Wilcao. The ship claimed that an outbound vessel had violated the Rules of the Road and forced it into the shallows to avoid a collision. Tad happened to be watching from shore and became an eye witness in the subsequent Coast Guard hearing. The two men emerged from the investigation with mutual respect and an easy friendship. Gardiner, at six foot two, was a little taller than Tad. His lean build, prematurely graying hair, and crisply pressed uniform gave him a formal, imposing appearance. This appearance was suitable for a man recently assigned to be Port Captain, but Tad knew him to be a warm-hearted, fair person.

Tad was lucky to find Commander Gardiner in his office and was ushered in by the receptionist who had met him at the public counter. "Hi, Bo. It's been a while."

"Sure has! I guess the last time I saw you must have been at that gig you had at the Taste of Portland."

Tad laughed, "Right. I sub as a drummer in that swing band and every so often I get to be in on a real performance. The regular drummer had a conflict of some kind so I got the call for that charity event."

"You ought to take over his position, you wild man!"

"No, we're all amateurs, but the other guy's a much better musician than I. Besides in the summer when the store's open evenings, I can't even make most of the rehearsals." Tad's grin faded and he sat a little straighter in his chair. "Bo, I need a favor."

"I figured this was something more than a social call. Tell me how I can help."

"A dear friend of mine – you might know him, Paul Castner –"

"Oh, yeah. A river pilot isn't he?"

"Yes, that he was. Paul was murdered, Bo!"

"My God!"

"Of course the police are on it, but I'm also looking into it on my own and I need some information about the ship he was working just before his death. Can you get me her registry and a list of her officers."

"Sure, easy enough."

"She's the Malaca Trader. I need more though. I want a copy of her cargo manifest and her stow plan."

"Hmmm…. that'll be harder, but I'll see if the agent will come across. If that doesn't work, I'll contact Customs." Gardiner paused to jot some notes. "I'll make the calls right away before my next meeting. Can you meet me around five at Jake's?" Gardiner asked as he jotted some notes.

"Great! Thanks, Bo. I'll see you there."

Jake's Famous Crawfish was a venerable restaurant on Stark Street beloved by Portland seafood lovers and young professionals. Tad liked the old mahogany bar overhung with oil paintings and the fine food, but could do without the noise of the animated diners and drinkers who invariably overcrowded the place in early evenings. He asked the hostess for a table at the rear of one of the less-crowded rooms for a little more privacy.

Gardiner arrived carrying a manila envelope about five minutes after Tad had been shown to his table. They ordered drinks and Gardiner said "I managed to get what you wanted. Since this ship visited my port, I'm more than a little curious what you think ties the ship's cargo to a murder."

Tad repeated Paul's comments about the mate appearing to be talking to a container. "I have no idea what was going on with this guy he saw or if there could be any connection to Paul's death. But he certainly reacted strangely toward Paul ... edgy and angry ...almost paranoid. And the police so far seem to be very conventional in their thinking and they apparently have no clues or evidence to work with. So I'm willing to spend some of my time poking around to see if anything jumps out as a reason for his death." He saw Gardiner's skeptical expression, but continued more forcefully, "The container incident is the only abnormal thing I know about. It's kind of suspicious on its face and it was observed by Paul. Then somebody felt the need to kill him and cover up any connection to his life or his job on ships."

Gardiner leaned forward across the table and lowered his voice. "You're thinking maybe a bomb in the container? Or undocumented aliens?"

"Like I said, Bo, I don't even have a theory. It smells of something illegal, though it's not easy to figure why Paul could be that threatening to whoever was behind it."

"Okay. My contact at Customs, Jason Elmore, was pretty curious too. I told him I was just checking on some stowage issues, but that I'd get back to him if I saw anything of concern to Customs. It doesn't sound to me like you know enough at this point to bother him, but if you turn up anything of importance, I expect to hear from you and we'll get Customs in the loop." He started to drink, then stopped and resumed, "Oh, I'm also acquainted with the top guy locally in the FBI. His name's Russ Bronson. I'll give him a call and tell him about you and why you're wondering what could be going on. Can't hurt."

"That suits me fine," Tad replied and they hoisted their glasses. "To a safe voyage and a quick return!"

At his motel, Tad studied the documents Gardiner had given him. He noticed a penned in correction to the ship's crew roster. The Third Officer's printed name had been lined out and the name Amed Krati was written beside the original name. By checking the cargo manifest against the stow plan, he learned who were the consignees of the four inboard containers on the weather-deck level at the number five hold. Three were consigned to Lawn King, Inc. in Troutdale, Oregon; the fourth to Tropical Furniture Imports in Portland.

Tad could not visit the consignees of the cargo until they opened for business tomorrow. He had not seen Davi for almost three days and wanted very much to hear her voice. His fingers hit the buttons on his cell phone.

DaVita Salloway taught International Relations and Near Eastern History at Clatsop Community College in Astoria. As the daughter of an American international-banker father and a Lebanese educator mother, she was fluent in Arabic. Her parentage, language skills, and early upbringing in Lebanon made her comfortable in choosing an academic career. After her husband was killed in the crash of a friend's light plane, the warmth of the residents and the community spirit of Wilcao made her decide that it was the best place to get past her grief and continue her life. That was nine years in the past and she had never regretted the move despite the somewhat longer commute to the college. Then, almost a year ago, she happened to be in The Breakers on an afternoon when Tad was minding the store.

Tad was attracted to this beautiful, dark-haired woman almost from the moment she entered the store. Her quiet smile and the soft curves of her figure held his attention in those first moments. They ended up sitting in the two easy chairs at the back of the store, sipping coffee and discussing the Alexandria Quartet. An hour passed before Davi chose a book to buy and left. Tad watched her go and marveled at the serene nature and obvious intelligence of his newest customer.

Davi returned to the store a week later and Tad invited her to take a short hike with him. Their relationship, so cautious and hesitant at first, had gradually deepened. Tad and Davi had each discovered they could love again. With Tad's small house and a drum set in the breakfast nook, they continued to maintain their separate homes. They had begun to consider marrying and looking for a larger house, but those decisions were still ahead of them.

He heard her answer the phone. "Davi, it's me. I'm in Portland."

"Oh, Tad. I heard about Paul. It's so terrible, so sad! Are you okay?"

"Not great, no. I'm so sorry I didn't call you right

away. I was helping Meg and, after that, I was in such a funk...."

"That's alright, honey. I know what a shock this must be and what you're going through. How come you're still in Portland? Do you have book business?"

"No. In fact, I'm taking some time away from the store. I'm ... well I guess it's kind of crazy, but I'm looking into his death. Sort of investigating. Maybe I can help discover who did this to him."

"I realize how close you were with Paul, but shouldn't you leave that to the police? You're not an FBI agent anymore!"

"Davi, I can't just go on with my life as if nothing happened. For now, at least, I owe it to Paul to try to help figure this out."

Davi well knew Tad's determined streak and his great loyalty to friends. "I understand, Tad. I could reschedule classes for a few days and come to the city to help you if you're set on doing this."

He very much wanted to say yes, but he didn't have a clear enough plan to see how she could be of immediate help. And, if there was something more sinister than random violence going on, he did not want her involved. "No, Davi. You stay there. I'll be fine... I'm just checking some facts. I'll call you tomorrow."

"I wish you were here, now. I love you," she said and they ended the call.

# FOUR

**N**AJEV AL SAID'S FATHER HAD INCULCATED HIM FROM his early adolescence with a hatred of Israel and its patron the United States. He stayed in the Palestinian refugee camp school through his teenage years despite an increasing realization that his future would be limited by lack of opportunity and regional politics. As he matured, his intellect was largely stunted by his sullen and vengeful persona.

Najev was eighteen and still living with his parents when word circulated through the camp that his father had been taken prisoner by Israeli commandos. The capture was never acknowledged by the Israelis despite inquiries through the camp administrator and the Red Crescent. That organization told his family that the summary in the commando unit's records for that day showed only that two Palestinian males were accosted on the Israeli side of the border, interviewed and then released. Neither man was identified. But Najev knew his father worked closely with their friend Aram as officers in the camp's "militia" and that they both disappeared on that day. He was never to see his father again or even to know whether he was still alive.

Two weeks after his father's disappearance, Najev asked to see his father's militia commander. He was ready, he said, to work for the Palestinian cause, to do his part in the movement. Najev did well in the secretive training sessions and was quickly recognized as a promising recruit. Four years passed and though he never was chosen for raiding parties or smuggling efforts, the commander valued him as a planner and organizer. It was then that Najev met the Egyptian.

The Egyptian was a corpulent man known simply as Al M'afid, although his contacts all suspected that was not his real name. He visited Lebanon on business visas ostensibly to sell cement mixers and used construction equipment, but spent only enough time meeting with contractors to build a credible cover. In the evenings and weekends, he was in the camps training, motivating, gathering intelligence and recruiting. The militia commander described Najev as a ruthless loner whose smoldering fury was held in check by above-average intelligence and a long-run viewpoint. At their first meeting, the Egyptian spoke with Najev for two hours in a stuffy room that smelled of tobacco smoke. Their conversation was intense and passionate. It revealed to the Egyptian qualities that he sought. Al M'afid found a better camp job for Najev and followed his progress in the militia. He managed to spend an hour with Najev whenever he visited Lebanon. Another year passed and Najev's mother died of lung cancer. Six weeks later, the Egyptian provided him with a slightly different identity, a new personal history complete with an Egyptian passport, and immigration papers to the United States.

When the message from Cairo was passed to him in the mosque, it was as if an intricately beautiful, vital butterfly had finally emerged from its chrysalis. After he arrived in the United States he never questioned the wait, the dormancy, the humiliation of the green-card process. Najev had hated his early sense of exclusion and the struggle to prove his competency to the bank that financed his inventory. In the rare communications from the Egyptian, Al M'Afid told him to be patient and to focus on imports from Asia. Al M'Afid had provided him with the initial capital to start the business in Portland, Oregon. He had simply required that Najev only employ other Muslims and that he try to find a place for himself alongside the infidels.

Over his seven years in the United States, Najev gradually made a modest success of the furniture importing business. Perhaps because of that success, he had, during the last year, started to wonder whether he still had the courage and the will to serve as a warrior in Al M'Afid's secret army. But lately, without anyone at the Portland mosque knowing of his relationship with the people in Egypt, the exhortations and fervor of some of those who worshiped there had re-instilled his sense of duty and mission.

After what he liked to think of as his "activation", Najev had little trouble identifying the people he would need. Bajehr had been his assistant in the business since the beginning. He was fiercely loyal to Najev and donated generously to several Pan-Arab causes. Zulanni did not work for Najev, but they had had many conversations and he knew she was intelligent, reliable, and deeply resentful of the United States' support of Israel. He considered her a jihadi just waiting to be operational. And he knew that Al M'Afid had given her financial support to start her dry-cleaning business. She would be on his team.

Sulien made too many clerical mistakes and had offended one of their better customers. Najev was ready to fire him anyway. He would replace him with Rudi. The young man was not too intelligent, but he was among the most radical of the young, disenchanted men who attended the mosque. Al M'Afid had suggested another Portland man, Taj and Najev promptly hired him to join the staff in the wholesale furniture business.

# FIVE

TAD VISITED A PRINT SHOP AFTER AN EARLY BREAKFAST and had two sets of business cards printed on a rush order. Tad headed for Troutdale with the cards in hand. The Lawn King address turned out to be a factory near the river where he saw lawnmowers being assembled. He asked to meet with the Purchasing Manager. An employee led him to the office of a woman in her forties. Tad told her that he was a representative of the Malacca Trader's liability insurer doing random checks on the condition of delivered shipments. Though surprised, she did not question his statement or ask for credentials beyond the business card. They conversed for a few minutes and she invited Tad on a brief tour of the factory floor. Walking down the immaculate aisle, he saw an overhead materials-handling system bringing body and control modules to be joined with wheel-axel combinations and engines. Assemblers manipulated power tools to accomplish the mating of the components. The factory appeared to have over a hundred employees on the floor. He saw the newly-arrived consignment of engines, still wrapped in plastic in an adjoining storage area. The Purchasing Manager said she had not received any damaged shipments in the last two years. Tad thanked her and headed for his car. The visit had given him no reason to believe there was anything out of the ordinary about the Lawn King operation or its consignment of engines carried on the Malacca Trader.

Tropical Furniture Imports was housed in a small warehouse about two miles from the Port of Portland container terminal. Before getting out of the car, Tad slipped some of the other business cards into his wallet. This set identified him as a buyer for a furniture store in Medford, Oregon. The building had a pair of loading bays to one side and a simple entry door centered and facing the parking lot. Tad opened the door and turned toward a modest office area to his right. A man with a darker complexion, a mustache and flashing brown eyes rose from behind a desk and introduced himself as the owner. Tad offered his card and explained he had come to Portland on a buying trip, dropping the name of another wholesaler. He said a contact of his had noticed the sign on the warehouse and mentioned it to him. Tad implied he had not yet made any final purchasing decisions and said he was particularly interested in seeing their line of tropical-style furniture. The manager looked momentarily uncertain. Tad used the suspension of conversation to absorb as much information about the office as possible: a desk calendar with some scribbled notes on the day's page; a small steel safe next to a file cabinet; a small shelf of manufacturer's catalogues; and a sizable portable radio that appeared to have short-wave receiving capability. Concentrating so hard on his visual inventory, he almost did not hear the man's somewhat reluctant agreement to show him their lines. The man flipped on overhead floodlights and led Tad to where samples were displayed. "These pieces are representative of the line we import," he said, gesturing at bamboo-framed chairs, lounges and tables arrayed along a wall.

Tad inspected the furniture, trying not to say anything specific enough to betray his lack of expertise. He asked for pricing information and turned to leave when his gaze fell on a large, capsule-like, fiberglass structure in the opposite bay. It was shaped like a giant oblong box with an access hatch at one end. The hatch was almost wide open and he caught a glimpse of a bunk against one wall.

Excited, but feigning idle curiosity, Tad asked, "What's that over there?"

The manager almost physically herded him toward the front door. "Ah, nothing....one of the employees is building himself a camper."

"I would've thought it cheaper to buy a used one already manufactured."

"I know, but he's kind of a do-it-yourself guy and he got the shell really cheaply from a salvage yard somewhere so I guess it's become his latest 'project'."

Tad then stopped and turned to face a solid wall at the back of the showroom space with a wide door signed "Employees Only". "More inventory back there?" he asked pointing to the door.

"Yes, just items ready for transshipment to our customers." The shorter man glanced pointedly at his watch, "You must excuse me. I'm alone here today and I have to leave for an appointment downtown."

As Tad drove away, his instinct told him something was not right about that wholesale operation.

He could not put his finger on anything specific and the furniture he was shown was real enough. He had seen other furniture, on pallets but still swathed in plastic, and that also looked legitimate. But the self-proclaimed owner seemed apprehensive and hardly showed any interest in gaining him as a new customer. He had not even offered Tad a business card! And then there was that strange fiberglass unit that the manager claimed was going to become one of his employee's camper. Tad decided to return after dark to take a closer look at the outside of the building. In the meantime, he would see what kind of a paper trail had been generated by Tropical Furniture Imports.

Tad's next stop was the County Assessor's office. He entered the five-story Multnomah Building, walked by a coffee cart in the lobby, and proceeded past the elevator bay down a wood-paneled hallway until he saw a sign "Records" to his right. After what seemed an interminable wait for his turn at the counter, he asked for ownership information on the warehouse. It was difficult because the building had no external indication of its address. A smiling clerk with an East-Indian accent showed him how to use the large-scale map that depicted the parcel boundaries and numbers. Once he identified the parcel, she consulted a computerized data base at a computer behind her and returned to the counter. Tad jotted down the owners' names, Patrick and Doris Severson, with an address and phone number in Sacramento. Tad waved a thank you and good bye to the clerk and headed for the lobby.

He felt lucky when the phone was answered and a woman identified herself as Mrs. Severson. "I'm with a lender considering making a loan to Tropical Furniture Imports, and we're doing a credit check on the company. They are housed in a building that appears to be owned by you and your husband," he said.

She responded, "Yes, I know they're our tenant in that warehouse we bought up in Portland, but we leave all the tenant selection and accounting to our property manager up there. Sorry, but all we know is that they seem reliable and they're current with the rent."

"Would you mind telling me who you use as your property manager?"

"Not at all. In Portland, we use Gilbraith Properties."

Gilbraith's office was in the Pittock Block building on Washington Street in downtown Portland. Occupying an entire block, the ninety-five-year-old structure had been carefully restored in the nineties to retain its stately grace. The Gilbraith reception room on the sixth floor was utilitarian at best. The grey-haired receptionist proved to be a formidable guardian of the inner offices. She asked the reason for his wanting to see the property manager and was not about to summon the manager to meet with Tad on his naked request. Tad gave her his best smile and the furniture-buyer business card.

"The company I represent is considering helping finance some imports through one of your tenants and part of our due diligence effort is to get background on the company's business arrangements."

This mollified her and, after he identified the property, she called a Mr. Jonberg to the front. Jonberg introduced himself and led Tad down a short inner hallway to his office. The large oak desk centered before the window was nearly covered with folders and computer printouts. A photo of Jonberg with a spread of pheasants hung on a wall. After confirming the reason for his interest, Tad asked Jonberg how Tropical had obtained the lease.

"Well, it was at least five years ago. The property had been vacant for several months at the time. They said they had seen our sign and they liked the location and the fact that it had a shipping dock. They didn't really attempt to bargain on much.... they seemed content with our ask on the rent. Didn't require any improvements, didn't ask for a TI allowance. One of the easier deals I've done."

"You checked their credit?"

"Of course. But they turned out to be okay. Been in business a couple of years. Nothing jumped out in their credit history. Their bank reference was fine. Seems they always had a healthy balance and the bank had approved quite a few letters of credit for import transactions over that period."

"Are they incorporated in Oregon?"

"Yes."

"How long is their lease?"

"Well, we usually do three years minimum, but they did ask for just two years, renewable. The Seversons had just bought the property and wanted to get it occupied. Mr. S. thought the market would be better a couple of years from then anyway, so they went along with the shorter term. It's rolled over since then with modest raises in the rent."

Tad left the building pondering what he had learned. Of the two consignees, Tropical seemed more opaque. It was newer and less well established. His visit there was met with some anxiety and little openness. The warehouse and the fiberglass module were more enigmatic than the bustling lawnmower factory and the manager he met seemed foreign-born, probably from the Near East. Tad felt handicapped by not having any contacts in Malaysia. It might help if he could learn something about the exporter. And he kept coming back to the question: why would a ship's officer be "talking" to a container whether it contained light engines or bamboo furniture?

———

Tad bought a black windbreaker, a cheap flash camera, a photo card, a pair of leather gloves, and a flashlight. He went back to his motel after dinner at an Applebee's restaurant and called Davi. He gave her a brief report on what he had learned. She again tried to discourage him from what she called his "snooping around". He was surprisingly tired and, after they ended the call, he lay down for a short nap, kicked off his shoes, and rolled under the bedspread. Sleep came quickly. Two hours later, he was startled by the unfamiliar buzzing of the bedside alarm. Working past the grogginess of awakening from a deep sleep, he put on the dark windbreaker, grabbed the flashlight and the camera and headed for the warehouse.

He parked the car two blocks away on a side

street. The streets were paved, but had no sidewalks. The night sky was overcast and there was no street lighting although a few of the industrial properties and warehouses had exterior lights. He saw no one about, but he stayed in the darkest shadows. He chose to keep even further from the street by crossing over a vacant lot and nearly tripped over a discarded water heater. The evening was cool, but the idea of trespassing into a possibly dangerous place left perspiration on his brow.

Tad could make out Tropical's warehouse about a block ahead on his right. At the cross street, he turned toward an alley that he hoped might run behind the warehouse. The alley was pot-holed and apparently little used, but it did run behind the warehouse. Tad saw an eight-foot-high cyclone fence surrounding an area about fifty feet wide adjacent to the warehouse. It was difficult to be sure in the darkness, but he thought he saw a paned window high on the warehouse wall facing the alley. He dimmed his flashlight's beam with his hand as he inspected the fence. It looked to have been installed very recently. Still wary, he turned off the flashlight. He could make out the remains of several packing cases, a dumpster, a small corrugated iron shed – and close to the building – a fiberglass module like the one he had seen inside earlier. What he had not noticed from his daytime visit, but now saw, was that a gated driveway connected the paved parking lot in front to the fenced area in back.

He very much wanted a closer look at the mysterious module, but he stuck to his original plan to work his way around the entire building before trying to enter the grounds. The building to the east butted up against the warehouse and was set deeper into its lot so that it almost reached the alley. That building was two stories high and appeared to be abandoned. It had many broken windows. There was a fire escape facing the alley further suggesting that the building was once an apartment complex. Tad continued through the alley and turned left on the side street and left again at the corner back toward the front of the warehouse. There were no lights on and he saw no vehicles parked in front. He crossed another vacant lot on the warehouse's west side to return to the alley. He stuffed the flashlight in a pants pocket and grabbed the mesh wire of the fence. Tad clambered over the top in a few seconds and dropped into the yard.

The shed had no windows and there was a padlock on its door. Moving to the warehouse and stretching to his full height, he discovered that the window-panes on the rear wall had been painted black. There was a triangular chip missing at the upper edge of one of the panes in the top row, but it was well above his eye level. Tad thought he heard a quiet electric motor sound through the wall. He wondered if the sound could be the motor of a small refrigerator. But why did a furniture warehouse need a refrigerator?

As Tad pondered that, he moved away from the building to the module. He tried the handle on the hatch and it turned. The hatch opened noiselessly and he shined his light inside. He saw a compact living quarters roughly ten feet by eight feet with a six-foot ceiling.

He stepped through the hatch opening, bumping

his shin on the coaming in his haste. He mentally inventoried what he saw: a bunk bed that could swing up like a crude Pullman berth, some sort of a chemical toilet, a secured-to-the-floor table, a chair, a storage cupboard and a frame apparently designed to support some equipment that was no longer there. But what he studied most was a five-inch diameter metallic disk about sixty inches off the floor in the end wall of the module. Next to the disk was an electronics jack. There appeared to be a heating unit affixed to the floor. He also saw a fitting that could have connected to a gas source, but no pressurized tanks could be seen. A pair of tubes ran from what looked like an enclosed fan manifold to the same end wall that held the metallic disk. Tad pulled the camera from his jacket pocket to take pictures when he heard voices. Several men were speaking in a foreign tongue and were close at hand.

# SIX

**T**AD TURNED OFF HIS FLASHLIGHT AND LEAPED THROUGH the hatch. The sounds of a truck engine and the clinking of a moving gate told him that people would be coming down the driveway almost immediately. On the run, he got as far as the shed when the headlights of a truck swept around the corner of the warehouse. Crouching behind the shed, he heard animated remarks in a foreign language as three men stepped out of the truck and stood around the module. One voice finally quieted the others down and repeated a phrase twice, then seemingly gave an order and the men started to attach ropes to the module. Tad was concentrating on memorizing the sounds of at least a few of their statements when he shifted his weight slightly and knocked over an empty packing case that had been leaning against the shed wall.

Cries of alarm rose from the three men and Tad knew he was facing serious trouble if he could not make it over the fence in time. Breaking cover, he sprinted the thirty feet to the fence. Tad was almost to the top of the fence when they spotted him. He flung himself over, knowing they were likely to pursue him. He landed hard, but kept his footing and raced east down the alley. Taking a quick look over his shoulder, he saw two of the men climbing the fence. Two shots rang out and bullets ricocheted off the alley in front of him. Tad was not in top condition, but he was strong and his long legs and a surge of adrenaline gave him a momentary advantage. He made it to the corner and turned South toward the next street. At that corner, he turned right again. He could see no one behind him, but he heard running footsteps nearing the end of the alley.

The street he had turned onto was even darker with no buildings on the south side of the street. Tad thought there might be a train track on that side. The buildings on the North side were all fenced off. He was too far from any late-night cafes or 7-Elevens to sustain a footrace to safety. That told him that he had only a few seconds to hole up somewhere. He angled across the pavement on a dead run to where he had glimpsed a deep ditch paralleling the street. He plunged, without hesitation, headlong into the blackberry bushes that filled the ditch.

His body tore through the vines and his fall ended abruptly and painfully when he crashed into something much more solid. He would have broken some ribs or ruptured some internal organ had the blackberries not cushioned his landing. As it was, the old railroad tie merely knocked the wind out of him. He fought to regain his breath and, light-headed from pain, tried to quiet himself. Tad sensed that he lay on his side partially wrapped around the tie and near the bottom of the ditch. As best he could see, the vines were mostly intact above him. He heard a car accelerating down the street in the distance. Tad hoped his pursuers would think that was he making a successful get-away.

He heard the voices of the two men, at first going further away, then returning closer to him. The voices sounded as though the men had separated, probably walking down opposite sides of the street. He saw a flashlight beam sweeping across the blackberries and willed himself to stop panting. The light moved on and he was able to suck in a new lung-full of air. Five minutes later, he heard the truck's engine and a distant conversation. Then the truck's doors closed and he heard it drive away.

Tad waited another ten minutes before attempting to climb out of the ditch. The pain in his solar plexus had diminished and was replaced by the lesser pain of dozens of scratches. It was not easy to right himself and untangle from the briars. He worried that they could have left someone behind to wait him out so he tried to move slowly to reduce any noise to a minimum.

Tad trotted toward where he had parked his car. Knowing it was just down the block on an intersecting street, he stopped to peer around the corner. It was then that he saw their truck parked with its lights out at the far end of the same block. He had left the car several blocks from the warehouse, but his was the only car on the street making it a likely target for their stake-out. Tad drew back from the corner and started running away from the area.

Ten minutes later, feeling safe but knowing he would have to rest soon, he spotted a neon "Budweiser" sign. He slowed and approached the tavern, checking to make sure the truck was not parked nearby. Stopping at the door, he glanced around the interior to be sure there were no Arabic faces inside. In answer to his question, and after a long look at his scratched face, the bartender offered him the bar phone. Tad punched in the number of a cab company. The dispatcher said it was a quiet evening for taxis and he could have a cab there in ten minutes. Tad used the restroom to clean off the blood from the blackberry scratches and the mud of the ditch. His pursuers would eventually decide he was not going to return for the car and would probably widen their search. It crossed his mind to spend the next nine minutes in the restroom but – even though he was now feeling more certain that his pursuers were somehow connected to Paul's murder and that their intentions toward him were deadly too – he could not see himself cowering in a stall. Besides, he realized, if they did enter the tavern, he would be safer amongst the customers. He found a stool at the end of the bar and ordered a beer. Ten minutes later, there was no sign of the three men and the cab pulled to the curb.

Tad told the driver to start driving and directed him to the general vicinity of his motel. He repeatedly looked back through the rear window, but saw no headlights. He told the driver to stop and paid him off when the cab was four blocks from his motel. Tad walked away from the direction of his motel. After a block, he turned to head toward the parallel street. There was almost no traffic and the street lights made it easy for him to see that he was not being followed on foot. He turned again and quickened his pace back to the motel.

They finally gave up on the stake-out of the vehicle.

Najev was nervous about their returning to haul the module away in case the intruder was still in the vicinity. He said they would wait a few hours and use a chain saw to cut it up in the very early morning. The noise would be risky, but there were no residences nearby and he wanted the pieces to be unrecognizable. No police patrols passed at three in the morning and they hurried to demolish the module. They loaded the debris into their delivery truck and took it to two different sites as soon as the waste disposal facilities opened in the morning.

# SEVEN

TAD CALLED A TOWING SERVICE BEFORE HE SET OUT FOR breakfast and arranged for them to tow his rental car to a supermarket parking lot a half-mile from his motel. He told the dispatcher, that the driver would receive a twenty-dollar tip if people asked him where he was towing the car and he told them that it was going to the police garage as a stolen car. As it turned out, no one had questioned the driver, but Tad gave him the twenty anyway.

Najev was angry that they had not found the intruder. They all had heard a car accelerating out of the area, but he was convinced that the man could not have had time to reach a car. He believed the man had evaded the searchers by going to earth in the immediate vicinity, waiting them out and then making his escape. He still thought that the car they staked out had been driven by the man they chased. They had the license number and knew it was a rental car. Najev said that they had to learn who the intruder was and where he could be found.

That morning, Bajehr parked down the block

from the Avis office and approached it on foot. He could see only two employees, a young woman and a man in his early thirties, at the counter. He loitered across the street until the woman disappeared through a door behind the counter. He entered and approached the man. Bajehr noticed the man had dirty fingernails and that his shirt cuffs were soiled.

"I need some information," Bajehr said in a low voice.

The man looked at him with a bored, but wary expression. "What do you want to know?"

"I'd like to know the identity of the last person who has rented a car with this license number from you." As he spoke, Bajehr passed the man a slip of paper with the number written on it.

"Well, we don't give out that type of information," he replied.

"I can understand that," said Bajehr, extracting a fifty-dollar bill from his pocket and discreetly laying it on the counter. "But this is rather important to me and I was hoping you might be able to make an exception."

The man reached for the bill and his hard lips curved in what might have passed for a grin. "Well, I suppose I could help you out this once."

Bajehr nodded and added, "I'll need the driver license number and address as well."

The man moved a step to his left and keyboarded some commands and the plate number. He studied his monitor for a moment, then reached for a note pad and wrote a name, a driver license number and an address.

Two hundred dollars to a fellow worshiper at the mosque who was rumored to be a talented computer hacker got Bajehr a digital copy of Tad's driver's license photo from the Department of Motor Vehicles' data base.

It was not difficult for Najev to obtain a credit report on Tad. Another fifty dollar bill on top of the standard fee greatly expedited the production and delivery of the report. Tad's bookstore proved to be a profitable enterprise. Najev had thought they had eradicated any complications by eliminating the river pilot. So why did this book person, Madison, take an interest in Tropical? Then his thoughts went back to the afternoon visit of the man calling himself a furniture buyer. The face he remembered was very similar to the photo. The man had seemed vague in his inquiries and hesitant in his inspection of the furniture samples. And, Najev now remembered, the visitor had asked a question about the module which was still inside at that time. This Thadeus Madison had to be found and silenced.

Tad collected his rental car and called Bowen Gardiner who told him to come right over.

"I think there's something going on with the Tropical Furniture people, Bo!"

"So what did you learn?"

"I went there posing as a furniture buyer. The manager could be an Arab and he seemed real uneasy talking to me instead of welcoming a potential buyer. Then I saw this strange fiberglass module ... a big thing – six-by-nine-or-ten – with sort of an access hatch at one end. When I asked about it, he claimed some employee was making a camper body!"

"That's kind of strange, but you know we can't move on that. Is there more?"

"Oh, yes! I went back there last night. They have a storage yard behind the warehouse and I found that module sitting out in the yard. I got inside the thing and it's outfitted like living quarters. But, most importantly, it had this odd metal disk in the end wall."

Gardiner nodded thoughtfully, "you're thinking this had something to do with the stethoscope-like communication device your friend saw?"

"Why not? That structure would fit inside a shipping container. And Paul mentioned a disk in the end of the container. You could easily install a life-support system inside. And the container Tropical's shipment came in is very likely the one Paul saw."

"So they're smuggling aliens?"

"That'd be my guess! But it looked like it could only hold one person. Must be a very important alien. Someone worth killing over."

"I wish you had pictures. That would help get Customs' and Immigration's interest."

"I had a camera with me, Bo, and I almost took some pictures, but the owner and two of his henchmen drove into the yard at midnight. I think they were getting ready to remove the module. I heard them coming and managed to get out of the module just before they entered the yard. I hid behind a shed, but I bumped into something that made a noise that alerted them. I climbed back over the fence and ran for it! They followed. One of them actually shot at me a couple of times! I got away, but it's clear they didn't want anybody snooping around. Those guys are definitely not just your everyday furniture importers!"

Gardiner picked up his phone and called Jason Elmore at Immigration and Customs Enforcement. He repeated Tad's story and gave Elmore the location including the alley and the rear storage yard. The Customs official said they could not justify a search warrant, but that he would have one of his agents check it out visually from the alley. Gardiner hung up and turned back to Tad. "So were you trespassing?"

"Uh, yeah, I was."

"So, despite the odd timing of their midnight removal effort, they can say they thought you were a burglar and chased you off."

"Well, maybe so, but they fired those shots well after I was over the fence and running down the alley."

"I don't like this one little bit, Tad, but you've taken it far enough! I'll let you know if Customs takes any action. You go home and cool it for a while. I'm going to see what I can learn about the officers on that ship."

Davi had gotten them tickets for the University of Oregon football game on Saturday and spending time with her sounded very good to Tad at that point. He gave Gardiner his home phone number, his cell phone number and Davi's number and let himself out the door. After a quick lunch, he left for the coast.

Reaching his house, Tad scooped up his mail from the floor under the slot in the front door. With fresh clothes after a quick shower, he set his lighting and TV timers. He heard Davi's car horn and was heading for the door when he saw the light blinking on his answering machine. He waved at her, then listened to three messages: one from his bookstore manager about a misdirected order, one from the swing band librarian notifying him of a change in practice time, and the third from Dr. Agnasi.

The doctor's recorded voice said, "... the police and Mrs. Castner okayed my telling you about my findings. We found two tiny punctures on the right side of your friend's chest. The skin was slightly singed around the holes. I've only seen such a wound once before, but I'm virtually certain that he'd been hit by a taser, a stun gun. And, as you predicted, there was no alcohol in his blood. We also know he did not die from the taser hit nor did he die of exposure. Without question, we know that he was asphyxiated...."

Tad's grief for Paul could hardly be intensified, but this laconic summation of the events leading to Paul's death nevertheless unsettled him. He shut the door and ran to Davi's car. She kissed him warmly and put her car in gear. Tad remained in a solemn mood most of the afternoon. Davi knew Paul's death was weighing on him. In the soft light of late afternoon and enveloped in the warm colors Davi had chosen for her interior walls, they sat on the couch in her living room. They talked about Paul and his family for nearly an hour. That had a cathartic effect on Tad. Davi wanted to help him through this and was glad to see him perk up when she poured them glasses of wine and lit the fireplace logs. The fire caught and Tad stood, smiling at her. Some strands of her shoulder-length, dark brown hair had fallen over her forehead and framed the chestnut pools of her eyes. He never doubted his growing love for this woman who seemed to read and support his every mood.

She rose and came to him and he enfolded her in

his arms. He felt the softness of her lips, the urgency of her tongue. His jacket fell to the living room floor and she pulled him by the hand toward her bedroom. She unbuttoned her blouse and started on his shirt. She was wearing an amber-colored bra and his fingers worked the clasp. He shrugged his shirt off and slipped the bra upward off her breasts, her nipples already taut and inviting. She slipped out of her slacks and pressed against his hardness as she loosened his belt.

It was late afternoon when, drained from their lovemaking, they languorously arose and moved into her shower. The suds on her glistening body and his hands soaping and caressing her rekindled their passion. The walls of the stall shower were close, but they were oblivious.

It was already dark when they dressed and prepared a dinner of lobster bisque, cracked crab, salad Nicoise, and chilled Riesling. They lingered at the table, savoring these few hours away from the tension of the past days. Tad called Meg Castner after they cleared the table. She had already spoken with Dr. Agnasi and understood his findings. Tad could tell she was stifling sobs as she spoke. He gave her an abbreviated report of his experience at the warehouse and assured her that he had advised the Coast Guard of what he had seen. Her grief moved him and rekindled his own sense of loss. Davi finished up in the kitchen and joined him just as he ended the call. He told her what he had learned from Dr. Agnasi and of his narrow escape from the warehouse.

Tad also repeated to Davi what he had overheard in the yard behind the warehouse. Despite the stress of that moment, he had tried very hard to memorize as many of the strange sounding phrases as he could and two had stuck with him. "I don't know the language, but maybe it's Turkish? Arabic? Can you make anything of it?"

"I'm pretty sure it's Arabic, answered Davi. "My sense of the first phrase may not be right, but it sounds like 'move the nest'. The second sounds like 'very four more days' or maybe 'just four more days'."

"'Just four more days until what? This has got to be more than just a smuggled alien. Something is going to go down in less than a week!"

Davi frowned, "but what kind of a 'nest' would they be moving in a week?"

"Maybe those two phrases weren't directly connected. In fact, I think the first one I repeated was said when they were starting to dismantle some of the stuff inside the module. Suppose they called that module a nest?"

"Yes, perhaps so, but that still doesn't help us much. I'm ready for sleep. Let's dream about Duck touchdowns instead of villains and their nests!"

"Yes, honey, I agree. But tomorrow, I'm going back to Portland to see if I can figure out if anything important is happening four days from now."

# EIGHT

**B**AJEHR AND TAJ PARKED THEIR TRUCK AT THE FAR END of the block and walked back toward the craftsman-style bungalow. The curtains were drawn, but they saw that some lights were on inside the house. As they came closer, they could hear the muffled sound of a television.

"He must stay up late," said Taj.

"Yes," answered Bajehr. "See those bushes over there? We'll wait there."

A Deodar cedar tree and a thick grouping of rhododendrons on the side of the lot afforded them cover as they crouched and held their ground. Five minutes passed and they saw the lights turn off and no longer heard the sound. Still, they waited until nearly one o'clock before they left their place of concealment and ran across Tad's lawn toward the garage. Bajehr shielded the beam of his flashlight and peered through a window to confirm that the car was inside. Moving on toward the rear of the house, they skirted a garden shed and paused outside the bedroom window. Taj had a pack over his shoulders and now he reached into it and produced a canister. With a nod to the other man, he heaved the canister through the window.

Hank Upson had been the Wilcao Fire Chief for longer than Tad could remember. He was also a good friend and had been a faithful patron of The Breakers ever since Tad had taken over the store. It was Upson's voice that Davi heard on the phone at two-forty that morning. Yes, Hank, he's here. What's the matter?"

Upson's voice was strained. He deflected her question and asked for Tad. She passed the phone to Tad who was now fully awake. Upson wasted no time on preliminaries. "Tad, thank God you're there. Your house has burned down!"

"Oh, my God!" Tad sat down on the bed. He had insurance, but photos and letters from his parents were irreplaceable. He was very partial to the bungalow and the way he had spruced it up; that planning and effort was now only a memory. Davi knew something was very wrong as she watched Tad's face.

Upson continued, "We think it may've been torched. Mr. Balducci down your block says he couldn't sleep and saw a white pickup truck parked across the street and it isn't there now. We've called in the Fire Marshal from Astoria and he'll know more definitively tomorrow. When it cooled down a little, we confirmed no one was inside so I hope you don't mind my calling Davi's number."

"No, don't worry about that, Hank." Tad's mind was in overdrive. He knew it was arson and he knew it was meant to be lethal for him. "Listen, have any reporters heard about it?"

"Surprisingly, none have showed up, but I'm sure they'll pick it up in the morning if not tonight."

"Hank, can you do me a very important favor? Can you tell them there was a fatality, believed to be the homeowner?"

"What are you talking about, man? Why should I do.... wait a minute! You're suggesting someone is out to kill you?"

"Look, it's my residence. It's the middle of the night. There's more that I don't want to go into right now. I'll talk with the Sheriff and try to explain it all to you later. But, in the meantime, releasing it that way will protect me, give me some time I desperately need. Don't worry, I'm not trying to outrun a gambling debt or a drug deal or anything remotely like that. I've just gotten swept up in something that's become very dangerous."

"All right, sure, I'll try. I know you're not involved in anything illegal! But you know the media people usually check with the medical examiner so they'll probably realize there was no death. Then they'll make a bigger story out of my saying there was."

"Well, at least you can shape the story for tomorrow's news. I need some time, Hank! And keep Davi's name out of it!"

"You got it! But get yourself a weapon... or a body guard!"

Tad thanked him effusively and hung up. Now, in addition to concern for his own safety, he was afraid for Davi. He told her he could no longer visit her at her house and had to keep her out of this.

Davi hugged him, but refused to stand off when he was in obvious peril. "Tad," she said, "these people have identified you! They know where you live. Even if you won't stay here with me and even if you feel you must keep looking into this, you have to find a secret place!"

"That makes sense, but I don't have a ready-made hideout."

"Wait! My sister's husband, Josh, has that duck-hunting cabin on Sauvie Island. I know they'd let you stay there, no questions asked. I'll call her first thing in the morning."

They slept fitfully and Tad was up before eight to meet with the sheriff. Unlike fire protection where Wilcao's station was manned by a professional/volunteer mix of local firefighters, law enforcement was contracted out to the Clatsop County Sheriff's office. This meant various deputies rotated through assignments covering Wilcao. They were well-intentioned and competent so far as Tad knew, but they had almost no local ties. Speaking to the sheriff, Tad recounted his activities and his theory of how Paul's murder and the attempt on his life were connected. Before Tad left, the Fire Marshall confirmed that an accelerant was used and the fire was definitely the result of arson. That fact added a lot of credibility to Tad's theory and the sheriff established an immediate liaison with Martinez and Peterson in Portland.

His interview with the sheriff over, Tad used his cell phone to call Betty Adams, his employee at The Breakers. She had already heard of the fire and he had to reassure her that he was fine. "Listen, Betty, they say the fire might've been arson and I'm pretty spooked by the whole thing. So, if anyone should be asking about me or my whereabouts, just tell them you don't have any idea where I've gone. And don't mention Davi either."

"Of course. I'll be like a fresh clam!"

"Thanks, Betty. The store's in your good hands. I'll be in touch."

Davi gave away their tickets to the football game and, since Tad's car had been badly damaged in the fire, she met him at the Sheriff's Office to drive them to his insurance broker's office. Following that, they drove to Tad's bank and then to a used-car dealer in Astoria. An hour later, as the new owner of a '99 Toyota Camry, he turned onto the Sunset Highway on his way to Portland. Davi had received approval from Josh and gave him written instructions on how to find the duck-hunting cabin. Tad promised to set up temporary housekeeping on the following night. On the highway, he used his cell phone to reach Jason Elmore at U.S. Customs. Tad introduced himself as Bo Gardiner's friend who had raised questions about the container consigned to Tropical Furniture Imports and asked, "What did your agent make of that module behind the warehouse?"

"I'm sorry, Mr. Madison, but there's nothing to evaluate. If such a thing had been there, it was gone this morning when we drove by."

Tad did not like the skepticism behind Elmore's remark. "I told Bo that they were getting ready to take it somewhere! They must have come back during the night."

"Even assuming that happened, you must realize the facts are circumstantial at best." Elmore realized that his attitude sounded borderline insulting to a responsible citizen who was just trying to be helpful, so he softened his tone. "Bo said you were hoping our surveillance would lead to a search warrant, but even if we'd seen what you described, I'm afraid no judge would issue one. We just don't have enough to connect the dots."

"How's this for a connection?" Tad asked heatedly. "Two nights ago three of them chased me away from that warehouse and all over the neighborhood. They actually fired a couple of shots at me! Last night, someone set fire to my house, almost certainly believing I was inside."

"My God, no wonder you're concerned! We may yet find a connection and, if we do, – believe me – ICE will be leading the charge. But, for now, surely these are matters for the local police."

"Yes, they're working on it." Tad was not ready to give up on Customs. "How's your x-ray program coming along? Any chance your people or Port Security looked at that container?"

"Well, we're still looking at mid-or-late 2019 before we have total screening. Right now we're just profiling, reacting to informants, following through on investigations… that sort of thing. The container you're interested in wasn't x-rayed or opened. The paperwork checked out. The designated contents were very normal and were repeats for that particular importer. The importer had been in business for over five years. No, the only thing even approaching the profile was the fact that the shipment originated in Malaysia. But that alone wouldn't call for physical screening."

"I see." Tad sounded resigned. "Look, there's one other thing. I forgot to tell Bo that I saw piping and venting inside that module that looked like it would circulate fresh air or evacuate fumes. Can you trace that particular container and see if it was fitted with a vent of any kind?"

"It can be done, though it isn't the easiest thing. The shipping company will cooperate, but it could take us several days to locate it. We'll give it a shot."

It did not sound to Tad like tracking down the container was going to be much of a priority for Elmore. He thanked him for listening and said goodbye. Tad's next call was to Bo Gardiner whom he filled in about the fire and his conversation with Elmore. "Bo, have you been able to learn anything about the officers on the Malacca Trader?"

"Yes, one interesting thing, at least. The Third Officer turns out to have been a last-minute replacement. And, get this: he jumped ship yesterday in Oakland! I've turned that piece over to the enforcement division of ICE and I tried to interest Homeland Security, but all they were willing to do was to check his name from the crew roster against their and Interpol's databases. If they don't get a hit, they'll lose interest fast."

"Thanks for pushing it, Bo. It doesn't clear anything up, but it adds another messy detail. Something's definitely wrong here. Murder is terrible enough and I feel we've just seen the tip of the iceberg."

"I have the same fear," said Gardiner. "I'm going to call the Special Agent in Charge of the FBI's Oregon office. I'll give him a heads up and tell him your name and what you've turned up."

"Thanks, Bo."

As he entered the outskirts of Portland, Tad pulled over to google the Portland Convention & Vistors Bureau. If two nights ago was "just six more days", he thought it was worth his while to find out what was happening in the metro area three days hence, on November fifth. A svelte woman in her late thirties wearing an Ann Taylor suit greeted him from her desk in the Bureau's office. He explained that he wanted to know all the significant events, public or private that would be occurring in a two-day period starting on the fourth. She motioned him over to a whiteboard with a calendar grid on it. "I'll get you a print-out, but you can see the simple version right here."

Tad saw a Trailblazers basketball game marked in on the first night, along with a regional dog show, and a Willamette Valley Grass Seed Growers convention. On the second day, there was the Tradewell Investing financial advisors national conference, an antique car show, a Pink Martini concert, and a microbrew festival.

"I've heard of Pink Martini," he said. "What kind of music do they play?"

"Where've you been?" she teased. "They're a very popular small orchestra with two vocalists and an international repertoire. They even perform quite a lot abroad. This concert's in a smaller auditorium, but they could draw six or seven hundred, easy."

"And what's this Tradewell thing?"

"It's a national franchise for financial advisors. This is their annual three-day meeting followed by unofficial workshops on the fourth day. It's at the Convention Center and it's a big one. The major hotels are all booked."

"And this microbrew thing, where will that be held?"

"Sunday afternoon at Tom McCall Park on the riverfront."

So, Tad thought, it could be the Moda Center

for the game or that Tradwell event. He figured it was not likely to be at an outdoor event. Or, he had to admit to himself, he could be way off. Could it really have been a local homicide unconnected to anything larger, the seeming tie-ins just coincidences? Surely the torching of his home could not have been a random act of violence given the timing and what he had been doing! The Wilcao and Portland police, at least, were now working together and believing in some kind of linkage. But no one, least of all the feds, seemed to be fast-tracking this. He was jarred from this troubled reverie by the woman.

"Here's the print-out. Is there anything else I can help you with?"

"No. Thank you. You've been very helpful".

He still had several more stops to make. The metro-area narcotics squad reported nothing on its radar screen for the days in question. The Oregon Furniture Dealers' Association knew of no gatherings or events in its domain. The Portland Port Authority gave him a copy of the listing of vessels arriving and departing from the fourth through the fifth. He saw nothing unusual in that traffic generally and was relieved to see there were no naval ships on the list.

Najev entered the "Employees Only" area of his ware-house where he stored tools, supplies and a small, electric, fork-lift. He locked the door behind him. Turning left, he walked toward what appeared to be a solid wall. A large metal cover plate contained a small door covering a circuit-breaker panel. Najev inserted a letter-opener's blade at a special place along the edge of the cover plate. There was a click and the left edge of the cover plate became unseated from the wall. The plate had a concealed hinge on its right edge and Najev swung the plate open. Bending over at the waist, he scuttled through an opening in the wall. He emerged into an eight-foot wide room running from the false wall to the building's exterior wall. He was proud that he and his men had constructed the enclosing walls that concealed this area and repositioned the circuit breaker in just four weeks. Their careful use of salvaged wood had allowed them to almost perfectly replicate the appearance of the other interior walls.

Inside, he nodded to Moud who stood next to the incubator reading a gauge. They spoke in English. "I found a news stand that sold the Astoria paper. There was an article that mentioned the fire and stated a correction to the morning radio news. It said that the firemen had determined that no one was home and no one died."

"Your people were so sure," Moud said.

"This Madison cannot have known that we found out where he lived. He must have spent the night somewhere else. I used a burner phone to call the bookstore. All they said was that he was taking a vacation. Perhaps there is a woman?"

"His getting involved must be because of the pilot. He is obviously suspicious. He will be like a leech! We cannot afford for him to dig any deeper. Send the woman to use some subterfuge at the bookstore. She must discover where he is so we can get to him!"

"Yes. I'll send Zulanni. We are too close to success to jeopardize the operation. If the FBI gets into this, there will be alerts, higher security everywhere ...

maybe they will even come here wanting to search the place."

"Are you still sure about the jobs?"

"There should be no problem at all. I've trained the others. We have the clothing. We've shown the catering manager the photos of Zulanni and him at the motel. Like all these American married men, he will do as we ask. And your part here... with the apparatus. It goes well?"

"Yes." Moud disliked Najev's arrogance. Al M'afid had put Najev in charge of carrying out the plan in Oregon, but he was only a merchant and his questions had increasingly seemed condescending. "We lost a small quantity when the C-O-two control was too imprecise, but I've fixed that. We will have more than enough and I've designed the culture to be robust enough to serve our needs."

"Excellent. Keep up the good work!"

Najev returned to his office and sat at his desk thinking with his eyes closed. Then he arose and summoned Bajehr. "I've been thinking about our difficulties with this man Madison. We must report this business to Al M'Afid. Take the photo enlargement we made from Madison's driver's license and fax it to him at this number". He handed Bajehr a slip of paper. "Just send the photo with no message. We cannot be sure when he'll arrive in the States so on the cover sheet put 'hold for arrival'. I'll call him on the message phone and explain what has happened."

"Do I use our fax machine?"

"No! Go down the street and ask to use Dobney's, but you do the transmission yourself."

# NINE

IT WAS NEARLY FIVE WHEN TAD DROVE UP TO THE SMALL shop on a back street. He had searched the internet for "security equipment" before he found what he was looking for – "surveillance; covert optics" – among the many products available. A young man with a beard came around from behind a display counter in a retail space crowded with electronics and self-defense equipment.

"Hi. I'm looking for something rather specialized. Do you have some kind of a viewer that can be inserted through a small opening and then controlled from the viewer's end as to the direction it's pointed in?"

"Yeah, I carry a couple of items that could do that. You a licensed PI?"

"No. Does that matter?"

"Maybe. Maybe not. You're not a perv I hope."

"No way! This is for a one-time project and nothing the least bit sexy about it. In fact, if you're interested, I'll even sell it back to you as used when this project's finished."

"OK. I'll go for the used goods buy-back." He could see a nice margin in this transaction.

"So what will it cost me?"

The bearded man walked over to a shelf along

the wall and pointed to two different optical devices. "The digital-camera version is pricey. Thirteen sixty-five. The use-your-own-eyeball version is just four hundred twenty. Both have lights on the head if you need them. Your choice ..."

Tad mentally reviewed the cash he had withdrawn that morning. He would have preferred a photographic record of what he hoped to see, but he quickly concluded that he could only afford the non-camera model. "Okay. The cheaper one."

He purchased a roll of picture wire, some duct tape, a crow bar, and a sturdy, old-fashioned curtain rod at a Home Depot. It was six o'clock when he arrived at a farm supply store just as they were closing their door. There, he bought some kerosene, a box of stove matches, and the last smudge pot in stock. Tad hoped his luck would continue to hold for the rest of the evening. He checked into a different motel even though it seemed highly unlikely that the forces against him had traced him to the motel he had used before. He went back to his room after a tasteless dinner in the motel coffee shop and called Davi. He summarized what he had learned. Her concern for him was palpable and he already missed her. After his conversation with Davi, he called Meg. She had spoken with detective Martinez who told her they had no new clues, but were still investigating.

Tad had not mentioned his narrow escape at the warehouse to the Portland police for fear they would forbid him to pursue it on his own. He knew the Clatsop County Sheriff's Office had talked to Martinez and Peterson that morning so the Portland police already knew about the fire at his house and conceivably knew about the warehouse incident as well.

Tad tried using the optical device that the manufacturer marketed as a "Spy Eye". With a little practice, he mastered manipulating the lens-head. He extended the curtain rod and wrapped the overlap with duct tape and he wired the sheathed fiber-optic cable to the rod so that it made a right-angle turn just before the directional joint at the lens-head. It was unlikely that he would fall asleep given what was before him, but – to be safe – he set the alarm for one in the morning and settled into his motel room's only chair to pass a few hours watching television.

Tad was determined to conceal his car this time. He cruised by Tropical's warehouse and through the alley noting a light in the window in the rear wall, confirming his guess that there was someone guarding the place. There was a car-repair garage three blocks away. He left his car in the deep shadows behind its structure and well out of sight from the street. Tad crouched low approaching the warehouse and ran toward the slight depression alongside the driveway on the west side of the building. He lay prone in the damp weeds and fueled and lit the smudge pot. He wrapped moist towels from the motel around the pot, positioning them where he hoped they would soon smolder.

In the alley, he confirmed what he had feared. A security system had been added to the fence. His planning had provided for that possibility so he moved toward the abandoned apartment building. He gained access to a hallway on the second floor by means of the fire escape and a missing window. Walking quickly to the first open door on the left, he shined his flashlight into the apartment and headed for an outside room. The carpets had long ago been stripped and his running shoes scuffed on the filthy underfloor. He raised the window with only one brief screech despite his expectation that the window would be stuck and require jimmying.

He lowered himself lightly to the roof of the warehouse three feet below the window sill. He moved, cat-like, to a position directly above the window pane with the missing corner of glass. Working swiftly, he lowered the rigid Spy Eye to the level of the pane. His guessed-at measurements would work! Lifting his jury-rigged device back to roof level, Tad dialed Tropical's number on his cell phone.

The ring startled Moud. He jumped off the cot and, rubbing the sleep from his eyes, picked up the extension phone. The voice at the other end was phlegmatic but serious. "This Tropical Furniture?"

"Yes, what? ...Who are you?"

"This is the Morrison Security Patrol. You're not one of our clients, but as I drove down your street, I saw a bunch of smoke coming from outside, alongside your building. Not worth a call to the fire department if you're already on the premises. Just thought I'd let you know."

"Yeah, Yeah. Thanks. I'll go try to put it out," Moud said as he reached for his pants and shoes.

Tad pocketed his phone and leaned over the edge of the roof to lower the Spy-Eye. He heard the front door opening less than a minute later. He failed in his first two tries at getting the optical head through the triangular hole. He was drenched in sweat despite the coolness of the night. On his third attempt, he steered the device into the hole. Looking through the eye piece, Tad saw a wall quite close ahead. Four white coats hung on hooks on the wall. Pharmacists' coats? Doctors' coats? Lab coats? He swiveled the head to the right: more hooks and a bulky yellow oversuit with a soft helmet attached. A hazmat suit! He heard the front door close. He did not have much longer. He swiveled the head to the left. There, he saw a cot and a microwave on a small table. A compact refrigerator sat next to the table. A larger table on which sat two stainless steel cabinets was visible beyond that. The larger of the two cabinets had an access door sealed by a gasket and a tube connected to some kind of a gas cylinder.

Tad spent two minutes concentrating on the far table and memorizing the details of the equipment when he heard a metallic clang from within the room. Hurrying too fast, Tad brushed the Spy Eye against the glass as he withdrew it.

Moud thought he heard a small sound as he re-entered the room and his gaze darted from wall to wall. He saw no one. He was getting jumpy, he thought, but he still wondered if the warehouse was under some form of attack. He decided to call Najev and tell him about the smudge-pot fire he had extinguished.

Tad walked softly toward the open window and climbed back into the empty apartment. He collapsed the curtain rod and stowed it and the Spy-Eye in his rucksack. Seeing that the alley was deserted, he climbed down the fire escape. Then it was a sprint toward the car-repair shop.

# TEN

THE SUIT WAS IMPORTANT. TAD KNEW THAT. NO USE OF finishes or solvents in a furniture warehouse would necessitate a hazardous materials suit. He swirled his morning coffee in the cup and considered what he had seen the night before, becoming more convinced than ever that he was dealing with some kind of terrorism. He had been thinking explosives or an assassination, but now his thoughts turned to a possible biological weapon. The information he had still might not be sufficient to support a search warrant. Without a camera, they would only have his description of what he saw through the limited aperture of the Spy Eye. Even the hazmat suit and the white coats were not, in and of themselves, hard evidence of any crime or conspiracy.

He realized who could help as he stood at the cash register to pay his breakfast bill. Dr. Michael Li had taken summer vacations at Wilcao for many years and had been a frequent customer at The Breakers. Tad had liked Mike instantly and they had become friends. The man's easy-going manner and mischievous sense of humor, belied his professional status as a brilliant biochemist. Li's parents had owned a small restaurant in San Francisco's China

Town and Michael had been the first of the three children to attend college. He followed his undergraduate schooling at the University of California, Berkeley, by obtaining a doctorate from Stanford. He did post-graduate work at the Oregon Health & Sciences University where he stayed on as a professor and scientist.

Tad called Mike's house and Mike's wife picked up the phone. "Alicia, this is Tad Madison."

"Well, Hi, Tad. Are you in town?"

"Yes, I am. How's everything with you two?"

"Just fine. We still have nice memories of that picnic with you and Davi last summer."

"Likewise! Is Mike around, Alicia?"

"No. He's gone to his lab. *I know*, it's Saturday, but Mike often goes in anyway, especially when they have ongoing experiments to fuss over. Do you want his office phone number?"

"Thanks anyway, but I already have it on my phone. I'll see if I can reach him there. Take care."

Tad drove through an evergreen/hardwood forest as Terwilliger contoured its way up the grade to reach OHSU. He left the car in the multi-story parking garage on the plateau that defined the one-hundred-forty acre OHSU/V.A. campus. Four major hospitals, several clinics, medical and nursing schools, and numerous research buildings were situated there and the area proved Byzantine to navigate for the casual visitor. Fortunately for Tad, Li had invited him up for a tour the year before so he remembered his way. Li's office was adjacent to his laboratory and offered a view across the campus and over downtown Portland.

"Mike, I really appreciate you letting me barge in on you on short notice."

"You said it was important, Tad. What's up?"

Tad lifted a few science journals off of the crowded office's second chair and took a seat. He recounted the developments of the last four days with few interruptions from Li.

"That's damn scary, Tad! You are smart to turn these matters over to the authorities, but I can understand your grief and your frustration," said Li.

"Believe it!"

"And you came to me because you are wondering whether these people may have smuggled in some kind of a biological agent?"

"Exactly."

"Given what you've seen, it certainly is possible. If a bacterium were lyopholized, if it were freeze-dried, it could be successfully transported on a cargo ship. They could turn it into a powder or perhaps even a liquid and dust or spray it on food or into beverage glasses. If they had a great lot of it, they could even try to disseminate it through an air-handling system."

"Likewise, a starter virus could be transported in a small flask if it was one of those stable enough to survive for ten or so days. After they got it here, they'd have to insert it into a bacterial artificial chromosome – we call 'em BACs – where they could clone it. Then they'd introduce it into a tissue culture so it could replicate. Once they'd incubated it for five or more days in the culture, they would have a highly pathogenic liquid. At this end, though, they would need a competent virologist or microbiologist to handle all those steps. When they were ready to use it, they could possibly make it into an aerosol for people to inhale. But I think it more likely they would want it to be ingested with food or drink."

Tad looked befuddled at his friend's science-speak. Mike smiled, "Well, anyway, it could be done. Their scientist would need some equipment, but nothing too large or exotic."

"And the hazmat suit?" questioned Tad.

"Those babies are expensive. It's very unlikely that a private party would own a suit except for a very specific reason. I don't think terrorists would need one to introduce the toxin, but they might want to use one while they were learning how to weaponize it."

"Can you infer what the agent would be?" Tad asked.

"Give me a couple of hours and I'll come up with a short list." Li frowned thoughtfully. "If I were in a terrorist's shoes, I'd try to develop a virus that was very contagious and highly lethal. One that could spread quickly, but had an in-host pre-symptomatic time of at least a week. And, if not actually weaponized, at least robust enough to be transported to and dispersed in public places."

"So where does that leave us?"

"Aerosols in outdoor places require planes or helicopters. For them to be really effective it would need to be a relatively windless day and a real large concentration of people like a football stadium or a huge parade. They'd be much more effective indoors delivered through a heating or ventilating system."

Tad leaned forward, "Like a Trailblazers game? Or a large auditorium?"

"Yes, those would be feasible targets. Liquids or powders are perhaps easier to insinuate into the human environment through food or drink like I said, but they are harder to deliver to large masses. If that's the vector they choose, they would rely more on widespread secondary contagion."

"Meaning what?"

"Well, with a five to seven day period before the first victims are symptomatic, the victims would have time to fly back home and go back to work where they would unknowingly contaminate even more folks ... and the cycle could continue!"

"Thanks, Mike. I knew I could count on you! I'm going to touch base with the Portland police and I'm going to try to get an appointment with the FBI this afternoon. I'll get back to you for that short list after that. If I can get the feds to take me seriously and get in gear on this, would you be willing to assist them?"

"Absolutely! You, the FBI, whoever! I hope there will turn out to be a benign explanation for all this, but if there isn't, we'll need every resource that can be mustered."

Business at The Breakers had been brisk all morning. Madeline Klein dropped in for her usual morning browse-and-chat around eleven fifteen and it was natural for Betty to ask Madaline to cover for a few minutes while she went across the street for coffee and a sandwich to go. Good friends of Betty and Tad like Madeline knew the store's routine and had covered before in this trusting small town.

Minutes later, Zulanni entered the store and approached Madeline. "Is Mr. Madison around?" she asked.

"Why, no. His house burned down last night so I suppose he's trying to straighten things out about the fire."

"Actually, I'm from his insurance company. We want to get right on this. Do you know where he'd be staying? Where he could be reached?"

"Well… I suppose you might reach him through Davi. DaVita Salloway."

"Does she live here in town?"

"Yes, she does."

Zulanni googled the name and found Davi's address. She jotted them down. "Thanks, I'll try her."

There were almost forty-eight hours before Davi's next class. She stopped at a supermarket in Astoria and bought food for three days. Reaching home, she changed into casual clothes, and threw toiletries and extra clothes into an overnight bag. She felt she should be with Tad in the hours ahead. The cabin would be a good hideaway, she was sure, but Tad was not one to passively wait it out. She wanted desperately to keep him safe. To do this, she knew she must convince him to stay in the cabin. If they stayed there and used their cell phones, she would argue, Tad could still make inquiries and could even try to keep apprised of developments at the law enforcement agencies.

Davi knew how to find the cabin and knew where the key to the door was hidden. If she left now, she could unload the groceries and build a fire to warm the place up before Tad arrived.

Zulanni had been watching Davi's house from her

car parked at the far end of the block. As she was beginning to believe her surveillance was fruitless, a very attractive woman drove up in a white Mustang and entered the house carrying a grocery bag. The woman was alone and twenty minutes later she emerged carrying a good-sized cooler and got into her car. Zulanni lay down on her car's seat until Davi had passed and then started her engine.

———

Detective Peterson brought an extra chair into Angel Martinez's cubicle and invited Tad to take a seat. The two detectives had already received a full report on the arson at Tad's home and told Tad that two sets of smaller footprints were found outside his bedroom window. Peterson subtly glanced at Tad's size 11 shoes. Tad caught the glance and hoped that they had not thought he had burned down his own house to remove himself as a suspect in Paul's death! As their conversation continued, he felt more confident that they no longer entertained that possibility. They seemed genuinely sympathetic and told him that, although they had no other new leads, they were now inclined to actively investigate the furniture wholesaler.

———

Tad reached the offices of the Federal Bureau of Investigation near the Portland International Airport in late afternoon. Not having a coded badge to open the entrance door, he stopped in the building's lobby. A guard pointed him to a wall-mounted phone and he used it to identify himself. He noticed a video camera aimed at the phone and guessed that his facial image, name and birth date were being run through some data base to "clear" him for entry as he waited for several minutes.

Russ Bronson had been the second oldest of five children in a humble, but loving, household in Tulsa. After graduating from Oklahoma State University, the earnest young scholar-athlete had applied to law school at the University of California at Davis. Even then, in the back of his mind, he had entertained the hope of a career with the Federal Bureau of Investigation. In any case, he realized that a law degree would offer attractive options for his career. Balancing the demands of athletics with a History major had made him both disciplined and confident.

He had been elated to learn that he had been accepted to Davis. In the first months of law school, that elation was quickly tempered by the heavy law school workload and the difficulty of absorbing an entirely new way of thinking and learning. After a disappointing first year, he had regrouped and finished in the top quarter of his class. He graduated and was more certain than ever that he wanted to work for the FBI.

Bronson had been infused with ambition and dedication as he finished the FBI training program at Quantico. At the end of the first year in his initial assignment, he thought it was time to buy a house. Marcy had been the first realtor he made contact with. He had not bought his house through her, but he had asked her for a date. They were married eight months later. Marcy and their son, Derek, had become the most important people in his life. Their lives were full of happiness until six years ago when Marcy was diagnosed with pancreatic cancer. Bronson grieved deeply for his beloved as she slipped ever deeper into the unholy depths of her illness. When it was evident that the chemotherapy was not going to save her and the dosage of pain-killing medication had to be raised, they knew her time was short. Bronson went on leave to be able to take Marci on short trips to their favorite get-away spots: The Heritage House on the northern California coast and a bed-and-breakfast in Carmel Valley. They made a video of Marci describing her favorite moments with the family. Bronson and Derek had watched it many times over the intervening years. Bronson had written her a long love letter in her last week. She had told him that she hoped he would feel free to remarry when the right person came along. Bronson had thanked her and agreed that would be a healthy development in time, but he had saved his letter to her. Sometimes, in the quiet of the late evening, he would reread the letter. His eyes might water a little, but he would return the letter to its place in his desk with a smile on his face.

Marci had passed away five days after he had given her the letter. In addition to dealing with his almost-overpowering grief, Bronson had to adjust to being a single parent. His job had become a stabilizing force as he fought to get past his loss and continue to provide a loving home for their teenage son.

Bronson's drive, imagination, and respect for others had not gone unnoticed in the Bureau. Those qualities, together with an ever-increasing record of impressive investigations, had assured his ascent through the ranks. The only reservations ever recorded by his superiors had centered on his occasional willingness to employ unconventional – though entirely legal and humane – means to further an investigation. His sometime straying from doing it strictly 'by the book' had given heartburn to some of those above him in the FBI hierarchy.

It was not unusual for Bronson, as Special Agent in Charge (Portland Division), to be working on a Saturday, but he had been clearing his desk in anticipation of leaving for home when he was told of Tad's arrival. Resigned to this extension of his working day, he asked the receptionist to let Tad in and show him to Bronson's corner office. A side table was laden with file folders, but the desk was clear and its walnut top gleamed. A framed photo, obviously a family portrait, hung on the wall above a row of file cabinets. There was a comfortable settee and a Hjellegjerde reclining chair to complete the furnishings with a less government-issue touch.

Bronson stood and walked around his desk to greet Tad. "Lieutenant Commander Gardiner assured me that you were a responsible citizen who had potentially important information to discuss. Please sit down."

Bronson was almost as tall as Tad and looked nearly as fit as when, twenty-nine years ago, he was one of the nation's best collegiate 800-meter runners. His warm smile was a bright contrast to his dark face, but his mien was all business as they settled into their chairs. "I understand there have been two attempts on your life and you believe you've stumbled onto some terrorist plot."

"That's right," said Tad launching into a concise narrative starting with Paul Castner's phone call to him on Sunday and ending with his consultation with Mike Li.

Bronson listened without interruption and openly studied the man across from him. When Tad had finished, he said, "I'm sure the answer is 'no', but I should ask. Can you think of anyone who might hate you enough to try to kill you?"

"No, absolutely not. I suppose somebody, somewhere, might be upset with me for something. But I honestly can't imagine who or why; and certainly no one I know would want to kill me!"

Bronson nodded, "Then it is quite probable that the same people who chased you away from the warehouse also torched your house. You understand that a naked attempt on your life is not within the FBI's jurisdiction, but I can assure you we'll look into this bioweapon angle. That unusual equipment you saw with your Spy Eye certainly isn't what one would expect in a furniture warehouse! I'll start by having one of our best scientists in D.C. set up a teleconference with your Dr. Li and myself. If she confirms that there's a feasible threat, we'll seek search warrants for the warehouse and for tapping their phone."

"That's what I was hoping to hear." Tad was elated that someone was finally willing to take action. "Mike said he would pull together some possible pathogens and contagion vectors this afternoon. I'm going back to see him and I'll tell him to expect your call."

Bronson stood to shake hands but, before Tad left, he said, "After Commander Gardiner called, I checked a little on you. Your work as an FBI counterterrorism agent was quite impressive. I can see you have a talent for this sort of thing! Do you mind if I ask why you left the Bureau?"

"No. That's okay. It was not an easy decision. The people I worked with were terrific! But, as the years rolled by, the stress never went away. And the inter-agency politics and conflicts were a constant source of frustration. I liked the highs of intelligence break-throughs and capturing those evil SOBs and my psych profile remained solid, but I started craving a more normal, more rooted life. Finally I just pulled the plug."

"Thanks for letting me pry a little. Sounds like the FBI's loss!"

Returning to the OHSU campus, Tad cruised all eight levels of the parking garage, but found no available stalls. He decided to drive right to Li's building where he remembered there were a few places marked "reserved". One of those spaces was empty. He parked there seri-ously doubting that he would be towed on a Saturday and thinking the risk of a parking ticket was well worth it. Li was in his laboratory, but a bearded post-doc offered to tell him that Tad was waiting to see him.

As soon as they were in his office and he had closed the door, Li said, "Here's a list. I can't tell you it's definitive in the short time I've had to think about it and check a few things, but I know it covers all the major possibilities."

Tad saw fifteen pathogens on the list. Each name was accompanied by a paragraph sketching its environ-mental requirements, its robustness, its toxicity-life, its lethality, and its primary vector and period of contagion.

Tad read the text and said, "I knew you'd come through on this! It's scary that there could be so many different ones. I had that appointment with the chief FBI agent this afternoon. Not surprisingly, he's a sharp fellow. Name's Bronson. He said he'd call and hook you up with one of their experts."

"Excellent! You look like hell, Tad. Do you need a place to stay? Alicia and I would be glad to put you up until all this is sorted out."

"Thanks so much, Mike, but Davi has arranged for me to lay low at a relative's cabin on Sauvie Island. You're right though. I've taken it as far as I can today and I'm pretty beat. Here's my cell number if you need to reach me. Otherwise, I'll call you tomorrow morning."

It was easy enough for Zulanni to follow Davi out of town. She was careful to let at least one other car remain between Davi and her once they were on the highway to Portland. As they neared the metropolitan area, Davi turned left and crossed a waterway. Zulanni was concentrating on the traffic and Davi's car, now two ahead, but managed to read a painted sign on a storefront: "Sauvie Island Feed & Fertilizer". Very quickly they left the developed area and traffic thinned. She lagged back as far as she could and still keep sight of Davi's Mustang. Zulanni started drawing a crude schematic of the road on a napkin as she drove. Ten minutes later, Davi turned down a dirt road marked "private" and disappeared into tree-covered terrain. Zulanni drove on past and, around a curve, pulled over to the shoulder where she called Najev.

"You have done very well," he said. "From now on, speak in generalities and use names like 'realtor' for the person you are observing. Do not go down the dirt road. Get careful mileage to the start of the dirt road from reference points that can be seen at night and phone me back on my burner phone's number in fifteen minutes. I'll send Bajehr and Taj to settle things this evening. In the meantime, you go back to the little community by the bridge. You know what her car looks like. Find a place where you'll not draw attention and watch to see if they leave. If the car leaves, follow it and call me immediately, speaking guardedly."

"I understand. I'll call you soon with the mileage."

Tad followed Davi's instructions and turned down a road marked "private". After driving four hundred feet and entering a young forest, he saw a cabin. He glimpsed, through the trees, what he assumed was the northern shore of the island. He was surprised to also see Davi's car. He was excited that she had come to him, but he knew he could not let her stay. She opened the cabin door and he took her in his arms. Wrapped in her warm embrace, Tad's resolve began to weaken. "Davi, Sweets, this is great!"

She led him inside and showed him around. There was a small kitchen and a living-dining room furnished with rustic simplicity. A chessboard on a small side-table and a CD player were the only concessions to more sophisticated living. Davi had laid a fire in the fireplace and the cabin was already warm. On the side facing the Columbia River, there was a bunk room for six with large paned windows.

Davi showed him the food she had stocked in the refrigerator and produced a bottle of wine. She was reaching for a corkscrew when Tad's resolve returned. "Listen, honey, I'd like nothing more than to drink some wine and … well, fool around, have dinner, have you stay here with me. But I said this morning that I don't want you connected to me or near me until this business gets resolved."

"But Tad, nobody knows about this place. I even swore my sister and her husband to secrecy about your being here! Besides, I don't want to worry about you from afar. I can postpone my Monday class."

Tad knew there was logic behind her position, but willed himself to argue against it. "I know this is a 'secret' location, but I still don't know who or exactly what we're dealing with. We're now fairly confident that it's some kind of a terrorist operation and they seem to think that what little I've learned about them threatens them enough to kill me. That tells me that they're up against some kind of deadline … those four days maybe … and that the stakes are very, very high."

Davi was unconvinced, "So we just stay here and keep in contact with the FBI by phone!"

"No! Try to understand! These terrorist actions would take planning, organization, resources. I agree that short of an FBI safe house, this is a good place to base myself, but suppose they have me under surveillance or have planted some kind of tracer bug on my car that I haven't been able to find? I'm prepared to look after myself, but I don't want them to discover any connection between us. If they do come after me, I don't want you in jeopardy also."

Davi realized she was not going to change Tad's mind. She felt he was being overly cautious, but she could see that her staying would only make him more tense. "All right. I think, and hope, that you're over-reacting, but I'll do it your way. Anyhow, let me fix us a good dinner."

"Compromise? How about a real quick dinner so you can get out of here before dark?"

"What a spoilsport, Tad! You win the microwave lasagna," she said and reached into the freezer.

They kissed good-bye as the sun was near to setting. "I'll call you tomorrow," said Tad.

In the softening light, Zulanni almost missed the Mustang. She started her car and called Najev. He picked up on the fourth ring. "It's Z. The realtor just left that house I was interested in. I'm going to follow her to her office."

"Did she bring her associate?"

"No, she was by herself."

"Keep your cell phone on in case the other realtor calls in."

Najev did not want distractions as their time grew short, but he knew Madison was a loose end that, if unsilenced, could unravel all of their plans. Taj had told him of the paramilitary training he had received in Afghanistan and Najev knew he could depend upon Bajehr. Those two had to succeed in their assignment this evening. He wondered, even if his two men were successful, to whom might Madison have talked? And what would he have been able to tell? More than some tenuous link to his friend's death? More than mere curiosity about the nest? He read Madison for a loner and thought it unlikely that he had reached a point where he would be ready to contact Homeland Security. And, he wondered, even if Madison had made such a contact, would anyone take him seriously?

Najev was cautious by nature and, as the chess champion of the mosque, it was natural for him to look beyond immediate problems to consider more remote contingencies. He knew they were running risks and knew that even well-planned operations could be derailed by unforeseen developments. Moud had back-ups for his biological process and he, Najev, needed a back-up for his part of the operation. He knew Zulanni had the stun gun in her car and he called her back.

"You still have that electrical device?" he asked.

"Yes. Why?"

"I want you to take the realtor to our second house. Can you do that alone?"

Zulanni paused for only a few seconds before answering, "Yes, I can do that. Shall I do it now?"

"Yes. Before she reaches her next stop. Call me when you are together there."

Zulanni had been able to draw closer to Davi's car in the gathering darkness. The two cars were nearly to where Davi would leave the highway for the less-traveled road to Wilcao when Najev called to give her his latest instruction.

Zulanni had been orphaned at age thirteen when her Palestinian parents had been killed in an Israeli air attack on a supposed Hezbollah ammunition cache in southern Lebanon. Al M'afid had met her in one of the camps and had soon realized her potential as one of his sleepers. Eight years later, even as a naturalized immigrant to the United States, her hatred of Israelis and their American supporters had not abated. She was a willing soldier in any vengeful operation against the Western establishment and especially in any attack on what she was certain was the Jewish-controlled banking and securities industry. It bothered her more than she cared to admit that this woman she was going to abduct appeared to be of Near Eastern extraction, but she told herself that Davi was an enemy who threatened the success of their plan.

The car ahead turned off the highway and proceeded on the county road. Zulanni tried to remember the terrain from her drive toward Portland earlier in the day. She was fairly sure she had about six miles of wooded roadside before they would reach the more developed area near Wilcao. There were no headlights ahead or behind them. She wore driving gloves and now she pulled a ski mask over her head and accelerated to pass Davi's car. There was a gravel shoulder almost the width of a car on each side of the road and then a drainage ditch before a short slope up to the beginning of the forest. Zulanni positioned her car's hood just ahead of the other car and swerved to the right. Her hands gripped the steering wheel tightly as if to will the vehicle to obey her in this dangerous maneuver.

Davi had been preoccupied thinking about Tad's safety at the cabin and had no idea she had been followed. She looked to her left when the passing car stayed nearly abreast of her and, for an instant, saw a person wearing a ski mask. Before that had registered, she felt a sharp jolt and fought to control her car as it was rammed toward the shoulder. She slammed on the brakes, but the car was already fish-tailing on the gravel. Davi was aware of the other car swerving back to the left and then the trees seemed to flash toward her.

Zulanni fought hard to control her car. She had

been careful that the contact was behind her front wheels so that her steering would remain intact. After the impact, she saw the other car crash into the ditch. There were still no lights in sight as she backed her car toward the wreck. She got out with the Taser in her right hand. It was obvious that Davi was in mild shock from the crash. Zulanni released Davi's seatbelt and used a pocket knife to cut away the air bag. Zulanni was strong for a woman of her size and managed to get Davi out of the car before she struggled. Despite her bewilderment and weakness, Davi suddenly realized that the woman pulling her out of the car was the same person who had rammed her. She knew then that she had to escape, but Zulanni dropped her and reached for the stun gun. There was an instant of great pain and what seemed like a white, searing flame in front of her eyes and Davi collapsed.

Zulanni feared that a car would come upon them at any moment. She grabbed Davi's limp body under the arms and dragged it to her car. Flinging a rear door open, she sat Davi on the door sill, then ran to the car's other side and climbed across to reach Davi from behind. It took all her strength to wrestle Davi onto the floor of the back seat. She used rope she had in her trunk to tie Davi's hands and feet. Davi watched with terrified eyes as Zulanni produced a chamois and stuffed it in Davi's mouth. Zulanni climbed behind the wheel, tore off her ski mask, put the car into a three-point turn and gunned it back toward the main highway. It helped that the damaged side of her car faced the shoulder and not the oncoming traffic, she thought. It also helped that, by then, it had become quite dark. She had to hope no one would connect her car to the wreck behind her.

They turned south well before reaching Portland. As the car finally slowed, Davi had recovered enough to work herself to a sitting position. Zulanni was concentrating on her driving and, at first, did not notice that Davi, though still on the floor, was able to look out the window.

Davi saw a Les Schwab tire dealership and a lighted sign on a building that said "Forest Grove Moose Lodge". She could see the back of the driver's head, but in the darkness and from her awkward angle, she could not see Zulanni's features.

At that instant, Zulanni pulled to a stop and, reaching her arm behind, roughly pushed Davi back down to the floor. "Stay on the floor!" she yelled. "You follow directions and you will come to no harm. If you disobey me, I will use the taser again! Do you understand?"

Davi nodded her head. Zulanni drove another half-mile and then turned down a driveway. She had driven them to a house she had recently rented for Najev in Forest Grove, some twenty-five miles west of Portland. The house was a simple ranch model in need of paint and its lawn showed neglect. It was set on a large wooded lot separated from its only neighbor by a tree-filled ravine. The house was screened from the street by the curving gravel driveway that wound through a thicket of young fir trees. Four weather-beaten dog kennels and a fenced run were situated on one side of the house.

Zulanni pulled the ski mask on and opened the rear door. She made Davi move into the house by a series of jumps. Davi pretended to stumble and, as she picked herself up, she peered at her surroundings. In those few seconds, she saw nothing but the kennels, an unkempt yard, and a rather run-down residence. Once inside, Zulanni led Davi to an unfurnished bedroom with an adjoining bathroom. She told her to lie face down and, under threat of another taser attack, to stay where she was, unmoving. Zulanni marched out of the room. She returned minutes later with a length of dog chain after a hasty search of the backyard kennels. She pried open the end links using pliers from her car and looped one end around Davi's waist and then joined the open link to the chain. She repeated the process at the other end after wrapping the chain around the base of the toilet.

She dialed Najev's number on her cell phone. "This is Z. I met up with the realtor and she showed me a place on the West side."

"Is everything fenced in there?" asked Najev.

"Yes. Quite secure."

"Good. Stay put on that deal. No further conversations with her. I'll be in touch tomorrow," he ordered as he ended the call.

She removed the chamois gag from Davi's mouth and untied her feet. "It will do no good to yell. The nearest house is vacant and there are no other neighbors. I'll bring you food in the morning."

"I'm so thirsty. Can I have some water?"

Zulanni wanted to interrogate her prisoner and holding out the promise of water would be a powerful lever. But Najev had obviously not wanted Davi to be questioned until they had a better idea of how involved she had been in Madison's investigation. "All right," she said, "I'll bring you some."

Najev sat at the desk in his office and concluded that the warehouse was no longer a safe place to be the base of their operation. He rose and headed for the hidden room at the rear of the building.

"Moud, could we move you and your incubator and the culture hood to a safer place this evening without disrupting your process?"

Moud frowned, "Possibly, if I have a little time to prepare the supernatant and adjust the apparatus. I know a move was part of our contingency plan, but we'll need to carefully maintain the $CO_2$ level during the transport. Can anything be left behind?"

"No. This room may be discovered sooner or later. If it were to be, there should be no suggestion that you or your equipment were housed here. We'll even take the furniture with us."

Moud's frown turned to a scowl, "The first priority must be to preserve the culture at a high level of vitality. Can Bajehr help with the furniture?"

"No. He has something else to do tonight. I'll help you. Zulanni rented another house in what's called the Sellwood district. It has a large attic that's wired for electricity. I want everything over there by morning."

Moud looked quizzically at Najev. "What has made you uneasy... the little burning pot?" he asked.

"That too, but mostly this man, Madison. I decided to move in case he has drawn the authorities' attention to this warehouse. Even if someone searched well enough to discover this room, they must not understand what we're doing. At first, I thought an out-of-the-way warehouse would be a better place for you than a neighborhood house, but now I think our last few days on this operation will be more safely spent in Sellwood."

# ELEVEN

TAD LEFT THE CABIN TO EXPLORE THE PROPERTY SOON after Davi left. There was a duck blind an eighth of a mile away on the left fork of the faint trail that led toward the water. He almost did not see it in the fading light. The marshy estuarine area began within a few feet of the blind. He retraced his steps to the fork and trotted down the other path to the bank of the vast Columbia River. He saw lights on the Washington side and, low to the East, he saw the lights of an airliner descending toward Portland International Airport. Breaking his reverie, he returned to the cabin.

Tad was tired. He planned to be in touch with Bronson in the morning and knew he needed to recharge his batteries. He read old Outdoor Life magazines for over an hour as the fire smoldered out, then checked his watch. It read 9:55. He decided to call Davi to confirm that she had an uneventful trip back to Wilcoa and then turn in. Before he had finished touching in her number, the lights went out. He knew a book distributor who lived on Sauvie Island and had heard him tell stories of their unreliable power on stormy nights. But there had been no evening wind. His instinct told him this was not the time to discount the threats he faced. He knew there could be a benign explanation, but he had to be in survival mode. Remembering a flashlight on the mantel, he shuffled toward the fireplace. Tad walked with his arms outstretched, waiting for his eyes to adjust to the darkness. He strained to hear any unusual noise, but the stillness of the night was broken only by the distant croaking of a bullfrog.

He had almost reached the hearth when the living room window shattered inward as a small, heavy object was hurled into the cabin. Tad knew he had only a second or two to escape the grenade's blast. He sprinted into the bunk room. Fortunately, he had not yet pulled the curtains across the windows. Wrapping his arms around his head, he dove at the slightly-less-black rectangle that he knew had to be the window.

The sound of splintering wood and breaking glass was totally lost in an almost deafening explosion. Later, he would wonder if the concussive shock wave from the grenade had helped expel him from the house. The wall of the bunkroom undoubtedly had shielded him from the shrapnel. Duff from two small fir trees softened his landing enough that he rolled to his feet and continued running. The moon had not yet risen and, in the darkness, he had no clear sense of direction. The crude path through the forest toward the shore led directly away from the rear of the cabin. His trajectory out the window left him running in that direction. He had no way of knowing how many men stalked him. If there were only one or two, the chances were good that they were still on the front side of the cabin making it impossible for him to reach his car. The duck blind might be his best chance, if only he could find it.

Tad crashed into tree branches and almost fell. It seemed that the forest was a little less dense and impenetrable to his right and he recognized that the trail was only a few feet away. He felt several cuts from the glass, but they did not seem to be bleeding badly and there was no time to take inventory of his injuries. Knowing that he had suffered only minor wounds fueled his determination to survive. He heard voices near the house. His attackers would surely be trying to verify their kill before leaving. In another few strides, the path forked and he knew he would immediately be out of sight even if they had powerful flashlights.

Tad fought for breath as he reached the blind. He careened down the internal entry steps and nearly fell to the straw-covered dirt floor. Regaining his balance, he leaned against the wall trying to silence his panting. If his attackers could not find his body in the cabin, they might realize the broken window was not caused by the blast. They would then start searching for him in the direction of the shore. Tad was strong, but he would be no match for armed men. Shining a light through the shooting opening or the doorway would immediately pinpoint him once they found the blind.

He saw a charcoal brazier and a skewer in one corner. He grabbed one of the briquettes from the brazier and rubbed his face with it to darken his skin. An unused shotgun shell, a roll of duct tape, and a duck call lay on the sill of the opening. He picked up the shell and placed it on the second step. In one corner, he found a length of camouflaged nylon netting and a sheaf of cat-tails. There was a chance he would remain unseen if he stood in the corner close beside the door, wrapped the netting around his torso, and set the cat-tails in front of his feet. Tad heard hushed voices just as he finished his preparations..

"The bastard is like a cat with nine lives! You go toward the shore, I'm going along this marshy area. If either of us sees any sign of him, call the other on the cell phone. And put your phone on vibrator. The less noise we make, the better the odds we can take him by surprise."

"I don't think it's so smart to separate, Bajehr."

"We won't be that far from each other and we have to locate him quickly. Just do it!"

Two minutes later, Tad heard a sudden exhalation of breath and a soft oath. No light shined in from outside, but the door swung open. Tad thought of himself as a wild animal, tracked back to its den: afraid, but needing to fight for its life. He steeled himself and felt a surge of inner strength. These people were evil. They had murdered his best friend. They had turned the last days into a living hell. He would do what he had to do. He was going to get off Sauvie Island alive!

Bajehr had left his flashlight in the car and his eyes had not quite adjusted to the blackness after leaving the cabin. He was not a duck hunter, but he guessed that he had come upon some kind of a hunter's hideout. He opened the door and could barely make out the floor level two feet below grade. Did Madison know about this place? If so, could he have reached it? Unlikely, he thought, but still he had to be very cautious. Holding his Baretta in his right hand, he ducked his head and put his foot on the first of the steep steps. He was placing his other foot on the next step and was peering into the interior when something moved under his foot. He instinctively looked down as he tried to regain his balance.

Tad stood like a statue with both arms upraised and free of the netting. As Bajehr tottered on the steps, Tad brought his palms together and crashed the backs of his hands into the other man's neck with all his might. Bajehr grunted and collapsed on the floor unconscious. Tad threw off the netting and straddled the unmoving man. He found his cell phone and put it in his pocket. He located Bajehr's gun after feeling around on the straw and stuck it in his waistband. He bound Bajehr's hands and feet with the duct tape and plastered it over his mouth. His adversary would almost certainly regain consciousness in the next few minutes. Working swiftly, he removed the man's shoes and socks.

Tad knew the second man could not be far away and could well be working his way toward the marshy area and the blind. His ambush had worked once, but he doubted it could be repeated, especially if the man on the floor was conscious and thrashing around. He had to abandon the blind and distance himself from the vicinity of the cabin. Tad remembered the duck call and picked it up. He jammed the skewer down the axis of the cylinder, tearing out the reed and silencing the call. He put it in his pocket and slid the skewer under his belt.

Tad flung the man's shoes and socks into the marsh as he fled the blind. The path had ended at the blind and now willows and brush forced him to run on the sparse grass close to the water's edge. He had gone less than forty yards when he felt the phone in his pocket vibrate. Stopping, he thought he could make out a soft voice ahead. He realized the second man must have overshot the blind, was now working his way back toward it, and was trying to reach his partner on the phone. Tad could barely discern a sizable stump a few yards ahead of him. Knowing it would afford him cover, he started toward it.

During the split second that his body was in midair, Tad knew he had stepped off the bank. He fell into the marsh with a noisy splash. Off balance and rotating as he fell, he landed on his back in ten inches of water. He sat up and sucked in a breath only to hear the man who hunted him moving toward the noise and closing fast. He reached for the gun and discovered it and the phone had slipped out of his pants in the course of his fall. He prayed that the breathing tube he had improvised from the duck call would work. The marsh water was cold and he dreaded lying back down, but he was out of options. He bit on the duck call and tried to seal it with his lips, then settled back under the water as Taj stopped fifteen feet away.

Tad needed all of his self-control not to hyperventilate like a novice snorkeler. He could see nothing through the dark water, but sensed that Taj had moved even closer. He had to hope that the water was deep enough and the reeds and cat tails thick enough that no part of his body showed above the surface. The icy water was already making him start to shake. Then he saw a diffused light sweep by where he lay. "Like shooting ducks in a barrel" was a simile that forced its way into his mind. The light moved on. Tad was beginning to think he had a chance when water started seeping into his mouth. He fought off panic and swallowed some brackish water. Somehow the duck call or his lips were allowing more and more water to enter his mouth. He had to get air! In a desperate attempt to clear the air passage, he blew hard through the call. Even that did not completely clear out the water. He would have to rise up for air in a matter of seconds!

Taj was sure the splashing sound must have been Madison falling into or running through the marsh. His batteries were low and the flashlight's meager beam hardly helped as he searched the edge of the marsh. He had just passed through the area that he believed was the origin of the noise, when he heard a wheezy, blowing sound. He spun around and froze, pointing his gun toward the marsh in front of him. Fear and uncertainty produced a prickly sensation over his entire body. He took another step forward.

Tad could see the light very close above him. Whether he would be seen first or would have to surface for a breath first hardly mattered. Getting off his back and standing up would be awkward and would place him at a big momentary disadvantage, but it had to happen now. He planned to throw as much water as possible toward the light when he leapt out of the water. This, and the element of surprise, might give him an equalizer.

Tad rolled to his right and lunged out of the water. He gasped a lung-full of air and then let out an animal roar as he gained the bank. In the microsecond of awareness that his adversary had been in the marsh after all, Taj stepped backward and instinctively raised his gun hand to protect his face from the pulse of water. The water fell harmlessly short, but in stepping back, his heel caught against a root and he arched backwards. He squeezed off two shots which were both well above Tad's shoulder. Tad's feet found better traction and as the other man staggered backwards, Tad hit him like a down-field blocker taking out a cornerback. They went down together with Tad on top. As they fell, a willow branch knocked the gun loose from Taj's hand.

Tad's fist hit Taj on the side of the head but did not stop his violent struggle. Taj reached up and got his hands on Tad's throat and they rolled over with Tad now underneath. Taj was much lighter and Tad managed to hook his legs over Taj's torso and break the choke-hold. He felt for the skewer, but it was not there. Tad knew it would not do him any good underwater somewhere in the marsh. Both men found their feet and Tad landed an uppercut that stunned his enemy. He hit him again and again. Taj backed off and reached to his calf. Tad was almost on him when he saw the knife. Taj swiped at him and narrowly missed. On the offensive, Taj darted in again thrusting high. Tad was no street fighter, but he instantly knew Taj's high thrust was a mistake and that he had to capitalize on it. He ducked and simultaneously swung his right leg with all his strength into Taj's' knee. Taj went down with a gasp of pain. They were now on the very edge of the marsh, almost where Tad had fallen in. Tad pounced on the writhing man, but could not grasp Taj's knife hand. He felt a sudden, fiery pain in his left arm just below the shoulder as his hands found Taj's throat. The two men slid off the bank into the water with Tad on his knees and Taj on his back under the water. Tad lost his grip on the other man's throat, but used his hands to keep the man's face below the surface. He got his knee momentarily on Taj's right arm, but not before he felt another stinging sensation on his left side. Taj's legs kicked wildly and he dropped the knife as he tried with both hands to tear Tad's hands off his chest and head.

It was over. Taj's struggling had lessened slightly and then stopped all together. Tad stood up. He was trembling from the cold, from the adrenaline rush, and from the knowledge his survival had required him to kill a man.

He slogged out of the marsh and stood exhausted on the bank. He was confident that he could find the area again to show the police. There was almost no current in the marsh so he decided to leave the body where it lay. When he had heard the men speaking, it sounded as if there were only two of them. Still, he felt it was too risky to return to the cabin and his car. Besides, he knew there was a good chance that they had disabled the car before they attacked. He hurriedly took off his sweater and shirt. His arm was oozing dark blood and it was starting to be harder to move it, but he could tell the wound was not deep. The skin also was cut over his ribs, but it appeared there was only slow venous bleeding. Tad tore his shirt to make crude compression bandages.

Davi had mentioned that the nearest neighbor was just off the paved road about a half-mile to the west. Tad walked as stealthily as possible. The new moon had risen and this helped him dead-reckon his way through the forest toward that neighbor. It was nearly one o'clock when he caught sight of the house.

# TWELVE

**B**AJEHR RETURNED TO CONSCIOUSNESS WITH AN OVER-powering headache. He recalled seeing a low structure near the marsh, but that was the last thing he could remember. He knew his hands and feet were bound and that there was tape over his mouth. Somehow, he had missed seeing Madison, and he knew he was lucky to be alive. He lay on his stomach on straw and concluded that he was now inside what must be a hunters' hideaway. His arms were behind him making it difficult to roll over. Once he did that, it was easier to regain his feet. Even in the darkness, he could tell that Madison had left. Despite the pain in his head, he needed to concentrate on how to free his hands. His eyes adjusted to the dark; but, after moving around the blind in short jumps, he saw no sharp objects with which to cut the tape. He hobbled backwards toward the door and felt along the jam for the hinges. He sat down so that, behind his back, his wrists were at the level of the lowest hinge. He methodically scraped the tape up and down against the hinge.

Many minutes went by with no noticeable weakening of the tape. He was becoming exhausted from his contorted position and the debilitating headache. Finally, he felt a little play in the bond. He took a minute's rest and resumed scraping at a faster rate. There was a tearing sound and he felt his hands separate. With numb fingers, he tore the tape from his mouth and then attacked the tape around his ankles. There were too many layers to tear, but he finally found the end and was able to unwind the tape.

His cell phone was gone, but Madison had missed his car keys. He remembered following a crude path toward the water. He climbed out of the blind and got his bearings. Without shoes, it was impossible to run, but he moved with a fast, tip-toeing walk. He located the path and turned back toward the cabin.

Tad felt weak as he stepped onto the porch and pounded on the door. Theresa Mallio was not a fearful person, but the evening news had carried a story about an escaped convict in the neighboring county so she was not about to open her door at two in the morning to anyone.

"Please," Tad said through the door. "I've been injured. Can you help me?"

"Go away! I have a gun and a German Shepherd," Theresa said with as much forcefulness as she could muster considering that she had no idea how to use her late husband's gun and her dog was a twelve-year old toy poodle.

"I understand it's the middle of the night, but I'm bleeding. Turn on your porch light and I'll show you at the window."

The light came on and Tad moved to the window. He saw part of her face as she looked through a gap in the curtains. He pulled off his wet sweater and showed her the bandages. "I'm still not opening the door," she said. "I'm calling the sheriff!"

"That's okay, in fact that's fine. But please tell them I'm hurt."

He heard no more and sat down on the porch step. He continued to feel weak and he worried about blood loss. Fifteen minutes had passed when he heard the cars approaching. Two squad cars pulled up the driveway and they turned a blinding spotlight on him. Tad stood up, raising his good arm in front of his eyes. An amplified voice told him to get off the porch and lay down on his stomach on the grass. Tad did as he was told and hoped he would not pass out before he had a chance to talk to them. Two deputies got out of each of the cars and ran toward him.

"He does seem to be bleeding," one said. "She got that right."

Tad started to roll over to look at the deputies.

"Stay right there! Don't move until we tell you to!

One of the men frisked him and said, "He's clean."

"So tell us your name and how you come to be here in the middle of the night."

Tad gave his name and wondered if they would believe what he would tell them about 'how he came to be here'. "I'm a retired FBI agent. I live in Wilcao near Astoria. You can check my driver's license on that. The short version of why I'm here is going to seem pretty incredible."

At that moment, they heard the sound of a heavier vehicle and an EMT's ambulance rolled up the driveway. The medical technicians interrupted the interrogation and, with the deputies' agreement, began examining Tad. When he was re-bandaged and hooked to an IV, the deputies asked to continue their questioning. The medics said they could have five minutes.

"I've had three attempts on my life in the last forty-eight hours. I've been working with the Portland and Wilcao police, the FBI and ICE, and we believe I've stumbled onto a terrorist plot."

"Oh, right" interjected the youngest of the deputies.

"No, dammit, it's true! For God's sake, check it out!" Tad did not have the strength to raise his voice, but he continued, "At least two men tossed a grenade into the Purvis's cabin where I was staying. I got out a split-second before the explosion. Then they chased me down to the marsh area. If you go back toward the river and a little east, in the marsh right at the edge, you'll find the body of one of them. He came at me with a knife after he dropped his gun. I had to kill him in self-defense. And there's a duck blind quite close to that spot where you'll find another one of them. I knocked him out and tied him up with duct tape. You'll also find their guns, one in the willows and one in the marsh, both not far from the body. The gun in the marsh will also have my prints on it because I took it away from the man I trussed up."

"That's enough, men," said one of the EMTs. "We have to get this man to the emergency room."

"Understood. But he's described a killing. He could be a homicide suspect, if this wild story of his doesn't check out. George, you go with them in the ambulance and cuff this guy to the gurney."

"Will do. You guys be careful looking for this crime scene. It's swampy in some places along the shore. And, if he's on the level, there could still be someone out there looking for him. I'll get back to the office on my own, but keep me in the loop."

Tad remembered, as they loaded his gurney into the truck, that he had not had time to mention his FBI contact. He motioned to the deputy they called George to bend over him so he could be heard. "Contact Russ Bronson at the FBI's Portland office. He'll vouch for me."

Tad was already feeling less woozy, but he was glad to be inside the EMT's truck heading for the emergency room even if he was handcuffed to the gurney. As the ambulance began to roll, he knew a lot depended on Bronson's willingness to stand up for him.

# THIRTEEN

BAJEHR WAS RELUCTANT TO FACE NAJEV, BUT HE KNEW that he must not fail to report. He believed no one had seen his car at the cabin but, to be safe, he parked a block away from Najev's home. Najev had been expecting their return and was sleeping fitfully and fully dressed in a living room chair. He answered Bajehr's soft knock almost immediately. He noticed Bajehr was barefoot and knew this meant they had some kind of a problem.

"Where is Taj?"

Bajehr winced. "It did not go well. I don't know where he is. There was only one cabin down the road so we knew it was the right place. Madison either was not inside or he somehow escaped the blast. We went searching for him in the darkness." He could not bring himself to admit that he had left his flashlight in the car. "Taj and I separated. I found a hunters' hideaway. I had my gun out and was going to check that shelter when he must have hit me. That's all I can remember until I woke up bound and gagged inside that little hideaway. I got loose and came back here."

"Fools! You shouldn't have separated. Why didn't you look for Taj?"

"I did not know where he could be and I did not

dare to call out. I think I was out for maybe ten or fifteen minutes. I had – still have – a terrible headache. I figured we'd lost Mad—"

"I don't give a damn about your head! You took the car. There's no way for Taj to get back. If Taj didn't get Madison, the place is probably crawling with police by now. We're in deep shit. Did you and Taj carry the capsules?"

"Yes! Yes! You reminded us. We know our responsibilities."

Najev tried to calm himself and think. The events of the night confirmed the decision he had made to move Moud's culture and equipment and furniture to the Sellwood house. He and Moud had completed the new installation two hours earlier. If Madison was still alive and not in some kind of protective custody, they had to keep trying to neutralize him.

⌒

The trauma surgeon told Tad that his injuries were not life threatening though he did give him two pints of blood. The wounds did not require surgery so the doctor cleaned and disinfected them and covered them with clean dressings. Tad was grimacing with the pain of that process when the doctor spoke.

"You're a healthy guy, Mr. Madison and I'm confident you're on your way to healing, but I'm still worried about infection from the marsh water and mud. I've cleaned you up, but I'm going to leave the wound open for a few days to facilitate drainage and to avoid any chance of an abscess."

"But I won't have to stay in the hospital, will I?" asked Tad.

"Well you can probably leave this evening. But we'll want to look at your wound in about three days. If it's healing properly and there's no infection at that time, we'll probably suture the wound closed."

"Well, I can understand the come-back-for-a-check-up part, but I've got to leave here right away. There are some things going on that I can't miss."

"I'm not comfortable discharging you right now. Can't you delay things for six or eight hours?"

The pain was subsiding and Tad faced the doctor. "Dr. Foster, you can't keep me here. I appreciate your caution. I'll be careful and follow whatever instructions you give me about changing the dressing, medications, whatever, but there are things going on that won't be postponed just because I'm not there. I have to leave!"

The doctor threw up his hands. "All right! I'll write you a prescription for an antibiotic and the nurse will tell you how to deal with the dressing. But you must not lift anything heavy and try to avoid using your left arm. Be sure to see your own doctor no later than Wednesday and sooner if you have a temperature, or great pain, or if you start bleeding."

"Thanks, Doc. I'm sorry I can't explain my situation better, but, believe me, it's important."

"Speaking of your situation, the Sheriff's Office has a law enforcement hold on you. There's a deputy in the waiting room. So you'll have to work out your freedom with the sheriff."

"Understood. I'll work on that," said Tad with a smile.

"Okay. I'll tell the deputy we're letting you go in the morning. In the meantime, I'm sending you to one of our beds down here where you'll get one more IV, a little sleep, and a hospital breakfast."

Tad was finishing his ham omelet when one of the deputies from the night before pushed the curtain aside and moved to his bedside.

"Mr. Madison, I'm Deputy Jellison. We found things pretty much as you said we would. The main room of the cabin has some heavy damage and it's lucky it didn't catch fire. We found a man's body in the marsh. Driver's license says he's Josef Abouti, but it looks to us like a fake. We'll check that further. And we found the two firearms. The prints were lost on the one in the water, but we can tell the other gun has been recently fired and there are two bullets missing from the magazine."

Tad hoped the FBI had been able to get useful information from the man in the duck blind. "So what about the guy I trussed up in the duck blind? Has the FBI questioned him yet?"

"Yeah, well I was coming to that. You see, we found the duck blind okay, but there was no one there."

"What!"

"Cool down. We did find quite a lot of torn duct tape on the floor. We think we'll be able to lift some prints from the tape. And we found some bare-foot prints heading back to the cabin. Last night, George, he called your Mr. Bronson. The fibbee was pretty excited to hear about this Sauvie Island business. In fact, his guys are swarming all over the place."

Tad asked, "So can I leave and get back to business?"

"Yes you can. The sheriff and Mr. Bronson have

worked that out. There *is* that body in the marsh, however, so our investigators will still want to talk with you, but they'll hold off for now. By the way, Bronson's men put air back in your tires. Your two 'friends' must have let it out. Get dressed and I'll give you a ride to your car."

"Give me a second or two to call a friend. I'll meet you in the lobby."

Jellison nodded and closed the curtain behind him. Tad dialed Davi's number. The phone rang until her answering machine kicked in. Surprised that she would be out of the house so early, he left a message that he had had a rough night with more trouble, but was alright. He said he was going to be on the move, but would call her later and explain.

Rachel Palowski was the FBI's Senior Scientist in the Biothreat Division. She had received graduate degrees from Cornell and began a twelve-year stint at the federal Center for Disease Control and Prevention in Atlanta. A recruiter for the Army's Medical Research Institute of Infectious Diseases in Maryland convinced her to direct her impressive research into antidotes and vaccines more toward national security by joining them at Fort Detrick. The slender woman with a ready smile and a near-photographic memory had quickly distinguished herself in her new role. Three years later, the FBI had enticed her away to lead the science staff at its division dealing with biological threats at Quantico, Virginia. She was surprisingly upbeat and outgoing considering the fell toxins she worked with at her lab.

Palowski spoke with Mike Li for a good half-hour. She finished their conversation sharing Mike's concern that there was a good chance some kind of a bioweapon was about to be introduced in the Pacific Northwest. She immediately assembled a team of highly trained technicians together with her own inventory of sophisticated analytic equipment. She told Bronson that they would be leaving for Portland on a FBI Gulfstream within two hours.

It was mid-morning, after conferring with Palowski, when Bronson gave Special Agent Clyde Morrisey the job of getting the necessary court orders and search warrants. Morrisey was one of Bronson's most reliable and experienced lieutenants. He had come west to Portland to start his legal career as an Assistant District Attorney for Multnomah County after graduating from the University of Iowa Law School. He had known, despite a fine record as a prosecutor, that his greatest satisfaction and ability lay in investigating crimes and gathering evidence. Three years later, he applied for and was accepted to the FBI's demanding training program. He was in the upper half of his class by the time he graduated from the FBI Academy at Quantico.

Morrisey had first worked with Russ Bronson in Cincinnati where Bronson had led an organized crime unit and Morrisey joined as a rookie. The two had been assigned to different districts two years after that but were reunited five years ago in Portland. Bronson had admired the legally attuned and imaginative younger man and had welcomed him to his District Office. Morrisey, even at a well-muscled five-ten, seemed overshadowed by Bronson's physical bulk, but he could not have been happier to work for his old friend and mentor.

Morrisey's first problem was to decide how to characterize the threat with which they were dealing. The murder and attempted murder were certainly local to Portland and the feared attack was certainly going to be against Americans on their home shore. These facts, taken alone would suggest "domestic terrorism". But he knew that this entire investigation grew out of the arrival of the container from Malaysia and the suspicion that an illegal alien was hiding inside it. And the rest of the suspects were of Near Eastern extraction, another fact that reinforced an "international terrorism" characterization. If they used the "domestic" approach to get warrants, wire taps, and phone traces, they would have to show "probable cause" to believe a federal law had been violated by the "targets". If they went the "international" route, the "probable cause" requirement would be somewhat diminished, and they would be applying under the Foreign Intelligence Surveillance Act (FISA) as amended by the Patriot Act. Bronson and Morrisey agreed that their highest priority was to act swiftly to prevent an attack in the immediate future. Conviction of the would-be perpetrators was certainly an important objective, but would be secondary to thwarting the scheme before it could be carried out. With its wide-open channel to the Attorney General in Washington D.C., FISA also offered them the fastest path to pursue the investigation.

Morrisey and Bronson concluded that their best

strategy was to seek an emergency search authorization from the Attorney General. Such an authorization, even if granted, would have to be backed up with an application to a judge on the specialized and secretive FISA court within seventy-two hours. Using a speaker-phone on a secure line, they reached the Director of the FBI and a conference call was set up with the Attorney General. Morissey had drafted the application to the court and had prepared an affidavit from Bronson that they faxed to the Attorney General shortly before the conference call began. After a minute of pleasantries, the Attorney General got down to business.

"Gentlemen, I have Phillipa Costillo, my Special Legal Advisor, with me on this call. I understand that you want emergency authorization for these searches."

"That's correct," said Morrisey. "Mr. Al Said is an American citizen, so we can't see how you could autho-rize the search without ultimately getting a court order. But, if we have their time-line figured out, we have to conduct the searches immediately for them to be of any value in stopping this thing."

Costillo interjected, "Sir, under section 1824(e) you have to let the FISA judge know you've approved the search and your approval can only last for seven days and you need to apply for a court order within seventy-two hours of granting approval. You've got to satisfy yourself, on a reasonable belief basis, that the FBI has to proceed right away and that the informa-tion you're after is necessary to our ability to protect against a potential attack by the terrorists or to avert a danger to the security of our country."

"Yes. And, given the remark about four more days and the seeming urgency of their pursuing Mr.

Madison, I'm comfortable with the emergency aspect. But I have a different concern. Nothing in these draft pleadings names any foreign government and the threat is presented there in Portland, not abroad. And you tell me the owner of the private residence is a naturalized citizen though he has an Arabic name."

"Yes, General Cartwright," responded Morrisey, "I see the problem you're having, but we think the solution is in the definitions section, 1801(a)(4). The term 'foreign power' is defined to include a group preparing for international terrorism activity. It no longer has to be actual agents of a foreign nation."

Castillo handed a copy of the U.S.Code Annotated to the Attorney General and said, "Quite so, Mr. Morrisey, but the expanded definition expressly relates to international terrorism, so are we back where we started? What makes this 'international'?"

"Well," Cartwright said, "look at the phrase about 'transcending national boundaries' as the means by which they would accomplish their objective. Does that get us anywhere?"

Bronson spoke up, "We have good reason to believe a person or persons were smuggled into the country from Malaysia in furtherance of the conspiracy. Moreover, there is evidence that the life support system that could have carried this illegal was seen at the warehouse. And, General Cartwright, we have an attempted murder by a man from the Near East with false identity papers. The man he tried to kill was Mr. Madison, the same man whom they saw prowling around the warehouse. We haven't yet discovered his real name, but a source at the local mosque has seen this man together with the owner of the warehouse at a cafe close to the mosque."

"I can see why you've approached this under FISA and the Patriot Act," said Cartwright. "I'm not quite convinced we have old-fashioned probable cause, but I think we must pursue this, and quickly, so the FISA court it is. As to the search warrant, I'm OK on the warehouse, but I'm a little more hesitant about Mr. Al Said's residence."

Morrisey said, "The Patriot Act helps us there, General Cartwright. It says you can give us the authorization if we allege, as we have, that a significant purpose of the search would be to obtain foreign intelligence information."

"All right. If you agree Phillipa, I'll authorize the searches under FISA."

"Yes, I do agree," she answered. "I think you're solid on that, Sir."

"Fine," Cartwright said. "You know the drill on the non-disclosure procedures, Mr. Bronson?"

"Yes, sir. We'll be scrupulous in that regard to protect our U.S. citizen's privacy."

"I'll also start the wheels turning to get an expedited court order for your phone tap including cell phones of the company and the owner under section 2511(2) of Title 18."

"Thank you, General Cartwright," Bronson and Morrisey said almost in unison.

"Sir, you'll have to certify that the tap will relate to intelligence gathering under FISA," said Costillo and added, "As for the trap-and-trace device, we'll seek that order under FISA section 1842 and, if we get the order, it's good for ninety days."

"Thanks, Phillipa," said Cartwright. "I can make

that certification. Call Judge Tasker as soon as you have finalized the pleadings."

They made arrangements for the Attorney General's office to fax the authorization and the court orders to Bronson and ended the call. When the faxes arrived, Morrisey called the three agents he had already placed on standby and gave them the coded phrase that cleared them to begin the searches. He turned to Bronson and sighed.

"It will be an unfortunate imposition on Mr. Al Said if he's an innocent victim of some bizarre coincidences, but it will be a hell of a lot worse if these guys are really about to unleash some catastrophic event and we don't discover it in time."

"So true, Clyde. But there've been real attempts to kill Madison so I'm not losing any sleep over the 'innocent' question. Whether they're involved in bio-terrorism is less certain, but we have no choice but to use all of our resources to get to the bottom of this."

"Absolutely, Russ! And we're ready to roll!"

# FOURTEEN

GENTS DAVE MORROW, NELSON CHANG, AND NORM Wilson found the parking lot empty and the door to Tropical Furniture Imports' showroom locked. They knocked loudly and then called the warehouse's number on their cell phone. When no one answered, they used a Speedkey to open the door. After two hours of opening crates, going through file cabinets in the office, and checking shelves and opening cupboards in the room marked "Employees Only", they had turned up nothing of interest. Nor did they see a bed or the apparatus Tad had described to Bronson.

"This looks like a dry hole," said Chang.

Morrow frowned in frustration. "Yeah, and Russ was sure we were going to find some incriminating equipment in that back room. But everything we've found is perfectly legit."

Chang thought for a moment and then started for the front door. "I'm going to check the back again. They could have stored things in that little shed."

"I'll go with you, Nelson," Wilson said.

Five minutes later the two men breathlessly came up to their lead. "Dave, we may've screwed up," said Chang. "We didn't turn up anything in that shed behind the building but, as we were walking back, we realized that storeroom in the back seemed too narrow. I guess we both assumed the wall we saw was the outside wall. We went back into that room and paced its width and, to be sure, we paced the width of the entire building. The building is some five paces wider! There's some space behind those walls that is completely sealed off!"

Morrow joined them as they broke into a trot heading for the "Employees Only" room. "So it must be some kind of a box-within-a-box puzzle," he said. "There certainly will be a way in. All we have to do is find it!"

They entered the room and saw that the ceiling was continuous and unblemished all the way to the wall. Chang moved on hands and knees along the bottom of the wall trying to slide a credit card into the seam where the floor met the plane of the wall. The seam was solid.

Wilson stood back and stared at the plate they already knew covered the circuit breakers. "Hey, guys," he said. "Isn't that metal cover oversize? I checked the breaker box by opening the little door and it looked to be normal dimensions for an operation like this, but the cover plate is too big."

All three of them peered at the edges of the plate and Chang ran a povket knife along its sides. As he worked the left side, he saw a small gap where the wall board had separated just a few millimeters from the steel plate. He gently inserted the knife blade into the crack. They heard a click and the edge of the plate sprung outward by a quarter of an inch. Chang grasped the edge and swung the plate open to reveal a rectangular opening between the studs. They shined a flashlight inside and determined that no one was in the space. Nevertheless, Wilson squirmed through the opening with his Glock drawn. Then he turned to face them and said, "welcome to the inner sanctum, gentlemen!"

The room was empty. There was no sign of the bed or the incubator and $CO_2$ tanks.

Tad discovered his cell phone – a waterproof model that he had paid extra for – was still working. But, again, he was left with Davi's message service. Getting back in his car, he drove to the FBI's secure garage to check out a loaner car. Bronson had pre-approved the loan knowing the terrorists had seen Tad's newest car. Tad arranged for them to temporarily store his car and said he would be back to use the FBI car later. Given the downtown parking problems, he thought it was easier to walk the three blocks to Bronson's office.

Bronson eyed the bulge of bandage under Tad's left sleeve. "I understand they came at you again last night and gave you a couple of knife wounds."

"Quite true, unfortunately. But the doctor at the ER said I'll heal up just fine."

"Glad to hear that! I'm also damn glad you got out ahead of the blast," replied Bronson.

"That makes two of us! And, Mr. Bronson, I want to thank you for clearing me with the Sheriff's Office!" Tad continued. "And for the loaner car."

"No problem! Call me Russ, by the way. We've talked further with the Wilcao authorities. They not only think you're a straight shooter, but the details they gave us on the arson seem incontrovertible. Our scientist, Rachel Palowski, in D.C. has had a talk with your Mike Li and they both think that this business could have a very deadly potential. She's already on a plane coming here. And we all agreed that we wanted you available to us and not cooling your heels in the Sheriff's office as a homicide suspect!"

Tad smiled, "That's great! I have no idea how they knew about the cabin on Sauvie Island. I understand your people have been looking around out there."

"You probably have to assume you were followed going out there. We found barefoot prints and tire tracks and evidence confirming the use of a hand grenade. We're running an international trace on the dead guy including our own terrorist watch list, but so far, nothing has turned up. We're discreetly showing his picture to people we can trust who worship at Portland-area mosques to see if we get any hits that way."

"What about the warehouse?"

"I had agents out there this morning with a warrant. There was no one minding the store which itself was pretty curious on a weekday. We got inside and found nothing out of the ordinary except for one exceptionally interesting fact."

"Yes?" prompted Tad.

"Get this. There was a hidden room in the rear of the building. Behind an oversize circuit-breaker box, our agents found an opening in the wall just large enough to squeeze through. It took our guys twenty minutes to figure out where that opening was. But once they got in, they found nothing. It had been cleaned out! The only good news is that our forensic team thinks they might be able to get some samples from vacuuming the room that could be analyzed."

Tad nodded. "I *knew* there was something very secretive about that place. And the fact that the furniture and equipment that I'd seen has been removed ices it! These guys are well organized and they're on full alert."

"I've got agents doing deep background on the owner, a Najev Al Said, and, through the Internal Revenue Service, we've learned who his employees are so we will be putting them under microscope too. Oh, and Bo Gardner called and said Customs finally found the container you put them on to. It does have two small, machined holes in the end and a thin metal plate nearby. Neither are standard."

Tad asked, "Where did it turn up?"

"They found it in a Long Beach container depot. They apparently needed more empties in California so it was trucked down there. I've got the L.A. FBI going over it. If they learn anything useful they'll let me know right away."

"Are you going to have agents on the ground at the events scheduled on the Visitors' Bureau printout?"

"Well, I've got twenty men assigned to the Trailblazer game and we're already talking with Moda Center security. We're vetting everyone on the maintenance staff and the concessionaires and ushers, and we'll be learning all we can from those that are cleared as to how everything works. We also have our team leaders studying the construction blueprints."

"And the Convention Center?"

"I have another team over there getting familiar

with the layout, the HVAC system, and the kitchen procedures."

Tad left feeling relieved that the FBI was now geared up to address the problem on all fronts. Following a wolfed-down lunch, he drove back to the same small shop where he had purchased the Spy-Eye. The pony-tailed sales clerk recognized him and asked if the Spy-Eye had been satisfactory.

"Yes. It worked fine."

They completed the repurchase and then Tad said, "Now I'd like to ask you a question."

Tad read some hesitancy in the young man's expression. "Well, okay, I guess. I gotta tell ya though, if you're interested in the business we do here, we consider transactions with our customers to be confidential."

"Well, let me begin with a general question. Do you sell stun guns?"

"No. We never have stocked them for some reason," he answered with obvious relief.

"Do you know of any place in Portland that does?"

"Yeah. I'm pretty sure Jamison's does and maybe The Gun Mart."

Tad asked for directions to those stores and drove less than half a mile to Jamison's. This store had a strong self-defense theme, advertised various classes, had an affiliated shooting range, and sold a wide range of sophisticated home protection devices. He introduced himself to an older woman behind the counter simply as an "insurance investigator" and offered her the same card he had used at the lawn-mower factory.

"We're checking into a death claim where it appears the decedent may've been attacked shortly before his death with a stun gun. I understand people may be able to get such a gun here. Have you sold any of those guns in the last few weeks?"

The woman looked a little nervous, but said, "We don't officially stock them for members of the public. They don't turn over too often in any case. Suppose we did sell one last week. Would that bring us any trouble?"

"Not at all." said Tad trying to sound business-like but not too eager. "Can you tell me who the purchaser was?"

"Well, I don't know that I should ..."

"The widow really seems to need the money from the life insurance. If this one odd fact can be dismissed, the insurance company will certainly pay off. I have to follow the lead, and, if it goes nowhere, the chances are very much better that she'll get her money. If there's no problem with the person who bought the gun, this lady should be able to collect on the policy."

Tad was improvising, but his widow story seemed to resonate with the woman. "There was only one sale and I know she didn't use a credit card. She paid in cash and told me she was an undercover police woman so I figured the sale was okay."

"Any way of identifying her?" Tad asked.

"Well, she looked as if she or her parents had come from the Near East or Middle East ... whatever. Anyway, she was young, brunette, kind of muscular, but not unattractive. You know, she dropped some bills on the floor and laid her wallet on the counter while she picked them up. I was kind of curious about her. I didn't touch the wallet or anything like that, but her driver's license was visible and I saw a name."

"That could help me a lot," smiled Tad. "Do you happen to remember it?"

"I'm not sure. I know I couldn't spell it, but I think it was something like Zulanni or Zulami and the last name might've been Hishadi or Hishodi."

Tad thanked her and moved on to check The Gun Mart. The manager there claimed they had decided to stop stocking stun guns eight months ago because of slow turn-over and had made no sales since then. Tad drove directly back to the FBI office.

S.A.C. Bronson was momentarily out when Tad arrived, but he was cleared into Bronson's anteroom to wait. Bronson strode through the door fifteen minutes later and nodded a greeting to Tad.

"Russ, remember I told you that the Medical Examiner had mentioned that my friend Paul had likely been shot with a Taser-type gun? Well, I checked a few places that reportedly sell them and one place said that within the last two weeks a Near-Eastern-appearing woman did buy such a weapon! And I got a possible name or at least some phonetic variations of a name."

"Nice work, Tad!" Bronson motioned Tad into his office and both men took chairs. "Give me the name and we'll run it against all the latest data bases. As you probably know, Arabic names do not make for easy computer searches, but we recently installed a new algorithm that has made a big improvement in picking up close spellings and minor variations."

"Good. I have another idea," said Tad. "Can you find out from the Corporation Commissioner the identity of the man who owns the furniture importing business?"

"Yes, I think we already have that. Sometimes the incorporators are just dummies for the real parties at interest. But we do have a person with an Islamic name. After the agents found that secret room at the warehouse, we immediately sent our people to the home of this guy, but no one was there either. We have it staked out and we have a tap on his phone."

"Glad to hear that." Tad hesitated, then continued, "Russ, I have two requests to make. The easy one is, may I use your phone to call Davi? The other one is that I think Mike and I could help you try to prevent anything from happening. Can we come along with you guys to the public events?"

Bronson frowned and thought for a few seconds before answering. "Of course, use the phone. As for coming with us, that's a lot trickier. I acknowledge that you've been on the right track from the very beginning. On the other hand, you've been victimized. By the book, victims can be too emotionally involved and could easily impede our efforts, especially when things start moving fast. Besides, you're no longer a federal agent!"

Tad started to interrupt, but Bronson held up his hand to silence him. "Nevertheless, I'm convinced you're one cool customer and I do want both you and Mike Li on my side. Here's the best I can do. You both can sign on as civilian 'consultants'. We'll fit you guys with armored vests and walkie-talkies. But I don't want you to get involved in any confrontational stuff or to carry a weapon. You can't use the radios to speak except in an extreme emergency. You can use them only to listen. I'm sticking my neck out on this arrangement, so you must obey my rules. Fair enough?"

Tad grinned, "More than fair. Now I want to call Davi."

There were several reasons why she might have been out of her house early this morning, he told himself. An early-morning jog or perhaps she had decided to go to her campus office even though she had no classes on Sunday. Still, Tad was uneasy as he heard the ringing. There was no answer. He waited for the sixth ring when he knew her answering service would cut in. Thinking she might be screening her calls, he asked her to pick up. Nothing. He left a message saying he would call again just before dinner. He called her office at the college and got her voice mail. He called her brother-in-law's house, but no one answered so he merely left a message saying he had tried to reach them. The police said they had called Josh Purvis to report the grenade damage, but Tad wanted to personally explain what had happened. He also thought her sister might know where Davi was. Finally, he called Betty Adams, his employee at The Breakers. Tad skipped their usual routine of having Betty report on the previous day's business, deliveries received, and local gossip.

"Betty, I'm trying to contact Davi and I can't seem to reach her either at home or at her office. Just wondering if she'd popped by the store by any chance?"

"No, Tad, I haven't seen her for several days," she said thinking she heard a bit of tension in his voice. "Anything wrong?"

"No. I'm sure she's just out somewhere. And no one has asked questions about me?"

There was an uncomfortable pause before she answered. "Well, actually there was someone from the insurance agency, I guess." Another pause. "Madeline covered for a few minutes yesterday morning while I grabbed a cup of coffee and a sandwich over at Raddemacher's. Tad, I forgot to tell her about your request to fend off any inquiries."

Tad steeled himself to hear the rest. "So what happened?"

"Well, I guess this woman came into the store and said the insurance company had an urgent need to reach you about the fire. Anyway, all Maddy did was to tell her that Davi might know how to locate you."

"Oh, shit," Tad half mumbled to himself. "You said 'this woman'. Did Maddy give you a description of this insurance person?"

"No, it didn't occur to me to ask. I'm so sorry I didn't think to warn Maddy, Tad."

"Yes, well, what's done is done. Listen, Betty, get hold of Maddy – track her down, close the store if you have to – and get her to give you the best description she can of the woman. And have Maddy call Russ Bronson at 503-224-4181 and give him the description also. He's with the FBI. If he's out, have her give it to his secretary. Tell her to use my name if the receptionist asks why you need to speak to Bronson directly. This could be very important, so both of you make it the highest priority."

Tad hung up and wondered if his assailants knew he was staying at the cabin because they had tailed Davi. He shuddered at that prospect since it also would mean they had identified Davi. He tried to convince himself that it would have been natural for an insurance claims agent to want to talk with him quickly after a loss, but Davi had not mentioned such a contact. He hoped the query was legitimate and continued to hope that Davi had just been away on some kind of a day-excursion when he called.

# FIFTEEN

AJEV USED A BURNER PHONE TO CALL ZULANNI AT nine o'clock in the morning. She heard the familiar ring-melody and opened her phone.

"He's still at large"

"But how can that be?" Zulanni interrupted.

"Later!" yelled Najev. "Have the woman call her man. She's to tell him we have her and that he must come to the empty shed in the south parking lot at the Washington County Fairgrounds at exactly three o'clock this afternoon. He should put a small ribbon on his car's aerial. He must come alone. If he fails to come or talks to anyone, anyone at all, about any part of this problem, he will lose her."

"You want her to make the call?" Zulanni asked uncertainly.

"Yes. He's no fool. He will ask to speak to her as proof of her situation. But be sure she sticks to the script! And if you don't get through the first time, call again for a meeting at the same place an hour-and-a-half later."

"Yes, of course. She doesn't show it much, but I'm sure she's frightened. I'll convince her, somehow."

She turned off her phone, put on the ski mask, and walked slowly toward the bathroom where she had chained Davi. She stopped to pick up Davi's cell phone and displayed its electronic phone book. Zulanni wrote down the number of Tad's cell phone. She slipped the phone into a pocket of her slacks and opened the door to the bedroom.

"I'll bring you some food in a while. But first there is something you must do. I want you to call your boyfriend, Mr. Madison, and give him some instructions."

"I'll never do that!" Davi said in what she hoped was her most resolute voice. "Besides, I don't know how to reach him."

"You think I don't know how cell phones work? We will use your phone. After I make the connection, you will talk. Here is why: if you don't call him, I will. But he will ask to speak with you. We mean neither of you any further harm. You have not seen me and neither will he, so you will not be threats to us. You will both simply be detained for a few days. If he does not meet with us, then we will have to take quick, decisive steps." She wrote the "script" in capital letters and handed it to Davi. "This is what you will say to him. This and nothing more!"

Davi reasoned that if the woman called Tad, he would probably do whatever she told him, anyway. She guessed they were going to try to take Tad hostage, but maybe he would disregard their demand and get the police to surround the place. But how could they find her? Possibly they meant what the woman said about not harming them. But how could she trust a terrorist? She feared that they would try again to kill him if he did not show up at the Fairgrounds. Davi felt quite sure they could not know about the cabin. Tad would be safe there, but he had said he was going back to Portland today. Then she remembered that she had been stopped on her way back from the cabin. With horror, she realized that they must have picked up her trail at the cabin.

"Give me some time to consider it," she pleaded.

"Five minutes. That's all. I'll be back."

Davi's headache from the car crash had not improved and that made it difficult for her to think clearly. Trying to ignore the pain, she concentrated. Their best odds might be for her to agree to speak with Tad. But she had to give him enough information to help her and to protect himself. But what information? She had no idea how to identify the house or her captor. Unless … she focused hard on what little she knew. She had just formulated her plan when the door opened.

"Are you ready to make the call?"

"Alright, but you must not hurt him!"

"We won't if he cooperates," said Zulanni, touching Tad's name on the phone's call list and handing the phone to Davi.

The ring continued for several seconds and then the message-taking program cut in. Davi looked up, "He doesn't answer."

"Leave the message," said Zulanni pointing to the paper.

"Tad, darling, this is Davi. Listen carefully. This is no Syl VanCoppice joke! They dogged my tracks and kidnapped me! They want you to meet them at an empty shed in the south parking lot of the Washington County Fairgrounds at three o'clock this afternoon. Put a ribbon on your car's aerial. You're to come alone and they stress that you are not to talk to the police or anyone about any of what you've been involved in or about my situation. Tad, I'm dog tired. I don't want either of us to get hurt. They say we'll be alright if you cooperate."

Zulanni yanked the phone from her hand. "Do as she says," she shouted and then broke the connection.

"You talk too much!" she scowled at Davi. "What was this Syl-Van-something business?"

"Nothing. We have a friend, Sylvia VanCoppice. She's a great practical joker. And Tad and I kid around. I just needed him to understand that this was completely serious. That's all."

"He'd better understand all right!" she turned and left the room. Najev had told her to confirm the call by calling him right back at his burner phone number. She was displeased that Madison had not answered his phone, but it was the best they could do. There were still three hours before the meet.

When Najev heard Zulanni's report, he summoned Bajehr. "I have a new plan for getting Madison. Get Rudi to go with you on this. We have his girlfriend locked up in the Forest Grove house. We've had her leave a message for him telling him to meet you at the Washington County Fair Grounds..."

"But, Najev, that's a big place..."

"Shut up! I'm going to tell you where! There's an empty shed – it's the only shed – in the south parking lot. We'll use that. You and Rudi must get there early to be sure there are no law enforcement people staking it out. Put on those ski masks before you approach Madison and search him carefully for a weapon or a wire or a homing device. Tie him up and take him, blindfolded and gagged in the trunk, to the house where Zulanni has the girlfriend."

"OK, I get it, but what if he doesn't show?"

"If he does not show up on time, wait only ten minutes and then leave. Zulanni will try to reset the meet for four-thirty. Go through the same precautions if you have to return. If Madison still does not show up, call me and speak so no one but I will know what you mean."

"Alright, and then?"

"Meet us at the Sellwood house"

Najev ended the call and frowned as he danced his fingers absently on the desk. Time was growing short and they had to neutralize Madison!

# SIXTEEN

MIKE LI CLEARED SECURITY AND JOINED BRONSON AND
Tad at the FBI's command center. The communications net now extended outward to Immigration & Customs Enforcement, Homeland Security, the Oregon State Police, the Portland Police, and the sheriffs of four counties. Bronson would have over a hundred men and women in the task force under his command within hours, as those from other FBI regions arrived. Many manned computers and communications equipment, even more got familiar with the layout of the Moda Center and the Convention Center, while still others were in the field working the few leads they had. Bronson had been presiding over several strategy meetings and was constantly on and off the secure phones.

They had converted a large room next to the FBI communications center for task force use. A briefing area in one corner was equipped with a large screen for power point or slide presentations together with a large whiteboard and rows of stackable chairs. Over a dozen desk-top computers lined the back wall. They had set up a table for smaller conferences and meetings. Along the window wall, they had desks to accommodate the visiting agents and Bronson's chief lieutenants.

Coffee carafes were quickly drained and replenished. They had established a secure link for Mike Li to access his own computer. He and Rachel Palowski, who had arrived from Washington D.C. minutes earlier, were already comparing notes. Tad stirred a fresh cup of coffee as Bronson approached. He poured himself a cup and looked soberly at Tad.

"We just heard from the lab. I pushed the techs to do the analysis really fast so they insist that we characterize their findings as 'preliminary'. The samples that came from vacuuming that secret room were almost infinitesimally small, at most just a trace, but it looks as though there may either be some anthrax or some monkey B virus or possibly some of each. I just now passed that on to Rachel and Mike."

Tad grimaced, "So this looks like the endgame. Can't we get them to postpone the basketball game and cancel the conference?"

"I'm going to talk to the Mayor and the team owner in about ten minutes," Bronson said. "The police would support postponing the basketball game, but the owner and the team president are apparently in Geneva for some Olympic Games meeting. It's late evening over there and they must be out socializing. We're still trying, but we haven't been able to reach them."

"But certainly someone locally must have authority to act!"

"Yes, you'd think the general manager has authority, but the team has been trying valiantly to rebuild fan support and enthusiasm. We're not in a position to go to the media with even part of the story and the GM says there's no way he's going to agree to turn away almost eighteen thousand fans at the last moment without an explanation."

"He's gotta be crazy!" Tad shook his head in disbelief. "If some lethal contagion gets loose and can be traced to the game and it becomes known that he was warned of the possibility, he can say good bye to fan support permanently!"

"I agree, but he seems to think the owner would support him if he could be reached."

Tad was amazed, "Can't the FBI or Homeland Security simply shut it down?"

"Sure, we could and would if we were fairly sure the Moda Center was the target. But Washington says we can't go around shutting down important events just because we speculate they might be targets. Politics, economics, avoiding panic ... they're all in the mix. I may seem overcautious urging a cancellation now, but if something goes badly wrong, you know the FBI will be the scapegoat."

"So it's on to the Moda Center?"

Bronson looked at his wristwatch. "I'm afraid it looks that way. We still have almost three hours, but our plans right now are based on the game taking place."

Tad had hardly slept in the hospital and was exhausted. Bronson arranged for a cot to be set up in a vacant office on the floor above and he virtually ordered Tad to try to nap. Tad called Davi and still got only answering machines. He called her sister again and learned that Davi had not contacted her. He decided to call the sheriff's office if he still could not reach her after the basketball game. Bronson hailed him just as he was heading for the elevator.

"Tad, I just got a call from a Madeline Klein.

She had a partial description of the woman who was asking how to locate you. Not much, but young, dark hair, dark eyes, and definitely Near Eastern. Sort of wiry, yet handsome looking, she said."

"What about the insurance company?" Tad interrupted.

"We checked with your carrier, Liberty Mutual Northwest, regarding your fire. Their local office said they have no claims agent fitting that description and that no one has yet started to work the file on your loss."

"Any background on that name I gave you this noon?"

"Not much so far, although we did get her driver license photo and she *does* look a little like an Arab. We know she's naturalized and she has no criminal record. She owns a small dry-cleaning business. Everything looks entirely normal on paper. And she too is not at her home. We'll find her, don't worry. I'll let you know. Now get some sleep!"

———

Two hours later, they reached the Trailblazer owner in Geneva and he too adamantly refused to postpone the game. The Moda Center was not quite full, but any game against the Los Angeles Lakers produced a good crowd. The FBI had vetted the catering and maintenance staffs and the concessionaires' employees. Some employees had been selected for further questioning, but the Agent in Charge had never uttered the p-word. No one they interviewed had raised their suspicions. By tip-off, agents were dispersed everywhere including key posts high up where they scanned the vast arena with binoculars and reported softly into their lapel microphones.

Agent Pilof Cirovich's assignment was to roam and periodically check certain critical nodes in the arena's heating and ventilation system. Moda Center maintenance men had shown him the fan rooms earlier in the day and he had noted their layouts. The rooms were sizable and quite warm. Situated high up on the east and west sides of the arena, their high ceilings vaulted under the curve of the Moda Center's gentle roof crest. The rooms were not routinely manned, but the maintenance staff had keys to access them and they had made copies for Cirovich.

On his second visit to the west fan room, Cirovich saw a movement from the corner of his eye. Someone had turned off the brightest of the lights and the remaining lights cast deep shadows behind the hulking fans and heat exchangers. Cirovich unholstered his Glock and shouted, "Who's there? Identify yourself!"

There was no response though Cirovich thought he heard a stealthy footstep behind one of the large fan housings. "This is the FBI! Come out with your hands in the air!"

For the benefit of the communication net, he added, "This is Cirovich. I'm in the west fan room. I've encountered someone, presently unseen." He heard in his ear piece, "Roger that. We'll have reinforcements there within ninety seconds. Stand pat, if possible."

Cirovich assumed a crouching position behind a large electric motor and listened intently for any further sounds. "I say again, come into the open with your hands high above your head!"

After nearly a minute, he heard shuffling steps

and a slurred voice, "Don't shoot, man. Don't shoot. Everthins goin be alright."

Cirovich trained his gun on the area where he believed the man would emerge. Two other agents cautiously entered the room, weapons drawn. A gaunt, bearded man in his early thirties waived his hands above his head and walked unsteadily around a huge duct. Seeing he was unarmed, the agents immediately overwhelmed him and forced him to the floor.

"Hey! I wazzant doin nothin! Take it easy!" the man yelled, the smell of cheap wine heavy on his breath.

They quickly searched the intruder and found nothing of interest. "Shit, Pilof! He's just a wino," said one of the agents who had taken the man down.

"Maybe," said Cirovich. "How did you get in here, Mister?"

"Hey, man, it's *cold* outside at night! Aroun five, they start makin deliveries. I just snuck in behind a delivery guy. I'd spent the night here once last year and knew how to find this room. Most times it's locked, but I got lucky again today. Look, it's just a place to keep warm through the night!"

"So you're homeless?"

"Well, yeah. I don't have a place to stay right now."

Cirovich spoke to his lapel mike, "Looks like he's really just a homeless guy. They'll bring him down for more interrogation and I'll stay here. Send up the chief maintenance guy. We need to check everything in here just to be sure."

Bronson had been patched into the communications circuit and gave a relieved sigh as he turned to Tad. "Looks like a false alarm. Apparently a homeless man who appears quite harmless."

He lowered the mike on his headset and spoke to another agent. "Manelli, find out how the hell that door was left unlocked! We stressed security with arena staff this afternoon and we can't afford another screw-up like that."

The game was fifteen minutes old when the Chief of Maintenance hurried up to Bronson. "We think we know how it happened, Agent Bronson. One of the sensors failed and it turned out to be one we didn't have in stock. Luckily, our vendor is located not far away. When my guy called him, he said he could run the new sensor right over. That was the good news. The bad news was the dumb shit figured he had fifteen minutes or so for coffee before the vendor arrived and he walked away leaving the room unlocked." Looking nervously at Bronson, he continued, "He was not one of my best guys. I sacked him."

Bronson asked, "So how'd this homeless guy stay in there while your man was replacing the sensor?"

"Well the sensor installation is right near the door. The homeless character must have hunkered down behind the big fans at the back and Hank just never noticed him."

Bronson gave a sigh of disgust. "Okay. Were all your HVAC systems otherwise in order?"

"Yes. I checked thoroughly. Everything's totally normal."

Bronson nodded, "Well, we dodged a bullet this time. But for God's sake, tighten up the reins. We're not through the evening yet."

Mike had come up to join Bronson and Tad. The three of them left the small meeting room that Bronson had commandeered for his command post and walked through a short corridor to the skybox area. They were standing in one of the few places where a walkway dead-ended between skyboxes with a view of the floor. Bronson swung his binoculars in slow arcs as he scanned the seats for any sign of unusual activity. He was mentally and conversationally detached from the others as he listened to the terse dialogue on the comm net through his headset. A modest wave of excitement spread in the crowd to their left. Looking over to see the cause, Mike focused on a five-foot blimp moving over the crowd. The scale model was maneuvered by small, swivel-mounted propellers. The crowd was excited because a "bomb-bay" door in the cabin of the blimp had opened and small Trailblazer favors were dropping into outstretched hands. At the same time, Trailblazer-red vapor was trailing the blimp like smoke from a stunt pilot's plane. Suddenly Mike stiffened and spun around. "The blimp!"

Tad and Bronson turned to see where Mike was pointing. "Right!" Bronson acknowledged and lowered the mike on the headset. "Find where they control that little blimp that's cruising above the crowd. Get there fast and go in hot!" He turned back to Mike and Tad. "Nobody told us anything about a blimp! Somebody gave me tickets to a game a couple of years ago, but I don't remember anything flying around. Damn!" He lowered the mike again. "All agents wear your breathing masks!"

A voice came over the comm net. "It's controlled from a room right next to the public-address announcer's booth. West side on the level just below the sky boxes." Bronson broke into a run with the other two following.

A grey-haired man hunched over the sill watching the blimp and delicately moved a joystick on his lap. He stood with alarm as the door behind him crashed open and two agents wearing breathing devices and with guns drawn burst into the room. "Stop the smoke!" one of the men yelled, then added, "Show us how to bring the blimp back here."

The operator shuddered and asked, "What do you want? Who are you?"

"FBI", said one of the men flashing the badge in his wallet. "Do what we say, now!"

"Okay! Okay!" the older man said. He pushed a button on his radio transmitter cutting off the red vapor. "I'll show you, but it'll take a minute or so for it to come back."

Before the second agent could lock the door, Bronson, Tad and Mike arrived. The first agent, with gun still drawn, frisked the operator and ordered him to identify himself.

"Herman Oldymier. I'm just a hobbyist! I have a contract with the Trailblazers to run my blimp at their home games."

"And this red vapor?" asked Bronson.

"I just added it this week. Pretty cool isn't it?" asked the man with a smile that quickly faded as he realized the concern behind the question. "Just dry ice vapor and some colorant. Took me a while to figure out how to expel it, but it's perfectly harmless. Honest!"

Bronson used the mike, "Check out Herman Oldymier with Trailblazer management. Find out if he's a contractor for the blimp and, if so, how long he's had the contract."

The first agent finally brought the blimp to the

window after some wrong turns and they tugged it into the room. Bronson heard a confirmation of Oldymier's contract status over the comm net. He gestured toward the blimp. "Mike, we'll get Rachel up here and she'll get samples from the smoke chamber on that oversize toy. Unless and until we get a clean bill of health on those vapors, everybody keep the breathers on. And we need a discreet, but de facto quarantine on this entire arena. Get cooperation from the local police if necessary, but nobody leaves without a clearance from me, the CDC rep or Dr. Palowski."

Rachel brought a very sophisticated instrument that could field test for over a dozen virulent pathogens. Within ten minutes, she was satisfied that the smoke was, as Oldymier had claimed, simply colored vapor from dry ice. Bronson told the group to take off the breathing masks and instructed the agents to cancel the quarantine.

"Maybe this wasn't the target after all," said Tad who was starting to feel the effects of his extreme fatigue.

"It's beginning to look that way," replied Bronson, "but we're staying here on full alert until the game's over and the crowd's gone home." He was already concerned that people had noticed his agents running through corridors or that those departing early had run into the momentary quarantine. Homeland Security had insisted every effort be made not to trigger publicity or general panic. Disseminating helpful information to stop or mitigate specific, localized threats was one thing but, at this point, any leaks or stories could be seriously counterproductive. Bronson told the law enforcement agencies to use a cover story if questioned by the media. They were to say that they had searched for a fugitive from an armed robbery charge reported to have entered the Moda Center, but they had not found him. They were to explain the masks as incidental to their possible use of tear gas.

The game ended with no further suspicious events and Bronson offered Tad a ride in his car. Tad had almost dozed off when he remembered he had to call Davi. Surely, in the evening, she would be home. When no one answered, he was about to confess his great concern to the other men. Then he realized she might have been trying to reach him while he was napping at the FBI office. He checked and found he had received five messages. He slumped in the seat as he heard the third message. It was Davi saying she had been kidnapped and was being held hostage.

# SEVENTEEN

**N**AJEV REALIZED THAT HIS GAMBIT WAS NOT LIKELY TO work when Bajehr and Rudi reported that Madison had failed to make the meet at either of the two times. Najev reasoned that Madison had not checked his messages or that he had already gone to the police or the FBI. To deal with the first possibility, he had told Zulanni to place one further call. Again, Madison had neither answered his phone nor arrived at the fairgrounds. If the second possibility had come to pass, holding the girlfriend or capturing Madison was of no advantage. He waited until after ten o'clock before making up his mind. He drove a mile away from the safe house in Sellwood and called Zulanni.

"Everything still OK?"

"Yes. Completely," she replied.

"This will no longer serve our purposes. Your friend must remain as she is, but you can leave now. We need you for tomorrow. Come to the other house. Do not bring a trailer."

"Understood. What will happen to … my friend?"

"She'll be fine. We can make a call tomorrow, afterward. Just make sure there are no art prints anywhere on the premises and leave nothing behind. We don't have the luxury of a cleaning crew."

Zulanni rolled up her sleeping bag and collected the garbage from their meals. She had worn gloves most of the time, but she nevertheless wiped down the kitchen counters. Looking ruefully at Davi, Zulanni determined that she could reach the bathroom sink. Zulanni filled it with water. She knew Davi could easily survive another twelve hours. She was confident that Davi could not escape or draw attention to the house, but felt it worth trying to inhibit any such efforts to be saved.

"I'm going to leave for a while," she said. "Don't try anything or you'll regret it when I get back."

Davi looked directly at the eyes behind the ski mask but tried to appear completely cowed. They had not brought Tad in and she trusted that he had never showed up at the fairgrounds. She thought it most likely he had not received the message in time. Would he find her before this woman returned? Would her message help him? As Davi pondered these questions, Zulanni closed the bedroom door and left the house.

Now totally awake, Tad sat forward in the rear seat and listened to the message a second time. It was far past the designated times for the meet. The last two messages were almost repeats of the earlier message in another woman's voice, but with later rendezvous times. The last attempt ordered a meeting at six PM. Was Davi alive? Should he enlist the FBI's help in trying to locate her? The more he thought about it, the more strongly he felt that his going to the terrorists only would have resulted in Davi's and his deaths. Besides, now he had no way of meeting with them. Their need to hold him, for some reason, seemed to have diminished with time passing and he no longer seemed so important to them. He straightened up in the seat.

"Russ, they have Davi."

"Oh shit! They left a message?"

"Yes, three times. It was Davi's voice on the first message. She was alive when the call was made. She sounded scared, but strangely collected. In fact, I think she was trying to let me know where she was being held!"

"What do you mean?"

"Well, she used phrases that were a little out of place. And mentioned something about a joke that made no sense to me. I'm going to listen to the message again and again until I make something out of it. You've got to help me find her!"

"Bet on it! I'll put Morrisey in charge of fine-tuning my plans for the Convention Center. We'll get a dozen agents on Ms. Salloway's situation right now and try to triangulate the pings to the cell towers. We have jurisdiction over any terrorist kidnapping. First thing, we'll get a transcript of that call."

By the time they reached the federal building and ordered take-out, Bronson had detailed an agent to contact all the county sheriffs from Washington County to Clatsop County regarding Davi's disappearance. The agent returned minutes later. "The Clatsop Sheriff's Office found her car in the ditch about three miles from Wilcao early yesterday evening. They thought she might be in shock from the crash and were looking for her in the vicinity. They saw no sign of her and that, together with some blue paint on the left side of her car, started them thinking foul play."

Tad interrupted, "Why didn't someone notify me?"

"Seems as though no one in the Sheriff's Office realized you two had a relationship. They'd heard from someone that she had a sister, but they did not know the sister's married name, so they didn't call her either."

"So all this time has gone by ...," said Tad with a mixture of sorrow and disgust.

"Well," the agent responded, "when they decided it might be a kidnapping, they did contact us. Unfortunately, the agent who took the call was also unaware of her connection to you so he routed it through other channels."

Bronson dismissed the agent and Tad listened to the recorded message several more times. He turned to Bronson. "Davi loves cross-word puzzles. I think this joke business is some kind of a puzzle clue. Obviously her captors were closely monitoring what she said. 'Syl VanCoppice' makes no sense by itself so I'm doing the puzzler's thing."

He printed the letters in the name. Nothing jumped out at him. He wrote them backwards. Still nothing. He tried synonyms and puns. The best he could tease out was unhelpful silliness. Then he tried conflating the first two words. "S-Y-L-V-A-N could be 'sylvan', you know, as in wooded, evergreen, forested," he said turning to Mike and Bronson. "But none of those narrow it down. Coppice is a glade or a copse isn't it?"

"Well, more like a grove, I think," offered Bronson.

"Wait a minute! Forested grove? No! Forest Grove! They're holding her in Forest Grove!"

"I think you're on to something," said Bronson.

"Still, that's a good sized town. We'll have to zero in before I can mobilize a team."

Tad nodded, "I understand. Now that I know she was trying to give me information, I want to think about the other parts of her message that just didn't sound normal." He studied the transcript of the call. "Most of it's very factual. Except for..."

Bronson interrupted. "Yes. She gets more personal in a couple of places. And look, she uses the word 'dog' or a variant twice!"

Tad looked at him thoughtfully. "Yes. That's got to mean something more than just what she's saying."

Bronson checked his watch. "I've already told our guys to talk to the wireless carriers. The carriers' computers can probably tell us whose phone was used to call you and the nearest tower to the caller. My agents will probably get some sleepy night shift person, but it shouldn't take long."

Tad started playing mental puzzle games with the word "dog", but after working through "canine", "puppy", "hound", "cur", "chase" "follow", and "determined", he stopped in frustration. He started writing down breed names on a sheet of paper. "Irish", "English", "Australian", "Newfoundland", "Afghan", "German", and "Scotch" suggested places, but they were certainly not places where Davi could be held.

Bronson poured a cup of coffee, black and strong and took his first swallow when an agent knocked on his office door. He handed Bronson a sheet of paper. "We have a tower location just outside of Forest Grove, Oregon. The carrier is Verizon. And the phone's owned by one DaVita Salloway."

Bronson nodded in appreciation. "Thanks, Doug.

So they were smart enough to use her phone. You were right on, Tad, about Forest Grove. Your Davi is plucky and smart."

The agent turned to leave the office, but Bronson held him. "Doug, tomorrow morning start working property titles in Forest Grove for this man Najev Al Said and for Zulanni Hishadi. In the meantime, check the wireless carriers to see if Hishadi has a cell phone. If she does, I want its number, a trace on all calls on it for the last two months and, if she isn't using a burner or hasn't removed the SIM card, try to get a fix on the phone's location. You'll need an emergency order from the A.G. Morrisey can handle that as soon as he's done with the preparations at the Convention Center. Tell him to apologize to the Attorney General for bothering him in the middle of the night, but this kidnapping is tied to the terrorists! We don't even have an hour to lose! Once we get the data, I'm particularly interested if she and Al Said have called each other and if either of them has called any realtors in Forest Grove."

It was a quarter to one in the morning when Doug Tashimoto returned to Bronson's office. Bronson sent someone to wake Tad who was taking a nap on the floor above. "I assume Morrisey got the order. Any links turn up?" the SAC asked.

Tashimoto smiled, "He did and, yes, boss, I think we have something. There were definitely a few calls between Hashadi and Al Said so they know each other. They've called each other eight times in the last two months. But – get this – six of those calls were yesterday!"

Bronson nodded and said, "Interesting for sure! How about realtors?"

"Yep. Got two hits to the same realtor, one day apart three weeks ago. A Sallie Ackerman with Brackton Realtors."

"Great work, Doug! Now you'll have to get Ms. Ackerman out of bed and find out if she sold or rented a place to Al Said or Hishadi. If need be, meet her at her office right away."

Tashimoto hurried out the door and Tad rose to follow, but Bronson raised his hand. "I know you want to find her more than anything else, but let him do his job. You can go with us, if we get a location, but you must understand it's our show."

"Okay. I know that's our deal. But could we listen in on his call to this realtor?"

"That would be alright. I'll get them to patch us in on my speaker phone. But no direct talking to this gal. This is going to be confusing enough for her in the middle of the night without multiple voices in her ear. Meanwhile, I'm going to check on the readiness of our SWAT team."

Five minutes later, the call commenced. The woman was somewhat groggy and highly dubious at first, but Tashimoto's patient firmness soon convinced her that his was not a crank call. He gave her an opportunity to call the FBI switchboard and ask for him as a way of reassuring her. After a moment's consideration, she agreed to continue.

"We really appreciate your cooperation, here, Ms. Ackerman. Now the question I need to ask you is have you sold or rented a property to a Zulanni

Hishadi or a Najev Al Said at any time, but especially in the last two months?"

"No. I'm pretty sure I'd remember names like that. What kind of property?"

"A residence probably. But possibly a farmhouse, or a warehouse. Probably something a little off the beaten path."

"No, I still can't even recall any contacts with such people. What's going on?"

"We're working on a kidnapping. More than that I can't say just now. Do you get telephone numbers of the potential customers who contact you?"

"I always try. It's good business. Even if you don't have anything that interests them right away, you might in the future. If we have repeated contacts, a name and number would make it to my Rolodex."

"Let me give you a number just in case it triggers anything for you." He read the number they had for Zulanni's cell phone.

"Sounds like a cell phone number, but I don't memorize them so it means nothing to me."

"I understand. Ms. Ackerman, we know a person of interest to us has called you on her cell phone. You've been helpful, but I'm going to have to ask you to meet me at your office so we can see if you can in any way connect a property with this phone number. Can we meet there in forty-five minutes?"

Bronson had left the room briefly, but returned shortly before the call ended. When they hung up, he told Tashimoto to stop by and pick up Tad. Two minutes later, he looked into Tad's worried eyes. "We're going to get her out safely, Tad. Count on it!"

"I'm willing to believe you can find her, but these

people are crazy, evil people. If they resist…. how can we keep her safe in a firefight?"

"I won't sugar coat it, Tad. You're right. There are no guarantees. But our tactical guys and our hostage negotiator, are all highly trained and very, very good at what they do. The team is already assembling for the trip to Forest Grove. We'll use the realtor's office as an assembly point. If we can't make a connection through the realtor, at least we'll all be in the community when and if something breaks."

Sallie Ackerman had only been in her office a few minutes when Tashimoto and Tad arrived. She was a handsome woman even without having had time to apply makeup or put on pantyhose. Her black hair had a slight tinge of grey and Tashimoto noticed a ready smile that he knew was an important professional asset. Tashimoto also observed that, even in the middle of the night, she had chosen an attractive, tailored dress to wear. He showed her his FBI identification and introduced himself and Tad. She studied the identification for a few seconds, then led them to a file cabinet beside her desk.

"It's entirely possible that this woman used a different name in dealing with you," Tashimoto said. "She's a naturalized citizen who came originally from a Palestinian refugee camp." He produced a photo they had copied from her driver's license. "Does the person look familiar?"

"Why, yes, I do remember that face! I showed her a couple of residences, rentals, but she didn't seem to want either one."

"Thanks, that's important. And you were going to check that phone number."

"Yes. Here's my Rolodex. You can start with that. I think I can remember the two places I showed her. They're both rented now, but sometimes I leave my contact notes in the files. Let me get them."

As Tashimoto flipped through the Rolodex, the SWAT team and the negotiator pulled into the parking area and Bronson arrived right behind them. The realtor searched in a drawer of the file cabinet and returned with two file folders. She opened them on her desk and studied the papers they contained. Then she spoke. "Sorry, no phone slips in either... wait a minute! Here in pencil on the inside of the folder ... yes, that's the name she gave me, Dorothy Michaels and isn't that the number?"

Tashimoto and Tad leaned over the desk. "That's it!" said Tad.

"So we know she was looking, using an alias, but she didn't close the deal on either of these houses," mused Tashimoto.

Bronson, looking thoughtful, said, "But somehow they found a place."

Replacing the folder on the realtor's desk, Tad knocked over a framed photo. He picked it up and saw a photo of the realtor and a beautiful Afghan hound. He spun around and asked the realtor, "Did either of the places you showed this woman have any dog runs or dog kennels?"

"Why yes, the owner of the place on Myrtle Road used to have a pet grooming business and there's a run and a few kennels beside the house."

Tad and Bronson exchanged glances. "The message!" Bronson said.

"Exactly! This has got to be the place!" shouted

Tad as he turned to Sallie Ackerman. "You said both places had eventually rented. Who rented the place with the kennel?"

Ackerman consulted the file. "A Nadine Fisher it says here. I never met her. Fisher's realtor closed the deal. When my client accepted the offer, the other side just sent me the signed rental agreement."

"Give us the name of the other realtor, please," said Bronson.

Tashimoto checked the phone book for that realtor's home telephone and made his second wake-up call of the night. Once awake, the realtor remembered the transaction and identified Nadine Fisher as "looking maybe like an Arab lady."

Ackerman agreed that the tactical team could gather in a conference room of the Brackton Realty suite. They waited there, with faces already blackened and weapons cleaned and checked. Tashimoto hung up and reported what the realtor had told him. Bronson almost sprinted to the conference room.

# EIGHTEEN

DAVI WAS TOO TENSE AND AFRAID TO BE HUNGRY EVEN though Zulanni had left her no food. She was puzzled that her captor had not returned. Had they abandoned her for some reason? She waited forty-five minutes, then tried to release her bonds. The chain was impossible to break without some kind of tool. Sitting on the floor and backing up to the toilet, she was able to use her hands to remove the plastic caps over the bolts. She found, to her dismay, that the nuts were rusted too tight to remove and the bolt-ends above the nuts were too short to use in prying the chain links. The ropes around her wrists gave her more hope at first. But there was nothing within her reach that was sufficiently abrasive or sharp to fray the ropes. She tried forcing the rope on her wrist lower so that she could reach it with her fingers. She finally worked the rope low enough that she could feel it with the fingertips of her other hand, but the knot was still out of reach. Davi yelled loudly, but soon concluded that she could not be heard on the paved road or across the wooded ravine.

Zulanni had taken Davi's cell phone when she left. The house was growing cold and it was totally dark. Davi fought the urge to cry, but she had no idea of whether she would be alive to see the dawn.

———

Bronson had spoken repeatedly to Washington on the question of attacking the house. There was a possibility, statistically almost negligible, that some innocent Near Eastern family had rented the place and would be terrified by the explosive entry of the tactical team. That was an outcome he did not want, but the slight risk had to be taken. Besides, too many factors converged on this house: the interest of Hashadi, the dog kennel, the isolated location on the edge of Forest Grove, and the physical appearance of the renter. It had to be the right place.

A FISA judge, also awakened in the night, provided a search warrant under the Patriot Act provisions. With Davi a hostage inside, there would be no knock on the door, no bullhorn from the front yard.

Sallie Ackerman provided them photos of the house and a parcel map showing the long driveway. Ackerman had also found a floor plan of the house, which the leader of the SWAT team was using to brief his men. An FBI helicopter arrived and its crew awaited instructions on a school ground a mile from the house.

"Listen up, guys!" The leader of the SWAT team gestured at the plan spread on the conference table. "This layout shows the front door entering directly into the living room. Looks as though there's a wide archway to the right leading to the dining area. And that area is more or less open to the kitchen in the rear with a back door opening onto a small deck.

This hallway runs the length of the house behind the living room. There's one bedroom at its far end on the left. Closer to the living room and off the hallway to the front of the house, right here," he pointed, "there's a bathroom and a utility room. And then the larger bedroom is off the hall at the end on the right with its own bathroom. Questions?"

The members of the team memorized the floor plan, but no one had any questions. Their leader went over some timing issues and, at ten minutes before three, the dozen agents on the SWAT team, Bronson, Tad, Tashimoto, a medic, and the negotiator left Brackton Realty for the house. All the agents wore flack vests and had blackened their faces. They parked their vehicles a short way down a private road a quarter of a mile from the driveway of the rental house and proceeded on foot. Bronson insisted that Tad wait in the car but gave him a walkie-talkie and promised he could join them outside the house once the area was cleared of any hostiles. The SWAT team leader assigned some of his team to circle around and cover the rear of the house. He ordered three others to approach from the ravine. The rest of them walked single file just off the gravel down the long driveway. The SWAT team activated their night-vision goggles as they got closer to the house. The team members used hand-signals when communication within the group was necessary. After what seemed to Tad like an eternity, laconic reports over the radios told him that everyone had reached their assigned positions.

A half-moon was behind thin clouds and its faint light illuminated the yard in front of the house. They could see no cars in the yard as the group paused behind the last of the trees. Looking through their night vision goggles, they confirmed that there were no sentries outside the house. One agent crawled toward the dog run and eased the gate open. He checked the kennels and signaled to indicate they were empty. Tashimoto nodded to the leader of the SWAT team and the leader motioned the unit on the driveway to approach the front of the house. Then, whispering into his walkie-talkie, he got all the units synchronized.

As his count-down from five ended, the teams at the front and rear simultaneously battered in the doors. The two teams were inside in less than four seconds and were already covering each other with overlapping planes of fire if the weapons had to be used. At almost the same instant, the team at the opposite end of the house threw a concussion grenade through the front bedroom window.

Davi had lain down to rest. She knew she would not sleep from the cold and her headache, but the length of chain allowed her to stretch out on the floor, half in the bathroom and half in the bedroom. At one point, she thought she heard a muffled word. She started and whipped into a sitting position. Tensing, she concentrated on hearing every sound. Her heart beat faster with fear. Two minutes passed and she heard nothing more. Before she had quite relaxed, there was the loud sound of wood splintering followed immediately by a deafening blast that came from the bedroom across the hall. Then blackness overcame her.

The back-door team moved quickly down the hall, clearing every room along the way. When they reached the large bedroom on the back side, they kicked the door in and swung their automatic weapons from side to side, fingers on the triggers. Their barrel-mounted miniature spotlights flashed around the room in controlled arcs. "There she is!" cried one of the men, pointing his light toward the bathroom door. Two of his team members ran to Davi and cleared the bathroom while two more entered and cleared the bedroom closet.

Davi lay motionless, but groaned slightly. A little blood dripped from her left ear. The front-door unit that had checked out the other bedroom called out, "Clear in every room!"

The team leader spoke on the radio to the men who had stayed outside, "We have her and there are no hostiles inside. Remain on alert and establish a perimeter defense. We still can't be sure there's no one lurking outside!" Then he radioed Bronson and Tashimoto. "We have her! She's alive. We encountered no resistance. None of them are inside and the house is secure."

"Great work!" exclaimed Bronson. "I'm coming in and the medic will come with me."

He called Tad on the radio. "They have her! She's alive! You can come to the front door."

Tad broke into a run.

Davi opened her eyes and frowned. The frown changed to a smile as she realized that she had been rescued. The men were already untying the rope around her ankles and another agent produced a Leatherman tool to work on the chain links.

The agents cut the rope binding her wrists and Davi painfully brought her arms from behind her back. They helped her to a sitting position. The medic examined her ear. "I'm afraid the concussion grenade ... the flash-bang ... may have ruptured your eardrum," he said. "But it will heal and you'll be as good as new."

The medic said, "Let's help her stand and get her to that chopper so they can take her to an emergency room."

Bronson looked at Tad and said, "If the medics agree, you can go with her."

Bronson smiled at Davi as they stood her up. "I'm Russ Bronson, Ms. Salloway. Your friend Tad has been a tremendous help to us and to you. Finding you unharmed made my day."

"Thank you so much. I probably owe all of you my life. Can I get something to eat on the way? After that, I could sleep for a week!"

Bronson nodded. "I can well imagine. I hate to delay your plans, but we think this matter is coming to a head very soon, perhaps even later today. That means we have to debrief you just as soon as the doctors finish with you."

Davi nodded, "Sure, I understand. You must stop them. I'm afraid I won't be much help though. That woman didn't say much to me and she wore a ski mask and gloves the whole time. Just once, in her car, I saw the back of her head and a little bit of the side of her face, but it was dark and my glance at her only lasted for a couple of seconds."

"We have a photo of her, but anything else will greatly help," Bronson said. "The car she was driving ... if she spoke with an accent ... her hair color. Try to remember any details you can and we'll have someone talk to you as soon as they finish with you at the emergency room."

Tad hugged Davi gently and said, "Babe, you're going to be okay. It's all over!"

"Oh, Tad. Thank God! I was so scared, Tad!" Davi said, finally allowing herself to cry. When her sobbing stopped, she looked at Tad and said, "I so wanted to believe you'd get me out of this. And you did! Who are these men? A SWAT team?"

"FBI, honey, a hostage-rescue team and they're very good at what they do. But I'm *so* glad they didn't have to fight their way in!"

Tad took off his jacket and put it around Davi's shoulders. With an agent at each elbow, they led her out to one of the cars. Bronson called for a forensics team and told one of the tactical units to continue securing the house and grounds until that team arrived. As Tad got into the car that would take them to the helicopter, Bronson came over to speak with him.

"Registration for that financial advisors conference starts at eight-thirty this morning. We'll be there at seven. Why don't you stay with Davi and you can get to the Convention Center as soon as you feel you can leave."

"Thanks, Russ, for everything you and your men did tonight. I'll be there around eight or sooner."

While Davi was being examined, Tad called her sister. He told her of Davi's abduction and rescue. She was horrified and angry. She also cried with relief, but Tad could tell that she blamed him for allowing Davi to have become entangled with these fanatics by his using their cabin, for the cabin being seriously damaged, and for not calling her immediately when he knew Davi had been taken.

"Diane, I'm so sorry this all happened. I suppose

I was stubborn about trying to find out what happened to my buddy, Paul, but I thought Davi and I had agreed that she would not come to the cabin. I tried my best to prevent her being identified, but Wilcao's a small town and somebody gabbed. And during the night, things were moving so fast and with so much security, I just didn't think to call."

"I do understand, Tad," the sister said. "Please forgive my little rant. None of us are prepared for something like this. This was just some kind of an evil vortex that sucked you both in! Give me the phone number and address of the hospital. I want to see her."

# NINETEEN

THE HOUSE IN THE SELLWOOD DISTRICT OF SOUTHEAST Portland was a solid, two-story bungalow constructed in the thirties. The kitchen and bathrooms had been modernized and a carport added in front of the narrow garage to afford off-street parking for a second car. Najev had Zulanni park her car in the garage. He wanted it out of sight given its damaged condition and the fact that Davi sooner or later might be able to identify it. The delivery truck had been wiped clean and left at the warehouse. He had been using Bajehr's car that was now under a nylon cover in the carport. Bajehr and Rudi had moved in enough furniture and bedding a week earlier so that they could all shelter in the house for a few days. Najev had sent Zulanni to a supermarket to purchase food and hair dye. It was six in the morning as Najev, Moud, and Rudi ate a simple breakfast around the kitchen table. When Zulanni and Bajehr joined them, the others saw they both had become blonds.

"The jackets and pants have already been altered, but try them on to be sure you each get the right ones. Zulanni, your outfit is the size you told us to get. After that, I want to do a run-through of how it's going to go. We also need a review of how we'll communicate with each other ... remembering that talk has to be kept to an absolute minimum. We'll meet in five minutes in the living room."

They took their plates to the sink and left the room. When they reassembled, Moud showed them how to use the small, finger-pump dispensers they would be using.

"There might be a metal detector and they will probably check your pockets and purses. They all dispense liquids in a heavy mist," Najev said. "Moud's liquid will be in the bottles which you will carry in your purse or your pockets."

"But won't they see them if they search us?" asked Rudi.

"Yes, if they ask you to empty your pockets or Zulanni's purse, they will look at them, but Al M'afid gave me an idea of how to handle that. I am giving each of you a special bottle. Zulanni, you have contact lenses and your bottle used to hold eye solution for contact wearers. You can easily claim your eyes are sensitive to the lenses and you need the fluid with you. Rudi, yours used to hold a spray mouth-freshener."

Rudy, who had notoriously bad breath, nodded and said, "Yes, I get it. If anyone questions it, I'll just breathe on them."

There was nervous laughter as Najev continued, "Bajehr, your bottle was for hand sanitizer. You can say you've always used it on food-serving jobs. As you probably know, I have a mild case of asthma. My bottle was an inhaler. If they ask you to dump out your pockets or packs or purses, don't hesitate. Just bring those bottles out matter-of-factly as though they are things you carry with you routinely. No one will probably even look twice at these bottles."

"But," questioned Bajehr, "what if someone sees me spraying an alcohol product on food?"

"Yes, of course, that would be a problem. That's why I had these new labels that I'm about to give you printed." He passed one to each person. "You'll see they are all just large enough to cover the original label. They all identify a product called 'Salad Fresh'. If anyone should notice you, your explanation would be that it's a product that stops the lettuce from turning brown and keeps it fresh looking. The new labels pull off the backing and are self-sticking. Put them on the bottles after you've cleared security. Just be sure to get them on straight and to fully cover what's underneath."

"And where should we put on the new labels?" asked Rudi.

"After you are inside, go to a stall in the restroom to stick them on. After the salads are put out, find some excuse to approach the serving tables. Straighten up the utensils or wipe a smudge off a bowl. When no one is paying you any attention, take out your bottle and squirt the liquid over the salads with lettuce. There should be several good-sized bowls of tossed salad at each buffet table so work quickly and apply a good amount. And for Allah's sake, do not lick your fingers or eat any food without disinfecting your hands!"

Najev turned to Zulanni. "You will probably have the most freedom to move about. You may be the only one able to pass any word among us. There will be four buffet lines: one in each corner of the ballroom.

If all goes as planned, there should be no need for us to speak to each other. We can't risk taking our little radios inside because they may wand the staff as they arrive."

Rudi asked, "Najev, is the schedule still the same?"

"Yes. Luncheon begins at twelve-thirty. A few people may wander into the ballroom as early as ten after twelve. The salads will probably be laid out around 12:15. That means we move between twelve-fifteen and twelve twenty-five. Later than that, there will be too many people around."

Najev drew closer and looked directly at each of them in turn. "If something goes off plan, you'll need to improvise. If you get a conflicting assignment, pretend to carry it out so that the lead person doesn't tie you up with an argument or follow you around. But as soon as you're out of sight, return to the plan. Once you've done your part, go back to whatever you were assigned to do. Don't allow yourselves to get paired up with someone during that time period." He paused. "Now, Allah forbid, if the police or FBI show up and try to apprehend you, try to ditch the jackets, then run like the devil himself is behind you. You've already memorized the floor plan and know how to get to the service exits. If they should grab you," he paused again, "you each have the pill. In the spirit of jihad, you must use it."

The others murmured, "Yes!"

Najev nodded with grim approval. "We must take our satisfaction and our reward in the devastation we shall wreak on the American financial community and the Jew bankers! Just think, they mingle in the conference, they board the crowded airplanes, they return to their busy offices and five days later, they and many of the people they've been in contact with all start to die!"

"Death to the infidel imperialists!" they shouted.

———

Davi was sleeping soundly with an FBI guard outside the door of her hospital room. Her doctor told Tad that, physically, Davi seemed to be recovering nicely, but he warned that emotionally, it could take longer.

Tad left the hospital a little before eight o'clock. The Convention Center was located near the east bank of the Willamette River not far from the Lloyd Center shopping area. Two graceful glass towers that arced skyward from the beveled roof punctuated the Center's two-block-long length. At night, illumination inside the towers made the Center a radiant and familiar landmark. Bronson had arranged a parking place for Tad in an area cordoned off in the parking garage. Tad hurried in through the north lobby, looking upward at the magnificent, full-size dragon boat suspended from the ceiling. During Portland's Rose Festival in June, racing club members would paddle boats like this along the river in the annual dragon-boat races.

Tad knew that the largest gatherings during the convention would be in the Portland Room on the second floor and, for lunch, in the Ballroom. Bronson's command post was in a smaller room further down the hallway past the Portland Room. Tad could see, as he walked toward the escalator, that the registration desks were getting ready to open and some early registrants were already milling around in the hallway.

He found Bronson talking with three of his agents. The command post was behind a key-pad protected door with tables arranged to form a large hollow rectangle with two other tables in the middle serving as a communications hub. Tad caught the aroma from pastries and carafes of coffee on a smaller table in one corner. Tad had snacked at the hospital, but he was still hungry. He helped himself to a cinnamon roll as Bronson approached.

"Doesn't look as though you made any headway getting the day's events cancelled," he said to Bronson.

"No. More of the same about the city's economy, its reputation as a convention city, the scheduling of return flights, yada, yada, yada."

"So what is the program for this conference?"

Bronson handed him a printed brochure. "Registration begins at eight-thirty. Some special-interest seminars and committee meetings run from nine to ten-thirty, then a break, then, starting at ten-forty five, their first substantive session begins in the Portland Room. At noon, they break for a fancy buffet lunch that starts at twelve-thirty in the ballroom with their keynoter beginning her speech as they eat dessert. Another break, then the afternoon sessions begin at two fifteen."

⌐

The service staff and catering employees were wanded with metal detectors, then patted down and asked to empty their pockets, and purses or tote bags on a table as they entered the Convention Center. Najev and his inhaler were passed through without question. When the agents handling security at the entrance first saw contact-lens fluid dispensers, they were somewhat dubious about letting their owners pass. But, by the time Zulanni's purse was emptied on the table, they had already seen three other such dispensers and waved Zulanni through. The agent checking Rudi had his own problems with halitosis and, after a moment's hesitation, decided to let Rudi keep his mouth-freshener dispenser. Bajehr was the last of the four through the entrance check. He placed coins, wallet, car keys and the dispenser bottle on the table. The agent reached for the bottle.

"What's this?"

"Just Purell. Hand sanitizer."

"What's in it?"

"I'm not sure. A dilute alcohol mixture, I suppose."

"Well, I don't think..."

"I... I have this thing about being very clean. I use it almost every hour. I handle food for a living. I know it may seem a little strange, but I'll have to turn down work today if I can't take it with me. Please let me keep it!"

The agent looked at Bajehr. The man was a little eccentric, but seemed genuinely concerned about earning his day's pay. The agent stared at the bottle in his hand. His wife was a veterinarian and he had seen her use the same product at her clinic. He decided Bajehr's compulsion was harmless and let him pass.

Jeff Malone had been working Vice for only six weeks. Jeff was an ambitious detective and he carefully

technicians specializing in bio-threats had, along with Mike and Rachel, carefully searched the equipment earlier in the morning and had taken samples from ducts and vents. A van down on the street was filled with sophisticated analyzers and each sample run through so far had been negative for toxins. They had connected smaller detectors to certain main trunks of the ducting. These sensors had wireless connections to the equipment in the van for real-time monitoring.

Bronson had insisted that each attendee entering the Convention Center pass through one of the metal detectors he had positioned at the entrances. Purses and ruck-sacks were to be searched and bodies were to be patted down. He also insisted that only speakers, conference organizers, badged attendees, certified members of the press, and serving staff be allowed into the Portland Room and the Ballroom. The Convention Center management had agreed with those procedures. The conference organizers had bridled a little, but Bronson made it clear that he still had discretion to cancel the event. This brought them around. The unusual precautions would surely be noticed and it was agreed that they would explain the procedures as a consequence of the nation-wide Orange Alert declared by Homeland Security four weeks previously. The irony that people would be comforted to know it was "only" due to the alert did not escape Bronson.

The vetting of the kitchen and serving staff produced only one suspect. Every other non-citizen had a green card that appeared to be legitimate. Bronson knew that forgers had been quite successful at replicating green cards. He also knew that it was hard for ICE to keep its database completely current. Input improvements and computer upgrades were in progress, but deaths, deportations, expirations, and voluntary relinquishments made it difficult to verify legitimate holders of green cards. Social Security's data base was considerably better, but even its records were behind in reflecting recent deaths.

One waiter, a Juan Felasco who had worked for the concessionaire for eighteen months, was found to be using the green card of a person who had been deported. He was immediately arrested and taken to a small room near the command post for inter-rogation. He quickly confessed to being an illegal immigrant. His cousin had been deported for stealing a car and had claimed that he had lost his green card. In fact, Felasco told them, his cousin had passed the card to him. Further intense questioning led them to believe that the man knew nothing of any terrorist plot. They handcuffed him and kept him in custody until Immigration agents arrived.

Bronson would have liked to require every member of the culinary staff to eat each item on the luncheon menu before the item was served. However much functional appeal this idea had for him, he knew he had no legal grounds to force such a test. He, Doug Tashimoto, and Tad had just entered the huge kitchen when an agent came trotting up to them.

"Sir, about half an hour ago, we got a call from Portland PD. It seems one of their vice-squad detec-tives was showing the Hishadi photo around and it was recognized by a motel manager."

"She used her real name?" asked Bronson.

"No. She didn't give a name at all. They have a

name for the guy with her that may or may not be his real name. Likewise a license number."

"Did you check it with Oregon DMV?"

"Yes, sir! The plate number belongs to a guy named Pershing in La Grande. When we called there, he told us he'd lost a hand in an industrial accident. We confirmed that with the State Industrial Accident Fund. Surely the motel guy would've noticed if the man had only one hand! We got different plates for the name Norm Adams, but that guy lives in Roseburg and he's seventy-five years old. So I'm thinking, okay the John used a phony name and made up a license plate number. But you know, sir, I've seen several cases in the past where the perps weren't too creative and simply moved the letters or the numbers of their real plates around, especially the letters."

"So you started manipulating them?"

"Exactly. There are six possible permutations on the letters. That leaves five besides Mr. Pershing's. We hit two in Portland and one of them is a high-school kid. The other was a Mitch Zacharia. Now he looks kind of interesting. He lives in a suburb of Portland, Wilsonville, and owns a business called Deluxe Banquets. He's forty years old. The business angle could be meaningful since the motel manager heard him bragging to the girl something about feeding lots of people."

Tad interrupted. "When your folks were vetting the kitchen staff and the serving staff, did they find out who was running the show?"

"Doug, you had someone on that. Please find out."

Tashimoto left and returned a minute later. "Bingo! Deluxe Banquets!"

Bronson said, "Get Rachel and Mike Li in here pronto! Let's talk to Mr. Zachariah."

Tashimoto held up his hand in a halt gesture. "I already asked for him. They said he never came in today. That's not unheard of, but they said he is usually on the site for large contracts like this one."

"We've got to find him and fast!" said Bronson. "Be diplomatic. At this point, he is only a person of great interest, but consider him potentially dangerous. We don't have any time to spare, so get the local police to help."

He turned to Tad, "This could mean that the delivery vector is through food instead of an aerosol of some kind. I may yet cancel that lunch!"

The tempo in the kitchen had increased to a near-frenzy by twelve-fifteen and an appetizing aroma of barbequed brisket permeated the room. Bronson ordered the bio-threat techs to start testing every item in every pot and pan before it left the kitchen. Additional agents had been assigned to be observers at the various stations in the kitchen. Bronson returned to the command post and Tad and Mike were left to walk down one of the main corridors. Mike asked Tad a question about Davi's captivity and Tad did not respond.

"Tad, I just asked you about Davi."

"Oh, sorry," said Tad looking back over his shoulder. "That waiter who just passed us. She looked sort of familiar, but I can't place where I've seen her."

"Well, we're all pretty wired. Maybe you're just imagining it."

Tad grabbed Mike's arm and turned them around. "Yeah, you may be right, but I want to see where she's going and maybe get a better look at her."

Zulanni was fifty feet ahead of them and financial advisors were starting to congregate in the corridor. Mike and Tad closed the gap and were almost even with her when a tall man waving at a woman on the other side of the hallway crossed directly in front of them. As she came back into their view, Tad saw her nod to a waiter standing near a coffee-and-Danish table and keep walking. Tad's eyes momentarily left Zulanni and fell upon the waiter. It had been dark the night Tad had knocked out his would-be assailant and trussed him up with duct tape, but he had no trouble recognizing Bajehr. The man had dyed his hair and cut off his mustache, yet Tad was almost certain it was he. In the same instant, he realized why he thought the woman looked familiar. It was the woman who had bought the stun gun and whose driver's license photo the FBI had circulated. She too had dyed her hair.

Without breaking stride, Tad whispered in Mike's ear, "She's one of the terrorists! Follow her and see what she does or to whom she speaks. If you possibly can, get the attention of one of the agents and let them handle it from there."

"Oh, my God! Okay. What are you going to do?"

"The man she nodded to back there is also one of them. He's the sonafabitch I got in the duck blind! I'm going back after him."

Tad had fifty pounds on Bajehr. Thinking of his shoulder wound, Tad hesitated for an instant but then decided to close in on him anyway. When Tad turned around, he saw Bajehr watching him. The man had been unconscious when Tad had bound his hands and ankles, but now he was unquestionably focusing on Tad. It was as if his psychic radar had picked up on Tad's intentions. To make his return seem as nonchalant as possible, Tad made a show of looking at his watch and checking the program as he walked toward the coffee-break table. Bajehr looked away and walked purposefully toward the kitchen. Tad started to run and had almost overtaken Bajehr when an attendee burst out in raucous laughter at a companion's joke. Bajehr looked over his shoulder at the source of the noise and, seeing Tad running toward him, broke into a sprint.

As much as anything to draw attention in hopes the agents would notice, Tad yelled loudly, "Stop him. He's a terrorist!"

There was some yelling and alarmed looks on faces, but people either got out of the way or dove to the floor. Tad had lost a precious few seconds and Bajehr turned into a doorway.

Too late, Bajehr realized he had chosen the wrong door. He intended to enter the service stairway to the floor below and the basement exit, but now he saw that he had but one choice: to climb stairs. He could not retreat with Madison close behind. He topped the flight of stairs and thrust open another door. Bajerh found himself in a small room with a large opening overlooking the Portland Room. Various spotlights and a control panel for a loud-speaker system and a motorized Power Point screen were before him. He had only a second to decide to jump twelve feet to the floor below where dozens of people were still in the room questioning the presenter. As he burst into the room, Bajehr had noticed iron rungs imbedded in the back wall leading to a square, hinged hatch in the ceiling. He heard Tad thundering up the stairs and he chose to go upward. He frantically climbed the ladder and pushed up the hatch.

Bajehr entered a vast attic. He saw a heavy roll of tar paper next to the hatch. He closed the hatch and shoved the roll over it as he heard Tad enter the control room and yell to the people in the large room below, "Call the police!"

Bajehr discovered the attic extended over all the vast rooms below. The gritty attic floor was crossed in places with plenums and ducting. In the dim light from a few overhead bulbs, he saw stiles crossing these barriers. There was a door at the far end and he raced toward it.

Tad did not wait to see if anyone in the room below responded to his shout. When he pressed on the ceiling hatch, it hardly moved. He's blocked it with something, Tad thought. Bracing himself on the rungs as best he could, he gave a mighty push. He felt pain from his wound as he clenched the ladder rung with his left hand. The hatch raised about four inches and Tad could see the tarpaper roll. Trying to support the hatch with his head and shoulders, he used his right hand to shove the roll aside. It finally slid off the hatch with a dust-scattering thump and he swung the hatch upward.

He climbed into the attic in time to watch Bajehr disappear behind a door at the far end.

Mike followed sixty feet behind Zulanni as she entered the ballroom and walked toward one of the buffet tables. As yet, no diners had approached the food. At the table, she repositioned a few serving bowls and seemed to inspect the salads. It occurred to Mike that she was taking too long to merely arrange things. Her right hand was obscured behind her body, but Mike thought her arm was extended over the buffet table. Then it hit him that she could be introducing some pathogen at that very moment! He broke into a run. Zulanni sensed the motion and looked over her shoulder. She saw an Asian man running directly at her with an angry, determined look on his face. Mike was almost upon her when she reached for a pitcher of salad dressing. She sloshed its contents into his face and dodged to her left. Surprised and momentarily blinded, Mike crashed into the table scattering croutons and pickled beets onto the carpet. He ended up with his leg tangled in the metal table legs as the table overturned. The pain in his ankle was immediate and so intense it almost made him black out. He tried to gather himself and, with a lurching limp, galloped after her. Mike was losing ground when he saw Zulanni turn a corner and disappear from view at least a hundred feet ahead. Zulanni had memorized her escape route via a service passage that reconnected to a different wide hallway. She stripped off her white jacket as she ran. She took a pair of tinted glasses from its pocket, tossed the jacket behind a sofa in the hallway and kept running. Entering a fire stairway, she took the stairs two at a time and, at the floor below, diverted to a restroom where she entered a stall and took off her black pants. Under them, with its skirt bunched around her waist, she wore a dress. She smoothed the dress, did her hair in a chignon, stuffed the pants behind a fire extinguisher, and re-entered the hallway.

Zulanni walked casually to an elevator and rode it the ground floor. Almost all of the FBI agents were still in the kitchen or the ballroom. The tactical coordinator was only then assigning some agents to station themselves by the doors to the street and the exit from the parking garage. Zulanni emerged from the elevator in the main lobby, walked outside and hailed a cab from the taxi queue at the curb.

~~~

Mike could not determine where Zulanni had gone. He sat on a chair in the hallway to have a few seconds off his feet. Then he saw an FBI agent he recognized from the morning meeting and told him about Zulanni's fleeing. The agent spoke into his lapel mike reporting her seeming escape. Still catching his breath from the exertion, Mike pushed on the agent's shoulder before he terminated the communication.

"It's not the cooks. It's the waiters! I think she just put something on the salads! Tell your people to prevent anyone from getting to the food or eating it!"

The agent relayed that information and then looked up at Mike. "You're Dr. Li?"

"Yes, I am."

"What if someone's already eaten their salad? There're always a few eager beavers that want to beat the line."

"You'll have to quarantine those people and get them immediately to the hospital! And have Rachel and your techs analyze all of the food on the tables, but especially the salads. I know she was at the table in the far-left corner. I don't know about the other tables, but they all should be closed off before people eat anything! Listen," Mike continued. "Tad Madison saw another one: the man who had thrown the hand-grenade at him out on Sauvie Island. He chased the guy and they disappeared into a doorway back toward the kitchen. Get him some help!"

"Right. Which side of the corridor was the door on?"

"On your left going back. Maybe seventy-five or eighty feet beyond the first coffee-break station going back from here."

The agent spoke into his lapel mike, "Madison is chasing a male terrorist and needs assistance." He described the doorway Mike had identified, then listened for a few seconds and turned to Mike.

"I'm Agent Vought, Dr. Li. Our coordinator says that there was some yelling from a balcony or control room or something in the west wall of the Portland Room and it appeared that a man was being chased or followed up a ladder to a higher level."

At that moment another agent approached them. Vought said, "Come with me! Dr. Li here says Madison chased someone through a doorway up ahead. We have to catch up with them!"

With a wave of thanks to Mike, they raced down the corridor.

In the hallway past the break station, the two agents reached to a door on the left. Vought tried the door, but found it locked. They ran another twenty feet and found the door with stairs on the other side. Pausing, Vought looked up the stairs. "This could be it, if Madison was the guy who yelled down into the ballroom. Let's try it."

They raced up the stairs and Vought recognized the room to be the control room described by the coordinator. Vought saw the opening in the ceiling and started to climb the ladder. Those in the Portland Room were now in a state of confusion. They watched in astonishment as two more figures dashed through the small elevated room and up the ladder. Vought went first with his gun drawn, cautiously peered over the sill of the hinged hatch, then gestured "all clear" for the other agent to follow. They saw two other agents emerging from behind a steel door on the east side half-way down the length of the attic space.

———

Tad scrambled over the first of the stiles and sprinted to the next one. His eyes had adjusted to the dim light and, having seen the man he was pursuing go through the far door, he was not worried about being ambushed in the attic. He cleared the second stile and saw only one more between his position and the door at the end. He slowed some as he got over the third stile. He doubted Bajehr could have brought a weapon into the building given the metal detectors. Nevertheless, he did not plan on rushing blindly through the door, not knowing who or what was on the other side. As he paused just short of the door, he heard over his earphone a report that the woman had eluded them. Tad's focus was certainly not on listening, but he also heard a report of two agents climbing a ladder on the wall above the Portland Room. Reinforcements would be welcome, he thought.

Tad eased the battleship-grey door open and looked around. He was at the end of a short hallway that led to a set of upward-climbing stairs. He heard running footsteps clattering on the metal treads of the stairs. He ran to the base of the stairs and looked up. They were inside one of the dramatic, glass-sheathed "horns" on the Center's roof. It was almost dizzying to look up the sweeping curve of the horn as it tapered in stages to its pointed tip fifty feet above. He saw Bajehr on the stairs some two flights above his head and started to climb.

Bajehr now understood that his first mistake of not finding the stairs to the utility entrance in the basement had been compounded by running for the door at the far end of the attic. He had hoped that he would make it through that door before Tad saw him. He had also expected the door to lead to a way down instead of a dead-end upward. All hope now gone, he could see Madison below him starting up the stairs. At the last landing, there was a vertical ladder leading to the highest of the light fixtures. On the landing there was also a small door opening onto an exterior, narrow walkway that skirted the tower. The door was unlocked and Bajehr moved outside. Madison had nearly reached the landing below him and he thought he could see two other men at the foot of the stairway. Bajehr slammed the door shut behind him and hurried on the walkway around the horn to its inward side where the descending flare of the structure offered him a fatal grace.

He wished that the American capitalists had had

their fill of salad by now as he climbed over the rail and plummeted downward. He caromed off the tower walls twice and a final thought flashed through his brain: "just like a roller-coaster". Then nothingness.

Tad opened the door in time to see Bajehr go over. He turned back toward the on-rushing agents. "He went off the ledge! He jumped!"

One agent stayed on the landing to preserve the scene and radioed what had happened. The other agent and Tad ran back down the stairs. The agent told Tad that she had entered the attic through a door along the east wall, but not as far south as the end wall and the door that led to the tower. They re-entered the attic, where they met Vought and his partner, and all ran toward the east door. By then, several other agents and a maintenance man had entered the attic. They all went through that door and down a flight of stairs leading to another, locked, door. The maintenance man produced a key ring and unlocked the door. They passed into a room filled with elevator machinery. Beyond the machinery was a third door that gave access to a lower level of the roof. They streamed through the door and ran to the South tower.

The man in the lead pointed to his right and yelled, "There he is!" They found Bajehr lying on his stomach, a pool of blood surrounding his head. He was quite dead.

Pilof Cirovich was within forty feet of a buffet table when he heard the coordinator's message. He drew his gun and ran toward the table. Najev had finished emptying his dispenser bottle over the four lettuce bowls when he looked up to see a large man with unruly black hair and a drawn Glock rushing toward him. He turned to run and tripped on his own feet. As he went down, he calculated his odds of escaping were nil. He had no desire to be shot, but he would never cooperate with the Americans. He reached into his jacket pocket. As Cirovich stopped and leaned over him, the gun pointed straight at his chest, Najev swallowed the pill.

⁓

As the crew was setting up for the luncheon, another waiter had spilled barbecue sauce requiring the tablecloth to be replaced. Silently, Rudi cursed his luck when one of the master waiters told him at fourteen minutes after twelve to fetch a clean tablecloth from the storeroom on the floor below. Rudi remembered Najev's briefing: if he faced a conflict in assignments, he was to appear to obey, then resume his mission as quickly as possible. Stealing a glance at his wristwatch, Rudi realized he could not do as the master waiter told him and still get to his assigned buffet table before the diners formed a line.

He hurried to the stairway as if going to the storeroom. He went down to the next level, then turned and ascended the same stairs. He had been assigned to the corner furthest from the doors. He thought that if he hurried as fast as possible without attracting undue attention, he could reach his buffet table before the crowd arrived. As he walked swiftly toward the table, he saw the salads clustered at its near end. The only problem was that there were two men standing with their backs to the table. One was resting one hand on the table and the other had his arms crossed over his chest in a very relaxed posture. They were casually, perhaps too casually he wondered, looking over the persons approaching the table as if searching for a fellow early-bird. He would have to tell them he needed to give the table a final once-over before it would be ready for people to start serving themselves.

"I'm sorry," he said, gently waving them away with his hand, "we're not quite ready to ..."

They were surprisingly fast. Their lethargic looks belied their cobra-like reflexes. They had him pinned to the floor almost before he realized they had made him.

As an agent led Rudi away in handcuffs, he told him that he was losing control of his bowels and begged to use the toilet. The agent escorting him relented and they entered a men's room near the top of the escalator to the lobby. Even with the agent outside the stall and with the handcuffs limiting his dexterity, Rudi managed to unclasp the watch on his wrist and attempted to flush it away. The agent had demanded that Rudi leave the door open, but tried not to stare at him. Even so, the agent saw a flash of gold disappear from Rudi's hand and ordered him out of the stall. As Rudi straightened up and clumsily started to pull up his pants, he leaned backward and depressed the flush handle with his hip. The agent checked to verify that Rudi's watch was missing, then radioed for assistance. They summoned a plumber, believing that the watch might have come to rest in the toilet's trap.

Bronson's men closed off the restroom with yellow "crime scene" tape and half an hour later the plumber was unbolting the toilet from the floor. "I could probably get whatever it is without doing this, but I don't want take a chance of losing it down the pipe," he said as he hefted the stool out of the stall and onto some canvas he had spread on the floor.

"No problem," said Cirovich who had taken charge in the restroom while the other agent took their prisoner away.

The plumber eased a flexible tool with a plunger-operated grabber on its end into the trap. "I feel something." A pause. "Yeah, I got it. If I can keep hold of it, should have it out in couple of seconds."

With a certain amount of triumph, he removed the tool grasping a gold watch. "I'll be damned! That's a nice watch!"

"Yes it is." answered Cirovich not wanting to get into specifics. He donned surgical gloves and said, "Please don't touch it. I'll take it off your device."

Before putting it into a transparent evidence pouch, he studied the watch. On the back he saw an inscription reading "To Paul, with love, Meg."

Bronson's agents collected all the food in an unused room next to the kitchen. Rachel and the technicians started work on the salads. They wore yellow biohazard suits as they took several samples from every serving bowl and ran each one through their analyzers. Bronson no longer needed to clear a shutdown decision with Homeland Security. The events of the last few minutes had changed any threat assessment from "potential" to "direct" and "actual". The task force's communications coordinator had already acted on Mike Li's vehement advice that no one be allowed to leave until they knew who might have already eaten some of the food. Bronson reiterated the seriousness of temporarily sequestering the attendees and ordered the luncheon canceled. A manager from Deluxe Banquets joined the conference organizer in a half-hearted objection, but neither had any enthusiasm for extending the risk when told of "an attempt to poison" people at the conference.

Tad called Davi in the hospital. Her voice sounded strong and he marveled at her physical resiliency. "Really, I'm okay, Tad. Four stitches for my scalp wound from the car crash, some IV fluids, and some ointment for where the rope chafed my wrists. They want me to stay overnight just for observation because they think I suffered a mild concussion, but they say I can almost surely go home in the morning."

Tad told her they had thwarted the plot to spread contagion by spraying a weaponized lethal virus on the luncheon salads. He also reminded her to only discuss with others those facts that had been released through television and newspapers. He ended the call saying, "I'll be over to see you in about an hour. I'll have to come back for more debriefing after that. The FBI always documents everything to the last detail. Then I'm going to use Mike Li's guest bedroom and sleep for eighteen hours. I'll be your chauffeur in the morning. I'll call around nine to make sure you're cleared to leave. I love you, Davi!"

"Darling, I'll be waiting for you. See you soon!"

# TWENTY

**M**OUD HAD FILLED THEIR BOTTLES JUST BEFORE THEY left the house in Sellwood. It was never part of the plan that he be present at the Convention Center due to his accent and the fact that he had lost some of his English fluency. He was in charge of disassembling the equipment at the Sellwood house. They would have disposed of the equipment and returned to their jobs if their roles in the operation had gone undetected. Bajehr would then drive him to a safe house in Los Angeles. From there, Najev had told him, a trusted contact would take Krati and him across the Mexican border. From there, they would make their way back to Malaysia.

If things went amiss, Najev's team was to return to the Sellwood house and remain there until it was safe to leave the state by separate routes, each with new identity papers. Given the meddling of the man called Madison, the mysterious smudge-pot fire at the warehouse, and Najev's determination to move their base of operations, Moud figured that Najev's home and the warehouse might be searched. He calculated the chances of success in the mission were high, but he thought the odds for the rest of them returning to their pre-attack lives were not at all good.

Moud had most of the equipment decontaminated and ready for disposal by eleven o'clock. No one had returned to the house or called him by early afternoon, and he began to worry that their plan had been derailed. He went to the small television in the kitchen and turned on the one o'clock news. There was a breaking story about a possible terrorist incident at the Convention Center.

Moud turned up the volume and heard the woman newscaster say, "I was here at the Portland Convention Center setting up with our camera crew to tape a short segment for the evening news on the keynote speech at the annual Tradewell Investing financial advisors conference when this horrific series of events began. The hallways were suddenly bristling with FBI agents and city police. We are told a man was chased up a ladder into the attic above one of the largest conference rooms. Two other men were wrestled to the floor and arrested right in this banquet room. There is an unconfirmed rumor that a fourth person, believed to be a woman, cannot be accounted for. It is believed that, in all, four terrorists were involved in a plot to somehow infect the investment advisors attending this national conference with a deadly virus. Apparently, two of the terrorists are now dead." She glanced down to consult her notes and continued, "The exact nature of the toxin or how it was to be introduced has not yet been disclosed by the Department of Homeland Security. We do know that there are many FBI technicians in the kitchen and in this room where the conference luncheon was about to be served. We also know that no one has been allowed to leave the Center. We will be updating this breaking story throughout the afternoon as more details become available, so stay with us at channel eight. For now, this is Sheila Davidson for Midday News."

A camera panned the Convention Center lobby, as the anchor woman segued to the next news story. The agents directed hundreds of nervous attendees to assemble in the lobby. They stood under a giant Foucault's pendulum swinging from a cable suspended high in the lobby dome as it slowly traced a complete circle from the end-points of its swings.

Moud collapsed into one of the cheap dinette chairs, his hands clutching his head. He wept the bitter tears of defeat. What would he do now? Why had Najev not given him a better back-up plan? He had false identity papers and he was thankful that he had kept out of sight so no one had seen his face. Moud concluded that he would have to steal some license plates and drive Bajehr's car south to Los Angeles. He had the name of only one person there, a name that Ali had given him as a last resort. The slender microbiologist knew it would be safest for him to leave after dark. Najev had hidden a considerable amount of cash somewhere in the house but had not told Moud its location. It was imperative to find that stash as he had very little American money of his own. He left the television going and started his search.

Najev had provided Zulanni with documents supporting a new identity. She had deposited them in a private box at a location in northeast Portland that also had storage units. She directed the cab to an intersection a block from the storage-unit complex and walked the rest of the way. Once there, she retrieved a new Oregon driver's license, a new social security card, bottles of titian hair dye, and her own savings of nearly $3000.

Zulanni took another cab to the Portland airport. She checked the departures board in the lobby and found a flight to St. Louis leaving in twenty-five minutes. She jogged toward the check-in counter. Slowing her pace and wiping perspiration from her forehead, she approached a ticket agent. She purchased one of the few seats still available. The airline agent noticed a late-arriving passenger with a wailing young child approaching the counter and hardly glanced at Zulanni – now Norma Henderson – as she processed her ticket and gave her a boarding pass. Nor did the agent seem concerned that Zulanni had paid cash and had no luggage to check.

Her plane was third in the take-off queue and was airborne an hour and forty minutes after she fled from the Convention Center. Once in St. Louis, she would take a bus to Kansas City and, there, get a flight to New York City. Morrissey had contacted airport security to hold anyone using the name Hashadi or meeting Zulanni's description. But word of this alert did not reach the ticketing counter for the St. Louis flight until ten minutes after the plane took off. The weary ticketing agent, who had started her shift at 5:00 AM, did not relate the alert to the glasses-wearing Norma Henderson.

Bronson's men and a specialist on loan from the CIA broke Rudi a little before five o'clock. He revealed that there were only six of them with Najev as their leader, that Taj had gone missing several days earlier, and that Moud had stayed behind at the safe house. He attempted to describe the house in Sellwood, although he could not remember the address and could only give the nearest cross streets. They turned him over to federal marshals for transport to the brig at Joint Base Lewis-McChord near Tacoma, Washington, where his interrogation would continue.

———

Bronson's team cordoned off four entire blocks in the Sellwood district and started, as unobtrusively as possible, working door-to-door. They ordered obviously uninvolved persons to leave for a few hours and to respect the blockade by not re-entering until it was lifted. They questioned everyone about new neighbors, asking especially if any appeared to be of Asian or Near Eastern extraction. Agents back at headquarters were canvassing all Portland realtors regarding recent purchases or rentals within the sealed-off area. By six o'clock, they had learned of two recent rentals and one sale. They made these three addresses their priority targets.

Moud was upstairs and only minutes before had found the money in a pouch taped to the back of one of the built-in drawers in a bedroom. He placed the currency in his money belt. He packed his suitcase and determined that it had become dark enough for him to steal a license plate when he heard the doorbell. Moud had no intention of answering. He opened a dormer window and considered, if he had to, how his chances would be of climbing out on the roof and dropping to the back yard. Below, he heard a loud pounding on the door and a demand to "open up." He eased himself out the window and felt the moss-covered shingles slick under foot. He was starting a controlled slide on his haunches toward the roof edge, when he saw two agents entering the back yard. They were checking behind the shrubbery and peering into the first-floor windows as he reversed his direction and quietly scrambled to the top of the dormer gable. He straddled the gable and lay prone, praying that he could not be seen from below.

Bronson had obtained search warrants from a helpful judge for all three addresses. The front door resisted the agents' speedkeys and Bronson gave the order to break it down. The door burst open with a splintering of wood and the agents crowded inside with weapons drawn. They discovered the incubator and the disconnected $CO_2$ tanks upstairs and knew they were in the right house.

Bronson noticed the open window. "Check the yard," he yelled. The leader of the team outside shouted back, "Unless he's already off the property, he's not in the yard."

"I want everyone on the larger perimeter to be especially alert. He doesn't seem to be in the house, but he may be close by," Bronson shouted into his radio. Then he added, "The team in the yard, do a visual check of the roof."

Less than a minute later, Bronson heard, "We can

see a shoe along the gable line on the south side of the roof."

Moud considered jumping but calculated that this would possibly break his legs and would not lead to his escape. The men in the yard were now yelling and pointing to the roof. it was obvious that he had been discovered. He reached into his pants pocket for the strychnine pill but could not find it. He remembered, with horror, that he had put on a clean pair of pants in the morning and had forgotten to switch the pill.

The FBI agents scrambled onto the roof within minutes. One agent nearly slipped off but gained some traction at the last minute. Moud was told to sit up and place his hands behind him. Someone produced a rope and, as soon as he was handcuffed, they tied the rope around his waist and eased him back down to the open window.

Bronson smiled as the agents shoved Moud through the window opening. Moud stood in front of Bronson with his head bowed and his eyes on the floor. Looking past Moud and out the window to the street intersection, Bronson saw the first of the television trucks brake to a halt just outside the barrier. His smile faded.

Homeland Security gave the media a much-truncated version of what had happened at the Convention Center due to lingering uncertainty as to how many were involved and whether related attacks might be attempted. Hundreds had seen federal agents racing down hallways in pursuit of people in food-serving uniforms and were aware of the temporary quarantine and the cancellation of the luncheon, so there was no way the events of the morning could be ignored. The stories that came out told of a small group of fanatics who had attempted to poison the food.

The FBI discovered an unclaimed car, rented under a false name, in a parking garage close to the Convention Center. The forensics team found fingerprints on the steering wheel and matched them to Najev's prints.

Inside the garage at the Sellwood house, the same team found Zulanni's car with damage on the right-side door and a paint transfer that, later, proved to match the paint on Davi's car. They also discovered a stun gun in the trunk of the car that matched the serial number of the gun sold to Zulanni. Forensics lifted a partial print from the taser that showed a high correlation to the fingerprints taken from the body of Taj. They also lifted a fingerprint from the flush handle of a toilet at the Forest Grove house that would eventually be matched to Zulanni's prints taken when she applied for U.S. citizenship.

Meg Castner identified the watch that Rudi tried to flush down the toilet as belonging to her late husband. Two days later, a forensic team scouring the furniture warehouse found a fragment of a credit card unburned among the ashes in the incinerator. The letters "…l Castner" could still be seen. A partial print on the card correlated with Rudi's fingerprint.

Federal agents located Mitch Zachariah at his beach cabin in Seaside, Oregon on the evening of the same day they had foiled the plot. They questioned Zachariah for hours and ran a thorough background investigation on him. In the end, they were satisfied that he was not privy to Najev's plan other than the adding of four persons to his serving staff for purposes not specifically known to him. He was arrested and subsequently pled guilty to a count of conspiracy. A federal judge eventually sentenced him to one year in prison.

Rachel's analysis of the salads and liquid in the Salad Fresh dispensers showed conclusively the presence of a strain of the monkey B virus. She briefed Bronson on her findings. "Amazingly, this virus isn't harmful to its natural hosts, macaque monkeys, but it is very stable in cultures and extremely lethal to humans," she said. "A dying person suffers the agonies of high fever and an encephalitic swelling of the brain. We know an antibiotic used against herpes simplex can be effective, but only if we can diagnose the disease in time. A good, timely diagnosis is really difficult because the symptoms presented and the results of routine tests will indicate many other far-less-threatening diseases. Those results mask the true pathology."

"Sounds like really evil stuff," said Bronson. "How long before the effects are felt?"

"Monkey B has a five-to-seven-day incubation period in the host and, of course, that makes it easy to transmit before any symptoms appear. It can spread from infected persons through sneezing, coughing, kissing, unclean hands, and unhygienic food-handling. You see, it is readily ingested through mucus membranes in the body such as in the mouth and nose."

Other agents conducted careful questioning of the attendees and serving staff. They found that nine persons had eaten salad before the buffet tables were closed down. Homeland Security immediately hospitalized all nine in a secure ward at Madigan Army Hospital at Joint Base Lewis-McChord. Hospital doctors put each person on a course of medication using acyclovire. One of those persons died of the virus eleven days after his ill-fated attendance at the conference. A woman, a thirty-two-year-old stock analyst successfully fought a prolonged battle for her life. A third person, a a forty-year old advisor, had only mild symptoms. After four weeks of observation and medication, he walked out of the hospital to return home and resume his normal healthy life. Those three tragically entered the ballroom and served themselves the tainted salad after Najev was taken away, but in the ninety-second period before the FBI secured the table. The other six persons served themselves at tables other than the ones covered by Najev and Zulanni. Most were released from the hospital quarantine after a week of further tests. Despite the tragic deaths, trading on the stock markets did not miss a beat.

The Third Mate, Krati, panicked trying to cross the border into Mexico. He had never been able to find the safe house in Los Angeles and had chosen to run for the border on his own. He had managed to buy a very old Toyota Corolla in San Pedro, California. At the border, officials asked him to fill out a form and present evidence of insurance for the car. He had none and when they denied him entrance, he broke from the car and ran. Mexican officials immediately apprehended him and turned him over to the U.S. Border Patrol. The Patrol captain contacted the FBI because he had seen the all-points bulletin warning that a Malay male could attempt to leave the country. Moud had never seen Krati though he had heard the men in the storage room of the *pasar* in Penang describe him. Thus, the bulletin was imprecise in identifying the man sought and the Border Patrol officers were uncertain if they were holding a key fugitive. The FBI arrived and felt confident they had the right person. Krati subsequently admitted enough details to support his being taken into FBI custody.

Tad drove Davi back to Wilcao two days after the raid on the Sellwood house. They arrived at her house in mid-afternoon. It was eight o'clock before they got around to dinner. Davi postponed her Monday, Tuesday and Wednesday classes, but she was back in her classroom on Thursday. Tad returned to The Breakers on Thursday, but said he had just needed time away after the arsonist had destroyed his home. The friendly faces of his customers had never looked so good. Each day he brought two dozen doughnuts and brewed pots of coffee to offer to his morning trade.

# TWENTY-ONE

**B**RONSON HAD FELT THE EFFECTS OF HAVING NO SLEEP two nights earlier. Last night, he put their best interrogation team on Moud at nine in the evening and then had gone home for a quick supper and a soft pillow. An interrogation team had arrived at Ft. Lewis and would resume the questioning of Rudi by mid-day. Forensics technicians continued their meticulous inspection of Najev's home and the Sellwood house. They were still in the field when he arrived at his office Tuesday morning. Bronson was elated by their success in averting the deadly contagion and in rescuing Davi, but he knew they must quickly move into the next phase. They had caught all but one of the operatives, the foot soldiers, but now they had to roll up the entire network and capture the facilitators who conceived the attempt and supported it. He already credited his Portland adversaries with a ruthless determination to further their cause. This ruthlessness might well pervade the terrorists' entire organization, but the cunning planning behind the operation convinced him that they were now looking for more sophisticated persons. Bronson had read the transcript of Rudi's interrogation and was especially unnerved by one sentence: Rudi said he had heard

Najev say, in passing, that their battle was here, but there would soon be "an event" on the East Coast as well. He had highlighted that item in his report to FBI Headquarters.

It was unlikely that Zulanni, detached from her Portland cell and its apparatus to culture the virus, could inflict large-scale harm, but she was nevertheless a very dangerous and determined fugitive. He had field agents combing the metro region for leads but, so far, they had turned up nothing of interest.

Bronson reasoned, between whatever communication scheme the terrorists employed and the news stories, however abridged, that the brains behind this attempt must surely be aware of the scheme's failure. The planners would review their actions to be sure there was no incriminating evidence that had to be destroyed, no linkages to be severed, and no as-yet-undiscovered conspirators to be extracted or eliminated. This meant that Bronson's people had to work fast. They had to scrutinize and probe everything the terrorists had done. They had to study whatever tangible evidence they could find at the warehouse and the homes of Najev and his fellow conspirators. They could take nothing for granted and should realize that not everything would be as it first appeared.

Bronson guessed that the killing of Paul Castner was a panicky over-reaction, suggesting the men and women on the ground in Portland were not highly-trained professionals. He presumed that whoever controlled those people would be insulated by layers of fronts and intermediaries. And, he reminded himself, as of today, they had no idea where control resided. Was it in the United States or Canada? In

Asia where the virus was originally cultured? Or perhaps even in the Near East?

FBI teams would also analyze communications and try to trace money transfers. Additional agents from the San Francisco office had arrived overnight and by ten o'clock he had teams starting those assignments. He set a meeting with representatives from the CIA and Homeland Security for one o'clock, but first he drove to the FBI's safe house where a team was interrogating Moud.

A trailing car made sure he was not followed and, after twenty-five minutes, one of the team met him at the gate on the private entrance road. "Any progress, Matt?"

"Yes and no, Russ. The man is scared and we think he'll be talking soon. He's alternating between almost hysterical denial and grasping for feelers as to how he can save his skin. He's given us a few crumbs already, but nothing of critical importance."

"Not too surprising at this stage of the game, I suppose. Is he intelligent?"

"Oh, yeah. He's smart all right. As Rudi said, he's some kind of science person … the guy who took care of the virus culture, knew how to grow it and sustain it. We also think he's been to the States at some time in the past. He has a pretty strong accent, but he has a little understanding of slang and idiom that he couldn't have picked up in just a few days."

Bronson considered Matt Jennings' information. "Set me up as a tyrant that would just as soon waste him as draw out the questioning, then let me have him alone for a while."

"We can do that. Give us ten more minutes and you're on."

Bronson entered the windowless den converted to an interrogation room and the two men who had been questioning Moud left. He could restart the hidden recorders with a remote out of sight in his pocket. "So you're the piece of shit they couldn't even afford to have at the Convention Center. What a pathetic band of amateurs! No wonder one of them turned you in. That'll probably save his life. The others, well, they'll be in prison until their trial, but you see ... it's kind of a special prison."

"Special?"

"The other prisoners there are exceptionally violent but, strangely enough, they all believe in America and, in their own way, they are quite patriotic. The guards find them almost impossible to control outside their cells. If your friends should live to stand trial, they'll .... they'll likely be very different ... maybe not so manly."

Moud could not stop himself from perspiring. Was this FBI man crazy? "But your court system... they'll know I was just living in that house.... no matter what the others may say, I didn't know what they were doing!"

"Listen to me, you turd! You can drop that innocent crap! The courts work slowly. You'll be in my special prison for years! We know you came in that capsule you call the nest. We know you grew the virus. We found you hiding on the roof! You tell us now whom you worked with in Malaysia and I'll keep you out of that prison. That's the way this works.

Now you have thirty seconds to decide what the rest of your life will be like."

Bronson's hand in his pocket activated the recorders. Moud wiped his brow. He started to stand up and then sat down again. He stared at Bronson's implacable countenance. "You're a black man. You know the capitalists exploit your people. You..."

"Time's up, asshole! What will it be?"

Moud visibly trembled and lowered his eyes. "We called him Ali," he said quietly. "I think that was his real name. We never used last names."

"What was his job?"

"A pharmacist."

"Where was his store?"

"I don't know. I never contacted him there."

"Where did you meet?"

"In a pasar in Penang."

"Who owned it?"

"I never knew."

"Where was it?"

"I can't remem..."

Bronson's fist hit the table so hard, Moud nearly leaped off the chair. "Don't start that 'I've forgotten' crap! You went to that place many times! We'll get a map. You will show us!"

"Yes. OK! I will try."

"Oh, yes! You *will* try and you *will* tell us what we want to know. I'm going to turn you back to my associates and you will tell them everything about yourself and your friends in Portland and Penang." Bronson turned off the recorder and then continued. "Remember that where we hold you awaiting trial depends entirely on whether you cooperate with us."

Moud spread his hands on the table top and nodded, then lowered his head to the table as his inquisitor left the room. Russ Bronson's first stop was in the bathroom down the hall. He rushed to the toilet and vomited his breakfast. He greatly disliked having to deal with another human being in that fashion, but he reminded himself that Moud had no compunction about trying to kill thousands of Americans. And time was of the essence. Whether he felt comfortable with it or not, his tactics had cracked the dike of silence and he believed it would totally crumble before the day was over. Bronson washed his face and hands to achieve an almost ritualistic cleansing. He dried with a paper towel and looked in the mirror. There's more to do, Russ, he thought. Much more.

The meeting at the FBI offices with the CIA and Homeland Security officials began soon after Bronson returned. There were two persons from each agency present around the conference table. Box lunches were open before them. The Deputy Director of Homeland Security, Dennis Borland, spoke first. "SAC Bronson, my boss and the Attorney General and the President all send their congratulations and commend you and your teams for the great work in stopping this fiendish attempt."

"Thank you, Sir. We had some critically important help from Mr. Madison and Dr. Li and we had some good fortune in overtaking the bad guys at the last minute. I'm very proud of our agents and technicians. They worked 'round the clock and deserve the praise. You can imagine how satisfying it is to prevent a disaster instead of having to react to one."

"Indeed. And with some of the terrorists in

captivity, we have a chance to roll up their whole network. Where do we stand on that?"

Bronson went to the whiteboard and diagramed the components of the next phase of the investigation and labeled the teams that he had deployed to work on each component. He then returned to his seat and summarized what little the interrogators had learned from Rudi and Moud.

Ginny Malstrom of the CIA asked, "Dennis, the Penang thing sounds like a decent lead. Can we help there?"

"Yes, FBI agents in California questioned the man, Krati, who tried to run across the border. He admitted to being the substitute Third Mate on the Malacca Trader, but claims he knows very little more than that. He was the physical minder for this Moud inside the container, but says he didn't even know his name. After many hours, he gave them a name of his contact back there, a Sallah M'adeen."

"I'll be in touch with our Legal Attache at the Embassy in K.L. later today," said Malstrom. "And, yes, we'll grab this M'adeen and get the identity of the pharmacist that Moud told your guys about before they both go to ground."

Bronson asked, "Do you folks have enough resources in Penang? I'm sure the FBI Lagat will want to have his agents on hand for any questioning."

"We do. My director will be contacting your director within the hour, but I already have informal authority to move on the overseas dimension of this. We will coordinate with the FBI as best we can."

Bronson inwardly wondered how timely and enthusiastic that coordination would be. Nevertheless, he personally believed that interagency sharing and cooperation were the best ways to enhance national security so this was no time to be acerbic about giving the CIA the lead. "Great, Ginny. I'll see that you get the transcripts and any written statements from our work here."

"How about our own opportunity to interrogate?" she responded.

"I want my guys to finish first, but you're welcome to have a go as soon as we're done."

The other Homeland Security official looked toward Borland, but spoke aloud to the group, "Wouldn't it be wise to get the NSA folks involved? Especially as we start back-trailing their comms?"

The junior representative from the CIA nodded and said, "I agree. It seems most likely they were controlled from abroad so that piece is bound to come into play."

Bronson sensed some rising tension, but he wanted to sustain the momentum of the meeting without getting into too many turf issues up front. "No question. My agency needs to stay on the domestic comm issues and to at least be informed of everything that develops on the international side. Ginny, I'll ask our communications expert, Patti Daisabi, to get in touch before you leave today and the two of you can make the contact with the National Security Agency."

The Deputy Secretary of Homeland Security, turned to face Bronson. "On the money trail, any ideas?"

"Well, the financial specialists in our D.C. Office will be handling that aspect with daily reports to me. It looks to me like the actual operation in Portland was fairly low-budget. The biologic equipment brought from Malaysia is a different matter. Right now, I'm thinking this furniture guy, Najev, was maybe a sleeper. That tells me we should be looking for early money, perhaps to set him up in business years in the past."

"Makes sense," said Ginny. "We'll look as best we can at financing in Asia. What about the local mosque?"

Bronson had asked Clyde Morrisey to attend the meeting with him, and Morrisey now spoke: "We started working that a couple of days before the conference, but we haven't turned up much. We think our informant is reliable and we've been very discreet so we don't believe he's under any peer pressure to clam up or feed us disinformation. So far, it looks as though some recruiting may have occurred at the mosque. This Najev was well-known there; he played chess, made donations, schmoozed. And the man who jumped off the tower, Bajehr, also attended the mosque and was an employee and friend of Najev's, but no other names or connections have come up. We think the man Madison killed in the marsh may be a tough guy named Taj who has been MIA around the mosque since that incident. Our informant has also heard a rumor that some messaging to Najev has come through the mosque. That's easy to believe but, so far, the rumor hasn't included names or times. We're going to be digging hard in that area."

The meeting ended after they worked for another half-hour on procedural details for interagency coordination. The blueprints had been shared and the dials had been calibrated. Now the cumbrous gears of the global anti-terrorism machinery would start to turn.

# TWENTY-TWO

TAD'S TIME BACK AT THE BREAKERS HAD BEEN A NECES-sary period of resting, both physical and psychic. But, as much as he liked the congeniality and intellectual ambiance of the book store, his friendship with Paul Castner meant that his brain was constantly re-engaging in the events of the past two weeks.

Russ Bronson had informed him that he would remain on a modest retainer to the FBI at least through the end of the month and perhaps longer as they progressed through the state-side aspect of the investigation. Tad was happy to accept the arrangement, but he guessed they would have little further need for him to consult. He was welcome to return to his life in Wilcao and he readily agreed to keep Bronson informed if he traveled and how to reach him. Tad was aware that the federal agencies had moved into high gear to trace the terrorist cell upward to its controllers in an effort to destroy the entire network.

Tad believed that the evidence that had turned up was going to point to Paul's immediate killer and he was glad that he had played a role in bringing the Portland terrorists to justice. He had spent many hours helping and consoling Meg Castner and had spoken at the celebration-of-life service for Paul the day after his return to Wilcao. But he also felt that his job was unfinished. There were even more sinister people still at large: the person or persons who conceived the plot and ordered its activation, perhaps even ordering the killing of his friend. On top of that, the woman who had kidnapped and held Davi, chained to a toilet, had escaped their net and was on the loose. And, there were still questions *he* wanted to pursue, details he wanted to discover, clues he thought he could spot.

Tad's thoughts for the past two days kept coming back to what links tied Najev and his men to their higher authority. His on-the-ground-with-the-agents privileges did not appear to extend to reviewing the items found in the searches or reading the forensic reports. He realized that his own exposure to the terrorist cell, though frightening and nearly fatal, had been limited to just a few – mostly action-filled – minutes. His focus narrowed to a short list of facts as he reflected on what he had actually seen. The terrorists he had encountered were all Near or Middle Eastern. At the warehouse, there had been imported furniture from Malaysia, a fiberglass module, a short-wave receiver, an ordinary office safe, a scribbled desk calendar, a white delivery truck, a hazardous materials suit, and some equipment to incubate the virus. He tried to visualize details from those mental snapshots. There was no brand name visible on the suit. In any case, the FBI would surely trace its provenance; likewise the equipment. The truck was most likely purchased locally by Najev or his people. The short-wave radio was too far across the room for him to have seen how it was tuned. The module's fabrication history would surely reveal important information, but that was for the CIA. The FBI specialists would work on the cell-phone logs, the computer drives and the contents of the safe.

That left the desk calendar. It was the first thing he noticed in Najev's office and he remembered trying to read it. What had he seen? The writing was a hurried scrawl. He concentrated. Had it been something about concrete? He tried to place himself back in that office as he fought to bring in the image more clearly. No. Not "concrete". "Cement"! Now he thought he could visualize the whole page: the day's date, printed, and the handwritten notations "Cement world" or "Cement work"? And a name, maybe "Sheridan" or "Sheraton" and "11/11-11/13". It was not much, but he had to start somewhere.

The media had not been told of Tad's involvement in stopping the spread of contagion across the country and his agreement with the FBI precluded him speaking to friends about it. His friends and neighbors did know that an arsonist had torched his house and a rumor had somehow traveled from the Sheriff's Office that Davi had been kidnapped. This was enough for everyone to cut Tad some slack if he was absent from the store for a while.

Tad sat in front of Davi's computer and called up his favorite search engine. He had already combed the Portland Yellow Pages and the state Contractors Board web site for cement finishers or contractors with the name Sheraton or Sheridan. There were none. There was one general contractor in Medford, Sheridan Builders, but it was two hundred miles from Portland and did not do its own cement work. The owner denied ever hearing of Tropical Furniture Imports. Tad was ready to cast a broader net.

Using the browser and trying "Cement World" he got seventeen hits, but most were simply adjacent words in other contexts such as "we must do all we can to cement world peace in spite of the fractious tribalism evident on every continent." He found three listings of seemingly greater potential. One turned out to be a high school rock group. Another was a trade magazine in Sydney, Australia. The third linked him to the web page of a trade show for the North Atlantic region that was held November eleventh through the thirteenth in Philadelphia. The show was over, but the web site had not yet been shut down. He clicked on accommodations and saw that the convention hotel was a Sheraton. To be sure, it was a tenuous lead, but the three elements of the calendar notation seemed to point to Philadelphia.

Tad left a message asking Bronson to call him and gave the number of his cell phone. A quarter of an hour passed before Bronson was free to return the call. "Tad, how you doin?"

"Pretty well, thanks, Russ."

"My men say things are absolutely quiet and normal with Davi. What's up?"

"I've got some news."

"Spill it," said Bronson with a little shiver of anticipation. He liked and admired Tad, but he was up to his ass in alligators with the investigation and he rather hoped that Tad was not free-lancing again.

"Tom, your troops vacuum-cleaned that office in the warehouse, right?"

"Yeah. Our forensics folks worked the scene and Tashimoto's team is examining everything tangible plus the computer memory and cache dumps."

"Did they find a desk calendar?"

"They did. But its top page was only for the last day Najev was in the office."

"Sort of what I expected. Remember I told you about my first visit there? When I first glimpsed that 'nest'?"

Bronson's mind was racing ahead. "Yeah. You saw something on that calendar?"

"Yes I did. I've been trying to recall everything I could about my run-in with these bastards, but it was only yesterday I started trying to recall small details like the calendar. When I was in his office, I was in super-snooper mode. I was trying to notice and take in *everything*. It wouldn't come at first, but I finally was able to visualize the…"

"Get to it, man! What was written there that has you interested?"

Tad chuckled. "Yeah, sorry. Well … I saw the words 'Cement Work' or 'Cement World'. I'm pretty sure the first letters were capitalized. It was sort of scribbled so the second word was not clear. And there was another word: 'Sheraton' or 'Sheridan' again with the first letter capitalized and then a range of dates: eleven slash eleven dash eleven slash thirteen."

Bronson was impressed, but was not sure how the calendar notes were relevant. "Doug is studying all the stuff we took from Tropical Imports. I'll tell him to focus a little more on that calendar."

"That's good to hear. But hear me out, please. I

started working the internet and I discovered this conference for the cement industry in Philadelphia that was held *on those exact dates*. I have a hunch there's a connection between Najev and his people here and that conference ... or at least someone who attended that conference. Russ, maybe at this stage, you couldn't consider this as part of my consulting duties, but I intend to go to Philly and snoop around. I'll do it on my own nickel."

"Yeah, I'm afraid you're right that I can't send you there but, as long as you don't represent yourself as an active agent, have a go at it. If you *do* turn up anything of interest, anything about the network or who's pulling the strings, let me know and we'll take a hard look at it and put our resources to work ... and I'll see that your expenses are reimbursed."

"Okay. That works for me. I'll stay in touch."

Tad had enough frequent-flier miles for a free round trip to the East Coast. There was a seat available on the evening red-eye. Davi had not liked the idea of any new initiative on his part even though she understood this "unfinished business" had been weighing on him. Now he really would have some explaining to do.

~

Davi neither wept nor raged. They argued all through dinner. Her position was that he was, at best, embarking on a 'wild goose chase'. On the other hand, she added, he had already risked his life. And people involved in the same conspiracy had kidnapped her as well. If his pursuing this was not a fruitless, quixotic, effort, it could, even more irrationally, place them in harm's way once again. She assured him that he had contributed mightily to the capture of Paul's killers. She reminded him that the remaining villains were being hunted by the most expert operatives of several federal agencies.

Tad did not openly dispute her points, but told her that he thought the effort was worth making. He offered a wry smile and said, "I hear you, Honey, but I'm so angry at these cowards and their preying on innocent people that I just want to do whatever I can to help choke this off right at the top! Besides, that woman who kidnapped you is still at large!"

Davi looked into his eyes and pleaded, "But, Tad, if you do discover something, you'll be in real danger again!"

"Not really. I plan to stay discreetly in the background... just follow up on a couple of things. I'll use an alias whenever I can and constantly watch my back."

"But you won't have a team of agents around you!"

"You know I have Bronson's direct phone numbers and I'll also get the number of the FBI office in Philadelphia. At the first sign that I've discovered anything connected to this network, I'll alert Bronson and let the FBI follow up."

"And you'll be so far away," Davi murmured.

Tad knew that Davi was brave and resilient, but he also knew how frightening her kidnapping had been for her. "Remember, Davi, Bronson has assigned round-the-clock bodyguards to protect you for another two weeks or longer if we feel they're needed. Besides, you're certainly no longer of any interest to these people's controller."

"Yes, I know that and I'm not really so worried about myself. It's just… you know… just this whole ugly business!"

Davi could see that Tad was set on making this one further effort. She choked up as she told him that she loved him and said she was not sure she could bear the thought of losing him and the happiness they had found together. Tad had struggled with his own feelings on that issue over and over as he had formed his intention. This was well beyond any quantitative risk assessment or probability of success. This was qualitative. This was his fury over the callous killing of his friend and the plotters' evil intention to harm thousands more Americans versus preserving and cherishing the love-filled focus of his life, his relationship with Davi.

He had wondered if he was no better than a compulsive gambler telling his fearful wife that he had to 'roll the dice just one more time' before quitting. Had he become a risk junkie? Was he morbidly fixated on vengeance for Paul and Davi? Was he being horribly unfair to Davi? As he had reflected on these questions in the preceding days, he became convinced that he was acting rationally under the extraordinary circumstances.

His wounds were healing nicely and he felt he could control his exposure to threatening situations. So long as he did not become a rogue or maverick, he could count on the FBI to do the heavy lifting if it came to that. Though he was very motivated to follow this lead, he also took some comfort in the probability that it was a meaningless dead-end with no risk to him beyond his time and money (and looking a bit foolish to those more removed from the situation).

Tad reached for Davi's hand and looked into her eyes. "I love you so much. I want to have this behind us as much as you do. I want our life to return to normal. But I need your support for this final push."

Davi gave him a small, slightly sad, smile and said, "I respect your feelings, Tad, and your determination. I just think we've been through enough."

"You must believe me that I think our relationship will be even stronger if I can see this through. And if this hunch of mine leads nowhere, I'll come right back to you and our lives together knowing I've done all that I could."

Davi took a deep breath. "All right," she said softly, "let's go from here." Tad kissed her and felt her tremble in his arms.

Their love-making was fiercely passionate. Tad was having second thoughts about leaving such bliss, but summoned the resolve to pack his bag. Davi drove him to the airport and left him at the curb with a tight embrace and a reminder to call her every day.

### 10:15 AM, THURSDAY, NOVEMBER 15ᵀᴴ, PHILADELPHIA

Cement World was a biennial convention and trade show for those in the business of constructing concrete buildings, foundations, highways, bridges, and airport runways. Most attendees came from the states of New York, Connecticut, Pennsylvania, Delaware, Maryland, and Virginia. Tad had called the convention headquarters number displayed on the web site before ordering his red-eye plane ticket. The woman answering the phone told him that the office was still operational and would continue to be so through the end of the month as they paid bills, processed records of the proceedings, and wrapped up customer services.

The business cards had worked for him before, so he used google to find the nearest print shop. An hour later and fifty dollars poorer, he drove the rain-puddled streets with a map on his lap searching for the Cement World address he had been given over the phone. He entered the trade show's office as Peter Lawson, an investigator for The Guardians. Fine print on his card stated that The Guardians was a non-profit organization devoted to supporting orphaned children.

The office was upstairs in a two-story frame building two blocks from the Sheraton Hotel. The suite was starkly utilitarian and was furnished with what looked like rental furniture. Stacks of unused vendors' brochures lined the far wall. Three women and one young man looked up from their work as he entered. "Good morning," he said unbuttoning his raincoat and leaning his umbrella against the wall.

A matronly woman with her graying hair arranged in a bun at the back of her head arose from the largest desk and walked to the counter. "Good morning. May we help you with something?"

"Well, yes, I'm hoping you can," said Tad offering her a card. "Our mission at The Guardians is to help finance the welfare, development, and education of orphaned children. Of course, we receive donations from generous patrons, but we also try to track down parents who, we have reason to believe, have abandoned their children."

The woman raised her eyebrows. Tad lifted a hand to disarm her concern. "We are not part of law enforcement. Obviously, our first step is to make sure of the parental relationship. If we are persuaded we have the right person, we seek voluntary settlements with some guarantees of continuity. Only if those arrangements fail, do we pass our findings on to law enforcement agencies."

All four of the staffers had listened with rapt attention, but their faces expressed puzzlement. "I think I get it," the older woman said, "but how can we help?"

"Please understand I'm just at the beginning of this particular investigation and our information is quite fragmentary at this point. But we believe this five-year-old boy's father is in the cement business or the cement equipment business. The mother is deceased but was an American citizen. We think the father is a non-citizen, probably from the Near East. We also think he's changed his name or uses a different name since fathering the child."

"OK. The cement business...?"

"Yes. We think the man does, or at least used to, do business in this part of the country. Can you tell me if there were any persons from the Near East registered for your convention?" Take it one small step at a time, he thought to himself.

"I suppose we could. That shouldn't be too hard. Debra, will you check the hometowns of the registrants?"

A younger, auburn-haired woman walked across the room to a desktop computer and keyboarded some commands to a data-base. She jotted down some details on a piece of paper and returned to where Tad and the older woman were standing. "We had three such persons. Two from Cairo and one from Bangalore, though I suppose one can't call India the 'Near East'. All three are vendors."

"Thank you. Your information will help us a lot," said Tad hoping to make it harder for them to refuse to provide more details.

The younger woman thrust the slip of paper at him before her supervisor saw what she had written or could object. He saw that Debra had included the names and addresses as well as the city names.

"What was the name you know him by?" asked the supervisor.

Tad was prepared for this question. "Ahmed Karuhl."

"Was that one of those three names, Debra?"

"No. Not that name."

Tad felt he had to keep the momentum of their cooperation going before the supervisor became too concerned for the privacy of the attendees. "I don't suppose you have any photographs of the registrants, do you?"

The woman stiffened and replied, "No. We don't do a picture book or photo roster or anything like that."

"But, Joan, with the new security protocols, remember we had to put their photos on the badges?"

Joan, the supervisor frowned. "Yes, but we don't keep the badges."

Debra smiled brightly. "True, but we used a digital camera! I was the one making the badges during registration. We decided to keep the images on the PC until the convention closed in case someone lost their badge. I haven't gotten around to deleting them yet so they should still be there."

Bless you, Debra, thought Tad. He said, "We received, from a distant cousin of the little boy, one rather blurry group photo with the father in it, but copies of your photos would let us see if we're on the right track here."

"Well, I don't know if we should..." began the woman named Joan.

"Ma'am, it's not easy to locate these deadbeat dads. And The Guardians always look out for more of these little tykes than the budget can adequately support. When their biological parents can afford to help out, we really need to find them and get them to fulfill their financial responsibilities."

Joan wore a wedding ring and Tad was betting she was a parent. He saw her face soften. "Yes, you're right. I still don't think I can give the pictures out, but you may look at them. Debra, can you pull those up?"

Tad really wanted copies, but thought he should not push his luck. "Thank you. Please know we're very discreet and if we don't have the right person, that portion of our file is expunged."

He walked around the end of the counter and followed Debra to a different computer station along the back wall where the young man had been working. Debra sat before the keyboard and Tad waited while she brought up the images. The first was that of the Indian man. Tad decided the man from Bangalore was less likely to be the controller, especially as he came from a predominantly Hindu area of the country. Nevertheless, he did his best to commit the face to memory. The next image was that of a man with a rather intimidating scowl, but he was still in his twenties. Tad studied his features, but felt he was too young to be the mastermind he sought. The third image showed a man in his middle-to-late fifties with a very wide face, bushy eyebrows, black hair, mustache, a goatee speckled with gray, and a bulging double chin. Tad asked Debra to pause on this picture and jotted a few lines in his notebook, then intensely studied the face once again.

He turned back to Joan. "The Guardians deeply appreciate your help. I don't suppose any of these three left a forwarding address?"

Again, it was Debra who responded. "No. If they had, I would've seen it in one of the fields of our database. They may've gone on to Nashville, though. A lot of our attendees will do that."

"Nashville?"

"That's the annual cement industry's national convention. It's in Nashville this year and starts tomorrow. We hold our regional meeting every other year and we always do it the week before the national."

"I see. What does this national convention call itself?"

"'NACC Expo'. That stands for National Association of Concrete Contractors."

"I get it. Well thanks for everything," Tad said with a friendly farewell wave as he picked up his umbrella and let himself out. In the car, he looked again at the scratch paper that Debra had handed him. The two men from Cairo listed the same address. Boss and assistant? But surely, Tad thought, if a bigwig was taking an intercontinental business trip, he would bring along a more senior executive. Maybe boss and bodyguard? The older man had registered under the name of Darius Mafousi.

His next stop was the Sheraton hotel. It was a quiet time in the forenoon and the attractive young blond at the reception desk was open to conversation with a handsome middle-aged man. "Hi, I'm hoping to reach Darius Mafousi. I thought he said he was staying at the Marriott, but he wasn't there. I know this was the conference hotel for the cement people, so I figured he might be here instead."

She accepted his casual reference to an acquaintance and made some keystrokes on her keyboard. "Yeah, he stayed here. Left yesterday though. Looks like you missed him."

"Damn!" Tad's disappointment was genuine enough. He knew there would be no easy way to trace phone calls, but thought he had nothing to lose by asking about faxes. "I wonder if our Portland office figured out where he was. They were supposed to fax him something. If it reached him here, I can relax a little bit and just hope I catch up with him later. Could you check that?"

"We keep a log of incoming faxes to be sure of delivery and to correctly charge the fees. I guess we could look." She smiled and motioned him around the corner to a small alcove behind the desk. She consulted a handwritten log for the days Mafousi had been a guest. "There's nothing here. But, you know, I remember that name. I think a fax came in earlier and the cover sheet said to hold it for his arrival. Yes, here it is, on the second; and it *did* come from Portland." she said pointing at a line in the log.

Tad's eyes followed her finger and he memorized the sender's phone number. "Well, that's a relief.

Looks like they got it to him when he finally got here. Thanks for your help!"

As he turned toward the lobby, she asked "Are you staying with us?"

Tad smothered his grin before he turned around. "No, they don't give us field guys the kind of expense account to stay here. Anyway, I'm leaving this afternoon."

"Right," she said with a trace of disappointment. "Take care."

"Will do. So long." Flattered by her interest, he left with a little bounce in his stride.

Tad had to fly under his own name given the increased security and identification procedures. He also had to rent the car under his own name since he did not have a false driver's license. The FBI had not seen any indication that this group of terrorists had the capability to hack into large corporate databases so those risks had seemed negligible. He did use an alias when he checked into a modest motel on Philadelphia's west side.

Tad had helped an old friend, Bev Taylor, replace a cooling pump and gas-gauge sensor on her boat last summer. Bev got many hours of pleasure boating on the Columbia River. Her day job, however, was more interesting to Tad at the moment. She was the District Manager for Comcast in charge of the Astoria office. She had wrapped up an early morning staff meeting when her phone rang.

"Bev, it's Tad Madison."

"Hi, Tad! So sorry to hear about your house. Is everything else OK?"

"I'm doing fine, Bev. Thanks for asking. Listen, I do need your help on one thing. I have a fax number in Portland and I need to know where that site is and who has that number. Could you find that out for me?"

"Sounds a little mysterious, but it shouldn't be hard. Except we aren't supposed to release that kind of data to just anyone ... so, if I can get it, you didn't hear it from me!"

"I'm trying to straighten out a business thing and, yes, it is a little mysterious. And, yes, I'll never say how I got it."

"Give me a couple of minutes. Where can I call you back?"

Two minutes later, she told Tad that the fax had been sent from an insurance agency, Dobney Insurance. It appeared, from the address, to be located about four blocks from the Tropical Furniture Imports warehouse. He thanked Bev and jotted down the business name she had supplied. He rationalized to himself that he had not really fibbed to her, just obfuscated a little. He considered what progress he had made. Najev had a calendar notation that possibly, though certainly not definitively, connected him to a man from Cairo. Was it a mere coincidence that that same man had received a fax from Portland, Oregon soon after they tried to kill Tad? Could Najev have sent the fax? And where was this Mr. Mafousi now?

It was time to call Nashville. Tad searched for the number of the Nashville Tourist & Hospitality Bureau. From them, he got the listing for the NACC Expo office. That office turned out to be in Washington D.C., but they referred him to their field staff at the Opryland Hotel in Nashville where they were already in the registration process. There, a harried-sounding woman answered the phone.

"Hello, can you tell me if Darius Mafousi has arrived yet?"

"That name sounds familiar. I think I just registered him about an hour ago. Is he a vendor?"

"Yes."

"Sure. Here he is. Already has his packet and he's probably setting up his booth by now."

"Is he staying in the hotel?"

"Let's see. Yes. He's staying here."

"Thanks a lot. We thought he might've been delayed. He must be too busy to turn on his cell phone. I'll catch up with him sooner or later."

Tad laid his phone on the bed and sat pensively. He could see no logical connection between importing furniture and the cement industry. Even if Najev had intended to pave the area to the rear of the warehouse, he would have used a local contractor and used asphalt rather than cement. Besides, In any case, Tad was sure Najev would not have been thinking of upgrading his property in the midst of their scheme to introduce the deadly virus. Tad had found no Sheraton connection to cement in Portland and had found one in Philadelphia. He remembered Najev's desk calendar had been a tear-off model rather than a flip-over model. So, if he had not seen it when he surprised Najev with his drop-in visit, the arguably sensitive notation would likely have been safely destroyed the next day. Even if Najev was intending to contact his controller, that person was not necessarily this man from Cairo. There had been at least three hundred people attending the Philadelphia conference and staying at the hotel, though the odds favored the controller being a foreigner. He had a temporary fix on the man from Cairo, but he needed a tighter link to Najev. He had to learn more about the insurance agency in Portland.

He considered asking Davi to look into it, but quickly dismissed the idea. There was some risk that the insurance agency was staffed by other conspirators they had not yet identified. After Davi's kidnapping, he wanted her to stay completely away from this business and under the watchful and protective cover of the FBI agents. Besides, she had not laid eyes on any of the group except the masked Zulanni and would not have access to any photos of the others. Thus she could not describe any of the conspirators if the insurance people did not know them by name.

Until then, Tad had reasoned that Bronson was fully engaged in the global effort to roll up the network and should not be distracted by having to listen to his speculative musings. But now, Tad had "something". It could be an important something if the fax could be tied to Najev or his people. If not, perhaps he had just been chasing a chimera, but at least he could offer the feds a further lead, however flimsy. In any case, he needed help to check out the sender of the fax. It was time to contact Bronson.

# TWENTY-THREE

THE MAN'S GREAT BULK MADE HIM WARM EVEN IN Autumn's cooler temperature. He reached in his jacket pocket for a freshly-pressed handkerchief and grazed his brow. The vendors' exhibits would not be open to those attending the conference until four in the afternoon. Mafousi and his employee, Salim Kadah, had taken possession of two crates from the customs agent earlier in the morning. The two of them had unpacked the crates in the exhibition hall's loading area and had one of the Opryland maintenance men haul the mixers to their booth. They had relied only upon color brochures, technical pamphlets and full-size cardboard placards to present their line of concrete mixers in Philadelphia. In Nashville, their needs called for two of the real products. They had chosen two models in the mid-sized range: one small enough to be loaded on the bed of a pickup truck with ease; the other, slightly larger, was fitted with a single axle carriage to be towed behind a truck.

Mafousi had attended the NACC Expo in several previous years, but had made little effort to make acquaintances. His prices were very competitive though there was inevitably some resistance to buying a product manufactured in Egypt. He seldom obtained more than a few dozen orders for his trouble. Even so, the trips were always worthwhile to Mafousi. This year's American trip was especially important to him.

A devout Moslem, Mafousi had already located the nearest mosque. He was a practical enough person that, when traveling, he usually made it to prayers only once a day. He had lost his father, a tank commander, in the Seven Days War. The bitterness had begun then.

Mafousi had been an intelligent young man and he discovered he had a knack for trading in used equipment. He learned quickly and became one of the shrewdest buyers at industrial auctions. He had a vast knowledge of machinery and had contacts all over the Mediterranean basin. Fifteen years in the past, he had formed a company to be a distributor for new cement mixers. This was a natural step and was a profitable addition to his business empire, but the company's value to him went far beyond the bottom line.

As with his girth and his balance sheet, the bitterness within Mafousi grew rather than diminished as the years passed. Not infrequently, he dealt with Israeli businessmen. He studied every dimension of his opposites in these negotiations: their strategies, their attitudes, and their integrity. They were clever, well prepared, and generally honest once the deal was struck. But even those not religiously or politically active, he felt were arrogant and condescending.

He believed his country's recognition of Israel to be a disgrace. He made generous donations to the P.L.O. and to other organizations that funded freedom fighters, as he called them, in Gaza, Lebanon and Syria. But these groups seemed to him too internally fractious, too inept in their targeting and too undisciplined in the field. Ten years ago, seven men contributed the seed money and worked quietly without a name or a slogan to patiently build the instrument of their vengeance. Darius Mafousi was one of those seven and their instrument was The Nile Trust.

They had placed sleepers in key locations. Their people, trusted and zealous, were in the United States, Malaysia, Turkey, Mexico and Israel. Soon, they would insert people into Panama. Their consortium had already established a successful counterfeiting operation for Israeli currency, exploded a bomb in the Australian embassy in Kuala Lumpur, arranged the assassination of two top Mossad operatives, and destroyed a supposedly secure N.A.T.O. communications center in Turkey. Outside funding had been plentiful in recent years as word of their accomplishments spread through discreet channels. They had been scrupulous in layering corporate entities and offshore banks so that the money-flow would be very hard to trace.

Mafousi and his six compatriots agreed on objectives, budgeting, general methods, and timelines, but the details of each man's operations were compartmentalized for the sake of their own security. They contacted those they controlled using cut-offs, couriers, dead drops, and secure phones. They always used work names. Mafousi was known by his underlings, sympathizers and donors only as Al M'afid.

Mafousi's group had rented a cottage on a lake near the southern tip of the Appalachian Mountains in Georgia partly for the purpose of having a phone with a password-protected answering machine. His "soldiers" could leave messages on the machine and Mafousi could harvest them remotely. It was to this machine that Najev had reported, in seemingly innocuous language, the intervention of Tad Madison and their failed attempt to kill him by burning his house. A second message told of Madison's escape from Sauvie Island.

Mafousi had been gravely disappointed by Najev's decisions to kill Castner and Madison. The Castner killing was without sanction from him as were the botched attempts on Madison. The latter, however justified after the fact, could have been avoided if Najev had not sent Bajehr after Castner. In trying to escape attention, they had ultimately drawn so much attention to themselves that Najev had felt it necessary to move the incubator out of the warehouse. To make matters worse, the attempts on Madison had cost Mafousi the life of his young cousin, Taj.

He had tried to calm his people in Portland with his return message. He had needed them to regain their focus on the financial advisors' convention Now he knew from the media that the entire plan had failed and some of the men were in custody. This Madison man was no longer likely to be involved as the federal agents would now be in charge and were, no doubt, furiously investigating. Still, he told his bodyguard, Kadah, to keep the photo of Madison that Najev had faxed him.

With the Portland attack defeated, Mafousi had to be extraordinarily careful, but he needed to continue with his current objective. He had two sleepers employed on Crescendo Cruise Line's newest megaliner based out of Fort Lauderdale and another two who owned a small construction business in Orlando.

Preparations for their operation would not be complete for another few months. Killing and sickening several thousand passengers on a luxury cruise ship would be an important victory, especially after the debacle in Portland. His people in Florida needed a sizable amount of money for preliminary steps that he had already approved. The cash he brought would be laundered in the construction business and available for their purposes in the months ahead.

His record with U.S. Customs over the years as a small importer of cement-mixing equipment was totally clean. That meant that his current shipment, even though originating in Egypt, did not raise suspicions. The two display models he had shipped to the NACC Expo had been cleared for sale during or after the conference. One of them would, in fact, be purchased by a particular buyer, the contractor from Orlando. The other would be a routine sale to anyone who made a decent offer. The mixer destined for Orlando had a unique compartment between the outer shell of the mixing drum and the interior shell. When it was cut open in Orlando, six hundred thousand U.S. dollars in various medium-denomination bills would be available to his people.

Mafousi and Kadah set to work to complete their display. The show was soon to begin.

⌒

Bronson's secretary told him that Tad Madison wanted to report and switched the call to Bronson's line.

"So have you picked up anything of interest in The City of Brotherly Love?"

Tad told him what he had learned. Bronson told Tad he still could not see a definitive link to this man, Mafousi, but he admitted the new facts were intriguing.

Then Tad explained about the fax from Portland. "If your men checked out the insurance brokerage, they might stumble onto more conspirators. Or the brokerage might be legit, but they would say they'd sent the fax as an accommodation to Najev or one of his people. Or, of course, they might simply say it was something else entirely .... something completely innocent."

Bronson was eager to follow up and told Tad he'd call him back within a few hours. Meanwhile, Tad was to stay in Philadelphia!

Doug Tashimoto stood to dismiss a progress-report meeting with the team analyzing the contents of Najev's home and office when Bronson's secretary tapped him on the shoulder. She whispered that Bronson wanted to see him.

Five minutes later, Tashimoto was studying the fatigued, but suddenly animated, face of his superior who said, "I just got a call from Tad Madison, Doug. He remembered something that led him to poke around back East. There's an Egyptian exporter who's presently in the States who received a fax from the Dobney Insurance Agency soon after the second attempt to kill Madison." Bronson went on to provide the address of Dobney's office and explained why the Egyptian might be a person of great interest. "What I want you to do, Doug, is find out whether this fax could've possibly been sent by or on behalf of Najev's group."

Tashimoto had been taking notes and looked up to ask, "So the Dobney folks or someone there might be in on it?"

"That's certainly a possibility so you'll have to get background on them first before you start any direct questioning."

"Looks like three possible scenarios to me, sir. One is that it was a totally unrelated communication in which case the Egyptian's connection disappears. Another could be that the fax was from Najev alone and the Egyptian will be a hot target. Or, it's possible that it was from Najev through Dobney meaning there're more local people we haven't yet collared."

"Exactly. Madison raised the same three possibilities. So begin carefully, but move as fast as you can. This could be a dead-end, but it's the first new idea we've had in the last week unless your team has turned something up in the last few hours."

Tashimoto shook his head with a sigh, "No, Russ, we're still grinding. Seems like they should have left some records or material related to this conspiracy, but they were very careful. They either destroyed such stuff or have hidden it elsewhere. We've thoroughly searched the Sellwood house and the Forest Grove house with the same result. That sketch of the various exits from the Convention Center that I told you about last week was the only thing we've turned up."

"The accounting guys in D.C. are still running the money trail," Bronson said. "I'm kind of hopeful there, but that always takes time. And Morrisey told me yesterday that we still haven't identified the body in the swamp beyond the obvious alias he was using."

"Anyone at the Mosque recognize him?"

"In general, they haven't been too helpful over there. One person thought he'd seen him a few times and thought his first name might've been Taj, but that's it. The one helpful person we have there had never personally seen him at all."

Tashimoto reassembled his team and gave them a new priority. He said he needed a total background on the Dobney Insurance Agency and its staff, hopefully within the hour. He parceled out assignments: checking business records with state agencies; checking with the Internal Revenue Service to see who was on the payroll; confirming Dobney's bona fides with insurers; seeing if any of the the Dobney owners or staff had criminal records or were on terrorist watch-lists; and learning if any of them were not American citizens.

Less than an hour-and-a-half later, they tentatively concluded that the company was legitimate and not likely to have been directly involved. Mike Dobney had taken over the business from his father who had started it nearly forty years ago. It was completely solvent and successfully handled accounts for several national insurers. Its six employees were all citizens and none had criminal records. There had never been a formal complaint filed against it. Tashimoto told them it was now appropriate to contact the staff directly. They could always consider a deeper probe, seek a search warrant, or even call for back-up if anyone acted suspicious during the interviews.

Agents Norm Wilson and Nelson Chang arrived at the Dobney agency shortly before five in the afternoon. They showed their credentials and asked if the agency kept a record of faxes sent and received. Mike

Dobney had emerged from his office as soon as the agents introduced themselves and answered with a frown, "Yes, we do. Helps the bookkeeper with the phone billings. May I ask why you're here?"

Wilson answered, "Sir, we're just following up on some loose ends. Probably doesn't even concern you or us. That's about all I can say right now, but we surely would appreciate your cooperation."

Dobney did not look especially reassured, but said "Of course. The log book is back here" as he turned to lead the way toward a back room.

Wilson nodded to Chang who remained in the lobby area and said "Mr. Dobney, we know you're about to close for the day, but may we ask that your employees hang around for a few more minutes until we're done?"

Dobney stopped in his tracks and turned back to face Wilson and Chang with an anxious look. "Yes. OK." He turned to a woman who had been standing close enough to hear. "Paula, will you ask everyone to stay?"

She nodded and the two men proceeded down a short hallway to the small, windowless room that served as a copy center. Dobney pointed to a loose-leaf binder on the counter next to the fax machine. Wilson opened it and found the page for faxes sent on November second. The third entry indicated a fax was sent to the number of the Sheraton Hotel in Philadelphia. Wilson said he would like to have the original, but Dobney could certainly keep a copy of the page for his records. Still mystified, Dobney agreed.

"Does one particular person in your office do all the faxing?" Wilson asked.

"No. Whoever of us needs to send something just uses the machine and makes the entry in the log."

Wilson hesitated. He did not want to show Dobney the exact line on the page that interested him. "May I have samples of your and each of your employee's handwriting? Perhaps filling out a mythical fax record?"

Dobney sighed. "Yes. I suppose so. I'll get them started."

It was obvious to Wilson as he scanned the seven samples that the entry had been made by an employee named John Sonneli. "I'm sorry to have held your staff these minutes. It shouldn't be too much longer. Could you send Mr. Sonneli back here?"

John Sonneli was in his early thirties and seemed more curious than apprehensive when he was left alone in the room with Agent Wilson. "Sorry for the inconvenience, Mr. Sonneli. I'd just like to ask you a few questions about a fax transmission."

"Sure. You can call me John."

"Right. So, John, think back a few days. It's the morning of Friday the second. The log suggests you sent a fax that morning to a number in Philadelphia. Does that ring a bell?"

"The second? I don't think so... oh, wait a minute. Philadelphia, you say? Yeah, I sort of pride myself on remembering area codes and that was one I didn't know so I looked it up just for the fun of it."

"That sounds like you didn't know where you wanted to send it," chuckled Wilson hoping to draw him out in a friendly way.

"Well, yeah. I mean it wasn't really my transmission."

"How was that?"

"Oh, we were just sending it for a client whose machine had broken down as an accommodation."

"Can you tell me who the client was?"

Sonneli wondered for an instant if there was some client privacy issue he should be thinking about, but decided that if a real FBI agent was asking, he was not going to beat around the bush. "I guess so. It was Tropical Furniture Imports. We've had their account for at least six years."

"I see." Wilson was careful not to let his elation show. "And who from that company brought it to you?"

"I think he is Mr. Al Said's assistant. Name's Bader or maybe it's Bajehr, I'm not quite sure."

"The log said it was just one page plus the cover sheet. What was it?"

"Well, I didn't really operate the machine. I thought that was kind of funny. Every so often we'll send a fax as a favor for a friend or a client. Most of the time, they just hand it to one of us. Not always though, and this was a time when he didn't seem to want me to handle it."

"Did you get a glimpse of it?"

"Not enough to really see it, but I thought it was a photo rather than text." Sonneli seemed to be warming to his subject. "You know, he was a little defensive about it. He even punched the buttons so I had to ask him for the phone number to write in our log. He claimed he'd already forgotten it!"

"But you *did* record it?"

"Well, you know, this machine has a little memory that tracks the last ten transmissions or receipts, so I just printed out the memory after he left so I'd have a number for the log."

"Very efficient of you!"

"Jenny, our bookkeeper, gives us the dickens if we

forget, so I just thought it would help make her life simpler. It only took me a few seconds."

"Just a couple more questions. Did this assistant come in alone that day?"

"Yes, so far as I know. We recognized each other and I was near the front that day so he just came up and asked me. I didn't see an extra car out front, so I assume he just walked over from their place."

"Right. And were there any other fax transmissions to or from Tropical Furniture Imports, before or after that time?"

"I can only speak for myself, but you could ask the others. As for me, the answer is 'no'. Are they in some sort of trouble?"

Wilson knew that whatever answer he gave to Sonelli would sweep through the office in a matter of minutes. "At this stage we're just looking into things about faxes from Portland to Philadelphia. I want to thank you for your cooperation."

Chang and Wilson questioned the others about faxes to or from Tropical Furniture Imports and apologized again for detaining them. Wilson phoned Tashimoto as soon as they returned to their car. Tashimoto knocked on Bronson's door within seconds of closing his phone. They conferred for a few more seconds and Tashimoto left. Bronson followed as far as his secretary's desk.

"Darby, will you check with our travel coordinator to get me on the first flight tonight connecting through to Nashville?"

He returned to his office and dialed the number of Tad Madison's motel.

# TWENTY-FOUR

ARON SHEVLIN HAD STOPPED SMOKING TEN YEARS ago when a colleague, Levi Nathan, had been killed. They determined that Nathan died because the PLO commander he had been stalking had smelled the cigarette odor from Nathan's clothes when the target first entered his hotel room. Nathan had picked the lock and waited inside in the darkness to surprise the man and take him into custody. Instead of acting like the unsuspecting prey Nathan anticipated, the man drew his gun and flicked the lights on, then off. In the split second of light, he spotted Nathan and fired three shots into his chest. Aaron and another colleague, acting as backups and loitering in the lobby, ran to the room and captured the commander, but were too late to save Nathan. Aaron gave up smoking the day after Nathan's funeral.

As one of the Mossad's top counter-intelligence agents, Aaron was known for his tireless attention to detail and his devotion to the safety and survival of his country. He was raised in France by an uncle after his parents were killed by a rocket attack as they worked at their kibbutz at the base of the Golan Heights. Aaron was five at the time of the attack. He returned to Israel at the age of seventeen. In college, he sharpened his innate intelligence and kept very much to himself. Aaron had worked ten months for an Israeli software company when a Mossad recruiter contacted him. He left the private sector a month later and stepped into the front lines of the anti-terrorism effort.

The Mossad's financial unit had first sniffed out donations going to The Nile Trust eighteen months ago. The trust's charter was duly filed with the Commissioner of Non-Profit Organizations in Cairo when it was first created. The charter authorized the trust to collect money for its declared charitable purposes. The charter also allowed the trust to invest the money pending disbursement for those uses. The charitable objectives were obliquely stated, but centered around historic preservation in the Nile Valley. The minimal annual reports the trust was required to file reflected the receipt of several large anonymous gifts, especially in the early years and again in the last two years. The report forms did not require identification of specific donors or the projects for which money had been disbursed. A covert examination of the Trust's bank records showed large transfers to two other entities. One was a real estate holding company; the other, a religious museum foundation.

The real estate company owned some land on the south outskirts of the city, but had done nothing to develop the acreage. The foundation did not operate a museum though it made small grants from time to time to religious history researchers. The Mossad delved further into the finances of these two entities and learned that both contracted with two consulting firms that charged exorbitantly for whatever services they rendered. The two firms did not have banking relationships, at least not in Egypt or Israel. These firms became the focus of Aaron and his colleagues' attention.

Each office was staffed with only one or two people. Sporadic intercepts on their phones had produced nothing of interest. Their offices were protected by very sophisticated security systems so Aaron and his associates had never been inside. Mossad's external surveillance eventually produced photographs of two men who made short, repeat visits. The men did not come together, nor did either visit only one of the firms. One man was of normal stature and weight. The other, despite his seeming agility, was very heavy – nearly obese. Aaron decided that the arrivals and departures during the quiet early-afternoon hours of these two well-dressed men made them worth following. There were a few other visitors, of course: bottled-water delivery men, and, once, a plumber, but none of them seemed likely to be of interest. Aaron also thought it notable that the "consultants" had relatively few clients.

It was the first day that Aaron's team was deployed to follow one of the men that two fellow Mossad agents were killed in Cairo by a bomb in their car. The Mossad pulled all of its agents in Egypt off their assignments to investigate the killings. They identified a woman who had manufactured the bomb and took her to a safe house for questioning. With the help of chemicals, she told them who had ordered her work. She could not, however, tell them anything of who had picked up the bomb from a secret drop or who had planted it in the car.

A day later, they picked up the man who had given

her the order as he strolled down a dark Cairo street toward the cafe where he played his evening game of backgammon. Two men in black clothing waited in a narrow dead-end alley. When the man passed the entrance to the alley, one of the waiting men pinned his arms to his sides while the other pressed a chloroform-soaked gauze cone over his mouth and nose. His struggling ceased within seconds and an older Mercedes swung around the corner behind them. The car lurched to a stop. One man opened the car's rear door and the other dragged the man's limp body into the back seat. The two men threw themselves into the car as it accelerated away. The driver of the Mercedes was careful to stay within the speed limit as they headed for the safe house. He made several small detours and loops to ensure they were not followed.

They strapped their captive to a chair inside the non-descript house on a quiet west-side street. They waited a few minutes for him to become fully awake. His initial struggles and curses diminished as he realized he could not escape. The questioning began. The interrogation technique changed when it became obvious the man would not give them the information they sought voluntarily. They draped a soaking wet towel over his head. The man in the chair did not appreciate the implication of this turn of events for the first few seconds. Then, as he gasped for breath, he knew he would very quickly suffocate. He tried to shout "Yes! Yes! I'll help you!" hoping that this was done only to frighten him. They yanked the towel off and the man gathered himself as he told a small lie. His interrogators were not deceived. They immediately replaced the towel. This time, they left it there until he nearly passed out. They gave him a few breaths of pure oxygen. As he revived and looked at them with terror-widened eyes, they had only to take the towel in hand. He started talking even before the urine trickling down his leg reached the floor.

He told them that the order and the money to pay the bomb-maker had come from a man he knew only as Al M'afid. They required him to describe this person. He said that he had sensed Al M'afid was a large man, perhaps even over one-hundred sixty kilograms. Aaron heard about this revelation two hours later and brought up the surveillance photo on his laptop. He printed the picture and joined the interrogation to show it to their captive.

"We met in the evening." The man looked anxiously at the wet towel, before he continued, "Al M'afid was inside a car. The window was darkened and only partially lowered as he spoke. I cannot be certain, but yes, he looked something like that."

When it was obvious that there was nothing more he could say about Al M'afid, a Mossad doctor injected the man and woman with heavy sedatives. The agents manacled the prisoners hand and foot, then loaded the two of them into a secret compartment in a truck that brought produce from Israel. Their colleagues would probe the captives' more general knowledge of Al M'afid's organization after they were across the border.

Aaron had spent four months trying to learn the whereabouts of this Al M'afid. Jewish bankers had been willing to help, but no one recognized the photo. Neither of the two visiting men returned to the consulting firms and one of the firms went out of business. Mossad agents followed the few other visitors to the remaining firm, but these persons' further contacts and their apparent reasons for stopping at the consulting firm looked to be legitimate.

The Mossad station in Beirut responded to an all-stations encrypted communique and reported rumors of a fat man who recruited people out of the camp militias. Another three weeks of work in Lebanon turned up a second reference to Al M'afid. Aaron's men had no access to passport control in Lebanon and the few clandestine photos they had from in-camp sources did not include an image of the man. Again, Jewish bankers in Beirut did not recognize the photos.

Aaron was back in Israel having a drink with a cabin attendant who worked for El Al one evening when it occurred to him that they should question her colleagues. They were not likely to get much cooperation from the attendants on Egypt Air flights, so they began with El Al flights to and from Egypt. Aaron happened to be present during the interview of the twenty-second attendant on their list, Sarah Kline. To make the attendants feel comfortable, the interviews were held in a small conference room. Audubon prints were on the walls and the chairs around the oak table were a matching set. A reporter with a digital stenotype machine recorded the proceedings and sat at one end. The agent who had interviewed most of the attendants sat on one side of the table, with Aaron on the other. Ms. Kline had come straight from the airport and was still wearing her uniform. She sat at the opposite end of the table from the reporter. The attractive thirty-two year-old woman sipped a mug of tea and sat primly upright in her chair. The news of the interviews had already spread among the cabin attendants so she was not nervous, though she could not imagine what they would ask her.

The other agent explained in very general terms that they were trying to identify a particular person who may have flown into Israel on El Al and showed her the picture of Al M'afid. "Do you recognize this man?" he asked.

"Yes, I've seen him before. It was well over a year ago. He was on the Tel Aviv flight from Cairo, I think. I remember because, even in first class, he wasn't entirely comfortable in his seat. He was very heavy."

Aaron took over. "That's good, Ms. Kline. Now I want you to try to visualize the seat he was in."

"Like I said, it was first class." She touched her hand to her temple and closed her eyes for a moment. "Yes, left side, second row I think. Maybe the third. Probably the aisle seat because I seem to remember his big leg in the aisle when I gave him an iced tea."

"How about the date? You said over a year ago."

"That will be harder. I know it was late summer, but that's all I can … wait a minute! I think that was the week that two of the attendants had emergencies of some kind and I got assigned to work two more flights right at the start of my vacation. They promised me extra days off at the end, but I remember being sort of ticked off. I had to change some of my plans and I was a little grumpy on that flight. I remember now that I thought 'oh boy, this big guy looks as though he'll be hard to please.' But I was wrong. He was perfectly nice to me."

"Thank you. That was very good recall."

Aaron smiled at her. He was handsome, she thought.

He had kind of a brooding, hard edge to him, but an attractive man.

"So do you remember when your vacation was supposed to start?"

"Mid-September, but Human Resources would have it exactly. They'd have my flight assignment too."

"Yes, and we'll be talking with them. Thank you for your cooperation. I must remind you again that you must not discuss the questions we asked or the answers you gave with anyone."

"Yes, I do understand that," she responded.

Aaron felt they were making progress at last. After his meeting with the Director of Human Resources at El Al, he had the dates of Sarah Kline's two flights from Cairo to Tel Aviv. The airline's data processing center dredged up the identities of the passengers in the aisle seats in the second and third rows on the left side of first class in both of those flights. Aaron ignored the one woman and considered the other three men's names. His next stop was Israeli Immigration. He knew that video cameras were used to record the arriving passengers at the immigration counter, but learned that the images were destroyed after twelve months. The digital cameras presently used to copy the passport pictures directly had not been installed the previous summer. He learned that the three names belonged to persons who had visited Israel more than once, but not often. Only one had returned to Israel between the time that Ms. Kline noticed him and the car-bombing. His name was Darius Mafousi and his occupation was listed as exporter of construction equipment.

Aaron checked personnel records to see whether

the immigration agents who had worked on the dates of those flights were still working for the government. There were five persons on duty when the flights had landed and four of them still worked for Immigration. It was the next day before he spoke with the fourth person, on the list, Sol Cabron. Aaron offered the man a brief and relatively inexplicit explanation and showed him the picture.

"Aw, you know, I see thousands of faces every year, Mr. Shevlin," he said even before he had glanced at the picture. Then he squinted at the picture. "Well, this man *does* look kind of familiar. He might've been a guy whose name I mispronounced. Yeah, I think so. I called him Mafarzi or something. He corrected me. I think it bothered him, but he was polite about it. I guess it was Masousi or Mafousi, something like that... his name, I mean."

"How about Darius Mafousi?"

"Perhaps, it's really only the last name that sort of stuck. Because of his correcting me, you know?"

Aaron left the interview like a dog with a fresh soup bone. He had a probable name and a face and a possible connection to the killing of the Mossad agents. He booked the next flight to Cairo.

Aaron learned in Cairo that Mafousi was a respected businessman credited with extensive knowledge about the value of new and used construction equipment. He worshipped at one of the more radical mosques, but had never been known to take part in demonstrations or violent protests. He traveled outside his country frequently, but that was not unusual given his several heavy-equipment enterprises. The Egyptian authorities had at one time, years ago, suspected him of being a sympathizer of radical movements, but had subsequently removed him from their watch lists. His offices were well-protected and Aaron's team could not risk any physical intrusions. They also found his home to be very secure. They had made five attempts to tail him when he left his home in the evening. Three times he went to innocuous cultural events or to the mosque where he spoke to no one beyond simple greetings. The other two times he had lost the tail. One of those times was in heavy traffic and they could not be sure if it was deliberate on his part. The other time, he had entered a parking garage and then immediately left, leaving the Mossad man assigned to follow him still checking parking stalls.

They discovered that he used a satellite phone/broadband connection and they requested the necessary equipment to attempt an intercept. Before it arrived, they learned of his pending trip to the United States. The intercept was held in abeyance and the Central Directorate gave Aaron approval for a two-person team to follow Mafousi to America. Aaron had asked for a four-person team, but his superiors said they could not spare the resources. He wanted a versatile partner if the team could only have two agents. He chose Julia Bergman. Julia's computer hacking skills were legendary. She was physically very fit and a crack shot as well. Five years ago they had enjoyed a brief affair, but Aaron felt that was behind them and, in any case, would not detract from their professional responsibilities.

They had booked into the Sheraton in Philadelphia, but did not learn anything of interest. In fact, Mafousi did nothing at all inconsistent with the ostensible purpose for his trip. He promoted his products and appeared to meet only with bona fide potential buyers.

The Mossad and the CIA had an understanding to share information about known terrorists on their respective watch lists. The Mossad had added Mafousi to its list as a "possible", but Aaron's superiors had not yet, Aaron knew, shared his name with the CIA or the FBI. Protocol also demanded that the FBI be informed and approve before the Mossad could engage in any anti-terrorism activity inside the United States. Aaron and his superiors had reasoned that they had not yet completed their case against Mafousi and were at most just passively investigating. They knew perfectly well that Aaron and Julia's trip was very close to the line and that the Americans would be furious if anything developed without their knowledge. Aaron's Division Chief told him that if he and Bergman turned up any more evidence pointing to Mafousi, they had to contact the FBI before going further.

Aaron had learned, by means of a substantial bribe to Mafousi's Cairo travel agent, that he and his henchman, Kadah, would go on to Nashville. Julia called the convention hotel, Opryland, and they were able to get a suite when a party cancelled at the last minute. They studied the hotel's map of its vast layout and realized they were almost directly across the lush interior garden from Mafousi's room in an adjoining wing.

On their first morning at Opryland, Aaron and Julia studied Kadah through binoculars from Aaron's room and concluded that he doubled as Mafousi's bodyguard. Later, they also noticed that Mafousi featured two medium-size cement mixers in his company's booth. They had confirmed, before they left, that his company had no distributors or warehouses in the United States. This told them that he had brought the mixers to the States for this show. Granted it was a national show in a major overseas market, but was it worth it for a relatively small company to go to the expense of shipping two heavy pieces of equipment?

Aaron still sometimes wished for a cigarette with his morning coffee. This was one of those mornings. He sat in a cushioned, wrought-iron chair in the outdoor patio of a French-motif cafe as he ate breakfast and kept an eye on Mafousi at a table fifty feet away. The patio where they sat was "outdoors" in the sense that it was outside the walls of the cafe and afforded a direct view of tropical trees and a fifteen-foot waterfall cascading into a lake. However, the entire setting – cafe building, waterfall, lake, trees – was under a towering glass ceiling that enclosed, like a gigantic greenhouse, the gardens and walkways between the several wings of the hotel.

Julia, in her mid-thirties and very attractive, made a mid-morning pass through the cavernous vendors' exhibition hall in hopes of striking up a conversation with Mafousi's assistant. She wore her dark hair down and had chosen a slightly revealing pantsuit that had already attracted attention from the male vendors. The room was not crowded at this early hour and she picked up a few brochures and business cards at other booths to give herself a veneer of credibility. Julia took a little extra time in a booth two down from where Kadah was stationed because he was engaged with two men. Seconds after they left, she resumed her stroll. Appearing to be distracted by the booth across the aisle, she almost bypassed

Kadah's booth. Turning back, she smiled at Kadah and stopped to study the larger mixer.

Kadah brazenly looked her over. She was sure that he noticed there was no ring on her left hand.

"Are you in the construction business?" he asked.

"Not really. My brother is and when he told me the trade show was at Opryland, I decided to tag along."

Kadah told her his first name was Salim. He was ready and willing to make the acquaintance of an attractive woman even though he wondered if she could be Jewish. He explained a few of the selling points of their equipment.

"So where do you go from here when this show is over?" she asked.

"Well, we probably will not go beyond Nashville unless we turn up some serious prospects for new business that would justify visits."

They chatted for several minutes more. When a man arrived at the booth with some serious technical questions, Kadah seemed almost sorry to have to turn his attention to a real customer. Julia waved good-bye and moved on.

At the restaurant, Aaron read the Tennessean's morning edition to stretch out his meal and make sure he did not finish before Mafousi. The man had eaten a prodigious breakfast, but finally signed the check and heaved his bulk from the chair. Aaron saw that he headed for the exhibition hall. Five minutes later, Aaron drifted into the hall and verified that Mafousi was in his booth along with Kadah. He turned and departed the hall. Once outside, he strode swiftly through the enormous atrium toward Mafousi's room.

Julia knew of Aaron's intentions and, finished with her brief reconnaissance of the booth and Kadah, she hurried back to Mafousi's room. The elevator lobby opened onto the corridor that led to the room at an oblique angle, blocking the sight-line down the hall of anyone emerging from the elevator. She found Aaron just around the bend in the corridor. They parted after a whispered few words. Aaron headed for the door of Mafousi's room and Julia posted herself near the elevator lobby holding a Grand Ol' Opry brochure.

There were no maids or guests in the corridor. A "Do Not Disturb" sign hung on the door handle of Mafousi's room. This caused Aaron to hesitate for an instant, before deciding that the sign simply meant that Mafousi did not want maids inside the room. Aaron had a device in his pocket that, in eight seconds, could read the door code and imprint it on the magnetic strip of a blank card. His luck held and he was inside the room in twelve seconds. A delivery from the Israeli embassy to their hotel room by courier had supplied Julia and him with Glocks fitted with silencers. Aaron hoped that they would not be needed.

He worked quickly, but not so fast that he would leave items out of place to cause Mafousi to realize that his belongings had been searched. He finished his search of the closet, the bureau drawers, and the medicine cabinet, but had found nothing that looked remotely suspicious or helpful. Mafousi must have the satellite phone on his person, he thought.

Both beds had been slept in and Aaron was confident that meant the bodyguard stayed in the room with Mafousi. He reached into his pocket and withdrew a tiny electronic microphone-transmitter that he attached to the underside of the sliding door of the closet. Checking his watch, he saw that he had been inside for nine minutes.

—

Mafousi made sure that Kadah had everything he needed in the booth and then remembered that there was a substantive session on a new technology that he wanted to attend. He had forgotten at what time of day it was to begin. Fruitlessly searching his pockets for the conference program, he realized he had left it on the table in their room. Telling Kadah he would see him later in the morning, he walked out of the exhibition hall.

Julia clicked twice on the walkie-talkie in her suit pocket the instant the elevator doors opened and she saw Mafousi emerging. Then she left the bend in the corridor and entered the elevator lobby. Pretending to study the brochure, she almost bumped into Mafousi.

"Oh, sorry!" She smiled as she spoke, but did not back away. "These stupid tourist brochures! I find them frustrating. Do you know anything about the schedule for the shows at the Grand Ol' Opry?"

Mafousi, taken a little aback by this friendly, but unexpected outpouring, stood and smiled back at her. She flashed the brochure at him as she saw the elevator door closing and continued "I'm waiting for my friend, but she won't know the schedule either. Have you been there?"

"You mean to the Grand Ol' Opry? No, I haven't. I know it's nearby. Perhaps you could go there and ask at the ticket office. Or try the concierge here?" He replied as he started to move around her.

"Thanks. That's a good idea." Just before Mafousi cleared the lobby, she laid a hand gently on his forearm. "If you haven't been there, you really should go. It's one of the things one must do in Nashville!"

"Yes, I must get around to that before I leave," he said with some finality as he separated from her and started down the hall.

Mafousi's ear for languages told him she was not a native American-English speaker. In fact, he thought that her very slight accent betrayed a Near Eastern origin. He, of course, noticed her beauty, but that too reminded him of the Near East and particularly of Israel. His thoughts returned to picking up his program as he inserted his key card into the slot on the door hardware.

Aaron had heard the two clicks on his walkie-talkie and leaped toward the door. He shut it behind him, stripped off his surgical gloves, and raced down the hall away from the elevators. Fifty feet ahead, he saw a stairway door. He pushed it open and took the stairs two at a time to the floor below. There, Aaron reentered the hallway and, with a conference program in hand, sauntered toward the elevator lobby.

Julia, consistent with her claim of waiting for a friend, stayed in the lobby area for another three minutes, before she took the elevator down. To her relief, Mafousi had not reappeared.

# TWENTY-FIVE

**B**RONSON TOLD TAD TO GET A FLIGHT TO NASHVILLE and confirmed that the Bureau would reimburse him. He had been able to get them reservations at the Fiddler's Inn Hotel just across Music Valley Drive from Opryland. They had adjoining rooms. Tad was to register using the name Michael Stauffer, consistent with Bronson's booking the room for him. Tad was to call back with his flight arrival time so Bronson could try to be back in his room by the time Tad reached the hotel.

Tad's taxi lurched to a stop at the hotel entrance just before lunch. Bronson had spent the morning in conference with SAC Sean McNertheny, who had come up with three teams of FBI agents from the field office in Knoxville. With McNertheny's twelve people, they hoped to conduct round-the-clock surveillance of both men. They had also set up a communications net with Portland and Washington D.C.

Tad checked in and, back in Tad's room, Bronson elaborated on what he had told Tad over the phone about Wilson and Chang's visit to the Dobney Insurance Agency. He also told him that agents in Philadelphia had secured the faxes-received log and a dump of the room-billing database from the

Sheraton and had seized the computer file containing the badge-photo file at the Cement World office. It was getting into the afternoon and Tad was hungry. Bronson and McNertheny had scheduled a further planning session so they told Tad to go ahead and eat while they got started.

While they did not ask him to stay away from their meeting, Tad understood it was primarily logistics and tactics they would be discussing and knew that he would have nothing to contribute. He wanted to see the NACC Expo convention hotel, and decided to walk there for his lunch. It was agreed that he would not approach Mafousi or his booth. He was staggered by the scale of the Opryland complex, and he decided to eat in the closest restaurant. "The Cascades", and save his orientation walk for after lunch. After a short wait, he was seated at an "outdoor" table overlooking a tropical "forest" and another waterfall.

⁓

Mafousi attended the session that interested him in mid-morning. Afterward, he rejoined Kadah at the booth. Around twelve-thirty, the big man returned to their room. Kadah would man the display while he ate and had his usual early-afternoon nap. He would order his lunch through room service, but first there was something he had to check. Looking carefully around the room and the bathroom, he saw nothing amiss. Mafousi approached the bureau and got on his hands and knees in front of it. He frowned and lowered his head for a closer study of the carpet. As he and Kadah left that morning, Mafousi had dusted white talcum powder on the off-white carpet between the bed and the bureau. By looking closely, he could see two disturbances in the talc, one clearly in the shape of a shoe sole. He sighed and reached for the room service menu. After calling for the meal, he sat in an easy chair to wait for its arrival while thoughtfully stroking the wattle under his second chin.

When Mafousi had finished eating, he went to the main desk and asked for a small case he had deposited in the hotel safe. Back in his room, he opened the case and removed a hand-held device with a retractable antenna and a small gauge. He pushed a switch and started walking slowly around the room. When he got to the closet, the needle in the gauge arced forward. When he walked past the closet, it receded to its baseline position.

Turning the device off and moving as quietly as possible, he made a detailed examination of the closet. He found nothing on his first pass. On hands and knees, he ran his fingers along every inch of the floor molding. Still, he found nothing. He removed an iron and a laundry bag from the shelf, then quietly lifted the shelf off for a closer inspection. He saw nothing. Back on the carpet, he lay on his side to squint at the underside of the door. This position was uncomfortable for him and he felt the need to take in a deep breath. He made a great effort to inhale quietly and it was then that he saw the bug. He did not attempt to remove it, but regained his feet and repacked the device in its case.

The atrium walk was a more appealing way to get back to the hotel desk. He had heard there was a national park in Costa Rica that featured a walkway suspended high in the trees just beneath the canopy of the tropical forest. This elevated walk through the tropical plantings in the atrium was clearly designed to afford guests some of the same exhilaration as must be experienced by the tourists in Costa Rica. Despite the pleasantly exotic nature of his path, Mafousi continued to brood over finding the bug. At its end, the walkway descended gradually and curved around on a level slightly below the terrace of The Cascades restaurant. Mafousi had nearly reached the curve when a waiter dropped a tray with a loud crash. Glancing up, Mafousi saw diners in freeze-frame as the waiter started to bend over. In the second row of tables, right beside the waiter, Mafousi's focus centered on a face he had seen before. He had seen it on the fax from Najev.

Bronson's meeting had evolved into a conference call on a secure, scrambled line between the Bronson-McNertheny group, Homeland Security and FBI headquarters. Since another convention site was implicated, the discussion focused on whether they should anticipate a second attempt to introduce pathogens. Dennis Borland, the Deputy Director of Homeland Security had reservations. "Look, we know this Najev guy sent some kind of image to Mr. Mafousi during the days preceding the Portland attempt. We know Mafousi is an Egyptian. Other than the missing woman, all the Portland players including the scientist are either dead or in custody. That's all we really know. We couldn't even hold Mr. Mafousi for questioning at this point."

Bronson frowned and said. "But, sir, the setting is the same. A large national convention."

"To some extent, yes, but a group of cement contractors hardly have the same symbolic importance as do investment advisors who are an intrinsic part of American capitalism. I just don't see these people as an attractive target," returned Borland.

The Director of the FBI chimed in. "I agree, Dennis, that it seems unlikely, but I want to send Rachel Palowski's biohazard team down there anyway. I realize the convention is already underway, but her team got their on-the-job training in Portland. We can have them testing everything in the kitchens and serving areas and we can put agents near the buffet tables if they have any."

McNertheny spoke up, "Sir, the attendees have very few meals together. An opening luncheon has already occurred. Since they're in a hotel with many restaurants, I guess they decided they would have more fun just going out in small groups. There *is* a final banquet Saturday night. We can certainly cover that meal with Dr. Palowski's team and reinforcements that I can bring up."

"I have no problem with that," said Borland. "We still have an Orange Alert going from before the Portland situation. We can maintain that and use it as a cover for your bio-hazard people. But you can bet the hospitality industry representatives will squawk big-time if we start shutting down conventions every time we have a lead or a suspect nearby."

Bronson was astounded. Did the Deputy Secretary not realize that they had just barely managed to dodge a very lethal bullet in Portland while fighting the same kind of keep-the-customers-calm reticence? "No doubt, they'll squawk, sir, but if the bad guys could pull one of these off, the hotels and caterers will lose twenty times the business in the future and lay the blame at our feet for not protecting their customers up front!"

Borland's political instincts were finally overcome by his sense of logic and responsibility. Instead of rebuking Bronson for his plain talk, he said, "That's true, of course. Let's do it this way. Mel, can the FBI pre-position some additional agents in Nashville? Then, if there's any evidence at all from Dr. Palowski or any other source that they will try it again, you can move them in immediately."

The FBI Director hesitated only a moment before replying. "Fine. It'll take us almost twenty-four hours to get the personnel to Nashville and logistically supported, but I'll order the deployment right away."

Bronson leaned toward McNertheny beside him and whispered in his ear. McNertheny nodded enthusiastically and Bronson said "Director Kirk, SAC McNertheny and I think the FBI should ask the Attorney General to authorize a search of Mafousi's hotel room and a tap on his phone."

The FBI Director answered, "I know that worked in Portland, but I'm not so sure he'd do that in this case. On our side, is the fact that this man has some connection to a real serious attempt that has actually occurred. Against us, is the fact that, apart from the fax, one Egyptian business man to another, we have nothing on this fellow."

Bronson replied, "Yes, sir, but I hardly see a business reason for a home furniture importer to need construction equipment or vice versa."

"I appreciate that. It is a little thin to be a legitimate business connection. I'll approach the Attorney General right away and give it a shot. I'll let SAC McNertheny know the results."

The call was brought to a close and the meeting broke up. Bronson knocked on Tad's door and brought him up to date on the plan for the surveillance of Mafousi and Kadah. As they sat in chairs in Tad's room, Bronson's cell phone rang. It was Clyde Morrisey.

"Boss, we finally ID'd that body in the swamp. As we suspected, Abouti was not his real name. We found a chess partner of Najev. This man prays at the mosque, but he's no Islamic radical and he was willing to help us. He'd seen a man fitting the description with Najev once. He just knew a first name, Taj, and he gave us a tea house where Taj might be found evenings. Showing a photo – the one the crime-scene people took – to servers at this tea-house led to a last name. We put that all together with immigration records and it looks solid."

"Good work! What's the full name?"

"Get this, Tom. It's Taj Mafousi!"

"I'll be damned! Does immigration show any ties to the Darius Mafousi we're looking at?"

"We didn't find any explicit connection in the file. And it turns out the name is not all that unique in the Middle East or even in ICE's own records. But we've started inquiries through channels with the Egyptian authorities."

Bronson had thought at first that they had found that extra piece of evidence that Homeland Security was waiting for, but he realized they were not quite there yet. "Thanks, Clyde. Keep after it."

Mafousi leaned over to Kadah and whispered, "Let's go for a walk. We can leave the booth untended for a few minutes."

Mafousi led him beyond the indoor gardens through the lobby and outside. Kadah could see the concern on the other's face. "Trouble?"

"Yes, Salim, you could say that. You know, after the debacle in Portland, I've been concerned that we could be somehow linked to Najev and that we might be under surveillance?"

"Yes, of course."

"And remember my little precaution in the room this morning?"

Kadah nodded.

"Well, we had a visitor. Then I checked to see if he had left anything the better to hear us with."

"You found a bug?"

"Yes, on the bottom edge of the closet door. Then, a few minutes later, as I walked past the main restaurant, I saw our Mr. Madison!"

"Allah be praised! How could that be? Did Najev talk before he died?"

"The newspaper said he took his own life before they could catch him. No, I don't think there was any leak through Najev himself. Possibly they found something at his house though I'm sure he knew better than to write anything down. And we couldn't be traced through the equipment. It must be something else, but you can be sure that it is no coincidence!"

Kadah scowled. "So your fears were right! He must

be here to watch us. Could he have traced us through the Portland mosque?"

"How? Our messenger has just passed through three times in eight years. He wouldn't be remembered at the mosque."

"Should I remove this man?"

"We need to know if he's got others with him. The FBI? The state police? Besides, we don't know this area well enough to isolate him here in Nashville. Anything in the hotel would be too risky. Right now, I can't even be sure he's staying at Opryland. You inquire discreetly at the desk to see if he's a guest here."

"I'll do that right away. I'll try to make a call to him on the house phone. If he's not staying here, they'll tell me that much. If they put me through, I'll hang up before he answers."

"Alright," Mafousi replied as he gazed into the distance. After a pause, he said, "I think we must tell Mr. Madison a little story that will distract him a bit."

"A story?"

"I left the bug in place. We must be very careful what we say in the room – and the booth as well – but we can say what we want him to hear, understand?"

"Yes. So what are you thinking?"

"I had one of the Orlando men, using an alias, buy a small cottage on a lake in northern Georgia. It was like insurance. A staging base or an escape hole and also a place for the message machine. Now we need to find a reason for Mr. Madison to go there and then you will make him disappear."

Kadah nodded. "When?"

"As soon as I can think it through. Now you must get back to the booth. Remember, we must say nothing of our other business even in the booth. Have you used your impressive talent for sniffing out contacts in the underworld to get yourself a weapon?"

"Yes, Mr. Mafousi. Took care of that last night. A nice clean Baretta with five clips and a silencer."

"Good. Meet me in the room in twenty minutes. I'll already be there. When you first enter, excuse yourself to use the bathroom. I'll hand you our script so you can read it over silently in the bathroom. When you come out, we'll begin."

---

By the time Kadah returned, Mafousi had prepared a script for them. After Kadah read it to himself a few times, he emerged from the bathroom and they began.

"I heard from Atherton this afternoon, Salim. He has the information we require."

"Excellent!" exclaimed Kadah.

"Yes, indeed. He will turn it over to us at the Carter Lake cabin. I told him to come alone. He said he would be there at nine this evening. I need to stay here, so you must be the one to pick it up."

"I can do that. I've been there once with you and I remember it's in northern Georgia. I can even remember the street.... Wildwood, isn't it? But I've forgotten the address and at night every cabin looks the same."

"You're close. It's Wilderwood Lane and the number is 163. This is a big responsibility. I want you to look the document over before you give him the money. He's a coward and he wouldn't dare fake it, but check it anyway."

"You can count on me!"

Mafousi waved a hand and picked up the script which had lain on the small writing table by the window as they read it. They lapsed into small talk as they prepared to leave the room. In the hallway, Mafousi tore the script into small pieces and stuffed them in his pocket to be flushed down a toilet in the exhibit hall later. He looked sternly at Kadah. "There is a large rock near the end of the road that would be the best place to wait. Better be out there at least an hour ahead of time. Memorize Madison's photo before you go. We don't want to have you get a neighbor coming over to borrow some matches! There are two anchors and plenty of rope in the boathouse. One of the anchors is probably on the boat. Use them to weight his body. Take it out a good distance, but not directly in front of the cabin before you throw him overboard. Call me as soon as it's over and say 'the new driveway has been completed'. Don't identify where you are. Erase anything that might be left on the answering machine including the greeting. Then lock up and come right back."

Kadah nodded and they reached the elevator lobby. "Oh, yes," added Mafousi, "be sure you aren't followed. We don't know what support this Madison may have. He may be a lone wolf, but, after Portland, we cannot be too careful!"

Kadah, whose many skills included a knack for very elusive driving, smiled and replied, "even if they do spot me leaving and try a rotation on me, I'll smell it. And I know plenty of city tricks to use on the way out of Nashville. I'll use a couple even if there's no...."

The elevator had arrived and as its doors opened

they saw an older couple inside. Kadah bit off the end of his sentence and they rode down wordlessly.

Mafousi did not go directly to the Exhibition Hall. Instead, he walked outside and headed in the direction of the Grand Ol' Opry Theater a few blocks away. Once sure he wasn't followed by anyone, he dialed a number on his satellite phone. It was the cell-phone number of the contractor in Orlando. He and his employee, both sleepers under Mafousi's control, were at the convention, but had studiously avoided direct contact.

"It's Al M'afid." The best-trained sleeper in Orlando, Bafir Nuwali, was the only one of his operatives in the United States who knew his real name. But Mafousi knew that even satellite phones could be intercepted, so he used his work name. Even the man's employee, Salim Toudani, knew him only as Al M'afid. "I want you to take the mixer today."

"Today? I thought the transfer was for tomorrow afternoon as the convention was winding down."

"That was the original plan. I'm changing that. I'll be at the booth until six. Do the paper work and take the mixer in late afternoon. And – listen carefully – do not use your van and trailer. Leave them for a couple of hours at the Elm Hill Public Use Area parking lot. Make sure it won't be closed when you get back. If it will be, choose another public park. I want you to rent a pickup truck with a hitch. Use your 'other' driver's license. Tow it..."

"What's the matter?" the man interrupted nervously. "Is there a problem?"

"Just listen! There are security cameras at the loading dock. I want no possible linkages for your sake. Tow the mixer by back roads to the Elm Hill place. You can study a map to find a way there. It's no more than twelve miles from here. You two can wrestle it into your trailer. Then you immediately return the rental truck and fly back to Orlando. Toudani can drive the trailer to your yard. Understood?"

Abashed by the vehemence of the instructions, the man answered, "Yes, of course. We'll do as you say. I'll come by the booth in an hour or so."

Mafousi had reached the parking lot for the theater. He slowed to a stop, wiped his brow with his handkerchief and turned to walk back to the hotel and his booth. He was a great believer in fall-back plans. He was comforted to know that he had a reservation at Reverson's.

McNertheny had spoken to the manager of the Opryland Hotel and obtained his consent to place a video camera and sensitive microphone in the high ceiling directly above Mafousi's booth in the exhibition hall. The work would be done during the night. Skeleton surveillance teams were already in place outside the hotel and the full complement would be in place by early evening. Bronson and McNertheny had just learned that the Attorney General had declined to approve a warrant to search Mafousi's room or place a wiretap on the room phone so that approach was not available to them.

In-hotel surveillance could not be operational until the next noon when more agents would arrive. McNertheny had persuaded the manager to relocate a young couple from Boise. That way, agents could occupy their room in the wing across the interior garden from the room shared by Mafousi and Kadah. From there, they would use binoculars. They also had a parabolic microphone that, with luck, would pick up, even through the window glass, Mafousi's and Kadah's voices. But the Boise couple would not agree to leave the hotel even with a free coupon to stay in a fine downtown hotel and their room would not be vacant until Friday. That meant the watching post was on hold until the next day.

Agent Mark Adderly had inserted himself as a supernumerary in a booth sixty feet down the aisle from Mafousi's booth. From there, he watched him settle his bulk into a campaign chair behind the table displaying his company's catalogues and literature. Adderly kept his gaze roving around the hall, but it always returned to the booth with the two cement mixers. His hidden lapel microphone easily picked up his softly spoken words. "The big man's alone. Watch the outside for his pal."

Agents Benneman and Lofton watched Kadah walk to his blue, rented Ford Taurus and start the engine. They ran to their unmarked Bureau car and left the hotel parking lot less than a minute behind Kadah. He had turned right, heading away from downtown Nashville. They saw his car a half-mile ahead and accelerated. There was a traffic light ahead that changed to red just as Kadah passed through. Stopped at the light, they could see an on-ramp to the north-bound parkway a few hundred yards ahead. A left-turn light turned green for the oncoming traffic and a tractor-trailer rig turned in front of them obscuring their view of the blue compact. Their red light at this busy intersection with the parkway on-ramp seemed interminable. As soon as the cross traffic slowed on the amber light, Benneman gunned their car through the intersection and headed toward the on-ramp. They surged past a truck, but saw no sign of the blue car. There were a few retail stores along the street paralleling the on-ramp. Lofton noticed a 7-Eleven, a pet store, a carwash, and a dry cleaners as they left the frontage street and raced onto the parkway.

Being fairly certain there was no surveillance car ahead of him, it was easy for Kadah to enter the car wash. He waved a twenty-dollar bill out the window and told the attendant "I'm in a great hurry. Skip the scrubbing and start me right in. Keep the change!"

Wide-eyed, the young men grinned and started Kadah's car into the tunnel of whirling brushes and spray just as Benneman and Lofton pulled past the truck. Emerging from the car wash, Kadah turned back south. He drove some twenty blocks on back streets before getting back on the parkway and, at the next interchange-ramp, onto U.S. 24 southbound. Chattanooga was two hours away and he was ahead of the late-afternoon rush. He repeatedly checked his rear-view mirror and was careful to stay within the speed limit.

# TWENTY-SIX

THE FBI AGENTS KNEW THAT KADAH HAD EVADED them and McNertheny had elicited the help of the Tennessee State Police to keep a look out for the blue Ford compact on all roads leading north. Tad had gone to watch the video from the ceiling camera and confidently stated that Mafousi's appearance matched the photo he had seen in Philadelphia. Bronson returned to his room after huddling again with McNertheny. He was just stretching out on the bed thinking of taking a cat nap when his phone rang. It was Tashimoto who sounded excited as he uttered the code word indicating that he was going to switch on the scrambler. Bronson did the same at his end and a short burst of static turned back into words.

"Doug, what've you got?"

"We got a slow start on some of the phone messages. The carrier misunderstood our request the first time and sent us the dope on Najev's home phone, but some other company's phone records instead of Tropical's. Anyway, we finally got the stuff for his company and we've been working our way through several months of phone calls."

Bronson was angry at himself for losing track of that aspect of their investigation. Had he known of the delay, he would have brought even more pressure to bear on the carrier to deliver the records sooner, especially given its screw up. He curbed his irritation. They could debrief on the delay later. "So, you found something in the records?"

"I think so. There were a fair number of calls but, when we ran them down, all but one cluster seemed legitimate business communications or pizza orders, that sort of thing. But we found this one, more unusual group: one call five months ago, one four months ago and then two just a few days apart in the days right before their failed attempt at the Convention Center."

Bronson's thoughts had already jumped ahead. "So who were they calling?"

"It was a number somewhere in backwoods Georgia! Place called Oakman. We got the address from Verizon. Turns out it's really at a nearby lake: Carter Lake. So we tried a subterfuge call. Got an answering machine: 'Richard and Paula aren't in right now'. Tried several more times. Always the answering machine. So we checked the assessor's records for that address. No Richard or Paula. The premises are owned by Wilbur Thordarson. Called Wilbur. Yes, he owns the place. Used to love bass fishing and used it for that. Too old now, he says, so he leased it out. Leased it for three years to a Richard Franklin. Thordarson and his realtor never met the guy. It was handled over the phone and by correspondence. Franklin pays the rent annually in advance by postal money order, realtor says. The lease was signed of course, but not notarized."

Bronson interrupted, "That process sounds deliberately opaque."

"Yes, it took some time, but the more we learned,

the more it got my interest, especially as the other calls checked out OK. So we tried Verizon again. Phone was ordered by a Richard Franklin. New to the area, no credit history with Verizon, so he puts up a healthy deposit. If there are any bills, they are sent to a P.O. box in Orlando, Florida."

Bronson was vitalized by this news. "Have you had time to check with the Orlando post office?"

"Sort of. The box was opened three years ago so no one remembers how or by whom. It's in the Franklin name and whoever opened the account at that time must have tied the box-holder's identity to an Orlando address. Box rentals are mailed in and paid by money order."

"This certainly sounds like somebody doesn't want to leave footprints. Franklin is probably an alias. See if you can trace the money order. Even if you can, it will probably end up with Franklin. If so, take the name as far as it will go. I'm going to head for some bass fishing!"

Bronson shook off the fatigue from his red-eye flight the night before as he hung up the phone. He studied a road map McNertheny had given him, then knocked on the door of Tad's room and asked, "How'd you like a road trip to Georgia?"

"Sure. You seem to have fire in your belly! Got a new lead?"

"Yes, and worth exploring." He summarized the call from Tashimoto. "McNertheny's men are all tied up between watching Mafousi and trying to find where the hell his sidekick went. This information from Doug is promising enough that I want to check it out tonight. If we get burgers to go, we can be there by eight-thirty or so. If no one's there, we'll at least get a good look at the place, stay overnight and try again in the morning when we can also talk to neighbors if need be."

"I'm in. Will you tell McNertheny?"

"Hell, yes!"

McNertheny was staying at the same hotel, using a suite of rooms as his command center. Bronson knocked on McNertheny's door. After identifying himself, he was admitted by a Knoxville-based agent. He saw McNertheny talking on the phone. As soon as the call ended, McNertheny gestured for Bronson to sit down.

"Anything new?"

"Yes, something that could be important. My people in Portland have found four phone calls from the Tropical Furniture warehouse to a residence in rural Georgia, on a Carter Lake. When they tried to learn whose residence it was, the paper trail got very convoluted and messy. And the calls were made at times of interest to us."

"So this could be how they reached their controller or at least it could be a communication link for the network," mused McNertheny.

"That's our thinking at the moment," said Bronson. "In any case, I want to get right on it. Tad and I are leaving within the hour. I want to interview the occupants and see why the phone records are so cloudy."

McNertheny listened with a mixture of interest and concern. "This sounds like a lead well worth investigating, but I'm troubled you guys are going there alone."

"I hope to get back-up from Atlanta."

That seemed to reassure McNertheny somewhat. On the one hand, a minimally supported approach could be risky. On the other hand, his plate was getting too full and time was of the essence if they were to roll up this network. Bronson was a savvy agent and Madison had proven to be both resourceful and cooperative. He shrugged his shoulders and grinned at Bronson. "Be careful and stay in close touch. The Atlanta guys are good and that should help. But if this place turns out to be the real deal, it may be heavily fortified."

"Right, we'll be cautious. And it's possible we won't even be able to make contact until tomorrow morning."

Back in his own room with Tad, Bronson used a scrambler and dialed the number of the Atlanta FBI office. They were closing for the day, but the Atlanta SAC had not yet left and the receptionist put Bronson through to Chuck Chavez. He introduced himself and they discovered they had a common friend in the San Francisco office. Cutting short the do-you-know conversation, Bronson filled in some background for Chavez including his working relationship with McNertheny, and then got right to the point.

"This contact may be nothing more than a third cousin or a furniture dealer that takes business calls at his vacation cabin, but the timing of these communications and the way everything has been so hard to trace suggest that these calls could have something to do with the terrorists' network. In fact, we think we may have the ringleader in our sights right here in the Nashville area, but it's imperative that we draw the net closed and the sooner the better! So one of our consultants and I are going to the cabin this evening. McNertheny's people are already spread thin in Nashville and the reinforcements from D.C. won't arrive until tomorrow. Can your office give us some back-up?"

"I'd dearly like to, but here's my problem. As we speak, I've got six people in the field in Savannah, one in the hospital with appendicitis, one on vacation in San Diego, two in post-graduate training at Quantico and only two able-bodied agents left here in town. And those two have both gone home for the day. I'll run them down and send them up there, but it could take several hours at best."

"That's better than nothing. Thanks, Chuck!"

They hammered out the details of rendezvous places and times and agreed on the radio frequency to be used.

When Bronson and Tad reached their rental car, Bronson opened the trunk and pointed to two armored vests that McNertheny had loaned them. "We'll wear those once we're there. Just in case Richard and Paula turn out not to be Ma and Pa Kettle!"

Around one o'clock, Aaron Shevlin observed a man of indeterminate ethnicity – perhaps Turkish, perhaps Greek – spend fifteen minutes talking with Kadah at the booth. Business cards were exchanged as they parted. Kadah absently laid the other's card on the table as the man walked away. Their conversation, though not furtive, appeared intense and they almost never referred to the sales literature or examined the mixers. At one-thirty, Mafousi returned to the booth, but then both men walked out of the hall leaving the booth untended. Aaron headed to the booth in order to steal a glance at the visitor's business card. Even if Mafousi should return while he was there, he was quite sure that Mafousi had never seen him. He signaled to Julia to follow the two of them to make sure they did not leave the hotel or make any secretive contacts. The card was still on the table. Aaron pretended to pick up a brochure and stared at the card. It read 'George Kapilos, Contractor, Chattanooga'. Openly checking his wristwatch, Aaron ambled down the aisle and out of the exhibition hall.

Julia sat in a lounge chair in the hallway just beyond one of the entrances to the hall, ostensibly reading a magazine. Aaron signaled to her to follow him to the atrium area. Once "outside", he stopped near a railing at the top of one of the large waterfalls and waited for her. She walked up to the railing a few feet from him and gazed at the waterfall. Without seeming to notice him, she spoke softly.

"They walked outside just talking to each other. Then they split up and Mafousi is on his way back to his booth. I thought it best to stay with him."

Still gazing at the waterfall, Aaron replied "Kadah had an intense conversation with a Mediterranean-type person at the booth about half an hour ago. Maybe it was nothing, but they looked quite conspiratorial. I got his name off his business card: George Kapilos, ostensibly a contractor from Chattanooga. I think you should go there right away and see if you can dig up anything about Mr. Kapilos."

"Alright. That'll leave you alone with the two of them, though."

"I know, but this could be the first promising development we've had. With luck, you'll be back here after dinner. Call me when you get there and keep your cell phone on."

Fifteen minutes later, Julia was headed south.

Aaron had to vary his location as he watched Mafousi. He had found a position on the indoor promenade from where he could watch all of the public doors to the exhibition hall. He could not monitor the interior hallway from the hall to the loading area from the promenade, so he had to stroll the aisles of the hall itself from time to time. He found an attendee's badge earlier in the day on the carpet near a hallway coffee table. Deciding that he needed it more than its owner, he clipped it on to give himself credibility in the hall.

Aaron was on his last walk through the hall when he made a man at a booth some sixty feet from Mafousi's booth. They were promoting a new type of styrofoam form for pouring foundations in this booth, but the man seemed indifferent to the potential customer with whom his apparent colleague was animatedly conversing. The man looked a little too fit and clean-cut for a salesman and his lips were moving. Aaron spotted the earpiece as he drew closer. The man had to be more than hotel security. Law enforcement? FBI? Could he be watching Mafousi too?

Aaron looked ahead and saw a pickup with the Opryland logo on its door ready to pull the larger cement mixer from Mafousi's booth toward the loading area. The man standing alongside the truck was a Near Eastern man whom Aaron had not seen before. He had an attendee's badge on his shirt and said "thank you, Mr. Mafouli. It's just what I need and your price was good." He spoke in American English with only a slight accent. Mafousi, hands clasped over his stomach, bowed slightly.

"It's Mafousi and you are quite welcome. Convention prices are always good. If you find you need other equipment, call me. My Cairo phone number is on the card. We'll always make you a good price!"

Aaron noticed that the other mixer now had a price placard on its frame announcing "Convention Close Out". He hurried out of the hall and found a door to the rear parking area. From behind a parked delivery van, he watched the loading area as the driver of the Opryland truck and the other man hitched the mixer to a white pickup truck. Aaron moved as unobtrusively as possible to a position from where he could read the truck's license number. He recorded the number in a small notebook and returned to the hall. Twenty minutes later, Mafousi secured his booth for the evening and went to a restaurant in the interior garden with a provincial Italian theme where he ordered an early dinner.

Aaron took that opportunity to return to his own room to listen to the recording of the transmissions from the device he had planted in Mafousi's room. The morning recordings were mundane. But the early afternoon recording had him hunched over the speaker and swearing at himself for not checking the tape earlier in the day. He replayed it twice and took notes. He located the lake on the Georgia page of a United States road atlas he had picked up in Philadelphia. Then he dialed the number of Julia's cell phone.

"Yes?"

"It's Aaron. Have you had your dinner?"

"No. I just finished checking out Mr. George Kapilos. He looks squeaky clean. Has a talkative office manager. He says Kapilos is American born, a veteran, and he's been in the contracting business for twenty-two years. Even attends the Greek Orthodox church and belongs to the local Rotary club. And the local Contractors Board confirms much of what the office manager told me."

Aaron listened with interest and complimented her on how quickly she had assembled the background information. He knew that it all might conceivably be a carefully constructed cover for a sleeper, but he was impatient to get her moving and refrained from probing her further.

"Forget Mr. Kapilos for now. I listened to the recording from our bug a few minutes ago. There's going to be some kind of a hand-off of information that Mafousi needs. It's to be at nine tonight at a cabin at Carter Lake in northern Georgia. The hand-off is from a man named Atherton. I can't get there in time, but you can if you leave soon. Buy a Georgia map and use your GPS to make sure you can find it. Got something to write with?"

"Yes. Go ahead."

"The address is 163 Wilderwood Lane. It's already dark and I have no idea how the streets around the lake are laid out or numbered so take a good flashlight."

"I have a powerful little one in my purse. I have that little digital camera too."

"Good. Just watch as best you can ... faces, license numbers, try to see what's handed over. Take pictures if that's feasible without using the flash. But don't place yourself in undue danger. If it looks like the real deal, call Ben Schuman at our embassy and tell him to get the FBI immediately in the loop. And call me too."

"Of course. I'll leave now."

"Sorry about your dinner. Stay well clear of the bodyguard!"

It must have been that pre-packaged egg-salad sandwich he had picked up for lunch, he thought. His gut was going wild. The rumbling had given way to cramps and now he had an urgent need to find a lavatory. He knew his relief would arrive in twelve minutes, at five o'clock, but he also knew that he could not wait that long. Agent Adderly gingerly left the booth hawking foundation forms and started his quest for the nearest men's room.

During the fifteen minutes that Adderly coped with his intestinal problem, the Opryland pickup truck had entered the exhibition hall, hitched up the cement mixer, and towed it out. Agent Carrie Tarvola was entering the in-hall surveillance rotation for the first time to replace Adderly. She had been briefed on Mafousi's appearance and the location of his booth relative to the foundation-form booth. She had also been instructed how to interact with the real salesman in the booth. She had even been given some of the sales brochures to study to afford her a modest cover if she was cornered by an interested potential customer. But no one had drawn her a diagram of Mafousi's layout or told her there were two mixers at the booth. As she entered the hall, she failed to notice a pickup truck towing a cement mixer just disappearing into the wide corridor leading to the loading area because she was distracted by not seeing Adderly.

Agent Adderly emerged from the men's room wan

and a little shaky. He re-entered the hall to see Tarvola already at her post in the booth. He explained
his absence to her and they conversed briefly on how
best to carry out the surveillance from that particular
booth. His shift then over, Adderly turned to leave
without glancing at Mafousi or his booth.

A few minutes later, Bafir Nuwali backed a rented
pickup truck into the Opryland convention center's
loading area. The Opryland maintenance man who
pulled the mixer out of the hall helped Nuwali hitch it
to his truck. Heading southeast, Nuwali finally found
Stewart's Ferry Road. From there, he knew it was a
right turn onto Pleasant Hill Road. Soon after, he
pulled into the park-like public use area at Elm Hill.
Their van with the box trailer was the only vehicle
in the parking area. A sign near the entrance said
the winter closing hour was seven o'clock. Toudani
stepped out of the van and immediately helped to
unhitch the mixer.

"You made good time, Bafir."

"Yes. And I saw no one following me."

The men lowered the door-ramp of the trailer and
pushed mightily to wrestle the mixer into the trailer.
On their first attempt, they could not quite muscle it
to the top of the ramp. On the next try, a raised lever
on the upper side of the mixing drum blocked them
from pushing the mixer further into the trailer. Unable
to hold the mixer on the slope of the ramp while they
repositioned the lever, they eased it back down to
the pavement. With the lever lowered, they gathered

momentum with a short approach and succeeded in getting the mixer into the trailer. After chaining it down, they pushed the door-ramp closed and locked it. The two vehicles left the parking lot, with Nuwali heading back to Nashville and Toudani turning south.

Salim Kadah would not admit it to Mafousi or anyone they worked with, but he had always liked American music, especially the big band sound of the swing era. He had heard the mullahs excoriate western culture and he knew that American music was thought to be particularly degenerate. Still, he greatly enjoyed hearing it. He thought of it as a secret vice and hoped it did not render him impure as a believer. Now, as he passed through Chattanooga, he thought of The Modernaires singing "The Chattanooga Choo-Choo" in front of the Glenn Miller band. Another closet aficionado of western music in Cairo had once told him that the words were no longer politically correct in the States. In any case, he found himself humming the tune as he crossed the river in the center of the city.

South of Chattanooga, at a town called Dalton, he turned off the interstate and drove east for a few miles, then turned back south on Highway 411. One further turn and he was nearing the lake. His only previous visit had been in daylight and he was not completely sure of his way in the darkness. It was seven-twenty when he thought he recognized the private driveway leading to the cabin. To be certain, he stopped to check the numerals on a weathered board nailed to a tree just where the driveway took off from Wilderwood Lane. Yes! There were the numbers 163.

He could make out the weathered cabin with its stone chimney at the end of the driveway. The front door opened to a simple porch and he remembered there was a comfortable veranda on the lake side of the cabin facing a patio. He circled the entire cabin to assure himself that no one was lurking inside. Then, he located the hidden key under the low porch and unlocked the door. Kadah turned on the entrance hall light and studied the interior. With gun drawn he checked out each room. The cabin smelled musty and appeared undisturbed. He had been uneasy with the idea of leaving his car near the cabin, but Mafousi had told him that if Madison was expecting a meeting, there had to be vehicles in evidence. The second vehicle needed to set their stage had presented a problem until Mafousi remembered that the owner's son had asked permission to store his motorcycle on the property. Kadah was to remove the tarpaulin that covered it and wheel the bike out near his car.

The sooner he was in place for the ambush, the better, but he wanted to check out the grounds first. He turned on the radio in the living room, tuning it to a talk show and then quietly left through the door to the veranda.

He felt that he was alone, but he could not be positive that Madison had not somehow arrived first or called ahead for some kind of help. The boathouse was a place he had to check in any event. He could see a quarter-moon from time to time through breaks in the clouds that drifted across the cold night sky. There was enough light that his eyes could adjust and he could see without using the flashlight he brought from the cabin. The door to the boathouse was never locked. To Kadah's dismay, it groaned a little on its hinges as he eased it open. He waited a full twenty seconds, but heard no sound from inside. He lowered himself to his hands and knees and crawled inside. His nose caught the very faint odor of grease and gasoline. He remembered the light switch to the left of the door. With his gun in his right hand, he raised his left arm and felt for the switch. He turned the light on and scanned the space in front of him. It was empty … unless someone was crouching on the far side of the boat. He turned the light off and crawled past the bow until he sensed he had a line of fire down the boat's port side. Then he raised himself to a kneeling position and used his left hand to take the flashlight from his jacket pocket. He switched on the light and saw that there was no one behind the boat. Kadah wiped perspiration off his face and stood up.

He climbed on board to inspect the bass boat. The key was in the ignition as the lease also provided for use of the boat. Kadah remembered from his previous visit that bass boats were strange looking, but very functional. This one was typical: a flat deck with fishing chairs, a sleek hull, and a powerful engine capable of racing its owner to prime fishing spots at the start of competitions. Mafousi had allowed Kadah to drive the boat just for the thrill of it during his previous visit to the cabin and he felt confident that he could get it started. Nevertheless, he worried about the motor's rumble in the quiet of the night when he would be dumping Madison's body. He decided to try using an oar to paddle the boat with the engine off. He also hoped that the moon would go back behind the clouds, since there would be no cabin to conceal his burden.

Satisfied that no one was on the lakefront portion of the property, Kadah continued his stealthy scouting in the area nearer the lane. This area also seemed clear. It was now nearly eight o'clock. His mouth was already dry from tension. He returned to the cabin to drink a glass of water. Making sure all the curtains were closed, he left the lights on and went back outside. He walked some fifty feet back on the entrance road until he came to the huge boulder that Mafousi had mentioned. In one of its clefts, he found a place where he could half-sit/half-stand. He broke off two pine branches from a nearby tree and, once he was wedged into the stony crevice, drew them over the top of the cleft. He knew it would be nearly impossible for him to be seen in the darkness. He laid the silenced Baretta against his leg and let out a deep breath.

# TWENTY-SEVEN

JULIA PUT HER CAR THROUGH A THREE-POINT TURN-around and regained the county road. The GPS in the rental car was not functioning well and that was the second time she had taken a wrong turn in the darkness. She knew she was close to the lake, but she could not find a road that connected to Wilderwood Lane. A ground fog was starting to form making her navigation even more difficult. Then she saw a road to the left that was signed Wilderwood. She had apparently been on the connecting road without realizing it. She could barely see some of the cabins set well off the lane let alone their house numbers. Then she noticed that most of the homes had family names and numbers posted on gates or trees where the driveways left the lane. She slowed down and used her flashlight to read the numbers 182 on the next sign. The next two driveways seemed to have no markings, but the one after that was signed 176. She was going in the right direction and was getting close. The majority of the cabins were dark and she assumed they were only seasonally unoccupied.

She slowed even more and turned off her headlights, using her parking lights to steer. Holding her flashlight, she picked out several more descending numbers and then 163. At the cabin down the driveway, the curtains glowed yellow. Kadah was there. Julia drove on past and looked for cabins where there were no lights. Her training had taught her to be leery of frontal approaches where there could be trip wires or other warning devices. The next four cabins appeared to be dark. The fifth one was lit up and she could make out an SUV in the driveway. She backed up and turned her car down the driveway of the third darkened cabin. Each cabin sat on a good-sized parcel. She guessed each lot was at least a half-acre. From this, she felt confident that her movements would not be noticed by anyone in either of the two occupied cabins.

She fitted a silencer to her Glock and applied black grease paint to her face and hands. She was fortunate to have been wearing a Navy blue pantsuit and dark flats when she left for Chattanooga. Her eyes had adjusted to the darkness by the time she got out of the car and walked carefully around a darkened cabin toward the lake shore. There, she found a canoe upside down on the planking of a modest dock. Trusting people, these Georgians, she thought. The canoe suited her purposes perfectly. Then she realized there was no paddle. She decided she could paddle with her hands as she needed to travel only a couple of hundred feet. As quietly as possible, she turned the canoe over and slid it into the still, black waters of the lake. With great concentration, she lowered herself into the canoe. She tucked her gun in her waistband and dipped her hands into the cold water. Five minutes later, in the thickening fog, she drifted abreast of Kadah's cabin. She could see the loom of a boathouse on the shore. She maneuvered the canoe to a spot on the narrow beach close alongside the boat-house, keeping it between her and the cabin.

Unlike the side of the properties facing the lane that everyone seemed to have left in a natural state, the area from the cabin to the lake was landscaped with a flagstone patio and a lawn. Julia could see the door to the boathouse was ajar. She opened it an inch further. Shielding the lens with her cupped hand, she turned on her flashlight long enough for a quick glimpse inside. She saw a rather odd looking boat in its berth and little else. Still worried about alarms, she dared not step on the patio, but thought she could safely get close to the lighted room on the front of the house. She moved to the front, but saw that the curtains com-pletely prevented her from seeing inside. Julia could hear voices, but it sounded to her like a radio playing. She doubted this Atherton person would arrive early and concluded that Kadah was possibly inside killing time by listening to the radio. An owl hooted some-where nearby. Uncertain exactly where Kadah was, she knew she had to conceal herself in the forest beyond the edge of the lawn to await Atherton's arrival. She crouched over and moved silently a short way into the natural area until she found a small windfall tree. With gun in hand, she lay down behind the tree. The luminous dial of her watch showed eight-forty.

Tad had offered to drive so Bronson could sleep. He accepted the offer and leaned his head on the window to doze, but kept awakening to rehearse various scenarios of their forthcoming confrontation. Bronson realized, as they passed south of Chattanooga, that they were fairly close to the Civil War battlefield of Chickamauga. If this all ended well, he promised himself a visit before returning to Portland. He had a bookshelf full of American history books at home and never tired of touring historic sites.

The freeway passed numerous suburbs for Chattanooga that were just across the border into Georgia. As they left the freeway to head east toward the southern tip of the Appalachians, Bronson was wide awake. The two FBI agents had left Atlanta and were on their way, but Tad and Bronson wanted to locate the address and do an observational pass even before they met with their backups. They approached the lake on a road that took them to its southern end. A tavern called Max's with a dozen cars in the parking lot faced them as they came to a "T" junction. This was the place they had agreed would be the rendezvous spot for meeting Chavez's agents. It was eight-thirty-five. From the bartender, Tad got directions to Wilderwood Lane and learned it began at a turning just over a half-mile from the tavern.

They almost passed the driveway before they saw the address on the tree. Tad slowed down, but Bronson told him to keep moving down the road another hundred yards and then look for a driveway to an unlit cabin on the side of the road away from the lake. They put on the armored vests as soon as the car was parked and pulled sweaters over the vests. Bronson re-slung his shoulder holster and then donned a FBI windbreaker.

McNertheny had loaned Bronson a portable

two-way radio and he used it to call the Atlanta agents. They responded saying they estimated their arrival at the tavern to be in fifteen minutes.

Bronson said, "We're already at the site. Madison and I are not going to attempt contact, but we are going to try to see how the cabin is situated and check the terrain on the half of the property nearest the road. We should get back to the tavern at about the same time as you are due to arrive. But, if we're not back in twenty-five minutes, you guys should come to the cabin, expecting trouble. I'll carry my radio tuned to channel six."

"Roger that, Agent Bronson. We'll see you shortly at the tavern."

Bronson and Tad walked down the road back toward number 163, talking only in whispers. "I thought I saw a light on in the cabin down that driveway, but it could've been a neighbor," Tad said. "I was concentrating more on the address signs."

"I saw it too," replied Bronson. "The good news is there will probably be someone for us to talk to. The bad news is, we don't know if it's just good ol' Richard and Paula or a died-in-the-wool, foaming-at-the-mouth terrorist."

They reached the driveway and stopped. Their eyes had started to adjust to the near darkness, but the moon disappeared behind a cloud and fog hugging the lake made it hard to see details.

"All the curtains are drawn," Bronson said. "Let's just mosey down this driveway sixty or seventy feet. We'll still be a ways from the cabin and I want a little better look at the approach so I can do some tactical planning with our two backups."

Tad nodded and they walked stealthily on the pine needles and compacted earth of the driveway.

Kadah heard the car drive past, but did not realize it had stopped. He was getting a leg cramp from his confined position in the boulder and was starting to stand to relax his muscles when he heard whispering. He froze and listened intently. He heard whispering again. They were coming nearer, probably walking down the driveway toward him. But Madison had brought someone with him! This changed the plan. Rather than a quick shooting, he decided to get as much information as he could about the second person before killing them.

Kadah looked at his watch and saw it was ten minutes before nine. Given the timing and the little play he and Mafousi had put on for the benefit of the hidden microphone, he felt that one of the men had to be Madison. Fortunately, the spill of the porch light reached the area of the drive near the boulder. He should be able to see faces and confirm that one of them was Madison. He was a little surprised they were coming right down the driveway, but their bold-ness suggested to him that they were armed. He retreated back against the rock and waited.

"That huge boulder over there would make a good firing position if there were to be any shooting," Bronson whispered. Then he added, "we'll stop just past there. Too much light if we get closer than that. I wish we knew something about the lake front."

"I saw an old poster at the tavern about a bass-fishing tournament last summer. Given that and Mr. Thordarson's reference to fishing, I'll bet every cabin owner has a dock and a boat," said Tad as they moved past the boulder.

Even in the weak light, Kadah could see the man nearest him was Madison.

Kadah stepped noiselessly out from the cleft in the rock. Although he heard nothing, Bronson had a strong sense that someone or something had entered his space. It was as if the primeval, reptilian center in his brain had fired off the fight-or-flight signal. He started to turn around and his right hand started to move toward his holster when Kadah snarled at them.

"Stop! I will kill you if you move! Raise your hands in the air, both of you!"

Bronson stopped in mid-turn and raised his hands. Tad tried to control his heart rate as he raised his hands. He estimated the man was no more than fifteen feet behind them. He wondered what their chances were of spinning off in opposite directions and charging the attacker.

"That's better," said Kadah. "There's a car next to the cabin. Walk slowly toward it and, when you're beside it, spread your legs and arms and lean into the car."

"We're FBI. Don't be foolish, this place is surrounded and ..."

"Shut up!" Kadah hissed. "Just do as you are told."

They spread-eagled against Kadah's car. He kept his gun on them while patting them down with his left hand. He felt Tad's armored vest and saw the "FBI" on Bronson's windbreaker. This meant the federal agents must be in Nashville as well.

Hoping that Kadah was momentarily distracted while frisking Tad, Bronson risked moving his left hand enough to press the transmit button on the walkie-talkie clipped to the front of his windbreaker.

Then he spoke again. "I have agents all around this property. You can't escape and harming us will not help your situation."

Kadah considered for a few seconds whether taking them hostage would allow him to escape. He knew that even if he could use hostages to get away from the lake, they would be the subjects of a tremendous man-hunt with no chance of his getting back to Egypt. Besides, he told himself, in the jihad, his duty was to fight and never to surrender. And, if the black man were lying and the two of them had come alone, he could still carry out Mafousi's orders and sink their bodies in the lake. They had already told him the most important fact: Madison was working with the FBI and they too must now suspect Mafousi. Kadah realized he would have trouble dragging the bodies of these two large men down to the boat and decided to improvise.

"Quiet!" he hissed and started to search Bronson. He felt Bronson's gun and radio and withdrew them. He put the Glock in his waistband and the radio in his pocket. He also found handcuffs on Bronson's belt. Moving quickly before Tad realized what was happening, he snapped one cuff on Tad's left ankle. As he reached for Bronson 's right ankle, Bronson gave as strong a backward kick as he could manage from his awkward leaning position.

Kadah took a heel to his cheek and reeled backward. Before Bronson and Tad could charge, he fired at Bronson and hit his leg. Then Kadah angled his gun to cover Tad. Bronson pitched forward grabbing his leg and lay between them. Tad stopped in his tracks, his fists balled and fury in his eyes. Kadah knew he had to change his plan again. He would kill the black man and make Madison carry his body to the boathouse. He looked at Madison.

"Drop your pants! Then lie face down over there until I tell you to move."

Tad complied, thinking their back-up would have missed them at the tavern by now and should arrive any minute. As soon as Tad was on the ground, Kadah pointed his gun at Bronson's head. His finger tightened on the trigger. There was the soft "phtt" sound of a silencer and the gun flew out of Kadah's hand as a wet, red circle appeared on the right side of his chest. He ran with a staggering series of lurches around the corner of the cabin.

Julia broke from the ferns beside the driveway and knelt beside Bronson. He appeared to be in shock and looked at her with great puzzlement. Tad had pulled up his pants and was on his feet starting after Kadah.

"Wait!" cried Julia. "He still has your friend's weapon. We'll go together, but first we must call an ambulance!"

The two agents from Atlanta waited only five minutes for Bronson to arrive before they decided to head for the cabin. The short-range radios usually had a range of only a mile, but they turned theirs on as soon as they left the tavern. A quarter of a mile later, they heard Bronson saying he had the place surrounded. Their tires squealed as they accelerated down the county road and veered onto Wilderwood Lane.

Tad asked Bronson for the phone number of McNertheny's dispatcher. Bronson was in shock and unable to remember it, but he looked at Tad and said, "glove compartment, in the car."

Tad ran to where they had left the car. He knew

the FBI dispatcher could route the nearest EMTs to them. Julia stayed with Bronson and used her blouse to make a tourniquet for his leg. Then she helped Bronson move off the road. She stood guard with her gun drawn in case there were other conspirators in the cabin that Kadah could summon to the attack. Bronson felt weak and on the verge of losing consciousness, but he wanted to speak to her.

"And you must be my guardian angel. Do you have a name, angel?"

Julia knew this was the time, perhaps past the time, for full disclosure. "Julia Bergman. Mossad, at your service. I see you're FBI."

"Mossad! I'll be damned! I'm Russ Bronson." He blinked and fought to continue. "I run … FBI office in Portland, Oregon. You people are … on this guy … too?"

"Yes. We've been investigating this man's boss for several months."

"The fat man? Mafousi?"

"Yes. Georgia's a long way from Oregon, I think."

"That's so …." Bronson started to shiver violently and his speech turned into a mumble.

Tad found the number in the glove compartment and reached McNerthney's dispatcher on his cell phone. The dispatcher forwarded Tad through to a fire station in Calhoun, Georgia. An ambulance was on its way. He was running back down the road when he saw a speeding car approaching. He stepped further toward the center of the road and waved his arms. The car was already slowing and Tad was silhouetted in its lights. The driver braked to a halt at number 163. Tad ran up to stand beside the vehicle.

The passenger side window moved down two inches. "What do you want?"

"If you're the agents from Atlanta, Russ Bronson's been shot! I was with him. I'm Tad Madison."

"We're the agents," a voice from within said. "Where is he?"

"Right down this driveway almost a hundred feet. The terrorist who wounded Bronson has been shot and ran away, but, right now, we aren't sure where he is."

"We'll see you there," the voice said and the car turned into the driveway.

Tad arrived seconds behind the agents who were already kneeling on either side of Bronson with their guns drawn. The men from Atlanta introduced themselves as agents Durgmore and Collins. Julia said she was with Israeli Intelligence. She also said she wanted to locate Kadah. This led to a low-voiced discussion on how they could best protect Bronson, clear the cabin, and chase down a wounded, armed Kadah. Before their discussion was finished, the roar of the bass boat's engine broke the stillness of the night. Julia, Tad and Collins ran toward the shore, momentarily heedless of the risk of not searching the cabin first. As they stood on the narrow beach, they thought they could see a figure slumped over the control console of the boat as it vanished in the gloom.

"Shit! We can't cover this whole lake! We don't even know how big it is or where roads touch the shoreline," said Collins.

"You could get local law enforcement to cordon off the entire lake area," offered Julia.

"Yeah, a full court press," said Tad.

Kadah was bleeding heavily. It had taken every bit of his remaining strength to push open the boathouse doors. He was sure he was going to die and would not need the pill in his pocket. But his duty was to call Mafousi. He dialed the number and Mafousi answered. "I've been shot. I'm hurt bad. Madison was with the FBI. They know about you. You must … " Everything was turning into a red blur. He could barely feel the boat's wheel in his hand. Was that the shoreline ahead? The red turned to gray and the gray turned to black.

Mafousi pushed the phone to his ear. "Yes, Kadah! Are you there?" The line went dead.

Tad, Julia and Collins could still hear the muffled roar of the boat. They had to return to Bronson, and Collins needed to use the radio to call the local sheriff. It seemed unlikely anyone was left in the cabin, but clearing it would be a further priority. The three of them spaced themselves out and, crouching low, gave the cabin a wide berth as they headed back to where Bronson lay. They made it past the cabin and were nearly to Bronson when an explosion echoed across the water. They turned to look toward the lake.

"The boat?" Durgmore questioned.

"Probably. He may've been wounded more seriously than I thought and just lost control near the far shore," said Julia.

"We still need the sheriff's help. I suppose it's

even conceivable that he torched the boat to create a diversion," added Collins.

Bronson was conscious again, but in obvious pain. Julia reached over to shake Tad's hand. "Well we've seen each other in our underwear and we're obviously working on the same side, but who exactly are you?"

Tad grinned. "Tad Madison. I got involved in this whole mess back in Portland when terrorists killed my best friend. Russ Bronson knew I had been with the Bureau years before and contracted with me to be a consultant to the FBI. One thing led to another and here I am on a foggy night in Georgia!"

"I see," said Julia. "So you're some sort of a criminalist or a specialist on terrorism? Or a profiler?"

Tad grinned again. "Well, back in the day, I had a stint on the FBI's Joint Task Force for Counter-Terrorism. Now, in between the times these nice folks have tried to kill me, I live a quiet life in Oregon running my own book store."

"I'm impressed, but it's a long way from Portland to here and how did that happen?"

"My friend's murder pushed me back into investigator mode and that led to working for the FBI."

"And these are the same terrorists?"

"Well, we think Mafousi is the brains behind the Portland attempt to kill thousands of people by introducing a deadly virus into the food at a national conference. And we've tracked him to Nashville."

In the distance, they could hear a siren growing ever louder. Agent Collins was already on his car radio calling the Gordon County Sheriff. Using a portable scrambler, Julia placed a call to the Israeli embassy and spoke in Hebrew for several minutes.

She finished that call and was about to call Aaron Shevlin when the ambulance arrived. The EMTs jumped out and immediately attended to Bronson. Julia's tourniquet had largely stanched his bleeding, but they nevertheless gave Bronson an IV to supply fluids. Tad hovered nearby. The lead EMT stood up and looked at Tad.

"We think he's going to make it and, with any luck, he won't lose the leg," he said.

Tad asked, "Where are you going to take him?"

"The Providence hospital in Chattanooga. We have the phone number in the truck and I'll give it to you before we leave."

A minute later, they lifted Bronson onto a wheeled litter and loaded it into their ambulance.

Tad stood beside the open rear doors and said, "Listen, Russ, you hold on. The FBI needs you! Hell, the whole country needs people like you!"

Julia too wished Bronson well. He looked up at her and forced himself to try to be coherent.

"Thanks again. His bullet had my name on it. Isn't every day … a man gets his life saved by a beautiful Mossad operative!"

Julia smiled. "It was an honor, Mr. Bronson."

As the ambulance drove away, the four of them formulated a plan for entering and searching the cabin. After optimizing their own safety in the face of possible resistance, they assessed a legal issue.

"I'm concerned that we might no longer be in 'hot pursuit' of Kadah," said Durgmore.

"But, look," said Collins, "we can't be positive that it was he who left in the bass boat. It could have been an accomplice instead of Kadah."

"Yeah, that sounds convincing enough to me," replied Durgmore. "The U.S. Attorney ought to be able to convince a judge that our entry into the cabin was in 'hot pursuit'."

"What's the big deal about this 'pursuit'?" Julia asked.

"Well, at this moment we have no warrant and we're about to enter a dwelling without the occupant's permission. Suppose we find something incriminating in plain sight once we get in. The court might not let the prosecutor use what we found in evidence unless the prosecutor could justify our entry as an exception to the warrant requirement. We can make an entry if we are chasing a person we reasonably believe to have committed a felony."

"Got it, I think," said Julia with a grin.

Durgmore glanced toward the cabin. "Tad, you're unarmed so you stay back by this car. Here's my jack knife. If you hear shooting or the sound of resistance from the cabin, knife a couple of their tires and run like hell. I'll kick in the front door. Collins, you do the same at the back. Julia, cover the side that has those larger windows."

They carried out Durgmore's plan flawlessly only to find the cabin deserted. They saw nothing out in the open that looked like incriminating evidence. They unplugged the radio and secured the entire property as a federal crime scene. Collins unplugged the telephone and its answering machine and placed it in an evidence bag. Later, with warrant in hand, the entire cabin would be examined by an FBI forensic team.

Finally, there was a moment for Julia and Tad to

compare notes on a professional level. "So the FBI had Mafousi's hotel room bugged also?" Julia asked.

"Not to my knowledge, no."

"But then why were you here?"

Tad told her of the cluster of phone calls to the cabin and how suspicious the identity trail had seemed. "So you and your partner had bugged Mafousi's room?"

"Off the record, yes. And we heard them discussing a hand-off of important information to take place here at nine this evening. My instructions from my lead were to just observe and to not directly intervene. Now, I think it was a set-up designed by Mafousi. They lured me down here to kill me!"

"I'm not so sure about that," said Tad. "Any reason to believe they knew you had them under surveillance?"

"No. Nothing back home. Over here, I made small talk with this Kadah in the exhibit hall one day, but I think he was too busy staring at my body to make me as a counter-terrorism agent."

"I believe you're right about this whole business being a set-up, but I think it could have been intended for me. They must have discovered your bug and assumed I was back in play. Though how they knew I was in Nashville, I don't know. Bronson has kept me pretty much on the sidelines. I registered under a different name and these guys have never seen ..." Tad frowned in thought. "Unless... Unless...You know, they faxed a photo of some kind to Mafousi at his hotel in Philadelphia. I'm wondering if it could have been a picture of me."

"Yes, I can see that as a possibility. Thank God I was already staking out the cabin when you guys arrived! I thought at first you were the man from whom Kadah was to receive the information. Only when he ambushed you and I heard Bronson say he was FBI did I figure out you were the good guys."

Tad's first call to the FBI dispatcher had been so focused on getting aid for Bronson that he simply told the man to patch him through to the nearest ambulance saying that he would call in a report to McNertheny as soon as they had cleared the area. He smiled at Julia. "I'm damn glad you got us sorted out! Now I've got to call the FBI agent who's running the show in Nashville. Mafousi will probably be expecting a report any minute from Kadah. The FBI will want to move in on him and they'll have to move quickly."

They both reached for their cell phones.

# TWENTY-EIGHT

**M**AFOUSI LAID THE PHONE DOWN. KADAH HAD NOT been able to tell him how he had been shot. Mafousi could not be sure that Kadah had not been captured and made to talk. Something had caused the call to end prematurely, but, even if Kadah was dead, the FBI would now be closing in. He had considered such an eventuality days ago and he knew that now was the time for him to put his escape plan into action.

Four years ago, in a Sybaritic mood, he had extended his United States trip for a week's stay at Reverson's. This exclusive spa was a gated resort for heavy men. It was not a "fat farm" in the sense that it offered weight-loss programs. On the contrary, it was a haven full of indulgences for its guests. Gourmet meals were served. One could relax beside the pool, play chess, poker, or croquet with other oversize guests, enjoy massages and therapeutic baths, listen to string quartettes, or watch films in the resort's small theater. He suspected that a few of the guests were gay, but this was not a purposeful aspect of Reverson's. In fact, he knew from experience that discreet arrangements could be made to have a beautiful young woman share one's room for an evening.

Reverson's did not advertise in travel magazines

and was unknown to most travel agents. Word of mouth was quite sufficient to keep its rooms filled. Mafousi remembered that when he stayed there previously, he had used an alias, Daniel Mellini. He had also paid cash. Interestingly, his method of payment had raised no eyebrows. He had made this year's reservation from Philadelphia and had booked a week starting the second day of the NACC trade show. If all had gone smoothly, he would have called in to say he was delayed a day and would arrive on Friday. Kadah would have flown back to Cairo and Mafousi would have enjoyed almost a week of western decadence and self-indulgence. But, after seeing Madison and setting the trap, he had decided not to delay his arrival. He dialed the Reverson's number on his satellite phone.

"This is Mr. Mellini. I'm sorry that I did not arrive this afternoon. I have been delayed. I ran into an old acquaintance in Nashville and we decided to have dinner. Is your car still available at this hour?"

"Yes, of course, Mr. Mellini. We were hoping everything was all right, but your room was held for you. Where and when may we pick you up?"

Mafousi gave detailed directions and asked for a pickup in forty-five minutes. He added one change of clothes and his toiletries to his large briefcase. The hotel had his credit card number and at this point, his personal safety was far more important than his leaving without closing out his bill. Besides, it would be better, when the FBI came looking, if the hotel records showed him as still in residence. He stepped into a taxi waiting at the lobby entrance. It was quite possible, he thought, that he was under surveillance. He gave the cab driver the name of a good restaurant on the east side.

Agent Brad Severs of the Knoxville team spotted

Mafousi as he crossed the lobby. McNertheny had arranged with the hotel that his people's cars could be parked in reserved spaces at strategic points around the hotel. Severs radioed his sighting to the dispatcher and headed for his car. The dispatcher announced that McNertheny had assigned two other agents to follow in cars behind Severs.

After a twenty-minute drive, Mafousi's cab stopped in front of The Hermitage Steak House. Severs watched him enter and radioed confirmation to the dispatcher and the other two agents. The agents parked their cars and agreed that two of them would enter the restaurant to keep Mafousi under direct observation.

Mafousi asked for a table away from the small combo playing in the front. He told the waiter who escorted him to the table that he was expecting a friend and also asked him the location of the men's room. Mafousi had been to the restaurant before and he knew that the kitchen opened off the same hallway that led to the lavatories. Down the hallway and out of sight of other late-evening diners, he pushed open the door to the kitchen. He strode past the surprised chefs toward the door to the outside. "Hey, sir, can I help you?" one of the chefs asked sharply.

"I, I'm feeling light-headed. I just need some fresh air."

The man was sympathetic and did not question that Mafousi still wore his coat and carried a brief-case. "Oh, sure. Want me to come with you?"

"No. Thanks. I'll be fine. I must have hurried too much getting here. Just didn't want to make a scene inside."

"No problem."

Mafousi stepped through the door into the alley.

The Reverson's car was waiting there as he had requested. The car was unmarked as he knew it would be. Discretion in all things was a hallmark of Reverson's. He settled into the comfortable back seat of the Lincoln Town Car and affably greeted the driver. "I appreciate your meeting me this way. Just finished supper with a business associate. Now our business is finished and it's none of his damn business where I'm headed."

"Certainly, sir. Understood."

———

Severs scanned the restaurant. Nothing. He walked through the bar area. Still nothing. He checked the men's room. "Shit!" he said to himself. He motioned to the other agent to go back to the maitre d' hotel's podium.

"We were supposed to meet a gentleman here. We're a little late, but we don't see him. He is, ah, shall we say, rather stout."

"Oh, yes. He said he was meeting someone. We showed him to a table in the back." He looked toward the back wall and frowned. "That's odd. He was there a minute ago."

"Is there a back door?" asked Severs.

"Well yes, but ...."

"No buts," said Severs flashing his FBI credentials. "Where the hell's this back door?"

"Right down that hallway and then through the kitchen."

The two agents sprinted through the tables and burst into the kitchen. "Has a fat man been through here?" Severs demanded.

"Yeah, less than two minutes ago. Said he felt sick and needed some air."

They ran past the cooks and a gawking waiter. The alley was empty except for a dumpster. Severs lifted the lid and peered inside. "Hellfire! He's pulled the old in-the-front-out-the-back on us. Must've had an accomplice back here with a car!"

The other agent said, "We had a mix-up as to which one of us was supposed to cover the back. We got it sorted out, but we just didn't figure he'd get out so fast. McNertheny's gonna spit nails!"

Severs said he would go around the block on foot to see if anyone had noticed a car leaving the area. The other agent cut back through the restaurant to hail the agent in the third car. Just as he opened the car door and started to tell what had happened, the radio crackled to life. The dispatcher said, "Mac's orders are to pick him up now. We just heard from Carter Lake. His sidekick ambushed Bronson. Shot him and maybe got away. Mac says we're through watching!"

Severs picked up the microphone. "I've got bad news here too."

⁓

Tad drove from Carter Lake to the hospital in Chattanooga. The trauma surgeon finally entered the waiting room and took off her green mask. "Hello," she said with a weary smile. "I'm Dr. Velstadt. Your friend is going to be okay. He lost some blood and the bullet damaged soft tissue, but it missed bones and arteries. He was lucky there. In a few weeks, he'll be as good as new."

"Can I see him?"

"Not now. He'll be in the recovery room for another hour and you should probably wait until mid-day."

"His family?" Tad realized he had never heard Bronson speak of his family.

"We didn't have much time to explore that. He said his wife had died some years ago of cancer. He did give us a number to notify his son in San Jose. My understanding is, the son's coming on the first flight out in the morning."

"Thanks, Doctor. I'm really glad he's out of danger. I have to return to Nashville tonight, but I'll call in tomorrow."

After the doctor left, Tad was alone in the waiting room. He poured himself a cup of black coffee and punched in Davi's number on his cell phone. It would be only ten-thirty on the West Coast. He had never loved her more than at that moment and he needed to tell her that.

⁓

It was two-thirty in the morning when a grim-faced McNertheny shook Tad's hand at his hotel-suite-command center. "Just after you called in from the lake, we lost Mafousi! He gave us the slip at a restaurant for cripes sake!"

"Have you heard from the other Mossad agent?"

"Yes. Aaron Shevlin. He's with us here. I'll introduce you in a minute. The big shots in D.C. are plenty pissed with the Mossad for working their investigation without clearing it with us first, but Shevlin seems like a pretty straight guy. They had no idea we had an interest in Mafousi. Tonight, he's told us a lot more about Mafousi than we knew before. Sounds like he could be a big player on the terrorist game board."

"So what was Mafousi's purpose in coming here?" Tad asked. "Hard to believe it was just to sell a few cement mixers!"

"I agree. Maybe just to look over the shoulder of the guys Bronson got in Portland, but Tennessee seems too far away for that. He might as well have stayed in Egypt. Shevlin thinks he could be running other sleepers in the States besides in Portland. And remember that Rudi guy we interrogated? He said he heard his local boss, Najev, say something about 'another event' coming on the east coast. Maybe he was bringing personal instructions or even more pathogens."

"Any word about the bodyguard?" asked Agent Novitsky.

"Yes," responded McNertheny. "The Atlanta agents, working with a county sheriff, found the bass boat burned to a crisp after hitting a rock outcropping on the far side of the lake. They found Kadah's body next to the boat. Burned some too, but they said it looks like he died from a wound. Exsanguination." Tad looked puzzled. "Coroner-speak for he 'bled out' from a gunshot wound."

"Suppose Shevlin's right. Did your people find anything in Mafousi's room or the booth?"

"Well, almost nothing. They found Shevlin's bug and, in the hotel's safe, in Mafousi's box, we found a device to detect bugs."

"That figures. Julia Bergman – Shevlin's partner – thought the trap was for her, but I believe they somehow knew I was here and thought I put the bug in their room and wanted to ambush *me*. Anything useful from your ceiling camera over the booth?"

"Nothing was passed to anyone except business cards. We missed the first couple but, after that, we had an agent discreetly interview everyone who got a card. All the people we talked to seemed like bona fide attendees, but we asked for their cards anyway. The lab checked them for microdots, but nothing turned up."

"And no Near Eastern contacts?"

"Well, Aaron had Julia check out a Greek man, but there was nothing there. That leaves only the man who bought the mixer. It was hard to tell from the camera angle, but he could have been of Near Eastern extraction."

"Hmm," mused Tad stroking his chin. Then his head snapped up. "That's it! Like the Purloined Letter! Don't hide it in a concealed place where trained searchers will eventually find it. Hide it right out in the open and let everyone take it for granted!"

"I see where you're going. It's the effing cement mixer! That's so big it could even be a dirty bomb! No, wait. I did have a guy make a pass on the booth and the hallway outside their room with a radiation detector. Nothing registered, so it can't be that."

"Well that's a relief!" said Tarvola sardonically. "How about the loading-dock area? Any security cameras out there?"

"Yeah, I'm pretty sure there are." McNertheny looked at Tarvola. "Carrie, check with hotel security. I want to see what's on their camera disks for the loading area this afternoon."

"I'm on it, sir," Tarvola said as she hurried out of the room.

Twelve minutes later, she was back, a little flushed from running. "I have something, Sir! A white pickup. Tennessee license RRG 729. I'll check with the Tennessee State Police in a second, but I'm thinking the RR could mean it's a rental."

"Good work! Even a rental should lead to a name and address."

Tarvola went to the adjoining room to make two calls, then returned, frowning. "Well, it was an Avis truck all right, but it was turned back to the Nashville office at six-twenty-five P.M. That makes it look like the delivery was local, but get this: the driver's license was a Florida license showing the car-renter living in Orlando."

Tad started thinking out loud. "Maybe the license is a fake and the delivery was local. Or, maybe the license is good, but they've switched tow trucks or transferred it to someone else either in state or out of state. Or, both the license was fake *and* they've taken it out of state. Is there a sales tax in this state?"

McNertheny answered, "Yes. You're thinking there'll be a tax remittance slip for the mixer?"

"Something like that. I'm guessing they'd want everything to look as normal as possible, especially yesterday afternoon when they probably still thought they could skate once they removed me."

"Well, we didn't find a copy of anything like that in Mafousi's room or the booth," offered Agent Adderly who had just joined the group. "He must have taken his order book with him when he fled. The fucker is not dumb!"

Tad turned to Tarvola who was still with them. "When did you say the truck was returned?"

"Six-twenty-five last night."

"So it was away from here for about an hour-and-a-half. If we put the Avis office on the map and assume he would not want to exceed the speed limits – adjusted for inside the city and outside – we could get a pretty fair approximation of the furthest he could go to deliver the mixer or make a switch."

"I like it!" said McNertheny. "But that still could be a hopelessly large area."

"I'm kind of intrigued by the Florida license, said Tad. "Even a fake license is likely to be obtained in one's home state. That makes me think…"

Agent Adderly approached and interrupted. "I was helping Carrie on the rental truck thing. I just checked with Florida State Police. Their computer says the name on that license belongs to a guy named Franklin who died six months ago!"

"Thanks! I'm more and more thinking that you are right about the cement mixer, Tad," said McNertheny. "That transfer and delivery seems a little too opaque to have been an innocent sale."

Novitsky chimed in, "I'd bet the mixer is heading to Florida as we speak. But we have to figure out how they're hauling it and where they made the switch."

Tarvola said, "Once it's light, we can get choppers up. Shouldn't be that hard to spot."

"That's true," said Tad thoughtfully. "So why would they take so much trouble at this end only to face that risk on a long drive?"

"They're going to stick to back roads? Driving only in darkness? Or maybe lay low around here for a few days before they start out?" wondered McNertheny.

"Logical enough, but somehow I don't think so,

Agent McNertheny," said Tad. "Especially if Mafousi has gone to ground. If they are sleepers and they need whatever is in this cement mixer, they'll have a good cover or front wherever they're from. Seems to me that they'll want to get out of this 'hot zone' as fast as possible and get to where they and the mixer won't attract attention."

"I see your point," McNertheny conceded. "I also have to admit that until we get any better leads, watching the main roads is the best we can do. Incidentally, the troops from D.C. will be arriving in about an hour so we will have more people to put in the field. And I'll ask Washington to call the Atlanta and Miami offices to get more bodies on the cement mixer part of it."

Something – he could not put his finger on exactly what – had been bothering Bronson for the last few minutes and he only half listened to McNertheny saying he would seek help in Florida. Suddenly he looked at the agent who had traced the driver license. "Agent Tarvola, did you say the dead man's name was Franklin?"

"Yeah, Richard Franklin."

"I haven't had time to tell you, but our team in Portland ran a check on out-going phone calls from the furniture importer where most of the terrorists worked. To make a long story short, a cluster of calls were to the Carter Lake cabin and the cabin was rented by someone using the name Richard Franklin!"

"Well that just about ices it!" said McNertheny. "And they all tie back to our friend Mafousi."

Aaron walked into the room and joined the group. McNertheny introduced him to Tad.

"Your partner saved our lives down there!"

"She's the best! Sorry we didn't all talk to each

other sooner. Might have made it less messy. Just now I heard you talking about a cement mixer. Like everyone else, I was preoccupied with this Carter Lake business and I forgot to mention that I got the license on the truck towing the mixer."

"Good thinking! Agent Tarvola here also got it from their security cameras."

They compared numbers and verified that they matched. Then they told him the truck had already been returned.

"I see," said Aaron. "Opens up quite a few possibilities. Agent McNertheny, what's going on regarding Mafousi, if I may ask?"

"You certainly can. But first tell us what you know from your work in Egypt."

"We learned that Mafousi is a businessman who's supposed to be very knowledgeable about the pricing of new and used construction equipment. He is secretive and has a lot of security for his office and home. He prays at a fairly radical mosque and travels abroad quite a lot. We had a tail on him once and he eluded my agents with some elementary tradecraft so he's sneaky and doesn't like being watched. But, most importantly – and this is highly classified – he's directly implicated in supplying the money to buy a car-bomb that killed two Mossad agents!"

"Good Lord! If Portland is any indication – and throw in your two agents – he really is an evil fuck!"

"That's how we see it, too," replied Aaron. "Now I'm very interested to hear what you're doing at this end and if you've got any idea on where he's holed up."

"In due course, Russ and Tad here will fill you in on the Portland business. As for his disappearance from Nashville, we've alerted all the airlines with copies of the photo that Tad saw in Philadelphia and we've covered the train and bus stations here and in Knoxville. We'll also notify the car rental agencies here as soon as they open. Obviously, our perimeter is not air-tight. It'll get better as we get more agents, but that's all I can say for now."

"What if he has a rental car already?" asked Aaron.

"Opryland issues its guests temporary decals for their car windows so they can leave them in the hotel lot. Mafousi's man Kadah only asked for one. So we're quite certain they had only the one car and that's the one we found at the lake place."

"Sir, I'll get started on that map of possible destinations Mr. Madison was proposing," said Tarvola. Receiving an emphatic nod from McNertheny, she left the group.

"Staying with my hypothesis that they are moving now and heading for somewhere in Florida," said Novitsky, "I'm still bothered by why they'd take the risk of being seen – no matter what vehicle they're using to tow it – with this cement mixer. And the more I think about it, the more I think they'd somehow hide the trailer. Camouflaging it or disguising it seems like too much work, would take too long, and probably wouldn't succeed anyway, at least not for a close-up inspection. So they have to have loaded it inside another truck."

"Makes good sense, Saul," agreed McNertheny.

"Since there are many hundreds of trucks on the road, maybe we should start by figuring out where they made the switch and see if anyone saw them," added Tad.

They walked over to the couch and sat down to brainstorm possibilities. Tarvola joined them with a road map in hand. "This is a little crude, but I used sixty miles per hour as the average speed. With a ninety-minute leave-to-return time, that's about one hundred miles or fifty each way. Once I got this maximum radius, I drew two circles using the Opryland Hotel as one center and the Avis office as the other."

She spread the map on the coffee table and they all leaned inward to study the overlap of the circles. McNertheny tapped the table with his knuckles. "If they had rented another house with a fence around it or a good-sized shed somewhere, we'll never find the place. So let's focus on things we have a chance of narrowing down. What if they accelerated the delivery once they figured out Tad was here? In that case, they may not even have planned on doing a switch. So suddenly they had to improvise. They may even have been willing to take a little risk in doing the switch in the open. But they'd at least have wanted to choose a place where leaving a truck parked wouldn't have attracted a lot of attention. Somewhere, in the darkness of early evening, they load that mixer into a truck."

"So, truck stops?" asked Aaron.

"Possibly. Maybe even the 'trucks' side of a rest stop," said Tad.

"But both of those places are only on the interstates, so they'd have to risk being on main roads until they made the switch," said McNertheny.

Tad looked back at the map. "So what other possibilities do they have, hmmm? Golf courses? Parks? Abandoned barns? Barns don't show up on maps and

I don't see them having the time to go hunting for one. That leaves parks and golf courses."

"And maybe school parking lots," added Tarvola.

"So how many are there inside these arcs?" asked Aaron.

They started counting as McNertheny took notes. When they finished, he summarized. "Three golf courses, nine parks, thirteen schools, plus three likely truck stops and one rest area on the freeways."

Aaron said, "If there's more than one driver, they already have crossed the Florida line. We've got to work fast. There won't have been any witnesses at schools that late in the day. Same for the golf courses. You're spread so thin, I wouldn't bother with the schools or golf courses. The parks, truck stops and rest areas are better bets."

"We will divide up and try our luck," said McNertheny. There are five agents still here. We need the dispatcher to stay here to run communications. But I'll go and I just heard that Tel Aviv and Washington have cleared a joint Mossad-FBI operation on this so you're included, Aaron and Julia. That makes four two-person teams. I know how Bronson felt about you as a consultant and I've heard about your days with us, but I can't have you out there alone and unarmed, Tad. Will you stay here with Dispatch? Or grab some shuteye?"

"That's okay. I understand. I'll hang out with your dispatcher, at least for a while … then maybe a cat nap."

They divided up the thirteen sites, and Tarvola tutored Julia and Aaron on using the FBI radios. McNertheny gave them each one of his cards on which he wrote that they were authorized to act on the FBI's behalf.

Tarvola was assigned to cover the three Public Use Areas on J. Percy Priest Lake. Following the idea that the terrorists would take the mixer to Florida, she decided to try the one that lay closest to a southern route first. This was the Elm Hill Public Use Area. At ten minutes before two in the morning, Tarvola knew that finding anyone to talk to would be a long shot. On arriving, the first thing she saw was that a pivoting pole had been lowered and padlocked to block the entrance to the parking area. Tarvola could see a road branching off to the left with a sign marked "Private". She wondered if there might be a caretaker's or park host's cabin down that road. She locked her car and ducked under the pole and took the left branch. Less than a hundred feet down the road she could make out the loom of an RV. There was a sign reading "Park Host" on its side. Sincerely hoping she was not going to badly frighten the occupant, she knocked on the door.

After a full minute, she thought she heard someone moving inside. For a brief moment, Tarvola conjured up the possibility that the terrorists had planted a conspirator inside this park. Thinking more realistically, she knew even the best planners could not have sprinkled their terrorist troops around every city in America just in case they were needed some day for a vehicle switch. In a calmer state, she heard an older man's voice coming from the other side of the door. "Who the hell is it? The park's closed! It's two in the morning!"

"I know and I'm very sorry to have to disturb you.

I'm here on FBI business and I must ask you a couple of questions."

"Well I suppose I could talk to you in the morning, but not now."

"I'm afraid this is urgent. Very urgent. In fact, it's a matter of national security."

"So how do I know you're FBI?"

"I have a business card and I can also give you the FBI's phone number in Knoxville. Or you can ask information for the number. Call there and they can patch you through to the chief agent in Nashville named McNertheny who's coordinating this operation."

"Hell, I'm awake now. You can ask any questions you want through the door, but I'm not gonna open it up this time of night."

"That's fine, sir. I need to know if you happened to see anybody come in here yesterday afternoon towing a good size cement mixer."

There was a short silence. "Well, yeah, as a matter of fact, I did. Came in late, startin' to git dark. After a few minutes, I walked down the road a ways and watched 'em for a while, but they didn't see me. Jokers were trying to get the mixer up a ramp. Damn near a clown act! I was almost ready to offer to help, but I wasn't sure it mightn't have been stolen. They seemed sort of jumpy and they were working pretty fast, so I just let 'em be. They left maybe ten minutes later."

Tarvola felt like she'd won the lottery. "You said they were trying to get it up a ramp. Did you see the truck?"

"Weren't no truck. They had one of them boxy trailers that people tow fancy cars or racing cars around in."

"I see. What color was it?"

"Oh, it was white. And the van they pulled it with looked kinda dark green."

"Did you get the license plate?"

"Naw. It was getting pretty dark and I wasn't that interested. I think it mighta been a Florida plate though. I seen quite a lot of them coming through here."

"What about the men? Can you describe them?"

"Well, not too tall. Sounded like maybe they had accents from somewhere. One had a ball cap on. The other was dark haired."

"Did you notice the time?"

"Well it was before six. I usually watch the news at six and it was just starting when I got back inside."

"How about the vehicle they used to tow it to the park?"

"I couldn't see it very well from here. Through the trees, it looked light colored and I think it was a pickup."

"Great. Thanks for your cooperation. May I have your name?"

Again, a slight pause. "I guess so. Jennings, Dave Jennings. So what's going on? These guys spies or somethin'?"

"Not exactly. But we're very interested in them. Thanks again, Mr. Jennings."

Tarvola ran back to the car and called the agent acting as dispatcher at the hotel in Nashville. "I struck pay dirt! Here's how they did it." She explained what Jennings had told her. The dispatcher said he would relay the information to McNertheny and call the others back.

Toudani was getting seriously drowsy. Even drinking coffee when he stopped to put gasoline in the van did not seem to help. It was almost three in the morning. He knew that Al M'afid had wanted him to drive right through, but if he drove off the road and crashed the trailer, that would be far worse. He saw a sign for the turn-off to Lake City. He decided to find a motel and catch two or three hours' sleep. Then he could complete the drive easily. He would not even stop for breakfast. He could be back in Orlando by eight-thirty or nine. Even as he made the decision, his head nodded. He flicked on his turn signal. Lake City it was.

# TWENTY-NINE

TAD HAD BREWED A NEW POT OF COFFEE WHEN THEY reassembled in McNertheny's suite. "Nice work Tarvola!" began McNertheny. "I've alerted the State Police in all of the adjacent states to watch for the green-van-white-box-trailer combination. And between our resources, the Army National Guard, and the Georgia and Florida State Police, we'll have eleven choppers in the air as soon as it's light over the interstates heading for and inside Florida. They'll be watching for any combination involving a white box trailer."

"What about the guy who rented the pickup?" asked Aaron.

"That's not going to be easy," said Tarvola. "He could be local, of course. But if he's an associate of the man with the trailer, he'll have to get back on his own to where? Florida?"

"I've got all the airlines agreeing to detain boarding passengers with Near Eastern appearances long enough to be interviewed by our agents at the airport," put in Agent Novitsky.

Tad frowned. "Bet you'll hear from the civil liberties folks for profiling. What if the interview causes an innocent person to miss his or her plane?"

McNertheny spoke up. "Of course we'll compensate

them in some reasonable way, but damn it, everybody is going to have to learn that the bad guys have very deadly intentions. Deadly for all of us, including Arab folks, here in the United States. Their weapons, their pathogens don't discriminate between races or ethnicities once they're turned loose. To be effective in emergencies like this, we have to play the percentages."

"Point taken," said Tad.

McNertheny turned to Novitsky. "Bus and train stations covered also?"

"Amtrak yes. And we're working on the bus stations. But even with planes and trains we have problems. Remember, Mr. Jennings was not able to give Carrie much of a description."

"Wouldn't he figure to be a little less conspicuous using a bus?" asked Aaron.

"That's so," replied Tad, "but I don't think these people are short on money and, like I said, I'll bet they want to get back to their normal environment as fast as possible. Besides, yesterday, in early evening, their scheme hadn't gone south on them. Maybe they moved up the pickup of the mixer by some hours, but they would not think the airports were going to be watched last night."

"So, Saul," questioned McNertheny, "are we checking passenger lists for Florida destinations on flights that may have already left between seven last evening and when your alert began?"

"Yes, sir," answered Novitsky. "That is what I've asked for and we should have that information from them any time now."

"Good. I suggest you all go to your rooms and get

a few hours of sleep. We'll meet for breakfast here at eight. I'll let you know if there are any developments."

They straggled into McNertheny's suite around eight o'clock. Room service had brought a hearty breakfast to the suite. McNertheny's lined face, his stomach starting to ride over his belt, and his graying hair advertised his fifty-six years. His subordinates knew that his gruff and formal exterior hid a warm and charitable heart. "Mac", as he was known behind his back, expected a lot from his people, but he was always ready to support and advance them. He was still dead tired, though a shower and shave had made him feel less like a zombie. But it was the phone call about half an hour earlier that had really energized him as the others arrived. He greeted Tad with a handshake.

"You and Saul were right on the button! He was heading for Florida. The State Police got him about forty-minutes ago on Highway 441 just south of Ocala. Our agents were in a chopper not far away and they're interrogating him now. His name's Toudani. He voluntarily opened the trailer and there sat the mixer!"

A cheer went up among the group. "What's his story?" asked Tad.

"Predictably, he said he was just a guy whose company got a convention sale price on a piece of equipment they needed for their business. He had a bill of sale. They're holding him as a material witness for the time being. And, as we speak, the wheels are turning to get a FISA court order for a search warrant of the business and his residence and for testing – destructive testing if necessary – the mixer." This brought more cheers from the group.

A phone rang in the next room and Tarvola went

to answer it. Her muffled conversation was followed by the sound of an incoming fax. When she returned, Tarvola held a sheaf of fax pages. "Delta may have something. They gave us the passenger lists of all outbound flights from seven last night forward. But it gets better. One of our agents out at the airport – it was Tony, I think – started calling all the counter personnel who were on duty last night. He asked about Near Eastern-appearing passengers who may've bought their tickets right there. One woman at the counter remembered a guy wanting to get on the last flight to Orlando. It was showing 'sold out' on her computer, but he wait-listed and seemed very relieved when he got on."

"So he's on the passenger list?" prompted McNertheny.

"Yes, Sir. Name's Bafir Nuwali. If we're lucky, that may even be his real name."

The group started chattering excitedly, but McNertheny held up his hand. "Let's not count our chickens. Could just be an ordinary fellow wanting to get home to his family. But you can believe I'll ask the Miami team to check him out from top to bottom. If he's from Orlando, they'll be able to find out where he lives and works. We're told these jihad guys hardly ever confess, but if there's any overlap with Mr. Toudani, either at work or at a mosque, they'll put him under the microscope!"

Julia Bergman knocked on the door and Aaron introduced her around the room. Tad said, "Julia's the one who saved Russ Bronson and me at the lake. Came out of the woods like Special Forces just in the nick of time!" They gave her a round of applause.

"Sorry, I wasn't a few seconds sooner," she said,

"but when I first heard the talk, you were over fifty feet away and I had to move through the underbrush without him noticing me."

"No need to explain yourself," said McNertheny. "We're damn glad you were there! Now let's have some breakfast and talk about Mr. Mafousi."

———

Darius Mafousi was thoughtful and farsighted like the accomplished chess player that he was, but he was also a believer in jihad. So too, he was imbued with an enduring hatred of the West and what he saw as its imperialistic ambitions. A more subtle trait was his stoicism. He still had several thousand U.S. dollars in his money belt, but his avenues of escape were fairly circumscribed. He prayed to Allah that his escape plan would work. If it did not, he knew what he had to do. He reasoned that the conventional portals of departure would be closely watched, especially for the next twenty-four hours. If, as he hoped, they had not already digitized the passport image processing at Philadelphia's ICE checkpoint, they would have no photo to publish on television or in the newspapers. He estimated he could safely bide his time at Reverson's for at least thirty-six hours. He relaxed in the hot tub on the private deck off his room, and went to bed. He found the extra-supportive mattress very comfortable and fell quickly into a sound sleep.

Soon after he awoke, he opened his toilet kit and produced scissors. Twenty minutes later, he appraised his face in the mirror. The goatee and mustache were gone. Only the driver of the Town Car and the night-desk man had seen him with facial hair. By the time they were back on shift, he should be gone. He knew that sooner or later some kind of a description of him would be circulated. Better to change what could be changed, he reasoned.

As soon as he finished dressing, he used the complimentary broadband connection and the in-room computer. There was a slight risk they might think to access the cache memory to see what website he visited, but he had little choice. After a few failed tries, he located the digital yellow pages for McMinnville, Tennessee. Looking under "charter flights," he found the number of a Humber Air Service. He picked up his satellite phone and dialed the number.

"Humber Air Service," said a voice with a soft drawl.

"Hello. This is Daniel Mellini speaking. What kind of aircraft do you fly?"

"Right now, only a Beech Baron. Twin engine. Where do you want to go?"

"This evening I need to go to Fort Lauderdale. Are your pilot and plane certified for night flying? And what's your range?"

"No problem, Sir. We often fly nights. I'm the pilot and I'm fully certified. We can go up to nine hundred miles. Lauderdale's only six-hundred-fifty miles. No problem."

"And your charter fee?"

"Let's see." There was a short pause and Mafousi could picture the man working a hand calculator. "I can take you to Fort Lauderdale for nine-hundred dollars. Remember, I'll have to sleep over there before I return. That's cash up front."

Good, thought Mafousi, he needs the business

and he likes cash. "That should be alright. I'm staying at Reverson's. Do you know the place?"

"I've heard of it. Near Shop Springs isn't it?

"That's correct. I'll throw in another one hundred if you'll pick me up here and drive me to your airstrip."

"Well, I guess I can do that. What time should I be there?"

"Five-forty-five, if you please. There's a gatehouse, but I'll be waiting on the road before you get to the gatehouse. They make a big fuss about letting non-guests in after five." Mafousi made a mental note to give the security person at the gate some story about overnighting – wink, wink – with an old friend, and being back by noon.

"Whatever you say, Mr. Mellini. My name's Terry Humber. I'll see you tonight at five-forty-five."

Mafousi broke the connection and tried to convince himself that the NSA was not listening to his satellite phone calls in real time. During the flight there would be an opportunity to offer Humber more money to entice him into refueling at some small airport with a self-service pump and going instead to The Turk and Caicos Islands. Despite the lethal operations he and his six colleagues organized, Mafousi had a distaste for personal involvement in violence. He would have to "borrow" a steak knife from Reverson's serving pantry, but hoped he would not have to use it to persuade the pilot to agree to the change in flight plans.

Mafousi admired the rich paneling on the walls as he descended the broad staircase to the dining room. It was time for breakfast.

The morning hours dragged on in McNertheny's suite with no further successes. They had three false starts. Two portly men – neither of them Arab-looking – were delayed in their efforts to rent cars as agents rushed to interview them. Agents held a heavy Latino man at the airport for interrogation, but released the man in time for him to catch his flight.

Aaron was particularly distressed with himself that he had not seen Mafousi get in the taxi to go to The Hermitage Steak House. For fear of insulting his new allies, he did not speak his thoughts, but his own instinct would have been to cover that alley immediately. He had lost a target once years ago who had used that gambit, and he had never made the same mistake again.

Tad called the hospital in Chattanooga and was able to speak with Bronson who sounded cheerful though weak. Tad reported Kadah's death and Mafousi's escape. Bronson wanted to strategize, but Tad could sense his new friend's fatigue. As a compromise, Tad quickly summarized the tracking down of the trailer containing the cement mixer and their interest in the two men from Orlando. A nurse arrived to change Bronson's dressing and they ended their call.

McNertheny's men verified through the airlines that Mafousi had booked his return to Cairo from New York on the following Friday. They would monitor those flights and also keep a watch on his room at Opryland, but no one seriously thought a man on the run would return to the hotel or use the tickets. Agents were sent to the Nashville mosque. A few worshipers saw someone of Mafousi's description two days earlier at evening prayers, but the man was a complete stranger and no one remembered talking to him.

At mid-day a call came through from the Miami team saying that Nuwali's company was the owner of the green van and its name was shown as purchaser on the bill of sale for the cement mixer. This was the tie-in between Nuwali and Toudani that they were looking for. Nuwali refused to speak to the agents and demanded a lawyer. Toundani was frightened and had started to talk. He denied knowing Mafousi, but did recognize the picture and said that he knew him as Al M'afid. He was still holding to his story that they had bought the mixer for the company's own legitimate use, despite being confronted with the FBI's knowledge of the swap at the Elm Hill Public Use Area.

McNertheny remembered Aaron had told them that Mafousi had used a work name that sounded a lot like Al M'afid. He passed that information on to the team in Florida. The Miami SAC said they expected the order approving the searches to come through at any time and that they already had both residences and the construction company's premises under twenty-four-seven surveillance.

# THIRTY

ESPITE THE PROGRESS IN FLORIDA, MCNERTHENY WAS frustrated that they had not flushed out Mafousi. Aaron's bleak countenance and Tad's restlessness were not helping either. They debated going public with the photos of Mafousi that Tad had discovered in Philadelphia and Aaron had brought from Egypt. Going public would have to be cleared through Homeland Security they were told, and McNertheny felt his frustration level rise. He favored taking that step and urged FBI Headquarters in Washington to seek that clearance. Between the politics and the fear of starting a panic that seemed to him to permeate the higher echelons of the federal bureaucracy, he feared more time and opportunities would be wasted.

A little before two, Julia said, "Even in a city as large as Nashville, he's got to be somewhat conspicuous. The guy's close to one-hundred-fifty kilos! Unless he's hiding inside some trusted friend's house, there should be some sightings. You now have over twenty additional people working the principal exit terminals and the hotels and motels."

McNertheny answered, "Dammit! Twenty isn't near enough. I've requested thirty more and Washington agreed. They're assembling them now and they should arrive in a couple of hours."

Tad said, "On Julia's point about a friend's house, doesn't this NACC convention move around the country to a different city each year?"

"Yes, I believe so," Tarvola replied. "I heard someone at Opryland saying to a friend that this year was much better than Denver was last year."

"So Mafousi can't have friends or fellow conspirators in all the major cities, " said Tad. "Though he could rent a house, I suppose, or possibly buy a prostitute's time for forty-eight hours and stay at her apartment."

Another agent spoke up, "Not likely. I used to work vice before I joined the FBI. Most working girls, even for money, don't let Johns into their apartments. They try hard to keep some part of their lives private. And the kind that live in their own crib? I don't think Mafousi is that desperate!"

"OK," said Tad, "and in any case, I bet we can rule out a 'trusted friend'."

"And I don't see this guy hitch-hiking his way out of town," added McNertheny.

"The man's devious," continued Tad. "He's surely aware that his size could draw attention. So if he decides not to make a run for it right away, where does he go to ground?" Tad's gaze became distant as he considered his own question. Others shrugged their shoulders or shook their heads. Seemingly oblivious of the silence in the room, Tad continued, "He finds some place where most everyone else is heavy also! Where he's pretty much the norm."

"That's an interesting idea, maybe even the right idea, but where would that be, Tad?"

"I don't know. Weight-loss clinics? Fat farms?" Feeling a little pretentious floating such a far-out theory, he added "sumo wrestling camps?"

The last possibility brought a chuckle from the group, but McNertheny looked interested. "At this point, what've we got to lose? Saul, see what you can dig up on those sorts of places. Let me know if you get a response from anyone that sounds even remotely viable before you take it any further. This Mafousi guy is a flighty old bird and we don't want him tipped off before we get mobilized."

Tad checked his watch. Davi would not be home from the CCC campus for at least another two hours. He could do nothing more around McNertheny's command center so he borrowed a pager and changed into jogging clothes. He ran at a decent pace and was soon warm despite the chill breeze. The trees, almost bare of leaves, gave the landscape a harsh look, especially after what he had seen inside Opryland's tropical atrium. Tad had covered about two miles and had turned to head back when the pager went off. He stopped at a cafe and bummed a friendly patron's cell phone.

Tarvola answered. "Better head back. We've got some interesting news from down south and Saul's discovered something we need to explore further."

"I'll be there in fifteen minutes!"

Entering the suite, Tad grabbed a towel from the bathroom, mopped his face, and walked over to McNertheny. "What's the development from Florida, Mr. McNertheny?"

"The Miami boys got their warrants. First they x-rayed the mixer. Saw something in the double shell. So they're thinking either bricks of heroin or else plastique explosive stuffed inside. The bomb team comes in and drills a small hole in the outer shell. They use a chemical sniffer and an explosives-trained dog for extra measure. Nothing. They don't want to cut it open with a torch, so they use a high-powered, diamond-bladed saw. Inside, they find money. American dollars. Over half a million of 'em!"

"I'll be damned!" said Tad.

"So our Mafousi may be the brains, but this time he was also a mule," said McNertheny. "Now we have to figure out what kind of evil deed that much cash was going to finance. I figure the Miami team will go over every square inch of those premises looking for the answer."

"Agent Tarvola said Saul had something?" Tad asked.

"Yes. Lay it out for all of us, Saul."

Saul Novitsky was a slender man in his early fifties with a Levantine visage. He looked up from reviewing some entries in a pocket notebook. "Well, I learned there are two residential diet clinics in town. Also a spa-slash-fat-farm, but it only caters to women. The two clinics didn't have any new patients admitted in the last twenty-four hours and they require a doctor's referral in any case. But at the second clinic I visited, there was a male nurse who was passing by the admitting desk and heard my question. He sort of hung around the area and when I was through talking with the administrator, he came over to me. Asked if I knew about a place called Reverson's. Said he used to work there as the medical-support person. So I said 'no, tell me about it.' He says it's out in the country about thirty-five miles east of here. Sounds like kind of an exclusive resort, almost a pleasure palace, but get this – it's only guests are fat men!"

"No shit?"

"I tried to find them in the yellow pages. No dice. Finally found a white-page listing in Lebanon. I checked with the Wilson County Sheriff. He confirmed what the nurse told me: very discreet, expensive, and kind of isolated. He said they took over an old estate and really spiffed it up. Thinks they can maybe handle a couple of dozen guests at a time. Rooms in the main house and seven or eight cabanas close in on the grounds."

"This fits another of your 'hypotheses', Tad," said McNertheny. "If he somehow could've heard about it, it sounds like a place he'd pick as a hidey-hole. I want someone to get us a good, detailed map of the area, and then ten of us will go out there. That way, we make the approach on-site instead of by long-distance phone. If this long-shot works, we're there ready to grab him. If he's not there or we learn he's somewhere else, we'll be in constant contact with dispatch and only forty minutes from town."

They did not have great confidence that they would find Mafousi, but all agreed the trip out there was worth the effort. It was five o'clock by the time they had the map and had formulated their strategy for covering the perimeter of Reverson's property. The evening rush hour slowed their travel on the interstate for the first fifteen miles. They could see gently rolling terrain and an occasional horse farm through the gathering darkness. By the time they reached the off-ramp at Lebanon, the sky was dark. A brief rainstorm earlier in the day had moved through to the northeast and they could see a few stars in the evening sky.

A brick fence began on the left side of the road a mile past the village of Spout Springs, A small unlighted sign told them they had arrived. Six of the agents were assigned to cover secondary entrances and a service road that ran along the rear property line. McNertheny, Tad, Aaron, Novitsky and Tarvola would go to the facility through the main entrance. The fence continued back from the road on either side of the driveway. Out of sight from the road and around a curve in the driveway, they arrived at a gatehouse and a closed gate.

Saul powered down his window as the security guard stepped toward them.

"I'm sorry, Gentlemen. We don't allow visitors after five."

Saul produced his FBI credentials. "We need to visit with your manager right now. Please open the gates and inform him we are heading up the drive."

"Well, I don't know. We've never had any problems with the law. Do you have a warrant?"

"There's no problem with Reverson's as such. Unless, of course, we don't receive cooperation. We're here on a matter of urgent national security."

"I see. Well, I'll call the manager and be right back."

"Thank you. And please tell him not to mention our arrival to anyone. Contact the manager directly, if you can. If you have to go through a reception desk or a switchboard, just say you need to reach the manager without explaining why."

They saw the guard on the phone through a window in the gatehouse. His gestures suggested he was trying hard to convey their determination to his boss. He returned with a forced smile. "The manager's name is Charles Hurlbut. He says to drive past the main entrance and stay to the right of the main house. He'll meet you by a side door."

Drawing to a stop at the side door, they saw a remarkably heavy man emerge and descend the four steps to their car. "Gentlemen, I'm Charles Hurlbut. To what do we owe this extraordinary visit?"

McNertheny introduced his group and proffered his identification. "Mr. Hurlbut, do you have an office or a room inside where we can explain this to you in private?"

He led them inside and down a back hallway to his office. One wall featured a built-in cherry bookcase with many books on psychology. A small Miro hung above an antique side-boy on a second wall. A Kermin rug was centered on the red oak floor. The only utilitarian items spoiling the ambiance of old-money luxury, were a computer on a movable table and a wide-drawer file cabinet. Hurlbut stood in front of his mahogany partner's desk and asked, "So, Gentlemen. How can I help?"

McNertheny looked him squarely in the eye and said, "We need to know whether you have any guest using the name Darius Mafousi, staying with you. We have a federal warrant for his arrest. If he's here, he likely would have arrived in the last twenty-four hours."

"And you have reason to believe this man is here?"

"No sir, no particular reason, but we are in the midst of an area-wide man-hunt under my direction," said McNertheny, "and, well, certain things suggest your resort as a possibility."

"He's a large man, then?" asked Hurlbut with a smile.

"Yes, around three-hundred pounds. I can't emphasize enough that this is a dangerous man."

"I see. Alright. We have no one here using that name. We have only had one new arrival in the last twenty-four hours. A gentleman named Mellini was due in yesterday afternoon, but he was late arriving. In fact, I saw in the records this morning that he requested our car to bring him over from Nashville."

"Mellini," McNertheny repeated. "Where exactly did the car pick him up? At the airport?"

"No. It was a little unusual. A restaurant, I believe. Shall I check?"

"Yes please."

Hurlbut reached for a loose-leaf binder marked "Transport" and turned to the last page. "Ah, here it is. The Hermitage Steak House."

Elation showed in all their eyes, but no one spoke. McNertheny produced the photo from an envelope. "Does this Mr. Mellini look like this?"

Hurlbut studied the image. "I only saw him one time, at luncheon, but no. He has no facial hair."

"Look again, if you would, please. Imagine this face without the mustache and goatee."

"Yes, I see what you mean. Yes, it could be him I suppose."

"We'd like to talk with him. What room is he in?"

"Upstairs, room sixteen, in the south wing. This will be terribly embarrassing if there's a mistake. We... we pride ourselves on the privacy, the discretion of Reverson's. Perhaps I should go with you."

"I understand that this is sensitive, but this is a very serious matter. If he is the man we seek, it could become dangerous. You may direct us to the room but, before we confront him, I must ask you to leave.

We will be as diplomatic as we can until we have a confirmed identification one way or the other."

Hurlbut squeezed his large hands together and said. "I see. Well then, I'll have to trust your good intentions, won't I? Either way this turns out, it seems to me this is going to be an unpleasant evening for Reverson's."

Hurlbut led them out of his office and down a hallway to a carpeted staircase. He stopped on a landing where the stairs reversed directions. "Mr. Mellini's room is down the hallway to your right at the top of the stairs. Number sixteen. I'll wait here."

Novitsky knocked on the door of room sixteen. There was no response. McNertheny returned to the landing and asked Hurlbut for a key to the room. Hurlbut winced, but handed him a passkey.

McNertheny's group found no luggage or toiletries inside the room. "All right," said McNertheny grimly, "Get Hurlbut to give us a floor plan and a grounds plan."

Novitsky returned a minute later with a schematic floor plan that McNertheny scanned. He looked up and spoke to Tarvola and Novitsky, "Check the lounge, the library, the card room and the dining room. If he's not in those places, we're going to have to search the entire place and the grounds!" He reached for his radio to inform the agents outside.

"Agent McNertheny," said Tad, "what about asking the gate guard if any of the guests have left since lunch, before we spend time on a search here."

McNertheny scowled at Tad, then shook his head with fatigue and nodded. "Yes. Good idea. Saul, use Hurlbut's phone and let us know right away."

Two minutes later, Novitsky hurried back to Mafousi's room. "The gate guard is supposed to register everybody in and out after five P.M. He has Mellini leaving the place around quarter to six on foot! Gave him a line about overnighting with a girlfriend and back in the morning. Said she was picking him up at the end of the driveway."

"That's it then!" said McNertheny. "Let's get back to the gate house, pronto! Tarvola, you stay with Hurlbut, in case we decide to do the room-to-room search after all. I'll have the people on the perimeter hold position until we can call them off."

The gatehouse guard, who introduced himself as Bill Patterson, seemed awed by the presence of the FBI agents and was obviously pleased to be the center of attention. They showed him the photo.

"Yes, I think that's him. He was clean shaven and he sort of stood off from my window in the shadow, but that could be him."

"Was he wearing a coat?"

"Yeah. A dark top coat."

"Was he carrying anything? Package? Briefcase?"

"I don't remember a package, but he could have had a briefcase."

"Did you see the car that picked him up?"

"Well ... yeah, I got a glimpse of it, I guess."

"You sound unsure."

"Well, you know, I'm not supposed to leave the gate here, but this whole thing was kind of weird. I mean these people come here to leave the outside world behind for a few days. They like the solitude and the company if you see what I mean. So here's this guy leaving and right before their fancy dinner, too."

"So you followed him?" prompted Aaron, impatient with the man's rationalizations.

"Well, let's say I was curious to see if he really had a woman to pick him up. Like I said, the whole business was just unusual. That curve in the drive is just a couple of hundred feet from here. When I got to where I could see the main road, I saw this light colored Jeep, probably a Cherokee. It was maybe fifty feet ahead when it started to pull away. He wasn't anywhere in sight, so I assumed he was inside."

"See the plate?"

"No, I didn't notice it at all."

"Any markings?"

"There was a symbol on the rear panel, kind of a star shape and some writing underneath, three words I think, but it was too dark to read it."

Tad pointed to the counter where a scratch pad and the log book lay. "Mr. Patterson, could you sketch that symbol?"

"Sure. I'm no artist, but I can try."

Staring at the drawing, Aaron said, "a cross of some kind?"

"I didn't draw that so hot. Each arm was sort of tear-drop shaped, I think."

"A snowflake?" Tad wondered out loud. "Oh! A propeller!"

"Yeah, it was kinda like a propeller," returned Patterson.

They looked at each other with sudden under-standing. "Shit!" shouted McNertheny. He's found a plane to charter!"

Tad asked Patterson, "Is there a small airport anywhere around here?"

"None that I know of right around here, but I'm pretty sure they have one at McMinnville."

McNertheny ran to his car, used the radio, and consulted a map. To his team, he said, "They've got about a fifteen minute head start on us. I called both choppers from Nashville to pick us up. Dispatch checked and says there's also an airport at Murfreesboro. So we have at least two to cover. I'll have dispatch call the county sheriffs and the airport towers to stop them from taking off. I'll send one chopper to each airport with three of us in each one. The rest of this team can divide up and travel by cars. McMinnville must be thirty, thirty-five miles from here. Murfreesboro looks closer: probably about twenty miles."

"I wouldn't count on there being a tower at these small airports, Agent McNertheny," offered Tad.

"If they have no towers or if their towers are not manned at night, that'll make it even tougher to stop him. Sonnovabitch, this guy's as slippery as an eel! And, Tad and Aaron, why don't you men call me Mac?"

McNertheny went back to the car and picked up the microphone. Novitsky identified a meadow across the road from the driveway where the helicopters could land. Using the GPS in one of the other cars, they determined the coordinates for McNertheny to radio to the helicopter pilots. They stationed agents with flares in the meadow to aid the pilots in their landings. McNertheny called Tarvola and told her to join them waiting for the choppers.

"It's a shell game," said McNertheny, "but I'm betting on Murfreesboro. It's closer and it looks like a little bigger community. Tarvola, Anderson and I will go there. If the chopper has room for five, Aaron, you come along. Saul will lead the group going to McMinnville. Blix and Wainwright will go with him. Same deal with the seats. If there's room for a fifth, Tad, you go with them."

Eight minutes later, they heard the distinctive sound of helicopters approaching. Each Bell Jet Ranger had a three-person seat behind the pilot and front passenger seat so Tad and Aaron climbed on board. The helicopters were on the ground less than a minute before lifting off. Tad had flown by helicopter several times in the course of his FBI anti-terrorist career, but he did not particularly like the experience. Even wearing earphones, the roar was distracting. In the darkness, they seemed to be buffeting along like a Disneyland thrill ride. Then he remembered that he had not had a moment to call Davi before they left for Reverson's. He realized his life had been lived in the fast lane in recent weeks. Tad was glad to be helping his country and satisfied to – at last – be resolving Paul's murder. Yet, when the adrenaline rush wore off, he knew that to be back with Davi and Wilcao friends and books was what he wanted the most.

———

From the air, McNertheny could see the blinking lights of the two-engine plane on the taxiway. Their helicopter, under his orders, landed on the taxiway in front of the other aircraft. Anderson leaped out and ran toward the plane with a battery-powered megaphone. He wore an FBI windbreaker and pointed to the large letters as he identified himself. He told the pilot to shut down her engines and keep the doors closed until the rest of them were in position. Then he instructed the pilot to have the passengers and crew disembark one at a time to be questioned.

The agents spread out and assumed firing positions from behind pieces of airport equipment. The plane's forward door opened and pivoted down to make stairs. The first passenger came down the steps shielding his eyes from the helicopter's spotlight trained on the plane's door.

"I'm James Dethridge. I'm President of Central Tennesse State University. What is going on?"

"President Dethridge, we're from the Federal Bureau of Investigation. Would you please tell us why your plane is leaving this evening and where it's headed?" asked McNertheny.

"I and our Vice President for Academic Affairs are headed for a regional college administrators' conference in New Orleans over the weekend. The plane does not belong to the University. A well-to-do alumnus donated his plane and pilot for our travel."

"How many of you on board?"

"Just the two of us administrators and the pilot and co-pilot. Why?"

"I can't really explain right now, sir, except to say that we are pursuing someone who might be trying to hijack a plane to make an escape. We'll need to check everyone's identification if you don't mind. And when we get everyone off the plane, we'll need to do an on-board search. If all goes well, you should be back in the air very quickly."

Ten minutes later they established that everything was as stated by President Dethridge. With apologies from the agents, his party re-boarded their plane and took off. McNertheny called his dispatcher to say they would remain there for a while, even though it now seemed unlikely that Mafousi would be using the Murfreesboro airstrip.

The helicopter carrying Tad slowed and started a controlled descent to the small airport at McMinnville. There was no control tower or flight controller. Tad was relieved to see the landing strip's lights were on. As soon as the skids touched the paving, everyone but the pilot climbed out, instinctively lowering their heads even though there was two feet of clearance beneath the decelerating rotors. They could see a two-engine plane over a hundred yards down the taxiway. Its propellers were not turning and they saw two figures beside it. One looked like a large man. Saul started running toward the plane and the others followed. In the distance, they could hear sirens.

Saul yelled, "FBI. Stay where you are!"

Terry Humber had been mildly curious about the helicopter coming in for a landing, but had already resumed his pre-flight external check when Saul yelled. At the sound of Saul's command, he turned back toward the approaching men and said, "My God! They must think we're on a drug run!" He looked over his shoulder to catch his client's reaction and was astonished to see the man he knew as Mellini was gone.

"Get down on your stomach! Now!" yelled Saul. "Where's the other guy?"

Humber quickly decided his best course was to obey their commands until they determined that he was merely an innocent charter pilot. He lay down beside the plane. "I don't know where he went. He was right beside me a few seconds ago!" he answered as Agent Blix searched him for weapons and extracted his wallet.

Blix spoke to Novitsky after checking the wallet. "This guy's name is Terry Humber. He has a pilot's license."

Saul said, "Mr. Humber, we're going to handcuff you to a seat in your plane while we look for your passenger. I'm sorry to have to handle it this way, but until we get this all sorted out, that's how it'll have to be."

Humber nodded. He had a clear conscience and had concluded that protesting at this time would be counter-productive. Two sheriff's patrol cars swung onto the taxiway and braked to a halt short of the plane. Three deputies got out and raced toward them. Novitsky explained the situation and they agreed on a methodical search strategy.

As soon as he saw the helicopter approaching, Mafousi knew his luck was running out. He leaped into the shadows and ran around the corner of the nearest hanger in the confusion of the agents' approach. He was no sprinter so he had to find shelter almost immediately. He saw pieces of old equipment laying abandoned in the overgrown grass surrounding the narrow ends of the hangers. Then he saw the cockpit of a helicopter standing against an end wall. The cockpit reminded him of the disembodied head of a giant grasshopper. He wondered if it had been left there so maintenance workers could cannibalize controls or instruments. In any case, he was running out of time. Mafousi pulled open the Plexiglas door and sat down with a grunt in the pilot's seat. He closed the door and fought to quiet the noise of his breathing.

The six law-enforcement types had broken into

teams of two and begun their search. Tad, unarmed, was the odd man out and was left behind. He felt that he best understood how Mafousi's mind worked: the cement mixer standing in the exhibition hall for all to see; his turning the listening device to his own advantage to set a trap; his choice to hide at Reverson's where his bulk would not attract attention. Even by himself, Tad thought he might have a good chance of finding Mafousi. To hell with staying at the plane; this malevolent man was responsible for Paul's death and Davi's kidnapping. Tad was joining the hunt!

He followed the route of one of the teams around the corner of the nearest hanger. Mafousi must have known he could not out-run the agents to get away from the airport. He would look for a way to get inside a hangar to hide. Tad found the first hangar to be securely locked. Checking for broken windows or loose panels of the corrugated steel siding, he quickly circled the first hanger passing an old aircraft engine and a part of a helicopter as he went. Tad soon appreciated that with planes and aircraft parts inside, all the hangars would be in good condition and well secured. He also saw that the windows were too high and too small for a person of Mafousi's size to use as entry points.

So he was in hiding yes, but, like the mixer, he was somewhere outside yet where his presence would be overlooked. Tad started walking down the paved area between the rows of hangars wondering if Mafousi had time to run that far; then he stopped. He could hear the muffled voices of the others as they moved even further from the taxiway. Something, almost in his subconscious, was teasing him as he tried to bring it into focus. What had he passed that seemed undeserving of his scrutiny? The engine, he remembered, was too small for anyone larger than a child to hide behind. There was also the front end of a helicopter. Just junk, but he had been concentrating on the hangar at the time and had not really looked it over. He retraced his steps back toward the old cockpit with its Plexiglas bubble so crazed and oxidized one could hardly see through it.

Mafousi had relaxed a little when the first team trotted by. But then a lone man came along checking the hangar walls. It was hard to see in the darkness, but the man looked like Madison! Whoever it was, he too passed by and headed for the back row of buildings. Mafousi knew he would have to wait, patient and as motionless as a statue. He was increasingly uncomfortable in the bucket seat designed for a smaller man, but he used his great self-discipline to remain unmoving.

Placing each foot with care, Tad crept around the corner to the narrow end of the hangar. The cockpit was a mere fifteen feet away. He stopped and stared at the Plexiglas exterior. Through the murky plastic there appeared to be a pilot at the controls! Was this a mannequin placed there as a joke? Were his eyes playing tricks on him? Tad knew better. He knew the figure was a man and he knew the man was Mafousi.

Tad sprung toward the cockpit and ripped open the door. He was certainly outweighed, but he had the advantage of being on his feet while Mafousi was wedged into a bucket seat. He fastened his grip on Mafousi's right wrist in case he had a weapon. Mafousi struggled mightily to raise the hand gripping the steak knife to Tad's throat. Tad yelled, "I've found him! Over here! At the old helicopter cockpit!"

Mafousi tried to gouge Tad's eyes with his left hand while still trying to force the knife point forward. Tad had to arch his head back to protect his eyes, but he kept his grip on Mafousi's right wrist. Novitsky and Blix sprinted to the scene and helped overwhelm Mafousi. After they freed the knife from his grasp, he managed to get his other hand into a pocket. Blix clamped both hands on Mafousi's left forearm. Seconds later, the deputies ran up and, together, they prized a small red pill from his fist.

Mafousi uttered no words throughout the struggle. Once he was handcuffed, he faced Tad, nodded and said, "You're Madison."

Tad stared directly back at him. Even if Mafousi intended his statement as a kind of complimentary acknowledgment to a determined adversary, Tad did not respond. He simply shook his head in bewilderment that an intelligent, successful human being could be so malevolent.

Saul reached the dispatcher through the radio in their helicopter and was patched through to McNertheny. "We have him! It's over! He had a plane ready to take off when we got there. He ran for it, but Madison found him. We'll take him to the federal office building in Knoxville and meet you there."

After asking Terry Humber how he came to be contacted and accepted the engagement with Mafousi, they decided he was just a pilot with a struggling air charter business; a man whose misfortune was simply that Mafousi found his company after an internet search. The handcuffs were removed and the agents apologized and shook his hand. He asked whether he should keep the money Mafousi had given him. Saul cocked his head in a moment of thought, then said, "Consider it a reservation fee. You were ready to go, he wasn't. Fee earned!"

# THIRTY-ONE

THEY HAD MAFOUSI IN A HOLDING CELL IN THE FEDeral building. All the agents had reassembled in a conference room on a higher floor. Tad had excused himself for the moment to make two telephone calls. He punched in Davi's number. It was after midnight in Wilcao, but he could not wait for morning.

"I'm so glad you called, Tad! I tried not to worry, but I'd hoped you'd call when I got home."

"Dearest Davi, I meant to. That sounds lame, I'm sure, but the FBI's been carrying on a multi-state man-hunt for these guys and it broke wide open this afternoon. It seems like I've been over half of Tennessee ever since."

"Is it over now?"

"Yes, you know I can't name names over the phone. But yes, it's essentially over. They got the man that controlled the people in our area. And it looks as though he had more sleepers planted in another state."

"Are you OK?"

"Yes, I'm perfectly fine. There *was* a scary moment. I'll tell you some of it later. I've done all I can in the way of helping. There's some debriefing tomorrow morning and with luck, I'll be on an afternoon plane out of here."

"Call me with your flight details. I'll be at PDX to pick you up, my love."

"That'll be by far the best part of my day!"

His next call was to the hospital in Chattanooga. They put him through to Bronson's room. "Russ, even your 'hello' sounded better than this afternoon. Seems like we only talked business then. How are you doing this evening?"

"Well, I'm not super comfortable at the moment, but all the news is good. I get to keep my leg! They say I'll be out of here in just a few more days."

"Did your son arrive?"

"Yes, he got here in late-afternoon. He's been great! Now tell me what's going on with our Near Eastern project."

"It's over for the most part. We found him a couple of hours ago. He led us a merry chase. You'll no doubt hear it officially before I see you out west, but I'll give you an informal version when we get together. He's downstairs in a cell and they 're starting to unravel what he was up to in Florida."

"I'm buying you dinner when we're both back home, my friend!"

"You're on, Russ! I'll look forward to that."

When Tad rejoined the others, McNertheny was finishing a conversation with the SAC Miami. As he laid down the phone, the room hushed. "Here's the latest," he said. "The owner of the company, Bafir Nuwali, is lawyered-up and isn't saying a word. But the other guy, Toudani, the man who towed the mixer, has started to cooperate. He's already implicated his boss, Nuwali. He claims not to know the whole plan, but he told them it somehow involved a cruise liner."

"They must have been planning another monkey virus thing!" exclaimed Novitsky.

"Looks that way. They went through Nuwali's office and found his cell phone. They opened the last-ten-calls register and started calling the numbers. All of them turned out to be uninteresting except one. Nuwali had called the Chief Steward on one of Crescendo's liners, one Harry Osgood."

The room erupted into excited comments. When things quieted a little, McNertheny continued. "So they spent the last few hours looking into Mr. Osgood's background. He's a naturalized citizen. Came from Lebanon. Changed his name to Osgood. Used to be Hasim Asgal."

"Another sleeper!" said Aaron.

"Possibly. Washington's sending a team to Fort Lauderdale. In the meantime, Osgood's boss is diverting him to some harmless shore-side project and SAC Miami is placing him under twenty-four-seven surveillance."

Tad said "And our fat friend downstairs?"

"Not a word," said McNertheny. "An interrogation specialist who speaks Arabic and a psychologist will be here in the morning so maybe we'll have better luck then. He'll have detainee status for the time being. When we do have to charge him, he's good for bringing currency into the United States illegally, being an accomplice to the attempted murder of a federal officer, conspiring to murder Tad's friend, Paul Castner, conspiring to bring in and conceal an illegal alien, conspiring to use a biological weapon, and conspiring to commit acts of terrorism. He ain't going anywhere!"

There was applause and cheering. McNertheny even led three "Attaboy"s for Tad. When the celebration subsided a little, Tad said "After what we went through in Portland, I can't help but ask if Rachel Palowski's team is still checking the food and drink at Opryland."

"Glad you raised that," said McNertheny. "They surely are still on the job. Absolutely nothing so far, but the testing and monitoring will continue today and will cover that final meal for the concrete people tomorrow."

Davi was among those waiting to meet the arriving passengers at the baggage claim carousel. Tad spotted her immediately and ran to her arms. They drove back to her house with happy chatter and laughter. Davi had rescheduled her Monday classes and Tad decided the bookstore could get along without him for three more days. One of the first things Tad did was to call Meg Castner and tell her they had the man responsible for the chain of events that cost Paul his life. That duty fulfilled, Tad and Davi spent the days happily together, eating, walking on the beach, playing games, and loving each other.

# THIRTY-TWO

IT WAS AN UNUSUALLY CLEAR DAY IN LATE MARCH WHEN Tad, Davi, and Mike arrived in the nation's capital. After checking into their hotel, it was a short taxi ride to the Ronald Reagan Building where Homeland Security is headquartered. After identifying themselves, passing their belongings through an x-ray machine, and walking through a metal detector, they were met by a senior FBI agent who escorted them to the fifth floor. There, the Deputy Secretary of Homeland Security, Dennis Borland, introduced himself and they entered his office. On his desk sat two small cases made of polished bubinga wood. After ten minutes of amiable conversation, he stood and motioned for Tad to stand.

"May I call you Tad?"

"Please."

"Tad, the nation owes you its fullest appreciation and thanks. You are a hero in the truest sense of the word. What you did and why you did it – to protect thousands of your fellow Americans from a horrible death, not to mention the chaos that would probably have ensued in the financial markets – was an act of great courage and resolve. SAC Bronson and SAC McNertheny tell me you were at the center of things virtually the entire time. He says you helped their people immeasurably, including personally cornering one of the Portland terrorists and catching the brains behind the plot in Tennessee."

Tad was starting to feel self-conscious and said, "Well, that's flattering, but …."

The Deputy Secretary waved him to silence with a smile and continued, "As I said, you are an American hero. Unfortunately, in today's world and given the jihadist situation we face, there will be no press conference, no standing ovation from Congress, no public ceremony at all. I expect SAC Bronson has explained that to you."

Tad nodded and Borland turned to Davi. "And you, Ms. Salloway. You were an innocent victim of these sinister doings. But SAC Bronson tells us that without your brilliant coded message, they would have had extreme difficulty in finding you. You too have our thanks for your cool head and your moxie. And I sincerely regret what they put you through".

"Thank you, Mr. Secretary," Davi said.

"And now, we have this medal for you, Tad." He lifted one of the boxes off his desk and raised the lid. "I'll be pleased to place it around your neck if you wish."

"No. It'll be fine if you just hand it to me," grinned Tad.

Borland pulled on the red-white-and-blue neck band to ease a heavy gold medal from its satin-cushion in the box and handed it to Tad. "It is my honor to present you with the Presidential Medal for Distinguished Service."

Next, Borland turned to Mike and lifted the lid of the second box. "Dr. Li, both Agent Bronson and Dr. Palowski have described the invaluable assistance you gave them. In fact, Dr. Palowski told me that it was your preliminary workup that really kicked our bio-threat operation into gear."

Mike raised a self-deprecating hand. "Sir, anyone in my position would've done the same. It was my privilege to help."

Borland extracted the medal and said, "Again, it is an honor for me to present you with this Presidential Award of Merit."

Moud was promptly tried in federal court and convicted. He was sentenced to a life term in prison. A Portland grand jury indicted Rudi for the felony murder of Paul Castner. After his trial, months later, he was convicted. Portland Police Detectives Martinez and Peterson testified along with federal agents at his trial and got the official credit for clearing the Castner murder case.

The FBI thoroughly questioned Krati, the substitute mate on the Malacca Trader, and he revealed enough that Malaysian authorities were able to arrest Ali and Sallah. The United States eventually agreed to extradite Krati to Malaysia where he was wanted on several felony warrants.

Darius Mafousi was tried in federal court on a multiple-count indictment. He was convicted on the money-importation count, the conspiracy-to-kill people on the cruise ship count, and the conspiracy-to-murder-a-federal-officer count. The judge gave him the maximum sentence of forty years in a federal penitentiary without a chance of parole. Mafousi was acquitted on the conspiracy counts involving the Portland patho-gens and the murder of Paul Castner. Several jurors felt his guilt was not proven beyond a reasonable doubt on those counts. The Israeli government filed a request for extradition to facilitate his trial in Israel for the assas-sination of the two Mossad agents. The federal judge denied the motion pending the end of Mafousi's trial in the United States. The Egyptian Internal Security Ser-vice began an intensive investigation of the Nile Trust and its donors and affiliated entities.

Salim Toudani made a plea deal to cooperate and his testimony led to the convictions of Barfir Nuwali and Harry Osgood as well as Mafousi. Nuwali was found guilty on a charge of conspiracy to import money illegally. If he once had the Richard Franklin driver's license, he had disposed of it before his arrest. Nuwali and Osgood were found guilty of a conspiracy to harm or kill persons on the Crescendo ship. They were given the maximum allowable sentences. Toudani pled guilty to the money importation charge and was sentenced to serve three years in a federal penitentiary.

Zulanni Hashadi reached New York City where she lived in the shadows and worked odd jobs under her new name of Norma Henderson. She could not obtain a New York driver's license without providing her nat-uralization papers under her real name. She was not willing to take that risk, and public transportation was readily accessible. Soon she was attending one of the more radical mosques and putting out feelers for contact with other jihadis. The FBI had a warrant for her arrest and a national alert for her whereabouts but, as one agent told Bronson, she was "in the wind".

———

Tad's insurance company paid on the fire policy, waiving the exclusion for acts of "terrorism". The insurer placed a lien on the Tropical Furniture warehouse by way of a subrogation claim. Josh's insurance company denied his claim for damage to the Sauvie Island cabin, citing its own "terrorism" exclusion. Bronson convinced the FBI Director to tap an obscure contingency fund to compensate Josh on the grounds that the loss was incidental to their campaign to identify and capture the terrorists.

———

A few weeks after their trip to Washington, Tad and Davi retained a realtor. It was time to look for a larger house... a home for them both with a nook for a drum set.

# ACKNOWLEDGEMENTS

Special thanks to my careful and supportive proof-readers: Del Thomas, Kathy Brault, and Susie Sivyer.

CPSIA information can be obtained
at www.ICGtesting.com
Printed in the USA
FFHW010633271018
48942774-53183FF

9 781629 015835